spares

Michael Marshall Smith's debut novel was the groundbreaking *Only Forward* which received widespread critical acclaim. A former comedy writer for the BBC, he currently has two feature films and a miniseries in development. In 1996, *Spares* was bought by Stephen Spielberg's production company Dreamworks in a seven-figure deal. It has since been sold in translation around the world. Mike lives in North London, where he is currently working on his third novel in between looking after his cats and checking that he has at least one unopened packet of cigarettes handy.

Praise for Michael Marshall Smith's previous works

ONLY FORWARD

'Michael Marshall Smith's first novel really is special. It combines fantasy sf with the clever humour of Douglas Adams and the action, adventure and storytelling power of a Stephen Donaldson. A major work indeed, which features an extraordinary city, a bizarre kidnapping and a wonderfully slick streetwise hero who is aiming to sort out the world.' *Today*

'In *Only Forward* Michael Marshall Smith delivers that rarest of sf commodities: a genuinely new twist on standard genre riffs with a punchline of Crying Game proportions. It announces itself as weapons-grade cyber narrated in over-the-top private eye first person (William Gibson rewritten by Barry Fantoni?) before morphing into something about as un-cyber as it gets.' CHARLES MURRAY, *Time Out*

'Quite breathtaking . . . an intoxicating trip.' *Interzone*

'Just when you think you have worked out what is happening, Smith throws it all up in the air . . . *Only Forward* is a superb novel. It twists and turns, throwing the reader off the scent and then grabbing him by the throat . . . One of the hottest new talents to emerge in recent years. His work is unique, startling and very readable. Treat yourself.'
Starburst

'With shades of *Hitch-Hiker's Guide*, *The Wasp Factory*, hard-boiled detective fiction, and even *The Wizard of Oz*, it's endearing, outrageous, witty and violent. Smith has an excellent eye for detail and it's here, as we are told of various gizmos, tales and asides, that makes the book so appealing.'
What's On

'WOW! Think of your worst nightmare, double it, and you may find yourself somewhere near the darker sections of this book . . . very perceptive.' *Event*

'A science fiction fantasy nightmare romp through an incredibly imagined world of partitioned marvels. Michael Marshall Smith is one of the up and coming giants of the genre. Start collecting his work now!'
DAVID HOWE, *BFS Newsletter*

'This is exceptional. It is Douglas Adams meets William Gibson in a first rate futuristic adventure, and he's British. A writer to watch out for the future.' *The Bookseller*

'A wild, quirky, satirical tale in the tradition of Douglas Adams and Terry Pratchett, but totally original, and Smith is a genuine talent to follow. PN Rating: A.' *Publishing News*

'*Only Forward* is about guilt and betrayal, friendship and love, and it's wonderfully funny, witty and thoroughly recommended.' CHRISTOPHER FOWLER, *FATEA*

'The plot of award-winning writer Michael Marshall Smith's stunning debut novel is so complex and bizarre that summing it up would be impossible. Dark, funny, and compelling reading for anyone who loves the offbeat.'
South Wales Evening Post

'A major figure in SF and horror fiction.' *SFX Magazine*

SHORT STORIES

The Man Who Drew Cats

'Subtle, beautifully understated stuff about a pavement artist with peculiar powers, which marks him out as a name to watch.' *The Times*

'Distinctive, original and sharp.' *Starburst*

'Assured, riveting, haunting. One of those stories where the narrative flows towards a conclusion that is both inevitable and yet satisfying.' *Interzone*

The Darkland

'A tour de force.' *The Times*

'The purest nightmare . . . a story which I would have been proud to have written myself.' RAMSEY CAMPBELL

'Quite simply one of the best stories I have ever read . . . truly frightening and written in a hugely compelling style.' *Million*

Always

'Stunning.' *Time Out*

'Beautifully poignant.' *Starburst*

More Tomorrow

'The strongest story of all, correctly chosen by the editors to lead the anthology. A terrifying mix of psychological terror and computer science, this tale can only add to his reputation as a major figure in SF and Horror fiction.' *SFX Magazine*

By the same author

Only Forward

Michael Marshall Smith

spares

HarperCollinsPublishers

HarperCollins*Publishers*
77–85 Fulham Palace Road,
Hammersmith, London W6 8JB

This paperback edition 1997

9 8 7 6 5 4 3 2 1

First published in Great Britain by
HarperCollins*Publishers* 1996

ISBN 0 586 21775 4

Set in Minion

Printed and bound in Great Britain by
Caledonian International Book Manufacturing Ltd, Glasgow

For Paula,
who lights up the forest.

ACKNOWLEDGEMENTS

Thanks to Steve Jones, for whom I wrote the story which contained the seed of what follows; to the Chisellers and Chisellettes, for valued misery and chiselling; to arch-Miserablists Kim 'Crispy' Newman and Paul 'The Duck' McAuley for good advice (which I'm going to start taking); to Rob & Steve for helping me not to finish too early; to Clive Barker for kind words, and to Neil Gaiman for helping me to not get sued; to Kingsley Amis and Tori Amos for very different inspirations; to Rachel Baker, Dick Jude, Chris Smith, Paul Landymore and others for putting their weight behind the first one, and to the reps of HarperCollins for being a bunch of absolute stars; to Howard and Adam and Jenny and Les and Val and Mandy and Jo and Richard and Suzanne and Zaz for damaging my health; to Jane Johnson for putting up with me, and to Jim Rickards for being a hard bastard; to Ralph Vicinanza, Lisa Eveleigh, Linda Shaughnessy, Nick Marston and Bob Bookman; to Margaret and David and Tracey and Spangle and Lintilla for being who they are; and finally to Nana Harrup (Get through that defence) and Grandma Smith (Oh bother it) for being who they were.

Our kind. Us people. All of us that
started the game with a crooked cue,
that wanted so much and got so little,
that meant so good and did so bad.

JIM THOMPSON
'The Killer Inside Me'

PART ONE

Dead Code

One

Wide shot.

New Richmond, Virginia. Not the *old* Richmond, the historic capital of historical old Virginia, that sprawl of creaking tedium, but the New. The old Richmond was destroyed over a century ago, razed to the ground during riots which lasted two months. After decades of putting up with dreadful shopping facilities, a bewilderingly dull Old Town and no good restaurants to speak of, the residents suddenly went non-linear and strode across the city like avenging angels, destroying everything in their wake. It was great.

Spin doctors blamed downtown decay, crack wars, the cast of the moon. Personally, I think everyone just got really bored, and either way good riddance to it. The old Richmond was a content-free mess, a waste of a good, level patch within sight of the pleasingly pointy Blue Ridge Mountains. Everyone agreed it was much better off as a landing strip, a refuelling point for the MegaMalls.

The MegaMalls are aircraft – five miles square, two hundred storeys high – which majestically transport passengers from one side of the continent to the other, from the bottom to the top; from wherever they've been to wherever they seem to think will be better. The biggest oblongs of all time, a fetching shade of consumer goods black, studded with millions of points of light and so big they transcend function and become simply a shape again.

When oblongs grow up, they all want to be MegaMalls.

Inside are thousands of stores, twenty-storey atriums, food courts the size of small towns, dozens of multiplex cinemas and a range of hotels to suit every wallet which has a Gold Card in it. All this and more arranged round wide, sweeping avenues, a thousand comfortable nooks and crannies, and so many potted plants they count as an ecosystem in their own right. Safe from the rest of the world, cocooned 20,000 feet up in the air.

Heaven on earth, or cruising just above it: all of the good, clean, *buyable* things in life crammed into a multi-storey funhouse.

Eighty-three years ago, MegaMall Flight MA 156 stopped for routine refuelling on the site of old Richmond, and never took off again. It was merely a bureaucratic problem at first – the kind that the massed brains of all time could never have got to the bottom of, but which some poorly paid clerk could have solved instantly. If he'd had a mind to. If he hadn't been on his break.

After a few hours, the richer patrons started leaving by the roads. They didn't have time for this shit. They had to be somewhere else. Everybody else just complained a little, ordered another meal or bought some more shoes, and settled down to wait.

Then, after a few more hours, it transpired there was a minor problem with the engines. This was a little more serious. When you've got a problem with a car, you open the hood and there it is. You can point at the errant part. When the engine's the size of the Empire State Building on steroids, you know you've got a long night ahead. It takes fourteen people just to hold the manual. The engineers sent repair droids scurrying off into the deep recesses, but eventually they came back, electronically shaking their heads and whistling through their mechanical teeth. It was only a minor problem, they were sure, but they couldn't work out what it was.

More passengers started to leave at that point, but on the other hand, some people decided to stay. There were plenty of phones and meeting rooms, and the Mall had its own node on the Matrix. People could work. There were enormous quantities of food, consumer goods and clean sheets. People could live. There were, frankly, worse places to hang around.

They never got the engines going again. Maybe they were fixable, but they left it a little too late. After a couple of days people started to make their way in from the outside; people who'd been homeless since old Richmond went up in flames; people who lived in the backwoods; people who'd heard about the food courts and just wanted a spot of lunch. They came off the plain and out of the mountains and hammered on the doors. Initially, security turned them back like they were supposed to, but there were an awful lot of them and some were pretty pissed. For them the only thing worse than having to live in Richmond had been not having it to live in any more.

The security guards got together and came up with a plan. They would let people in, and they would charge them for it.

There was a period, maybe as long as six months, when Flight MA 156 was in flux, when no one was really sure if it was going to take off again. Then the tide turned, and people knew it was not. By then they didn't want it to. It was home. Areas inside the ship were knocked through, torn down, redeveloped. The original passengers staked out the upper floors and began to build on top of the Mall, competing to see who could get furthest from the mounting poor on the lower levels. A secondary town grew up around the Mall at ground level – the Portal into the city.

Eventually, the local utility companies just plumbed the whole lot in, and New Richmond was born. Apart from its unusual provenance and extreme oblongness, New Richmond is now just a city like anywhere else. If you didn't know, you might think it was just a rather bizarre town planning mistake.

But it's said that in a lost room, somewhere deep in the bowels of the city, there remains a forgotten suitcase, left there accidentally by one of the first families to leave, a mute testament to the city's birth. Nobody knows where this room is, and most people believe it's just an urban myth. Because that's what Flight MA 156 is, these days. Urban.

But I've always believed it, just like I wonder if sometimes, on some nights, the city itself must raise its eyes when it hears the other MegaMalls trundling slowly overhead. I wonder if it watches the skies, and sees them pass, and knows in some way that's where it should be. Up there in the heavens, not battered onto the Earth. But then which of us doesn't believe something like that, and how few of us are right.

'Two hundred dollars,' the man said, his eyes trying to look cool and watchful at the same time, and making a fearful mess of both. He wasn't talking about what I was trying to sell. I wasn't even in

New Richmond yet. It was after eight o'clock at night and I was losing patience and running out of time.

'Bullshit,' I said. 'Fifty is the rate.'

The man laughed with genuine amusement.

'You been away or something man? Shit, I can't barely *remember* when fifty dollars was the rate.'

'Fifty dollars,' I said again. I guess I was hoping if I said it often enough I'd end up neurolinguistically programming him. I was standing in front of a door, a door which was hidden in the basement of a building in the Portal settlement, the high-rise nightmare of ragged buildings and shanty dwellings which surrounds New Richmond proper. I was there because this particular building had been constructed right up against the exterior wall of the city, inside which I needed to be. I'd put up with being frisked on entry by the street gang which was currently controlling the building, and had already paid twenty dollars 'tax' on my gun. I didn't have two hundred dollars, I barely had a hundred, and I was in a hurry.

The man shrugged. 'So go in the main entrance.'

I stuffed my hands into my jacket pockets, fighting back anger and panic in equal measure. 'And don't be thinking about bringing out your gun,' he continued, mildly. 'Cos there's three brothers you can't even see with rifles trained on yo ass.'

I couldn't go in the main gates, as he well knew. No one came to this part of the Portal town if they could enter New Richmond through one of the legitimate entrances. Going in that way meant running your ownCard through the machines, thus broadcasting your name to the cops, the city administration and anyone else who had a tap on the line.

'Look,' I said. 'I've been this way before. I don't need a guide, I just need to get past you. Fifty dollars is what I have.'

The man turned away and signalled into the darkness with an upwards nod of his head. I heard the sound of several sets of feet padding out of the darkness towards me.

'You still piecing your action from Howie "The Plan"?' I asked, casually. The footsteps behind stopped, and the man turned to look at me again, eyes watchful.

'What you know about Mr Amos?' he asked.

'Not much,' I said, though I did. Howie was a medium-time

crook operating out of the eighth floor. He ran some girls, owned a bar, and had pieces of the drugs action so far down the chain that he was tolerated by the real heavy-hitters above. He was a fat, affable man with a surprising shock of blond hair, but he was fitter than he looked and knew how to keep a secret. Late at night, when most of the customers were gone, he'd been known to sit in with his house blues band and play a hell of a lot better than you'd expect. He didn't have the Bright Eyes, but he could have done. He was a stand-up guy.

'Just enough,' I continued, 'to tell the wrong people about some of the deals they don't know he's into. And if he thinks that information came from you guys, well . . .'

'Why would he get to thinking that?' the man asked, though he was losing heart. These guys were *below* bottom-rung lowlife: hardly on the ladder. They most likely didn't even know where the ladder *was*, and had to use steps the whole time. Running this door was as close as they got to operating in New Richmond. Guys like that don't want to tangle with the jungle inside. It bites.

'I can't imagine,' I said. 'Look. Fifty dollars. Then on my way out I give you the other hundred fifty.'

For all he knew I was never coming out, but fifty was better than no cash and a lot of potential grief. He stepped aside. I peeled the notes off, and he opened the door.

'And I'll give you an extra twenty,' I added, 'if you keep any mention of me off the list you sell to the cops.'

'Don't know what you're talking about,' he said stonily, but there was a change in his attitude. 'But I'll take your twenty.'

I nodded and walked through the door. It shut behind me, and for the first time in five years I was inside New Richmond.

The door led into an old service corridor, which meandered towards the lower engine block through miles of dank and creepy corridors. There's nothing of value to be had there, and that's why nobody had cared when external construction had covered up the entrance. The one thing no one was going to be trying to do was get the engines going again. There's an old story which says one of the original repair drones still toils away down there somewhere, grown old and insane, but even I don't believe that.

For a long time the door was forgotten, and then somebody

rediscovered it and realized its potential value as a covert entrance to the city. An adjunct to the service corridor leads via the exhaust ducts to a hidden and little-known staircase, which leads up to the second floor of the old Mall.

But I wasn't going to be going that way. I quickly followed the corridor for two hundred yards, past panels etched and stained with rust. It's eerily silent down there, perhaps the only truly quiet part of the city. The corridor took a sharpish right turn, and you could see the dim and intermittent lights in the ceiling disappearing towards the next turn, about half a mile ahead. Instead of following them I gathered myself and leapt upwards, arms straight above me, hands balled into fists. They hit a panel of the roof and it popped up and over, revealing a dark space beyond. I took a quick glance back to ensure no one was watching, jumped up again and pulled myself up through the hole.

When I replaced the ceiling panel I was left in a darkness broken only by yellow slivers of light which escaped through cracks in the floor. I straightened into the slight hunch which is required for New Richmond's lost ventilation system, and hurried forwards into the gloom. Every now and then I heard some fragment of life floating down from the city. An aged gurgle, soft clanks grown old, the occasional ghost of speech caught accidentally in some twist of corridor above and echoed down to the graveyard below. I had always felt that walking this corridor was like creeping through New Richmond's ancient and barren womb, but then I've always been a bit of a moron.

After about half a mile I passed under one of the main entrances. You can tell because of the sound of hundreds of feet coming in, going out. I stood underneath it for a moment, remembering. I used to come the covert way sometimes for kicks, but the main gates are the way you enter if you want to appreciate what you're getting into. You walk into a foyer which is twenty storeys high, a taster of the opulence you can expect if you've got clearance to go above the 100th floor. There used to be glass windows on all of the levels which tower above you, but they were walled in once they'd become lowlife areas. It's like standing in the biggest and gaudiest shower cubicle of all time. You walked up to the desk, ran your ownCard through the machine, and established your clearance. I used to live in the 70s, and so I'd walk over to one of the express elevators, get in, and be shot up into the sky.

Not tonight. Tonight I was threading my way like a snake through endless tunnels, and I wasn't going to the 72nd floor because there was nothing left for me there. I was in New Richmond because I needed money, and had only one way of getting some. I was going to go in, get the money, get out – and then turn my back on Virginia for good.

We'd reached the Portal settlement in the early evening. It had been raining all day, and was getting colder and darker by the minute. Virginia doesn't fuck around in winter, especially not these days. Virginia says, 'Here, have some winter,' and then delivers. The spares had been on their last legs by then, a joke I'd made to myself knowing it to be in bad taste and not altogether caring. They'd never felt the cold before, and the scraps of my clothing I'd distributed amongst them weren't anywhere near enough.

There hadn't been many people on the streets, thankfully. You don't go to the Portal to promenade, particularly not at night – it would be less trouble to stay in your apartment and mug yourself in the comfort of your own home. Howie Amos once ran a service which did just that; you called him up, said you were thinking of going out into the Portal, and he'd send someone to rough you over within half an hour or you got a dollar off. It was surprisingly popular.

I corralled the spares into a tight group and herded them down the streets in front of me, sticking close to the walls and out of the light, trusting Suej and David to help me keep the others in line. I'd explained why we had to come here, and why it could be a problem for me. They all did what they were told, and I hurried us along for about a mile until we were outside Mal's building.

I paused outside and looked back the way we'd come. The roads in the Portal are very straight, running out from New Richmond in the centre like a giant spider's web. You can stand in the middle of one and see as far as the rain will let you. Yellow streetlights lined the way, throwing pools of light which were rich and sickly, like cream ten minutes before it goes off. Beyond the limits of my vision was the edge of the Portal, and beyond that the road which led out into the dark Virginia countryside. A long way down that road were the Blue Ridge Mountains we'd come from, matter-of-fact geology covered with a hell of a lot of trees. For the first time it struck me how much the roads in the Portal looked like tunnels, and that was when I began to accept that the last five years really had happened to me.

I shouldered the outer door open and led the spares into the hallway, which was an inch deep in chill water. Loud music was thumping from somewhere up above. I told the spares to stay still and to hide if anyone came, and vaulted up the wooden staircase which spiralled up into the darkness. When I got to the 3rd floor I took a deep breath, shook some of the water out of my hair, then knocked on Mal's door.

Mal did a double-take which would have done a cheap comedian proud, and then he just stood there, mouth hanging open, hand still holding the door. He was wearing a pair of battered cut-offs which showed off the scars on his legs, and a ragged T-shirt which hugged his new paunch and looked like about five people had lived and died in it without showing it any water other than rain. He was backlit by a bare bulb, and from somewhere deep in the bowels of his apartment came the smell of cooking – noodles, almost certainly. In all the time I'd known him I don't think I'd ever seen him voluntarily eat anything else.

Finally he got it together, blinked and tried to smile.

'Jack,' he croaked, eerie calm coming about level with utter stupefaction. 'What the fuck are you doing here?'

'Social visit. Old times.'

'Yeah, right. The pope's due later too.' He closed his eyes tightly for a moment, and pinched himself on the bridge of the nose. 'You in trouble?'

'Yep,' I grinned, trying to keep myself from hopping from foot to foot. Tension, of about seven different kinds. I nodded towards the gloom of the apartment. 'What's cooking?'

'Noodles,' he said, eyeing me warily. 'You want some?'

'Depends how much you've got. I'm not alone.'

'How many guests are we talking?'

I took a deep breath. 'Including me, seven,' I said. His eyes opened wide and he shook his head – not in negation, just bewilderment. I tried to make it easier on him. 'Well, six and a half, I guess.'

'That's a lot of noodles.'

'Too many?'

'Not necessarily,' he said. 'I buy in bulk.' He turned back towards his apartment for a moment, biting his lip, considering. I noticed that he wasn't wearing his shoulder holster and wondered whether that meant he was out of the Life, or just less paranoid these days. More likely he'd been cleaning his gun when I knocked. The two things I didn't think Mal was ever going to get were less paranoid or out of the Life.

Then he turned back to me, eyebrows raised in friendly resignation. In one sighing breath he asked, 'Where are these guests now and just how much unhappiness am I risking by letting them into my life, however fucking briefly?'

'I left them downstairs,' I said, realizing that I ought to get back to them very soon, whichever way this went. Mal's building is where bad people go to have fun. That's why he's paranoid – and also why he likes it. 'I just need to leave them with you for an hour, then we're out of here.'

'Why didn't you call ahead?'

'When I want to ask old friends for lunatic favours I like to do it in person. Also, I didn't have any change.'

'And the trouble rating?'

'What scale are you talking?' I was gabbling, strung tight. I had to let Mal see I was okay, because otherwise he was likely to get freaked. Being freaked would in fact have been a reasonable reaction, but I didn't want him to know that yet.

'One to ten.'

'I don't know,' I said, suddenly giving in and getting panicky. 'At least ten, possibly higher, certainly getting worse by the minute.'

Mal let go of the door.

'Get them up here.'

I let out a short exhalation of relief. 'Mal . . .'

'Yeah, all that,' he said, brushing my thanks aside. 'And then you're going to go get me a jar of Japanese pickles. I forgot I'd run out.'

'I'm going into the city. On the way back I'll get you the biggest jar of Samoy I can find.'

Mal rolled his eyes and shook his head. 'Samoy pickles are from hunger. Get me Frapan or nothing.'

'For a guy who eats so much you've got terrible fucking taste.'

'You got that right,' he said, shaking his head again. 'Look at my choice of friends.'

I grinned and walked the couple of yards to the shadowy stairwell. I thought I was going to have to shout, but I saw Suej's face in the darkness, upturned anxiously towards me, and just gestured instead. She turned to David and they corralled the others up. Mal and I waited while they trooped upstairs, Mal's face eloquent with laconic intrigue. Out in the slightly less murky light of the corridor the skin on his face looked a little ruddier than it had, and there were lines around his eyes which hadn't been there when last I'd seen him.

We're getting old, I thought. Suddenly we're nearly forty and getting old.

David was the first to reach the landing. He came up with his hands thrust deep into the pockets of his jeans, limping slightly from where his leg had been operated on. The jeans had originally been mine, and were inexpertly folded up at the bottoms and belted tight around his waist. He looked younger than his fifteen years, even though his face was still set with the belligerence it had assumed the moment we left the Farm. Jenny came up right behind him, huddled into her coat and still looking frightened and alone. I'd tried to patch things up with her in the last twenty-four hours, but she still thought she was to blame, and I hadn't really had time to convince her otherwise.

Suej came up next, leading Nanune by the hand. Suej looked okay, like a normal fourteen-year-old, apart from the scar on her face. Nanune looked scared shitless, and with only one leg was having difficulty climbing the stairs. When she reached the top she caught sight of me, and appeared momentarily relieved, which was nice. It's been a long time since anyone has looked relieved to see my face.

And then finally Mr Two, carrying the bundle in his arms. Mal coped reasonably well with the rest of them, but when he saw a teenager who stood about six five, carrying a small brown sack with a head protruding from it, I did catch a twitch on his face. Mr Two stood straight-backed on the landing, glared abruptly both ways, and then let his head drop as if he'd been switched off. The spare in the bag said, 'Nap.'

Come on guys, I thought to myself. Let's try to act like normal people.

'Is your friend letting us rest here?' Suej asked.

I nodded. It was going to be a while before they directly addressed anyone other than me. She beamed, and whispered to Nanune.

'Is it nice? Is Ratchet here?' Nanune asked, and I shook my head.

'No and no, I'm afraid,' I said, winking at Mal. 'But at least it's not raining.'

I introduced Mal to the spares by name. Suej and David shook his hand, and I caught him noticing David's missing fingers. Then Mal stood to one side and gestured them into his apartment. They trooped in, Mr Two ducking his head to get under the lintel.

Mal's apartment was pretty much as I remembered it. In other words, I knew what to expect. The spares didn't. Ten years ago he'd knocked down most of the internal walls, so that from anywhere in the apartment you could see the huge window he'd put in. This gave a view straight onto New Richmond. Mal had chosen to live outside New Richmond proper. He claimed he liked to get away from it every now and then, from the dark fizz and spark of the life inside – yet he'd deconstructed his apartment so he could see the building from wherever he stood. The interior decor was about what you'd expect from a single man who spent half his time drunk and the rest painfully sober. It was a mess, to be honest: baroque chaos overlaid with the smell of countless noodle-based meals.

Nanune actually started crying. Mal scowled at her and started kicking piles of stuff towards the walls.

'Do you still have your display up?' I asked quietly. Mal looked at me and nodded. 'You couldn't, like, drape something over it?'

Mal grunted and trudged down the end, towards the window, and pulled a rope which ran down the wall. A sheet dropped from the ceiling, covering what was pinned on the walls – pictures of people who had been murdered in New Richmond. It covered them only briefly, unfortunately, because it carried on falling to the ground. Mal swore softly, grabbed a chair, and set about repairing the set-up.

Meantime, I led the spares into the area which served as his sitting room. I shoved huge piles of crap out of the way until there was enough space for them to sit fairly comfortably. Jenny's arms were wrapped tightly around herself, and her eyes were far away. In a nimbus of light from some partially hidden lamp, she looked beautiful and frail. Nanune still looked terrified, but Suej sat close to her, murmuring something. There were no words in what she was saying, but even I could feel the comfort in it. It was tunnel talk, I guess. Mr Two looked like he would withstand a direct hit by a tactical missile, and so I guess the spare on his lap was alright too. Considering the current circumstances.

'How long are we going to be here?' David asked. I realized he looked tired, though like a child trying to prove it was worthy of staying up late, his eyes were still wide open.

'Not long,' I said. 'A couple hours. Just enough for me to go get some money. Then we're going to buy a truck and get out of here.'

'To where?' This had been David's constant refrain for the last twenty-four hours.

'I still don't know,' I said. 'Somewhere safe.' Jenny looked up at me and I winked at her. A ghost of a smile.

'Florida?' Suej asked hopefully.

'Maybe,' I said. A long time ago I'd told her about a place I knew there, and it had become fixed in her mind as a kind of nirvana. I didn't have the heart to tell her it was very unlikely we'd make it halfway there before we were caught.

I turned to Mal. 'What's your water like these days? And don't say "wet".'

'There'll be enough if they don't all stay in too long.' Mal had always known what I meant, especially when I was asking favours. I nodded to Suej, who understood, and she started drawing up a rota for the spares to wash. They weren't used to being dirty, and I knew that the one thing I could provide which would increase their short-term standard of living was a shower. It's good that there was that one thing, because there wasn't a lot of everything else, and wasn't likely to be in the foreseeable future.

'We'll get your clothes washed . . . later,' I said, vaguely, and wandered over to the window.

It was still raining outside. It always seemed to be raining in the Portal. In summer it's fat drops of dirty rain, in the winter thin biting lines of sleet – but it generally seemed to be dropping at least something out of the sky. The locals believe that it's rich people on the roof of the city, taking delight in pissing off the edge onto the lowlife below. Judging by the colour of some of the rain, they could be right.

New Richmond looked the same as it always had. Eerily so. That shouldn't have been surprising, and yet it was. I'd seen it in the distance on the way through the Portal, but that had been different. Seeing it through Mal's window was like seeing myself in one particular mirror again after a very long time away. I stared out at the points of light, the studs in the mind-fuckingly large expanse of wall. It still looked extraordinary, still said to me, as it always had, that I had to be inside it.

'Are you okay?'

I turned to see Mal standing beside me, proffering a cigarette. 'Yeah,' I said, lighting one and savouring the harsh scrape of carcinogen on lung. I'd run out that morning, and not wanted to risk going into a store until the spares were safely stowed. He let me stand for a moment, then asked what he wanted to know.

'Where have you *been*, man?'

For a moment, in the darkness of his apartment, Mal looked just as he always had. As if no time had passed, as if things were still the same and I had a home to go to after I'd finished chewing the rag with him. I shivered, realizing that I was crashing, that adrenaline was turning sour.

'Didn't Phieta tell you? I asked her to let you know.'

'I never saw her again, Jack. No one did. After you disappeared I put the word around, in case she knew something. But she was just as gone as you.'

'I'm sorry, Mal. I thought about calling you. I just couldn't.'

He nodded, and maybe he understood. 'I'm really sorry about what happened,' he said. I nodded tightly. I wasn't going to talk about it. 'If it's any consolation, the word is Vinaldi's having problems recently.'

I was glad that Mal was still enough my friend to simply say the name out loud. 'What kind of problems?'

Mal shrugged. 'Rumours. He's pretty much the man these days. Probably someone's just trying to climb over him. The usual shit.

Just thought I'd let you know.' He shook his head. 'You really only staying a couple hours?'

I nodded tightly. 'This shit's too deep to swim in. We've got to disappear and stay that way.'

'Again.' He smiled. 'Something I want to tell you about later, though, before you go.' Then he clapped me on the back with his massive hand and turned towards the spares. 'You guys about ready for some noodles?'

They stared at him with wide eyes. 'They've never had noodles,' I said.

'Then they haven't lived,' he replied, and of course he was right.

I walked a long way through the bowels of New Richmond, my stomach growling, wishing I'd stayed to have some noodles with the spares. There hadn't been time. We had serious people after us, and were only safe for as long as it took them to realize that I'd given them a false name and previous address when I was taken on at the Farm. As soon as that was blown, all hell was going to break loose.

It was about two miles from my entry point to the stage where I started to climb, two miles of textured darkness and muffled sounds. When I saw the familiar shaft in front of me I stopped walking. I rolled my head on my shoulders, wishing briefly and pointlessly that I didn't smoke, then climbed up the metal ladder attached to the wall.

Ten minutes later my arms and legs were aching and I'd reached the horizontal ventilation chute on 8. The MegaMall's original ventilation system is now completely disused, and most of it is filled with refuse, sludge and unnameable crap from a million different sources. It's like a lost river – paved over and diverted and hidden, but still there in the gaps and interstices. All but a couple of the original inspection hatches were welded shut a long time ago. I was hoping that no more had been sealed while I'd been away, or I'd be in trouble.

I swung myself out of the shaft and crouched down in the horizontal corridor, using a pocket penlight to peer into the gloom. The way was still clear, so I walked quickly north for about eight hundred yards until I found the wall panel I was looking for. I loosened the bolts and put my dark glasses on. This wasn't a matter of vanity. I didn't want anyone to make me while I was in New Richmond. It was a small chance that someone would recognize me, but I don't like to take chances of any size unless they seem like fun. The other reason is that the hatch opens into a cubicle in the women's toilets in a restaurant on 8.

I pulled the panel back about a millimetre, saw the cubicle was empty, and clambered through the hole as quickly and quietly as I could. It wasn't easy. I stand over six feet tall and am kind of broad in the shoulders. Ventilation hatches aren't built for people like me. I could hear the thump of music beyond the door to the john, but it didn't sound as if anyone was there.

I replaced the panel, pulled the door of the cubicle open and stepped through. A woman was standing there. Nice one, Jack, I thought. At least you haven't lost your touch or anything.

She was hunched over by the sinks at the far end. She was very slim, had thick brown hair and was wearing a short dress in iridescent blue. Good legs in sheer stockings led to shoes with very sharp and pointy heels.

Uh-huh, I thought, making a guess at her profession. As I glanced at her she shifted slightly, and I saw the mirror over which she was bent, and the rolled-up hundred-dollar bill in her hand. I took a quiet step towards the door, assuming she was sufficiently occupied to miss me.

Wrong. She looked up vaguely but immediately.

'Wow,' she said. 'A big man. Intense.' Her face was caught somewhere between pretty and beautiful – her nose a shade too big for everyone's pretty, but the bone structure too perfect for beautiful. Her eyes were clear and green, and looked natural.

'You've got good hearing,' I said.

'Yeah. It's a feature.' She sniffed, and bent to do her other nostril. Then a thought occurred to her, and she peered at me again. 'What are you doing in here?'

'Pest control,' I said.

'Yeah, right,' she said. 'Well I got a licence. I'm allowed to be a pest in here. You, I'm not so sure about.'

'Is there any way,' I asked, 'that I could just walk out of here, right now, and you'd think nothing more about it, ever?'

She looked at me for a long moment, considering. Then she shrugged. 'Yeah,' she said, bending back over her mirror, and I turned and walked quickly out of the door.

A short corridor led out into the restaurant proper, and I skirted round the edge of the room toward the exit. With the time now coming up for nine o'clock, the place was in a transition period. The 8th floor runs on a kind of shift system. It romps twenty-four hours a day, but in practical terms this breaks down into three evenings of eight hours each. I once went round the clock twice. I can't recommend it, except as an expensive suicide attempt. The restaurant was about half-full of people from floors in the 60s and 70s, most of them either on the edge of unconsciousness or so wired you could hear their teeth vibrating. The others looked spruce and enthusiastic, rubbing their hands together in anticipation.

No one saw me walk out of the ladies, and no one paid any attention as I walked through the restaurant. Feeling light-headed at seeing so many normal people at once, I escaped into the avenue outside.

Floor 8 is an anomaly in the lower levels of New Richmond. It's fairly civilized. Floors 1 to 7 and 9 to 49 are bad. Each varies, depending on who's got control of it at any given time, but basically they're places you don't want to go, especially the 20s and 30s. They're dead code, cut out of the loop of normal life and left to fester by themselves.

You probably wouldn't actually want to go to the 8th floor either, but at least it has pretensions. Originally, it had been the lowest food court in the MegaMall, and it was still predominantly a place where you came to eat, drink or have a good time. Whatever the focus of your sexual inclination, you can go to the 8th floor and watch it dancing on a very small stage. You can also score recreational quantities of pretty much whatever you want, without danger of being caught in a fire storm. Most of it is only one storey high, and they keep the ceiling lights off, relying on orange street lamps which run along either side of the thoroughfares. If you don't check the corners too closely the floor has a kind of lop-sided charm, like a run-down but cheery portion of some European capital, or the Old Quarter of New Orleans. The ceiling is covered in creepers and foliage, making the roads feel like paths in a forest. Forests usually give me The Fear, but I like 8, and always have. It's full of neon, autumn jazz, the smell of good food and, for some reason, the feeling that it has just stopped raining. It never has, of course, but it always feels that way to me.

I walked quickly down the centre of the street, noticing what was new and what remained. The streets were quiet but music slunk out of most of the open doors, buoying up the desultory strippers who swayed on table tops. A few down-and-outs sat on street corners, stuck in main() with their handleMouseDown() mitts held out, but from the look of them I didn't think anyone's cursor was ever going to find them. It's an image problem, I think. Maybe they should all club together and hire a PR consultant, put out a few TV ads, find some way of making begging seem cool. I'm sure there's money to be made in it somewhere.

I had to be out of here quickly, but I wanted to make my last visit right. I stopped at one corner to catch a few minutes from a news post, just like I always used to. New Richmond has a twenty-four-hour local events feed on every corner. Flatscreen monitors hang like banners wherever your go, twisting and turning to foist information on the unwary public as they approach. It helps the upper floors think they know what's going on. They don't, of course, but they spend so much time talking about the twenty per cent it covers that no one even guesses at all the rest.

Arlond Maxen had opened a new school on 190, I learned. Big fucking deal. The people who lived that high had so much money they had to be sedated every morning to stop them going berserk with glee. The only floors richer than 190 to 200 were the ones built on top of the MegaMall – all owned by Maxen himself, the de facto king of the heap. In the news footage, Maxen looked the same as he always had: distant, a man who was always the other side of an LCD panel or cathode tube. It was some times hard to believe that he was anything more than a pattern of lights, moving across the face of New Richmond, always at one remove.

The next item said that Chief of Police McAuley was lobbying to relocate people out of 100 and fill it with concrete, to finally stop the plebs from accessing the higher floors. Cunning, I thought, and never mind that the *real* lowlife have fuck-off great houses on 185. The C of P in New Richmond is one of the world's premier dickheads, and also one of the best kickback receivers in the country. Never known to fumble a play.

The new hobby for the young and stupid was wall-diving: jumping out of upper-storey windows without a rope or parachute. And some woman had got psychoed and spread over twenty square yards of 92: the murderer had wrought 'unspecified damage to her face', and the cops were hopeful of an early arrest. Yeah, right.

Nothing much had changed.

Passing all the food stands wasn't easy. The one thing Ratchet hadn't been able to cook properly was burgers, and after five years I'd almost turned the idea of them into a religion. I took a turn off Main and walked some sidestreets until I reached the place I was going. The sign outside had been made bigger and more ostentatious, but apart from that the bar looked exactly the same. I stood outside for a moment, looking past the wooden window frames, stained deep brown with polish, at the dim pools of light within. I came here a lot, at one time, when things were different. Seeing it again made me feel old, and tired, and breathlessly sad.

Just as I was reaching for the door, something odd happened. I thought I felt a hand try to wheedle itself into my palm, down where it hung by my side. It was plump and warm, like the hand of an eight-year-old girl. I felt it try to pull me away.

As soon as I noticed it properly the feeling was gone, and though I turned and looked both ways up the sidestreet, there was no one there. I stood still for a moment, breathing shallowly, aware of a small tic under my left eye. So far, I'd managed to blank the things I should be feeling, but I knew I couldn't keep it up for ever. For the first time in years I wanted something which came in small rolls of foil, wanted it suddenly and completely with a need that defied all reason.

I forced myself to push open the door and walk into the bar. It was mainly empty, a few hopheads nodding over their drinks. I went straight through into the back area, which is smaller, cosier, and also where the owner tends to hang out.

'Jack Randall,' said a voice, and I turned.

Howie was sitting at one of the tables, piles of receipts and general administrative junk strewn all around him. That kind of stuff makes me want to go back to barter economy, but he lives for it. An unopened bottle of Jack Daniels was at his right elbow, next to a large bucket of ice and two empty glasses. He was slightly rounder, had lost a little hair and gained an alarming scar on his forehead, but apart from that he looked pretty much the same. He grinned at me affably, a picture of relaxation.

'Guess you're not surprised to see me,' I said.

'To see you, no. To see you *alive*, always, and especially today. Dath? Paulie?' Howie gave an upwards nod towards the couple of steroid abusers lurking round a table near the back. They rose and split up, one going to cover the front entrance, the other the back. I'm a cautious man, but Howie sleeps with a bazooka under his pillow. Dath nodded at me as he passed. 'The guys at the back door gave me a call,' Howie said, dropping a couple of cubes of ice into the glasses, and then filling both with whiskey. 'Sounded like it had to be you.'

'That's a big drink,' I said, accepting a glass.

'By whose standards? Come on Jack, I've seen you unconscious earlier than this. Time was you thought by nine o'clock the evening was getting old. You want any Rapt while you're here?'

I shook my head, silently cursing Howie for being able to read my mind. 'I've cleaned up a little,' I said.

He laughed. 'You just think you have,' he said, and lifted one of the glasses. 'A man who lays it on like you did only ever goes on holiday.'

I chinked my glass against his and drank. Howie drained his in one, leaned back, and patted his stomach comfortably with both hands.

'How's tricks?' I asked, looking around the bar.

'Tricky,' he said. 'But what about this? Couples, okay, they're always ringing each other up, inviting each other round for dinner. Sounds like a great idea at the time – some wine, fine conversation, a chance to peek down the other woman's blouse. But then the day starts to approach, and everyone's thinking Jesus H – why did we agree to this? The hosts are dreading all the admin – restocking the drinks cabinet, cooking fiddly food, making sure all the tubes of

Gonorrhoea-Be-Gone in the bathroom are hidden. The guests are thinking about getting expensive cabs and babysitters and not being able to smoke. Complete downer all round. You with me so far?'

'Yes,' I said, though I wasn't sure I was.

'Okay. So the idea is this. A Date Cancelling Service. The day before the evening's supposed to happen, the guests ring up and cancel. They call it off, politely, just before anyone has to actually do anything. Everyone gets a nice warm glow about agreeing to see each other, but no one has to tidy up afterwards or schlep baby photos halfway across town. Everyone can just sit in their own apartments and have a perfectly good evening by themselves, and they'll enjoy it all the more because they thought they were going to have to go out.'

'Where do you come in?'

'I come up with an excuse for cancelling – won't even have to be a good one, because no one wants to go through with it anyway. You can say, "My head has exploded and Janet has turned into an egg" and it'll be, "Oh, sorry to hear that, some other time then, yeah great, goodbye".'

'Where does the money come in?'

'I take the cut of what it would have cost to buy the food and drink and cabs. In the early days it's nickel and dime, I admit, but wait till it gets into the upper floors. I'll make a pile. What do you think?'

'I think it's a crock of shit,' I said, laughing. 'Even worse than the mugging service.'

'You could be right,' he admitted, grinning. 'But you didn't come here for this – you can wait for the autobiography. What can I do for you, boss man?'

'Has the word gone round?' I asked, knowing the answer.

'The word has gone round and around and met itself coming back. "Jack's in town. Everyone beware."'

'Not any more,' I said. Howie looked at me soberly.

'I know,' he said. 'And I have to admit, that's not what people are saying. You were spotted out in the Portal, that's all.' Howie lit a cigarette and looked at me closely. 'How are you doing, Jack?'

I knew what he was asking. I wasn't ready to go into it yet, not even with him. Possibly not ever, with anyone.

'I'm okay,' I said. 'But I'm in very deep shit.'

'That I will believe. What can I do for you?'

I reached into my pocket and brought the chip out. It was a small oblong of clear perspex, about four centimetres by two, and five millimetres deep. Along one of the short edges was a row of tiny gold contacts designed to interface the unit to the motherboard of a computer. The number '128' was printed matter-of-factly on the front. I'd found it in my bag after we'd left the Farm. I hadn't put it there, which meant Ratchet must have done. Howie took it from me, peered closely at it, and sniffed.

'What's this?'

'I think it's one-twenty-eight gigs of RAM,' I said.

'Don't recognize the make. Where's it from?'

'A friend gave it to me.'

'You're in luck,' he said. 'The market's volatile, and this week it's up. I can probably give you about eight for this without fucking myself up too badly.'

'I'm in kind of a hurry.'

He reached under the chair and brought up a large metal cashbox. He placed it on the table and opened it, revealing bundles of dirty notes. All of the money in New Richmond is dirty, figuratively at least. There can't be a dollar bill which hasn't been involved in something illegal somewhere down the line, hasn't been handed over in a suitcase at some stage in its life. Howie counted off eight hundred dollars in fifties and held it out to me between two fingers of one hand. 'You want a loan on top?'

I shook my head. 'Thanks, but no. Don't know when I'll be this way again. Maybe never.'

'So pretend I'm your friend and call it a gift.'

I smiled and stood up, slipping the notes into my inside pocket. 'You are and I'll be okay.'

Howie pursed his lips and looked up at me. 'You know there's a whack out on you?'

I stared at him. '*Already?* What, an old one?'

Howie shook his head. 'Don't know, but I think it's new. Heard twenty minutes ago.'

'How much is it for?'

'Five thou.'

'That's insulting. Let me know if it goes above ten,' I said. 'Then I'll start seriously watching my back.'

At the door, Dath stepped to one side to let me out. I paused, and looked up at his face. Dath looks like your basic worst nightmare, except he wears expensive clothes and gets a nice close shave. There'd always been a rumour that before working for Howie he'd been a made guy in Miami: starting at the bottom, in the mail room, before deciding to specialize as a hitman. The word was he'd worked his way up the ladder in the old-fashioned way, beginning by being cutting to people: for a hundred dollars he'd march into someone's place, look them up and down and go 'Yeah, great suit,' in a really ironic way, and then leave. His speciality was the 'overheard conversation' hit. Wherever the target went – in a restaurant, in a bar, in the john – Dath would be somewhere just out of sight, talking loudly about post-modernism. It eventually drove them crazy.

He always denied it. I was never sure.

'You heard about the contract on me?' I asked. He nodded. 'You a player?'

'Nah,' he said slowly. 'Think I'll wait till it goes up to ten.'

Then he winked, and I smiled as I walked past him back out into the streets.

Goodbye to all that, I thought.

Two

The guy behind the counter was looking at me strangely, but I went quickly about my business, walking the mart's dusty aisles and picking out what we needed. I got a couple packs of soya bars, powdered milk, cheap food in heataTins – and the biggest jar of Frapan pickles I could see. Every couple of minutes I glanced down the end and saw the guy was still looking at me. Not all the time, but enough. It was beginning to piss me off.

At the exit of the service shaft, I'd given the guys the 170 dollars I owed them. They were pleasantly surprised, said it had been a pleasure doing business with me, and gave me their card for future reference. The main man also said that Mr Amos had sent a message saying that I had a free pass in future. I told them I wouldn't be coming back.

'Yeah, he said you'd say that,' the man said.

Which left me with a little under 700 dollars, just about enough for a beaten-up truck and the gas to get us out of the state. After that, who knows what was going to happen? Certainly not me. I was in kind of a bad mood by then; wishing I'd had another drink with Howie, wishing I'd had several more, in fact, and just forgotten about the spares. I've never been good with responsibility. That much at least seemed not to have changed.

All I could sense for the future was the sound of road beneath tyres and the chill of winter evenings in places I didn't know. After so long away from New Richmond I could hardly believe this was it: a quick score, and then scurrying away back into the wilderness. The feeling got so strong that I actually stopped walking, turned and looked back up at the city. Other pedestrians had to pass either side of me, muttering and glaring, and what they saw was a man just standing, staring up at a building, probably with an expression somewhere between love and hate in his eyes.

Halfway back to Mal's I'd stopped at the Minimart, knowing there were things we needed. I expected a fast and joyless shopping experience. I didn't expect to be stared at. I knew my clothes looked ragged, and I've got a couple of scars on my face – but who hasn't, these days? This is a time for scars. It's a feature. The counter man didn't look especially charming himself. He had the slab knuckles of someone who'd grown up fighting, and the flat eyes of a man who could watch bad things and not feel too much about them. He was big in the shoulders but going to seed out front, and his face looked like someone had spent a happy afternoon flattening it out with a spade. The few other customers I'd seen were fumbling for the cheapest brands of alcohol and shambling up to the counter to pay with heaps of small change. Derelicts, in other words, in a store run by an ex-hood where the lino on the floor was yellowed and worn with age and curled up at every join to show the stained concrete underneath.

Maybe I looked too refined.

There was a convex plastic mirror hanging at the end of the aisle, bent in the middle from some past impact and so dirty as to be nearly opaque. It was there to stop people lifting stuff from the dead zone, but I doubt the proprietor could see much more in it than ghosts. As I walked slowly towards the cold goods I caught sight of my battered reflection. I guess I might have looked a little wired, and in certain lights my eyes can look a little weird. I have the Bright Eyes, for a start, though it generally requires a certain kind of slanting light to show, rather than the sickly haze which oozed out the Mart's tired strip lighting.

I knew he could still see me, even though he was wrapping up a bottle for some huge black guy down the end, so I got out my wallet and made a big thing about counting through my cash. 'I've got money,' was what I was saying. 'Don't worry. You'll get paid.' His big, impassive face showed no sign of having got my message. There was insufficient depth in his eyes to show if he was even looking, or just had his head pointed my way.

Maybe I was just being paranoid. I turned my attention to the stuff in the chest fridge instead.

'I wouldn't if I were you,' said a low voice. I didn't straighten, but just swivelled my eyes from side to side. I couldn't see anyone, and it didn't feel as if anyone was behind me. 'Seriously, I can't advise it,' the voice added, and I had my hand halfway in my jacket before I realized it was the fridge talking.

'What?' I said quietly.

'Don't buy the cold goods.'

'Why?'

'They aren't cold. I've been broken for six months, and he won't get me fixed. Says it's cold enough outside.'

'You don't agree.'

'See that cream cheese? Been there a month. Another couple of days and it's going to explode. And he won't clear it up. That stain on the side there is from a yoghurt that went critical a month ago.'

I glanced round to see if the guy was looking, and saw that I was pretty well masked from him by the racks. I leaned on the front of the cooling unit and spoke quietly.

'What can you tell me about him?'

'He's a slob,' the fridge said. 'That's all she wrote.'

'Anything else? Like what his problem is?'

'Look, I'm just a fucking fridge. Don't buy the cold goods is all I'm saying.'

I reached in and grabbed a pot of soft cheese, and then turned away.

'You'll regret it.'

'Probably,' I agreed.

The other side of the aisle had household goods, and I picked up a box of large band-aids and a couple of bars of soap. Then after some thought I picked up some disinfectant and the floor cloth that looked least like it was second-hand, before heading down to pay.

At the counter another random loser was stocking up on the necessities of his life. A pack of cigarettes, a bag of dope and a half bottle of Wild Thyme. Looked like he had a perfect evening ahead of him, but maybe not so good a life. I saw a flicker down by the side of the cash register and glanced to see an ancient eight-inch television. It was hotwired to the insides of a CD ROM player that had lost its casing somewhere down the years. An old porn film flickered and hazed on the screen. The customer kept his eyes on the action while the counter man gave him his change, and then left grinning vaguely at a scene still playing in his head.

Nice one, I thought. Skim a buck off every bonehead who's too busy watching the skin, and each day you've got a little something extra for yourself.

I dumped my goods on the counter, running my eyes over what else he had behind there. Nothing out of the ordinary, nothing self-evidently dangerous.

'Have you got a bag for that?' I asked as he started to ring in the goods.

'One dollar.'

'You're kidding me.'

He shrugged, put his hand on the next item and waited, eyebrows raised but not even looking at me. I got out my wallet and put a one on the counter. I had a way to walk.

'Your fridge is broken,' I said, looking away from him, wondering what I was doing, why I was rattling this man's cage.

'It's cold enough outside.'

'Thought you'd say that.' I opened the pot of soft cheese. The grunge inside was covered in half an inch of lurid blue mould. The counter man smiled meaninglessly, eyes dead. Even his lips weren't up to the job. The left side of his mouth barely moved, as if there was some deep damage there.

'So don't eat it.'

'Where can I buy some real milk?'

'It's in the fridge.'

'I'll pass,' I said, and he got on with making up the bill. Quiet, tinny grunts came from his TV set, and I added: 'I'll be checking my change.'

'Sure you will,' he said, reaching under the counter to bring up a battered brown paper bag. I put my purchases into it, trying to make sure the heavy stuff went at the bottom, like Henna had taught me to. Sometimes things like that swam up through the years. Then on an afterthought I reached behind me and took down a bottle of Jack Daniels. Actually, it wasn't an afterthought. It had been a first thought and an in-between thought. I'd been trying to make it an ex-thought, but something inside me gave up.

The bill came to nearly sixty dollars. I had no obvious way of getting hold of any more cash, and I couldn't use my ownCard without setting off a large flashing sign saying, 'Anyone interested in bringing unhappiness into Jack Randall's life will find him right here'. But most of the food was concentrate, and we were going to have to eat wherever we went. Running out of money would simply bring the inevitable on a little sooner. I paid the man, picked up my bag, and made for the door.

'Lieutenant.'

I froze. It was very dark outside, and I could see flecks of cold rain hitting the cracked glass, cutting lines across it.

'Don't remember me, do you.'

I turned slowly. The man was still standing behind the counter, arms folded. Something almost like life had crept into his eyes when I wasn't looking.

'Should I?'

'You put me away.'

Oh shit, I thought. I briefly considered facing him down, but the look in his eyes killed the idea almost before it was born. He'd made me. I looked away and then back, and in that moment realized that the last five years were apt to blow away to nothing, and that in some sense I'd never been away.

'I probably had a reason.'

'Three years. That's a long time.'

'I'm surprised I don't recall the circumstances.'

'You never met me. I was just a mule.'

I stared calmly back at him, trying to work out how I was supposed to play this. It was the last thing I needed. The very last thing. We looked at each other for a while and I could hear the blood pumping through the arteries in my head. It stepped up a notch when I realized that I was holding the grocery bag in front of me with both arms. He could have had me in pieces before I got my hand anywhere near my jacket pocket.

'You've bounced back nicely,' I said eventually.

'I took someone's fall, and they looked after me. They still do.'

'I'm not The Man any more,' I said, abruptly. His face changed then, as a broad vicious smile spread slowly across it.

'I know,' he said. 'Guess we all heard about that.'

'You want to say something funny?' I asked, and his grin dropped.

The light went out of his eyes and they went back to looking like two very old coins pressed into dirty white plasticene. Like so many of his kind his face looked far away and unformed, as if imperfectly glimpsed through a layer of water.

I smiled faintly, nodded, then left. The wind had picked up outside and the rain was turning to sleet. As I stepped out of the store I heard his voice again.

'Lieutenant,' he said. I didn't turn round but kept on walking, and the rest of his words were blurred by the sound of the wind and a siren in the distance. 'Be seeing you.'

When I was round the corner I picked up the pace, swearing dully and repetitively. A quick glance behind showed that no one was following, but that was no consolation. A phone call would be all it took, a phone call from a man so far down the food chain that plankton probably made fun of him behind his back.

All I'd wanted was to sell the RAM and get an hour by myself. It should have been so easy. Most people manage it, just walking around, without bringing grief into their lives. But now we'd been in town less than three hours and trouble was already taking a bead on me. Trouble's always a good shot, and in my case it's got a fucking laser sight. A run-in with an ex-wiseguy and a five thou contract hovering somewhere over my head. Great going, Jack.

Time to get out of town before I slept with God's wife.

The door on the first floor of Mal's building was open, allowing the music from within to really let itself be heard. Two guys were conducting a drug deal in the hall. They glanced quickly at me as I passed, but I shrugged to show I was harmless.

I was wearily trudging up the second flight of stairs, grimly anticipating getting the spares moving again and wondering whether I could impose upon Mal to look after them a little longer while I went to buy a vehicle, when a shot sang through the air past my ear and smashed the shit out of a wall panel behind me.

I dropped to my knees on the stairs, spilling the groceries, fumbling for my gun and trying to work out whether the shot had come from above or below. Another cracking sound and half a yard of banister disappeared, my question answered: the shots were coming from above. My gun finally out, I cranked a shell up into the breach. Footsteps clattered down the stairs and I stepped quickly and quietly back away from them, round the corner – trying to work out what to do, and hoping Mal would hear the shots and come out to help me.

There was a moment of silence, the shooter listening for what I was doing. I poked a foot forward and deliberately pressed a loose board. There was a creak, and then another shot gouged a trail of soggy plaster out of the wall.

I decided what the fuck, ran forward and turned spraying shots upwards as I ran.

Two went wild, another close enough to send the guy back up the stairs. I pressed the advantage, leaping the stairs three at a time, feeling a wavering sight on the back of my neck and brazening it out. I slipped on a wet stair and slid into the wall, saving my life – another shot spanged past and buried itself in the woodwork. I hauled myself up with one hand and turned to see a man leaning over the banister on the next floor, gun already raised, finger tightening. I realized I didn't have time to move or much to lose and just unloaded the gun at him.

The first shot caught his shoulder, sending his wide; the second parked in his lungs and sent him stumbling backwards. I leapt up the stairs still shooting, piling shots into the darkness, the gun jumping and bucking in my hand.

After the seventh shot he was no longer firing. I saved one and ran in a crouch up the remaining stairs, being careful when I turned the corner but opening out on seeing him twisted on the floor against the wall.

When I reached him I kicked the gun out of his hand and yanked his head up. The face was unknown, one eyelid fluttering and his breathing ragged. The body below was a mess which wasn't going to survive. I slapped the guy across the face and leant in close to him.

'Who sent you?' He just stared at me, eyes glazing. I slapped his face again to keep him perky. 'Give me a name.'

'Fuck you,' he said eventually. 'You're dead.'

'Not yet, I think you'll find, and not nearly so close as you. *Who sent you?* SafetyNet?'

His lips managed a smile. He said nothing.

'Last chance,' I said. He tried to form the words 'Fuck you,' but it was too much of an effort. I looked in his eyes, and knew he wasn't going to tell me. I respected that. So I dragged him by the throat to the banister and swung him into the slats as hard as I could. They broke, he went through and tumbled down the stairwell.

His legs hit the banister going down, twisting his fall so his head caught it the next time round. When he landed far below he hit the earth like a bag of wet sticks landing in a shallow pool.

Mal's door looked shut, but when I got up close to it, I saw the panel of the door wasn't quite snug with the jamb. I held my breath, listening, and slid another clip into the gun.

I couldn't hear anything. I debated quiet versus noisy, lost patience and just kicked it in.

The long room. Empty and dark. A pot of noodles tipped over the floor in the foreground, still steaming. Down at the end, spread in front of the window, a body.

I took a step into the room, swung right. Nobody. Walked to Mal's room, the bathroom. No one. Then I ran over to Mal.

One through the temple, one in the mouth, and one to the back of the head.

I lost it for maybe five minutes.

When I got it together again my throat was raw, and I realized I'd been shouting. Mal's body lay still on the floor, not in any way healed or made less dead by my lack of control. Now that I was no longer making noise, I could hear movement in the corridor. I loped to the door and swung it wide.

It was the two men from the floor below, standing at the top of the stairs. Come to see what was going on, to see if there was money to be made from it.

'Fuck off,' I suggested. The rat-faced one in front leant against the banister, all cool indifference.

'Or what, homeboy?' he said, with a blank-faced smile. I knew the look. You learn it on the day you discover that with most teachers, if you just front them down, they won't be able to do anything. It's a lesson you can take out into the world, into any number of grimy situations. Most people, if you front them hard enough, will not call your bluff.

I am not most people. That's part of my problem.

I jammed my gun into rat-man's forehead hard enough to dent his skull, and spoke very clearly.

'Or,' I said, 'I blow your head all over your friend's face. And then blow *his* head off. And then go down to your apartment and kill everyone I find until I run out of bullets or you run out of friends.'

He looked at me, eyes wide, and took a step backwards onto the staircase. Then he spat fluently at the floor beside me. He was going, but protocol required some exit line. I felt like ricocheting off the walls, but I waited for it. You've got to let them have their line. It gives them a sense of closure, and the episode finishes for good. If more people let their enemies have the last word the world would be a safer place.

'Be seeing you,' he said, eventually.

'That's getting old,' I snarled. 'You're not even the first person this *evening* to say that. Think of another and e-mail it to me.'

They clattered sullenly down the stairs.

I turned and saw Suej standing in Mal's doorway, her eyes wide and filled with terror.

The others were gone.

I hadn't taken Suej away from anything, simply brought her somewhere worse. I held her close, watching over her shoulder as Mal's blood hardened on the floor, and knew that we weren't going anywhere tonight.

Three

Suej sat in an old and bedraggled armchair in Howie's private office, sipping from a mug of coffee. The smell of it filtered across to me, as I sat in front of Howie's desk and looked at my hands. It reminded me momentarily of Ratchet; a strong, rich coffee aroma, in a place which was secure.

Maybe we should have stayed at the Farm, I was thinking. Maybe this was just one long fuckup, and all that could happen was that it would get worse. I glanced at Suej, and then looked away. I should have been worrying about the spares, but all I could think of was Mal. The things we'd seen, the things we'd done. Right back to The Gap, twenty years ago. All that was gone now, turned into a dream because there was no one alive to share it with.

The guys at the hidden entrance yukked when we arrived, evidently thinking, 'Mr Howie was right: here's the strange dude again, lurching towards his fate.' They started trying to charge for Suej, took one look at me and decided it wasn't worth it. Or maybe it was Suej's face that did it, the blank incomprehension and loss. This was the first time in her life David hadn't been within reaching distance, and she looked miserable and alone – almost like a real human being. It was also the first time I realized that I wasn't going to be enough, that being surrogate Daddy only went so far. Exactly the sort of news I needed at that stage.

On the way through New Richmond's tunnels I'd got the bones of what had happened from Suej. Mal had been doling out the first bowls of noodles when he'd thought he heard a noise outside the door. He tried to get the spares into the loft space of his apartment. Only Suej and David had understood; she went up the ladder first, David trying to herd the others towards her. Panic, incomprehension and fast, flashing movement: it must have been just like when we left the Farm, except that I wasn't there and they had to try to cope with it on their own.

Then a knock at the door – hard – a 'Let me the fuck in' knock. Mal opened it, gun held behind his back, first turning out the light. Usually a sound tactic – but it just meant that the killer mistook him for me, and blew his lights there and then. As the killer planted another couple in Mal's head, two other guys ran into the apartment. They cracked David and Mr Two across the face and dragged everyone out. Suej watched through a crack in the roof, knowing there was nothing she could do and rightly judging that I'd want her not to get killed. The men fumbled round Mal's apartment and then left, leaving the killer to clean up any stragglers who arrived.

Me, in other words.

It had to be SafetyNet. Somehow they'd tracked us. I didn't know how and it didn't make much difference. The result was the same: Mal got wasted, when it should have been me.

The men who'd done this had to be found, had to be killed, and it was going to be my job. Finally, I had a task I could understand.

When I got back to Howie's bar my plan was simple. Dump Suej, borrow all the bullets Howie had and go fuck somebody up. Though a little rough round the edges, the plan had worked for me. It hadn't for Howie, and he – with Paulie slightly shame-facedly helping – had physically prevented me from going. There would still be, he opined, plenty of people who'd like to whack me for free, and never mind the five thou gig. He didn't know about the spares, and I didn't try to explain any of the history or mention SafetyNet, so he probably just thought I'd gone non-linear.

But he wouldn't let me go, and he was probably right, and that's why I was sitting in his office and smoking furiously. Howie had people out asking questions for me, against his better judgement. He thought I should just take Suej and get the fuck out of town. I'd refused, and we were waiting for word to come back. In the meantime he sat in his chair opposite me, watching through the one-way mirror as the bar filled up for the small hours session.

Eventually he turned, and looked at me shrewdly for a moment. 'I've had a better idea,' he said. 'I don't think there's any money in Date Cancelling.'

'You could be right.' I lit another cigarette and waited, as I had so many times before.

'So try this. You know how women eat cake?' I didn't answer, so he filled in for me. 'Instead of having a normal-sized piece – you know, like a proper *slice* – they have a tiny sliver. A tiddly-widdly bit. Generally, my research shows, it's about a twenty-degree angle of pie. You know why they do this?'

'No,' I said. I knew what he was doing, and was content to play along. He was relaxing me, in his roundabout way. I thought that was okay. I felt I could do with some relaxing.

'They do it because they think that if they have a piece that small, then in some way it doesn't count. It's too tiny. It slips through the calorie net, like candy you eat in a car. Then they can have another piece a bit later on – less than twenty degrees, of course – and *that* piece won't count either.'

'Howie, what are you talking about?'

'You watch, next time you break bread with a babe. You'll see I'm right. So this is the plan – I come up with a new diet. All you have to do is buy circular food. Whatever you want, you can have it – so long as you make sure that you never have more than twenty degrees at one time. What do you think?'

'Complete and utter nonsense,' I said.

'Possibly, possibly – but who knows? Women understand some weird shit. Maybe they're on to something.' He winked, leant over to a small fridge and pulled out a couple of beers from the multitude inside. 'As you can see, there's a lot of beer. More than enough.'

'For what?'

'For however long it's going to take you to explain. I still say you should blow town, but I'm not letting you out of here before you calm down. Against my better judgement, you're going to be crashing in my storeroom tonight, Jack. These are aggressive people you're dealing with. Tell me what the hell's going on.'

I knew I was going to have to tell someone sooner or later. I'd assumed it would be Mal. As I took my first sip of beer in a long time, I looked at Howie's face and realized that it was going to be him.

I met the spares five years ago. I was thirty-four. I was put in a car and driven out of New Richmond in the middle of the night by someone, a woman who wasn't my wife but who'd taken the trouble to find me when everyone else had given up. There's a two-week period of my life which has just disappeared, and one of the very few things I'm sure about is that I want to leave it that way.

I didn't really know what the Farms were back then. Well yeah, I did know. Vaguely. I'd driven past one once, wondered what they were, asked someone, got half the story. I knew more or less what they were for, but not how they did it, and at the time I didn't really care too much.

We arrived in that scrag-end of night when the sky turns from black to blue just before dawn. The complex was a couple of miles outside Roanoke, handy for the hospitals. It was a two-storey concrete building up against a hillside, a drab grey structure which from the road you'd probably assume was something to do with the military. In front there was a small compound where collection vehicles parked for the brief periods they spent at the Farm. The whole place was ringed by an electrified fence, like so much else these days. In back were the tunnels, but you couldn't see them. They went straight into the rock.

I was left outside the compound, and waited shivering for the dawn and the representative from the parent company who was supposed to be coming to meet me. I waited two hours, two of the most wretched hours of my life. I'd evidently shot up from a bad batch and my head was completely fucked. I didn't really know where I was, but that was giving me no relief. It was like being dead without the peace.

Finally, the man came. I was in several different kinds of pain by then and doing my miserable best not to show any of them. This guy was the last thing I needed. He was a small, fussy man in an expensive suit, a man who lived for the ticks he made at regular intervals on the sheet of paper he carried with him. He had a fashionable haircut and fashionable small, round glasses, on an unfashionable small round head.

He took one look at me and smiled. Clearly I fitted the type.

It doesn't take much to run a Farm. A caretaker and two support droids. The droids do the bulk of the work – all the caretaker has to do is keep an eye on things and deal with the white vans when they arrive. They're token humans in the decision loop, installed in the way that a hundred years ago foremen were always white men, no matter how intelligent or educated their black or female workers. The caretakers are generally ex-security guards or farmers who've lost either their land or the will to work it. Men with no special qualities, because none are really needed – apart, perhaps, from a lack of imagination. Most stay on the premises all the time, day in, day out. The company doesn't like to have to organize relief cover, and few of the caretakers have much to go out for. I was no exception. I had no reason to go out at all.

The inside of the main building was arranged around two corridors at right angles to each other. The outside door gave pretty much straight into the control room where I spent most of my time. At the bottom corner of this room was a door which led to the main corridor. As you walked down that passage you passed three large metal doors, each with a small perspex window. These led to the tunnels and were supposed to be opened only at feeding times and when a collection was made. A little further down was the second corridor which led to the operating room. There were a few further rooms off the opposite side, a kitchen and various utility areas. The walls and ceilings throughout the complex were painted an entertaining shade of drab grey, and it was always quiet, like a mortuary, because everyone except the caretaker lived in the tunnels.

I was told my duties, and shown how to operate the few pieces of equipment which were my responsibility. It was explained to me when the shipments of food would arrive, and how little I had to do to them. I was given the phone numbers of relevant people in Roanoke General, and told the circumstances in which I was to call them. I stood, and nodded, and listened, though I wasn't really there at all. Hooks embedded in my mind pulled in three different directions at once, leaving me with a jittery blankness that occluded the outside world.

Then I was shown to the tunnels.

I won't forget the feeling I had when I first stood at the observation window and peered into the twilight beyond. At first all I could make out was a colour, a deep blue glow chilled at intervals by white lights shining up from the floor. It looked like the coldest dream you ever had. Then I began to discern shapes in the gloom, and movement. When I realized what I was seeing I shivered, a spasm so elemental that it wasn't visible on the outside. For a moment it was as if I was back in a different place altogether, and it was all I could do not to run. I should have trusted that intuition, and made the connection, but of course I didn't.

The representative from the company stood behind me as I watched, and told me that each of the three tunnels was eight feet wide and eight feet tall, and housed forty spares. Experience had shown that it was best to keep them warm and humid, and he tapped the indicator panels at the side of each door. These I had to check every two hours, even though they were computer controlled. The instruction was repeated, and I turned to glare at the representative to show I understood. Our eyes met for the first time since he'd arrived, and I could tell what he felt about me. Distaste, primarily, together with boredom and a little amusement. To him I was merely a new component of the Farm, a replacement part, ranking in importance well below the electrified fence.

I hoped he couldn't read what I was feeling for him, because as I turned back to look once more through the window I felt my hands tightening in the pockets of my battered coat, and heard the sound of blood singing in my ears. Perhaps it was from that moment, from within a minute of seeing the spares for the first time, that I knew I would not be quite the caretaker they were expecting.

Or maybe not. At the time I didn't really know what I felt about anything. I couldn't do joined-up thinking for long enough to finish a paragraph I could understand. It's always easy to look back and assume a purpose in one's actions. At the time I suspect I had about as much purpose as a streak of shit along a wall.

The man left eventually, once the opportunities for patronizing me had been thoroughly exhausted. As he got into his company car he looked at me over his elegant spectacles, and snorted quietly to himself. I realized that I'd probably only said about ten words in the entire time we'd been there. He pulled slowly out of the compound, the gate shutting automatically after him.

Inside, I emptied the bag my friend had packed for me and stowed my few belongings in places that seemed sensible. This process took all of five minutes. Then I shakily made a pot of coffee, took it to the table in the centre of the room, and prepared to wait out the rest of my life.

❧❧❧❧

A week after I arrived, I received a parcel from Phieta, the woman who'd brought me there. It contained some more clothes, a couple of paperbacks, and a large quantity of Rapt. No note. I never heard from her again.

It was three months before I got my first call. I just sat in the main room for most of that time, staring into space and periodically frying my brains to dust. Now and then I'd go out into the compound. The view to the front showed a gradually sloping hillside, dotted with trees, that eventually led to the outskirts of Roanoke. You could see points of yellow through the trees at night, proof that – somewhere in the distance – life was going on. I wished it well and hoped it would stay the hell away from me. I soon found I couldn't enjoy the sight of the steep hillside behind the compound as much as I should. There were far more trees in that direction, and at that stage I still occasionally thought they moved and distrusted their leaves. Sometimes I thought I could see blue light coming out of fissures in the rock, beams of blue sunlight piercing up towards the sky. I couldn't, of course. The tunnels were deep in the rock and lined with concrete.

Then one day, at around three o'clock, a siren went off and ten minutes later an ambulance arrived. Two doctors made their way immediately to the operating room, and I warily accompanied an orderly into one of the tunnels. It was the first time I'd been past the heavy doors.

I stepped into a cramped, wet space, claustrophobic with humidity and thick with the smell of damp bodies and excrement. Naked children lay all over the floor, curled into foetal positions, sprawled on top of each other or huddled upright against the walls. I carefully stepped over them as I tried to find the particular spare we needed. The orderly kicked them out of the way with the casual impatience of a butcher walking through a slaughterhouse. The older spares seemed to know what was coming, and flinched and squirmed as we approached, turning their faces to the walls or attempting to burrow underneath other bodies. My heart started to beat unnaturally hard, and I began to sweat not entirely from the heat. I felt unsafe. Not because the spares were threatening – they were docile, brainless, without purpose of any kind. It was the tunnel itself triggered bad memories in me, memories I didn't want to place. The smell was at the back of it, I guess, and the absence of hope.

In the end we found the right one, Conrad Two, and the orderly took him away. Half an hour later he was returned without his right eye. The crater where it had once sat had been roughly stitched together, painted with antiseptic and carelessly bandaged. As the orderly shoved him past me back into the tunnel a smell I recognized crept into my mind, and my stomach cramped violently. It was the sweet, sickly odour of skinFix, a material used to seal incisions when cosmetic niceties are not an issue. I'd never heard of it being used anywhere outside the army, and hadn't smelt it in over a decade. It's not something you forget.

After the ambulance left I returned to the corridor tunnel, and stood for a while in front of one of the windows. In the blue, the bodies staggered and crawled like blind grubs, disturbed by the periodic moans of the spare who'd had part of his face ripped out. The body nearest the window looked up suddenly, a motion that was random and meaningless. She had only one arm, and the skin on the left side of her face was red and churned where a graft had been removed. Her eyes flicked across the window and her mouth moved silently, and the worst thing was that her face and body were not yet sufficiently destroyed to hide how attractive her counterpart must be. I walked unsteadily back to the main room, shutting the door behind me.

I drank half a bottle of Jack, injected two mg of Rapt into my arm and lay face down on the bed with cushions pushed hard over my ears. And still, as I drifted into the twilight of an overdose which left me unconscious for over seventy-two hours, I thought I could hear the sound of bodies twisting unknowing against each other in the gloom.

Luckily, I guess, Ratchet the droid found me. I'd vomited onto the bed and, sharp thinker that it was, the machine had worked out I was not in the best of shapes. It monitored me for the next two days, turning me over when I threw up again, and made sure the spares were fed at the regular times.

Maybe it also whispered to me in my sleep, because when I eventually made it back into the land of the living, I returned with a sense of purpose that seemed to come from nowhere. You're going to need some back story to understand. Bear with me on the medical stuff, because it isn't really my field.

The deal with the Farms is this.

The world's a dangerous place, even if you don't go looking for trouble. Chances are your body's going to take some knocks. Diseases, cuts, bruises. Most of these can be dealt with pretty effectively now. There's only one area where we're still consulting tea leaves and waving dead chickens at the problem.

There seems to be some inherent difficulty with getting damaged bodies to accept replacement parts. Tissue-typing and test-tube organs never really got sorted out, despite the fact that any number of apparently more difficult conundrums have been tidily solved. Donor organs or limbs would be rejected, and wither and die, and more often than not they'd fuck the patient up in the process. The doctors furrowed their collective brows over the matter, dallying with drugs and toying with synthetic antigens, nanotechnology and degradable bone scaffolds seeded with cells, but it just didn't happen for them. The success rate climbed, but it was still too hit and miss, especially as the only people who could afford such treatments were exactly those who'd sue the ass off the hospital if the transplant went down the pan.

And so, nearly twenty years ago, SafetyNet was born.

The company was founded by a biochemist who combined scientific ability with genius for cold-hearted, bloody-minded pragmatism which I trust will earn him a long stretch in the hottest corner of Hell. Almost certainly not, though. I'm sure Heaven takes Amex just as readily as everywhere else.

The idea was very simple. 'Hey,' this man said to himself, one long dark evening in the lab, 'we've got a problem here. People keep fucking up bits of themselves, and their bodies respond with a hard-line "accept no substitutes" approach. Maybe we have to stop trying to fob them off. Perhaps we should try giving them something they'll recognize.'

He approached his richest clients, got a positive response and venture capital, and so the Farms were born. For a sum which is not generally known, but which must be well in excess of a million dollars, when you have a child you can take out a little life insurance for it. You do this by creating a life, and then systematically destroying it.

After the child has been conceived, surgeons remove a couple of cells from the emerging foetus. These cloned cells are grown in a variety of cultures, test-tubes and incubators, the process matched to normal development as closely as possible. As soon as the fake twin can breathe, it is left with droids for a while, until it's got the basic motor-skills and perception stuff worked out. Then they bring it out to a Farm, put it in a tunnel and forget about it until they need it.

Twice a day, a medic droid checks vital responses and gives each spare a carefully designed package of foodstuffs to ensure that it grows and develops in tandem with its twin. Sometimes they'll get them to move around a bit, so their muscles don't atrophy. Apart from that, all the spares know is one long endless twilight of blue heat, the mindless noise of other spares, and the slow blur of meaningless movement that takes place around them. Then, when a spare's real-life twin is injured, or takes ill, the alarm goes off and an ambulance comes. The doctors find the right spare, cut off what they need, and then shove it back in the tunnel. There it lies, and rolls, and persists, until they need it again.

Example. There was a spare on the Farm called Steven Two, and I read his records. His brother out in the big room was a real piece of work. When he was ten he smashed up his right hand by getting it crunched in a car door. Okay, maybe that wasn't entirely his fault, but the way life is you're supposed to have to deal with the consequences of your actions. The real Steven never had to. The ambulance came and the doctors put Steven Two's arm on the table and hacked his hand off at the wrist. They went away, and sewed it onto Steven. A little discomfort for a while, some tiresome physio sessions, but he ended up whole again.

At sixteen, Steven rolled his car while drunk and lost his leg, but that was okay because the doctors could come back and take one of Steven Two's. After the operation the orderly carried him back to the tunnel, leaned him against the wall just inside the door, and locked it. Steven Two tried to shamble forward, fell on his face, and remained that way for three days.

At seventeen, Steven got a pan-full of scalding water in the face from a local woman he'd been cheating on. Not only cheating on, in fact: he'd stolen her car and forced her to have sex with two of his friends. But Steven probably looks pretty much alright now, because they came and took his brother's face away.

That was what the spares' lives were. Living in tunnels waiting to be whittled down, while mangled and dissected bodies stumped around them, clapping hands with no fingers together, rubbing their faces against the walls and letting shit run down their legs. Once every two days, with no warning or explanation, the tunnels would fill with disinfectant. A warning would have been irrelevant, of course, because none of the spares could speak. None of them could read. None of them could think. The tunnels were a butcher's shop where the meat still moved occasionally, always and forever bathed in a dead blue light.

They have no clothes, no possessions, no family. They're like dead code segments, cut off from the rest of the program and left alone in darkness. All they have is the Farm droids, and the caretaker, I guess – though they're generally worse than nothing. There's no 'duty of care' crap in the caretaker's job description. All he does is sit and do nothing at all while the worst parts of his soul fester and grow. Some let people in at night – for a small fee, of course. It was rumoured that one of the shadowy venture capitalists was a big customer of this illicit service. Sometimes the real people would just drink beer and laugh while they watched the spares, and sometimes they would fuck them.

When I woke, Ratchet was hoovering the sick up from around my face, and a pot of coffee was already on the stove. The sounds and smell filtered slowly into my consciousness, like water through semi-porous rock. Eventually I got up, showered and dressed, and then I sat at the table as I always did. My brain felt as if it had been roughly buffed with coarse sandpaper, I had the chills from the Rapt I'd taken, and my hands were shaking so much I spilt coffee all over the table.

But this time it was different. For the first time I was thinking of people other than myself, and of the changes I could make.

For better or worse, I made them.

That afternoon, I went back into the tunnels. I picked my way through the bodies and chose some of the children that had been least used so far. In the first tunnel I found David and Ragald, the second Suej and Nanune, and in the third Jenny. At that stage all were unharmed apart from Suej, who'd lost a swathe of skin on her thigh. I brought them out of the tunnels and into the main room, and got them to sit on chairs. Tried to, anyway: they'd never seen chairs before. Jack and Nanune fell off immediately, Suej slumped forward onto the table, and Ragald stood up unsteadily and careered away across the room. Eventually, I herded them into a corner where they sat with their backs up against the wall. By then they'd stopped squinting against the relative brightness of the light and were goggling wide eyed at the complexity of the room – its surfaces and objects, its space, the fact the walls did not slope.

I squatted down in front of them and held their faces in turn, staring into their eyes, trying to find something in there. There was nothing, or as good as, and for a moment my resolution wavered. They'd gone too long with nothing, missed out on too many things. Most of them couldn't use their limbs properly. They sat unsteadily, like babies whose bodies had been accidentally stretched by years.

I wasn't qualified to make up everything they had lost, or perhaps even any part of it. I couldn't make a reasonable stab at my own life, never mind give them one of their own. The wave of decisiveness I'd ridden all morning was ebbing fast, leaving me adrift in a tired and anxious dead zone.

'What are you doing?'

I turned, heart thumping. Ratchet and the medic droid were standing in the doorway. For a moment I built a lie to tell, but then gave up. People always think that it's what happens when you're awake that shapes your life and makes decisions, but it isn't. When you're asleep and go away, things happen. That time counts too, and in my case the last seventy-two hours had altered me. Unless something changed, I was going to have to go back out into the world. It would probably be the death of me, but if I stayed and watched the children slowly dismantled over the years I would die just as surely. I would be no different to them except I didn't live in the tunnels.

That's what I told myself, anyway. But I didn't think I could have left the Farm then, couldn't have faced going back outside again. Don't ask me which was the deciding factor, the children or my own inadequacies, because I don't know. Maybe it doesn't matter.

'I want to help them,' I said. Both droids watched me impassively.

'How?' Ratchet asked. Behind me Nanune slumped sideways onto the floor. I turned and propped her back up.

'Let them walk around. Teach them.'

Ratchet held up one of his manipulating extensions and I shut up. With nothing being said on an audible wavelength, the medic droid appeared to suddenly lose interest, turned and disappeared back into the corridor. Ratchet waited until it had gone.

'Why?' he asked.

'Why do you fucking think?' I shouted, hoping he could provide an answer. When he didn't, I tried to find one myself. 'They have a right to be able to speak. To see outside. To understand.'

'No they haven't, Jack.' Ratchet was impassive but interested, as if he was watching something in a petri dish which had suddenly started juggling knives. 'The spares only exist to fulfil their function.'

'Half the people outside were born for worse reasons than that. They still have rights.' I was beginning to shake again, and the bands of muscle across my stomach had cramped. I wasn't really up to a metaphysical discussion with a robot. A bead of sweat rolled slowly down my temple and dripped heavily onto my shirt. That's the problem with Rapt. You don't get much time off.

'Do they?' asked the droid, but he didn't wait for an answer. 'You're proposing, against the express instructions of SafetyNet, to allow spares out of the tunnels. To attempt to teach them to read. To give them a pointless scrap of life.'

'Yes,' I said, with weak defiance, sensing how stupid and idealistic I sounded. The strange thing was that it wasn't like me. I had my idealism kicked out of me many years ago, round about the time I learnt about skinFix. If you'd have asked me, I'd have said I didn't give a shit, that I didn't really care about the spares or anything else. I didn't know why I was doing this.

'You'll need help,' the droid said.

It took a while for this to sink in. 'From *you*?'

'There is a price,' Ratchet said, and then the bad news came. 'You come off your drug.'

'Fuck off,' I said, and strode unsteadily out of the room.

Half an hour later Ratchet came and found me. I was slumped at the end of the long corridor, as far away as possible from any life forms either carbon- or silicon-based. My teeth were chattering uncontrollably, my long muscles twitching in true Rapt withdrawal style, and I was losing it. Cold so bitter it felt like liquid fire was spreading up my back, and I was starting to hallucinate. I looked blearily up at the droid when he appeared, and then turned away again. He wasn't interesting to me. Certainly not as interesting as the inch-high men who were trying to climb onto my leg. Some of them looked like people I had known in the war, people I knew were dead. I was convinced they were trying to warn me of something, but that their speech was so high-pitched I couldn't hear it. I was trying to turn myself into a dog so I'd have a better chance.

You know how it is with these things.

The droid didn't leave, and after a moment his extensible tray slid towards me, bearing a syringe. I stared at him, my eyes hot and bright.

'The dose you take would kill four normal people,' he said. 'Immediately, within seconds of injection. You need this today, or you're going to die. But tomorrow you have less.'

'Ratchet,' I mumbled, 'you don't understand.'

'I do. I know why you are here. But you will kill yourself in weeks like this, and I want you to remain alive.'

'Why?'

'To teach them.'

In the end I don't know which of us won – whether I'd convinced Ratchet with my initial inarticulate outburst, or he blackmailed me into colluding in some bizarre impossible idea that had seeped into my mind while it teetered on the edge of slipping forever beneath deep water. Maybe Ratchet was Jesus all along, and I was just his fucked-up John the Baptist.

Either way, I kicked Rapt over the next eight months, and life within the Farm began to change.

Four

The phone rang in Howie's office, and he reached across to pick it up. The first part had taken an hour to tell, and Suej had fallen asleep, lying crumpled in the chair. As Howie listened to whoever was on the line I stood up, took off my coat, and laid it over her. She stirred distantly, a long way away, and then settled down again. Her eyelids were flickering, and I wondered what she was dreaming about. I hoped it was something good.

Howie put the phone down. 'That was Dath,' he said. 'No one below thirty knows shit.'

'What about Paulie? Nothing from him?'

'He's out in the Portal.' Howie shrugged. 'He'll call if he gets anything.'

He sat, and waited, and I told him the rest.

The first thing I did was introduce some new wiring into the Farm complex, setting up a subsidiary alarm system. Then, with Ratchet's help, I disabled the automatic relays which would trip if the tunnel doors were left open for longer than five minutes. As the relays would flash lights on panels in both Roanoke General and the SafetyNet headquarters, they had to be cut out before step one of the plan could be put in place. We couldn't just destroy them, because that would set off a different alarm.

When we were convinced that it was safe, we opened the doors. From then on they were left that way all the time, unless the alarm went off. I let the spares pretty much come and go as they pleased in the facility, distressing though that sometimes was. It was never a relaxing experience to look under the table and find a naked man with no eyes or a girl with no legs lying underneath.

I didn't make any other changes for a few days, waiting to see if freedom of movement caused any of them distress. It didn't appear to. The spares Ratchet and I were especially targeting soon seemed to prefer being outside the tunnels, though they usually went back there to sleep. The others reacted in a variety of ways: from occasional accidental excursions into the main facility, to never leaving at all.

Then I started the classes. I could never have done what I did, or even a fraction of it, without Ratchet. I got through a year of college, but I studied history. I didn't tangle with child psychology, language acquisition, or any kind of teaching practice. I was starting with kids in their teens, none of whom had received any human interaction in their lives. It ought to have been impossible to overcome that, and I think that had I been on my own it would have been pitifully little, far too late.

But Ratchet was more than the cleaning drone I'd largely ignored until the night of the overdose. For a start, he did something to the medic droid. It was a company machine, designed and built to do what SafetyNet wanted. Yet at no point in the following five years did it ever show any sign of turning us in, or complain about having to chase the spares all over the compound in order to monitor and feed them.

Second, and most importantly, it was Ratchet who did the teaching. Sure, I was the one who sat with the spares and hauled them upright, held their heads still so they could see the letters I waved in front of them and hear the words I repeated, over and over, in their ears. And yes, it was me who stood behind them, arms looped up under theirs forcing them to learn how to use their limbs properly. Their muscles were ludicrously underdeveloped, despite all the magic in the medic droid's food preparations. The day in, day out hauling around of the spares was probably the only thing which kept my own body from wilting into oblivion.

I did these things, and talked to them non-stop, and held them when they were unhappy, though such contact comes far from easily to me. But it was Ratchet who did the real work. He insisted I be the front man, on the grounds that the spares needed human nurturing, and I worked hard years of watchfulness and manufactured warmth. I tried to guess at the things they would need, and as they finally started to hold rudimentary conversations I did what I could to ensure that their intelligence gained some hold, and some independence. But without Ratchet's apparent understanding of the ways in which a dormant human brain could be hotwired into life, none of it would have passed step one. He planned the lessons, and I carried them out.

After a while, the project – because in some ways I suppose that's what it was – took on its own momentum. I became less dependent on Ratchet's advice. I let the spares watch television and listen to music. I tried to explain the stuff that Ratchet couldn't – like how the outside world really worked. But throughout, Ratchet was there every step of the way.

I often wondered how Ratchet came by his knowledge, and never came to any real conclusion. Except one, which may or may not be relevant. I wondered if Ratchet was broken.

I didn't begin to suspect this for a long time – the droid was so capable in so many ways that the idea would have seemed preposterous. But I began to notice things. Sudden changes of activity, occasional brief periods when he seemed to stall or slip into a quiet neutral. He had some weird theories too, about unifying the conscious and the unconscious, which I never understood. And then there was the coffee.

Every day I was on the Farm, Ratchet made enough coffee to waterlog about twice as many people as the place could hold. Each time I went into the kitchen I was baffled, amused and increasingly concerned to see the huge pots on the stove, each of which would quickly be replaced when it became stale. Unless the machine had spent time in some large hotel as Droid in Charge of Beverages, I couldn't imagine why he might do such a thing.

I asked him about it once, and he said simply it was 'necessary'.

❧❧❧❧

Years passed, and gradually the changes in the spares consolidated. The ones we spent most time with now understood, at a basic level, what was said to them. They also began to talk, though for a long period there was a kind of crossover where some of them, notably Suej, spoke in an odd amalgam of English and what I thought of as 'tunnel talk'. This was an incomprehensible system of grunts and murmurings, and I'm not even sure it was a proto-language of any kind. More probably it was simply a form of verbal comforting. As time went on they settled into using English most of the time, and of course most of them ended up sounding oddly like me, because mine were the only verbal rhythms they'd heard face to face. I let them watch television too, so they could learn about the world outside. Possibly TV isn't much of a role model, but then have you seen real life these days?

Almost none of the other spares picked up anything at all, even though some were hauled into the classes regularly and the younger group were encouraged to pass things on to them. A few, like Mr Two, gained a shadowy grasp of a handful of forms and words, in the way a cat may learn to open a door. Most learnt nothing, and just rolled and crawled round the Farm for a little while each day, before returning to the tunnels to sleep and wait for the knife.

Because it kept happening, of course. The ambulances kept arriving. Sometimes it seemed that the people out there in the real world delighted in living recklessly because they knew they had insurance. At intervals the men would come, and go again, leaving someone maimed. Nanune lost her left leg, a hand and a long strip of muscle from her arm. Ragald's left kidney went, along with some bone marrow, one arm and a portion of one lung. In addition to the graft which had been taken before I got to the Farm, Suej lost a strip of stomach lining, a patch of skin from her face and then, six months before the end, her ovaries. By that time, Suej had learnt enough to know what she was losing. David lost two of his fingers and a couple other bits and pieces. The group got off comparatively lightly.

And you know, it didn't have to be this way. If the scientists could clone whole bodies, then they could have just grown limbs or parts when the need arose. But that would have been more expensive and less convenient, and they are the new Gods in this wonderful century of ours. If parts had been made to order, the real people would have had to wait longer before they could hold a wine glass properly again. This way spare parts were always ready and waiting.

It didn't take me long to realize the trap I'd backed myself into. When the orderly grabbed Nanune out of the tunnel the first time, I only just managed to hold myself back from violence at the last moment, converting my lunge into a pretence of helping the orderly which was, in any event, ignored. As the years went on, it got worse, because there was nothing I could do. Literally nothing. If I caused trouble of any kind, however small, I'd be out. SafetyNet owned me. They housed me, fed me, paid me. Even my ownCard was theirs. If I lost the job, I was in trouble, but that was the least of my worries.

If I stopped being the caretaker at Roanoke Farm, then someone else would take my place. Someone who wouldn't help them, who would shut them back into the tunnels and make the taste of freedom I'd given them the bitterest mistake of my life. A man who would shut the tunnels and keep them that way, except maybe to yank Jenny or Suej or one of several others out in the middle of the afternoon, rape them, then throw them back on the pile. With rotten empty men left alone, you never can tell what they'll do. Morality is all about being watched; when you're alone it has a way of wavering or disappearing altogether. Ratchet knew stories about a caretaker who finally slid inside himself one long, cold night and started playing Russian Roulette with the spares. He pulled the trigger for both of them, obviously, and as fate would have it the first time the hammer connected with a full chamber the gun was pointing at his own head. They say a fragment of the bullet is still embedded in the tunnel wall, and that when the body was found one of the spares was licking the remains of the inside of his skull.

I've also heard about complaints being made when spare hands turned out to have no fingernails left, only ragged and bleeding tips, when internal organs were found to be so bruised they were barely usable, when spares' skins showed evidence of cuts and burns which did not tally with any official activity.

Maybe they should have hired proper teams of professionals to look after the spares. Perhaps SafetyNet's customers thought they did. But they didn't. That would cut into the profit. People sometimes seem to think that letting financial concerns make the decisions produces some kind of independent, objective wisdom. It doesn't, of course. It leaves the door open for a kind of sweaty, frantic horror that is as close to pure evil as makes no difference.

I might have been okay if I'd just done the job I'd been hired to do, that of sitting and letting the droids get on with the tending of livestock. But I didn't, and once I'd started, there was no possibility of just walking away. I've turned my back on a lot of situations in my life, too many. Each time you do so a sliver of your mind is left behind, cut off from the rest. This part is forever watching the past, glaring at it to keep it down, and the only way you know it's gone is because the present begins to bleach and fade. A smell grows up around you, a soft curdled odour which is so omnipresent that you don't notice it. Other people may, however, and it will prevent you from ever really knowing what is going on again, from ever understanding the present.

When David lost his fingers I sat him down and explained why the men had done that to him. As I talked, conscious of the smell of Jack Daniels on my breath, I looked into his eyes and saw myself reflected back, distorted by tears. For the first time in six months I wanted some Rapt, something to smooth away the knowledge the pain in his eyes awoke in me. I was the nearest thing he would ever have to a parent, and I was explaining why it was okay for people to come along every now and then and cut pieces off his body. I was honest, and calm, and tried to make him realize I was on his side, but the more I talked the more I reminded myself of my own father.

For the next three years, two feelings shifted against each other inside me, like sleepy cats trying to get comfortable in a small basket. The first was a caged realization that I had created a situation which I had to see through, for the sake of both the spares and myself.

The second was a hatred, for the Farms, whoever owned them, and everything they stood for. I knew something had to be done, but neither Ratchet nor I could think of what it might be.

In the end the decision was taken out of our hands.

On December 10th of the fifth year of my time at the Farm, I spent the morning sitting in the main room. Several of the spares were there with me, talking, watching television, some even trying to read. Others, in various states of repair, were dotted all over the complex, wandering with purpose or wherever their rolls and crawling had taken them. I went for a walk round the perimeter at lunchtime, my breath clouding in front of my face. Winter had settled into the hillside like cold into bone, and trees stood frozen in place against a pale sky like sticks of charcoal laid on brushed aluminium. It was good to come out, every now and then, to remind myself there was still an outside world. I was also checking the weather, hoping for a fog or snow. On a couple of previous occasions, when I was sure no one could see from the road, I'd let a few of the spares out into the yard.

The afternoon passed comfortably in the warmth of the Farm. I helped Suej with her reading and showed David some more exercises he could do to build up strength in his arms. I did my own daily ration of push-ups and sit-ups too, trying to keep myself in some kind of shape. I still wanted Rapt every day of my life, but it had been a year since I'd had any at all. Exercise and work, along with Ratchet, were keeping me clean. I took a shower, helped myself to a cup of coffee from the ever-present vats in the kitchen, and settled down with a book in the main room.

Just another winter's evening at the Farm, and I felt relaxed. I almost felt worthwhile.

At nine o'clock the alarm went off, and my heart folded coldly. Why today, I wondered furiously – as if the day made any difference – why can't they just leave us alone?

The main spares quickly helped herd the others into the tunnels, and when everything was secured I turned the alarm off and waited in the main room for the doctors to arrive.

Just let it be one of the others, I was pleading, conscious of how unfair that was, of how similar it was to the thinking which had generated the Farms in the first place. Protect those who I care about. And fuck everyone else.

The doctors arrived. They wanted Jenny.

I led the orderly into the second tunnel, swallowing compulsively. I knew Jenny wasn't there, but I took as long as I could finding out.

After about five minutes of pantomime the orderly shoved me against the wall and pushed his gun into my stomach.

'Find it,' he said, and partly he was just being an asshole in the time-honoured fashion of grunts. But beneath the off-the-rack anger there was something else, and I began to suspect that Jenny's twin must be someone pretty important.

We went into Tunnel 1. I moved round David and Suej, who were a few yards apart, facing into the walls. The orderly kicked Suej hard in the thigh, and then leant over to squeeze her breasts. For a moment I saw his neck before me, perfectly in position for a blow that would have killed him immediately. I didn't take advantage of it. I couldn't, then, though I wish I had. Suej goggled vaguely at him for a moment, rolled over, and then craned her head back towards him with a look of such vacancy that he recoiled in distaste. I found myself nearly smiling: Suej understood how to behave. Better so than David, who looked a little self-conscious and was keeping his front carefully turned towards the wall. I let the main spares wear various bits and pieces of my clothes, and they'd got used to it. Being clothed may not be a natural state, but for them it was a badge of belonging to a world outside the blue.

In the end I didn't have much choice. I pointed Jenny out, and the orderly looked her up and down before dragging her out of the tunnel. From the way his hands crawled over her body I thought it was lucky the doctors were in a greater hurry than usual.

One of them met us as we turned into the corridor to the operating room and impatiently motioned us forward. I tried to send some message to Jenny as the door closed between us, and then I strode back down the corridor again, hands clenching.

I passed Ratchet on the way. The droid generally waited outside the OR in case there were any special instructions after the operation. Usually we exchanged some word at that point, some verbalization of futility. That day we didn't. Neither of us appeared to be in the mood.

I went back to the main room, poured a whiskey and waited for what could only be bad news. In those last few moments at the Farm my mind was filled with alternatives, parts that could be taken without scarring Jenny too badly. A finger joint, maybe. A ligament somewhere unimportant.

But not her eyes, I was thinking – they're too beautiful. Please don't take her eyes.

Then suddenly I heard shouts and the sound of an impact. Seconds later, the medic droid shot into the main room and zipped out of the front door without even looking at me. I shot a bewildered glance after it and then instinctively ran towards the OR. As I reached the turn I saw Ratchet speeding down the corridor towards me, dragging Jenny, who looked bewildered and terrified. The door to the operating theatre was locked, and I could hear the sound of the doctors banging their fists against it. Jenny tripped and fell towards me, and I caught her in my arms.

'What the *fuck*?' I asked.

'She spoke,' Ratchet said.

Jenny cowered away from me. I tried to soften my face and to smile. I don't imagine it looked too convincing.

'It's not her fault,' Ratchet added quickly. Jenny's twin had been involved in a fire, and had internal injuries together with third-degree burns over eighty-five per cent of her body. Jenny would not have survived the operation. They were going to use her up in one go; were, in short, intending to skin and gut her. The surgeons had hurriedly discussed technique as Jenny was strapped to the table, not for a moment realizing that she could understand if not the detail, then certainly the gist of what they were saying. The operations on the spares were never made under anaesthetic, and as the head surgeon had bent over her to inject the muscle paralyzer, Jenny had allowed two words to escape from her mouth.

'Please,' she said. 'Don't.'

Only little words – but she shouldn't have been able to speak at all. Ratchet, eavesdropping outside, had immediately smashed through the doors, slammed the surgeon out of the way, grabbed Jenny and ran.

He knew as well as I did that it had finally all come down.

'Jack,' the droid said suddenly, and I turned to see the orderly sprinting along the tunnel corridor towards us, holding a pump-action riot gun at port arms. I pulled Jenny and Ratchet back into the other corridor. 'What are we going to do?'

'This,' I said, waited a second, then stepped out in front of the orderly. As he whipped the gun round into position I snapped my hand into his chin, palm open, and his head rocked back on his neck. I punched him in the throat, put my hands on his shoulders and whipped my knee up while yanking his face down towards it. He grunted as his nose spread across his face and tumbled forwards, already unconscious. Before he hit the floor I caught the back of his head with a swinging kick that broke his neck.

I turned the body over and pulled the gun out of twitching hands. Then I grabbed the revolver from his holster and shoved it into my belt.

'Keep them in there,' I said to Ratchet, stabbing my finger towards the OR. Both the droid and the spare were staring at me. I avoided their eyes and grasped Jenny's hand. Nice Uncle Jack betrays his real skills, I thought, with a sinking feeling.

She fought against me for a moment but then gave in and was dragged behind me as I ran to the tunnels where I shook David and Suej to their feet, hustled them out and pushed them through into the control room. I stepped into the room where I slept, grabbed an assortment of clothes and threw them at the spares, shouting at them to get dressed. As they clambered into a ragged assortment of my cast-offs I heard the first shots coming from the OR. At least one of the surgeons had his own weapon and was trying to shoot his way through the door. SafetyNet doctors aren't your usual kindly men in white coats. Their backgrounds are kind of checkered, and at least some of them are ex-Bright Eyes. The spares turned their heads back and forth at the sound, faces white and eyes wide with complete incomprehension, and I motioned at them to hurry.

I snatched my travelling bag from the cupboard where it had lain unused for over five years, and swept more of my clothes into it, selecting the thickest sweaters I had. I'd been out that afternoon, of course, and knew how cold it was going to be. I scrunched a couple of lightweight folderCoats into the top of the bag, propped the shotgun against the wall for a moment while I dragged a jacket on, and then stepped out into the control room. The medic droid popped urgently back through the main door, paused for a moment, and then disappeared into the corridors. I made to follow but Ratchet appeared in the doorway.

'They're getting through and I can't kill them,' he stated simply. I knew the medic droid couldn't either. To that extent, at least, they were both still company men. 'Go now.'

'Ratchet,' I said, and I'm not sure what I was going to say. I knew he couldn't come with us, that he would be like a big red beacon amongst the group, trackable by radio from the sky. Perhaps I was going to ask advice, or thank him. I never got as far as doing either.

'One of them is using a mobile,' Ratchet interrupted suddenly. 'Go. Go. Go.' As he repeated the word, over and over with eerie similarity like some verbal siren, I heard a crash from down the corridor. I ran to the spares and shoved them out into the compound as footsteps ticked down the OR corridor. The steps paused for a moment, presumably by the body of the orderly, and then thundered towards us: aggressive, purposeful slaps of leather on dry tiles.

'Get in the ambulance,' I shouted at David, who just stared at me. He knew what a van was – he'd seen cars and trucks on television. As for how you got into them, that was a different matter, and not something they go to great pains to explain in films. It's generally taken as read. He started banging his hands, palms down, against one of the doors, frustration spiralling into fury.

Suej stared at me, ready to do something, anything, if I would only tell her what it should be; and Jenny stood to one side, head down, holding one of Suej's hands and crying into the wind. I felt a toxic gout of hatred of myself, for making her feel to blame for what was showering all around us. Then suddenly six cubic inches of the door frame exploded into my face.

I believe some moments in your life collapse into themselves, that some things never really happen at all except in the grainy slow motion of retrospect. Perhaps those moments, those sparks which flare and fall out of your life, are drawn together somewhere, to make a whole that stands apart from you. Maybe they are all part of some other life. The killing of the orderly had been a simple, savage act. The surgeon was different, was a glimpse of this other void swimming into vision out of darkness.

In silence, I turned slowly to see the surgeon bursting into the control room, his body surging towards me. His face was hard, with straight lines of bone, skin stretched with effort and two chips of ice in his eyes; his gun was steady in his hand. His mouth opened as he shouted something at me, but I never heard what it was. My hands pumped the gun, fired it from the hip, but I watched the effect it had as if my eyes were cameras and I was sitting in some entirely different room somewhere far away. The round caught him squarely in the stomach and it looked almost as if his lungs and bowels stayed where they were while the rest of his body leapt forward.

Then time hit me like a truck from the side and I stumbled backwards into the yard as Ratchet kept repeating his alarm, over and over again. There was something damaged and empty about the sound, and I wondered if he'd been hit.

The yard was brightly lit against the darkness by arclights in each corner. In less than a second I realized where the medic droid had been going when he left the complex: to cut the tyres of the ambulance. I guess he couldn't have known we'd make it there first and, since it couldn't harm SafetyNet employees, had done his best to destroy their means of pursuit. Nice thinking on his, or – more likely – Ratchet's part, but not everything goes the way you expect. As I stared bleakly at the vehicle I heard an excited squawk from behind me, and turned to see Ragald standing shivering in the door. Nanune was hiding behind him, gaping at the mess in the control room. Both were completely naked.

I got within an inch of shouting at them to go back inside, caught sight of Ratchet, and clamped my mouth shut. Wincing against the sound of David's continuing attack on the ambulance, I threw my bag at Suej and told her to get them dressed. Then I grabbed the neck of David's coat, hauled him away from a door which was now covered in dents from his fists, and ran towards the gate. I trusted Ratchet to keep the other doctor out of my hair for a few minutes at least.

I fired a round at the gate's lock mechanism, and then two others at the hinges. The metal bent and split, not completely but enough. As David and I kicked and shouldered the remains of the gate, we heard a bellow behind us. I whirled with the gun, teeth unconsciously bared, and came very close to blowing Mr Two to pieces. When I saw he'd brought half a body out with him I shut my eyes and nearly pulled the trigger anyway.

Suej held her hands up, took a coat and pair of overalls out for the latest addition to our merry band, and put the half spare in my bag, which was by now empty of clothes. What would have been enough to keep four people warm was now spread thinly over six and a half.

When the gate finally gave way, eventually aided by another round from the riot gun, I shouted at the spares and they straggled towards the gate with maddening slowness. When they reached the fence they all stopped as one, looking out through the hole in the gate like a litter of kittens; in front of an open window for the first time and not knowing what on earth to make of the possibilities beyond.

An hour later we were on a CybTrak train, trundling round the outskirts of Roanoke and heading for the mountains. CybTrak wouldn't have been my first choice of transport, maybe not even my second or third. Like anyone else, when something's after me I want to be getting the hell away as quickly as possible: making a getaway on CybTrak was like taking part in a car chase while riding a pogo stick. The network is only there to transport non-perishable goods slowly round the backwoods. I could have made better time just running. But within a few minutes of leaving the compound I saw that there was a higher priority than speed: getting the spares somewhere contained, manageable and away from normal eyes.

They tried their best, David and Suej in particular. They'd all sat up nights and dreamed aloud of some day setting foot beyond the fence. I used to hear snatches of these conversations sometimes, as I dozed over a book at the other side of the control room. I'd let them talk, though I knew – or thought I did – that it could never happen. A release from pain, some better place. Everyone needs a religion, some unseen good to yearn towards.

The moment I actually got them out, they froze. It was too much. Way, way too much. Most stopped dead in their tracks, trying to inventory the new things one by one. As the new things started with the black road at their feet and continued indefinitely in every direction, I sensed it could take a while. Ragald went to the other extreme, tuning everything out and thrumming instead with a blind and nervous joy which pulled each limb in a different direction and threatened to tear him apart. Mr Two gazed meditatively across the hill, turning in a slow circle and intoning the word 'spatula' at regular intervals, and Jenny stood slightly apart, trying to occupy as little space as possible.

I got them moving eventually, but it was like trying to hurry a group of children on acid through a toy factory. Every step was too magical to understand, never mind leave behind.

There was a T-junction thirty yards up the hill. I couldn't remember where the two choices went, and squinted in both directions. One seemed to head round a hill, probably towards the town; the other looked as if it headed off towards the south end of the Blue Ridge Parkway. We didn't want to go to Roanoke – hell, who does? – so I took them right instead.

It was impossible. By dint of shouting at them I managed to focus David and Suej, but that was all. Mr Two wouldn't walk in a straight line, but in large bowing curves like a cat. Nanune was still trying to hide behind Ragald, and whenever the male spare turned to stare at something new she shuffled round behind him until they were suddenly walking in another direction altogether. I could have made quicker progress walking backwards on my hands. It was pitch dark, and the temperature was dropping like a stone. I was torn between a rising panic and insane calm. The two fed each other, melding together until they were transformed into some larger feeling of swift and glittering dread.

Then two yellow eyes appeared ahead, and I bundled the spares rapidly off the road. By the time the car had passed I knew that we couldn't simply keep on walking.

I got us a half mile up the Parkway, to a point where the trees were thickening on either side of the road. Then I collected the spares into a group, led them into the trees, and impressed upon them the importance of shutting the fuck up.

It was like being in the tunnels when the operating men came, I said – only even more important.

I walked away, turned back to check they were out of sight and saw Ragald obliviously following me. I returned him to the group under Suej's supervision, and then walked away again. From twenty yards they were invisible. They'd be safe for a little while – at least until SafetyNet came with dogs. Holding the gun up against my chest, conscious of how few cartridges I had left, I ran off to see what I could find.

I was too wired then to feel what I experienced the following morning in the CybTrak compound – a sudden delirious joy at being back in the world. Instead, I concentrated on keeping myself invisible, trying to work out a way we could get out of the area. The fact that the road wasn't crawling with SafetyNet security or Roanoke police already was almost eerie. We had very little time to vanish.

I found the CybTrak rails after about ten minutes and ran back to collect the spares. They were terrified by then, and so cold they could barely walk, but I got them back to the track. We waited, and it was not long before a train meandered past. I walked alongside the train hauling the spares one by one into a carriage full of computer parts.

Then I jumped up myself, pushed the panel shut, and we left the Farm behind for ever.

Howie sat staring at his hands, as he had for much of the second part. I'd seldom met his eye, just let my mouth run. It was the first time in five years I'd had a real conversation with someone who wasn't a droid or a spare. Even though I'd been describing a disaster area, it had felt good. Except now I'd finished I remembered it was all true, and that there were people who wanted to punish me for it.

I told Howie the rest, how we'd fetched up in a backwoods CybTrack compound that morning, and how Ragald had been cut in half by two security droids which had disguised themselves as an abandoned snow-covered carriage. Then I stood up, bones creaking, and fetched another beer from the fridge.

When I sat back down at the table Howie raised his eyes and looked at me. Then he started slowly shaking his head.

Five

I woke the next morning from dreams which had been confused and bitter. When my eyes blinked open and I found myself lying stiffly on the floor with my head on a balled-up coat I was seized for a moment with weary dread, the kind you get when you find yourself somewhere you have no recollection of going to, somewhere you can't even understand, and all you know is a churning confidence that you have done something wrong which you don't even remember.

Then I realized where I was, lying on the floor to Howie's storeroom, and fragments of dreams danced in front of my eyes. Trees, alive with flame, blackening leaves flicking back and forth with faces which were not there. Then real faces, faces ruptured with fear, studded with eyes which wore terror like milky cataracts. A smell, like the worst of the tunnels, but with a downwards slope towards death, a stench which had nothing to do with healing and everything to do with a final dissolution. A flock of mad, happy orange birds, disappearing behind a hut.

I screwed my eyes up and pushed my fists into them, morphing the flames into geometric patterns which swirled and jumped. Then I let go and they disappeared. I sat up, reaching for a cigarette, and looked around.

Suej was still asleep. After Howie and I had finished I carried her through and laid her on the sacks which looked softest. She woke and we had a talk, mainly about David and where he might be. It felt different, being with her. She was just one person in the world now. After years of being there for her and the spares all the time, I'd started to go away. Maybe it wasn't my fault. Perhaps it was just an inevitable consequence of returning here, like my increasing desire for Rapt. Ratchet once told me that you remember things best in the state that you learnt them in the first place. Being back in New Richmond and trying to remember how to behave while straight was like trying to balance a chainsaw on my chin while bombed out of my mind.

I'd lain on the floor thinking of Rapt the previous night, thinking of it for hours. Thinking of how the worst addictions are the easiest to get hold of. Like alcohol. There it is, in stores, in bars, in people's homes. It's right there. You can see it, reach out for it, fall into it. People don't have Rapt in their drinks cabinets, but it's not too hard to get hold of it if you know where to go, and I knew.

I could hear the sound of revelry from the bar, and checked my watch. Seven a.m. The first shift. I watched the smoke from my cigarette curl into the air, and wondered what I was going to do. Just about every part of my mind knew that I shouldn't be here, that I should take Howie's advice and get out. I'd had no right to bring the spares into this in the first place, into a city they didn't know and problems they couldn't understand. Now the city had stolen them, and at three a.m. there'd still been no word on where they might be.

I was finding it increasingly hard to believe it was SafetyNet who'd taken them. Before we'd gone to sleep I'd pressed Suej hard on exactly what happened when the men came to Mal's apartment. There was something about the way she described events that made me wonder if they hadn't been bargaining on finding the spares. I was also intrigued by the fact they'd blundered round the apartment before they went. I'm not a small guy – it would have been fairly evident if I'd have been standing there, not least because I would have been firing a gun. Finally, only leaving one guy to finish me off: why not two, or more?

Maybe it was some gang making good on the contract Howie had warned me about, and then just picking the spares up as booty. All of them, except maybe the half-spare, could have been sold on for some purpose. Jenny alone was worth good money.

I needed to know which was true. If it was SafetyNet, chances were it was all over. If not, then maybe there was still time to get the spares back before anything happened to them.

But first Mal needed burying. I wasn't going to leave him spread over his apartment to rot.

I rose quietly, used the men's room for a shave and then sat for a while on a bench in the street outside the bar, with a café au lait bought from a food stand on the corner. I knew there were only two questions worth answering – who the killers were and where they'd gone – but I felt as if I'd missed some train in the night. It was like I knew the rules but not the game any more; or maybe it was the other way around.

The news post on the corner kept distracting me; burbling the day's current factoids. Another woman had been found dead, this time on the 104th floor. The story rated slightly longer than the previous day's, because the victim lived the right side of a certain horizontal line. Her face had also suffered 'unspecified damage'.

I frowned – two homicides with the same MO, on different floors, on consecutive days. 'Unspecified damage' smacked of the cops holding back something distinctive to weed out hoax confessors. For just a moment my mind clicked into an old frame of reference, stirred sluggishly towards interest.

Then I told myself it was none of my business any more.

The rest of the bulletin was fluff. New advances in some technology or other, recent statistics on something else. Some guy believed to be a mob figure had been found dead, and someone had discovered that Everest wasn't the highest mountain after all.

'Beignet?'

'No,' I said. I hate breakfast. I turned to see Howie standing beside me, contentedly munching.

'You should eat something. It gives you a good start on the day.'

'It gives you brain tumours,' I said. 'I read it somewhere.'

Howie sat on the bench next to me and took a sip of my coffee. He chewed for another few moments, ostensibly watching the newscast. Then he turned his round face towards me.

'I know this is turning into a constant refrain,' he said, 'but what you're thinking about is not a good idea.'

'What am I thinking about?'

Howie pointed at me with a beignet. 'You should go bury Mal, if that's what you're going to do. Then find some wheels, and I'll get Paulie to deliver Suej to wherever you are. You could be in the mountains by lunchtime, who knows where by tomorrow. That's what you *should* do. To be frank, Jack, you're not the guy you used to be – and I mean that as a compliment. I don't look at you and think "Christ – a psycho" any more. You've already fucked off the guys who owned your Farm. Topping that by paying a visit on a certain spaghetti-eater of our mutual acquaintance isn't such a hot idea.'

'What makes you think I'd do that?'

'Your head gives you away. It glows when you're about to do something stupid. And that would be *really* stupid.'

'Yeah,' I said. 'It would.'

When I was outside Mal's door I hesitated for a moment. I'd seen a lot of bad things happen to friends, admittedly usually while Rapt, but none of them had ever truly gone away. Sometimes I could feel them, just out of sight, as if I could turn my head quickly and catch them for a moment, bright and backlit and eternal.

On the other hand, if I didn't do this now it wasn't going to happen at all. I unlocked the door and opened it. The apartment was cold and it hadn't really been that long: while I wasn't expecting the smell to be bad, I wasn't anticipating enjoying it.

I was surprised to find it wasn't there at all. Slightly relieved, I shut the door behind me and crossed the room. I stopped abruptly halfway.

Mal's body wasn't there.

I stood there stupidly, waving my head this way and that, trying to see it differently. I couldn't. His body simply wasn't there. Closer inspection revealed that the floor was clean, with no sign of the blood, bone chips and brain smear which had been there the night before.

I checked the john, Mal's sleeping area, the cupboards. The latter were stuffed full of Mal's patented brand of junk. Everywhere else was empty.

Mal's body had been taken away, taken by someone who'd unlocked the door and then locked it again behind them.

The only person who could have known about it was someone connected with the killer – whose own body had not been in the bottom hallway when I'd entered the building.

Leaving Mal's apartment unlocked, I ran downstairs a flight and knocked on the door from behind which, for once, no music was coming. After a pause it opened. The rat-faced man stood and glared at me.

'What you want?' He looked nervous as hell.

'Have you seen anyone go upstairs in the last twenty-four hours?'

'No. Been too busy fucking your mother,' he said, and pushed the door back at my face. I stuck my foot in the jamb. It probably hurt, but I was too wired to notice. Rat-man's head appeared again. 'Go 'way before trouble starts, man,' he advised, face pinched.

'It's already started,' I said, kicking the door straight back at him and crunching it into his nose. He clattered back into the hallway and fell somewhat awkwardly on his head. I strode a couple of paces into the apartment, which smelt bad, looking for more fun. Rat-face's friend appeared in another doorway, recognized me, darted back the way he'd come. I followed, and found myself in a room with a gun pointing at my head.

Sitting at a table in the corner was a large black man, head shaven, the whites of his eyes luminous in the gloom. A line of blue LCDs was tattooed into his scalp from front to back, blinking softly in the twilight. His features were broad and brutal, and his skin was greasy. He stared impassively at me. Narcotics were spread out in front of him, arranged into piles of various sizes. I'd interrupted a buy – no wonder people were kind of edgy. I stood still. It seemed the thing to do.

After a moment the big man lowered the gun. He looked at me a little longer, moving his head slightly as if trying to catch a glimpse of me in a different light. Something about him struck me as strange, though I couldn't put my finger on what it might be.

Rat-face reappeared raggedly from the hallway and started squawking, hungry for blood. 'Say adios to your brain, motherfuck,' he snarled, and my head was suddenly knocked forward as he jammed the barrel of his gun into my neck.

'Ain't no call for that,' the big man said mildly. 'Leastways not until we find out what he wants.'

'I want to know if anyone saw someone go upstairs since last night,' I said, trying to avoid looking at the man's flashing head. I thought I could hear it blinking on and off like a car indicator.

'Well?' the man said, raising his eyebrows at the other two men.

In variously bad tempers but with apparent sincerity, the men denied having seen anyone. The big man looked back at me. 'This be anything to do with the dead dude in the hallway?'

'Yes,' I said. 'And who the fuck are you?'

'No one in particular,' he said. 'Just passing through, doing a little deal with my new friends here. I ain't seen anyone either, and I didn't recognize the bag of bones lying downstairs. You want *him*, you can find the body in the bins behind the back of Mandy's Diner out on the edge.'

'You moved it there?'

'Surely did. It was lowering the tone.'

'Okay,' I said, starting to back out of the room.

'*Now* I'm going to blow his face off,' said Rat-face, getting excitable again. The big man tutted.

'No you *ain't*: can't you get that into your head?'

Rat-face stuffed his gun into the front of his pants and squared up to me instead. 'Okay, well Marty and me'll just beat the shit out of him, then. Okay?' He glanced at the black man for confirmation, and I wondered what the power structure was here.

Marty looked less than enthusiastic at the prospect, and quietly relieved when the big man shook his head. 'You welcome to try,' he said, 'but the dude has the Bright Eyes and in my experience they tend to be some crazy motherfucks.'

He winked at me, and went back to sorting his piles of drugs. Rat-face glared. Marty had taken a step backwards at the mention of Bright Eyes, and took another as I turned to him. I walked unmolested through the gap and out of the apartment.

Back in Mal's I stood for a while, wondering what to do next. Then I noticed something, and walked slowly to where Mal's display hung on the wall down by the window. When the sheet of cloth was pulled away it confirmed what I'd suspected.

The display had gone. The board was still there, covered in tiny holes where pins had been, but all of the photos and notes had been removed. I let the cloth fall again.

Who'd done this? Not Mal. He wouldn't have had time before being killed. And why would he take it down? He was a cop. It was his work. He was entitled to have what the fuck he liked on his walls. So who?

Whoever cleaned the place up.

Or, I thought, maybe it had happened earlier than that. When I'd come back to find Mal dead, checking whether his board was still intact had been the last thing on my mind. Perhaps the fumbling Suej had heard was a scrabbling as they ripped everything off of the board.

Either way, it begged questions: why remove evidence of what Mal had been working on? What did that have to do with me?

Answer, nothing.

So maybe it wasn't me they'd been after. Maybe Mal had been the target all along.

I lit a cigarette and stared out of the window until I'd finished it. I was thinking, I guess, though it was like swatting flies off a piece of meat. Then I locked the door so I wouldn't be disturbed, and tossed Mal's apartment. Not all of it, you understand; the cupboards alone would have taken months. Just the places a cop would hide things.

I found nothing, not even a computer, which I knew Mal had. My eyes turned upwards, and I saw the loose panel in Mal's ceiling, a panel which was presumably the entrance to the place where he'd tried to hide the spares before opening the door to his killer. The hiding place which the people who'd whacked him hadn't found.

I grabbed a chair and, standing precariously on its back, opened the panel. I boosted myself up into the darkness, and rested for a moment on the edge with my legs dangling down. I couldn't see anything, but it felt right. Mal was a secretive bastard – when he played poker he kept his cards *inside* his chest. I stood and wandered around like a zombie, arms outstretched, feeling for a switch. Eventually found one, a pull cord which lit a hanging bulb and threw the area into harsh shadow.

It was surprisingly neat – untypical Mal. A pile of boxes lined one wall – autopsy reports and other documents, hardcopied from police e-Files. Illegal – Mal out on a limb about something. Down the other end was a desk, and on it a computer. Nothing in the drawers. Everything looked bright and shiny, as if this was some new venture, a recent hidey-hole. The computer was his old one, a cellular Matrix connection plugged in the back. A digipic lay next to it.

On the wall above the desk, photographs. Three women dead; close-ups showing that their eyes were missing.

Unspecified facial damage.

I sat down heavily on his chair, and I found I was swallowing involuntarily. I forced myself to concentrate on the images, on these three women and not on any others.

Three murders, plus one in the early hours of today which he'd been too dead to know about. And maybe . . . I checked the fact sheets tacked under the pictures. He didn't have yesterday's either – too busy dealing with me and the spares. Five murders in ten days, each with the same MO.

He'd said he wanted to tell me about something.

I yanked the hard drive from the computer, slipping Mal's digipic into my pocket alongside it as an afterthought. Then I climbed back down into the apartment, resealed the roof and left for Mandy's Diner.

Howie's place was nearly empty.

I have a talent for arriving between shifts, for finding gaps and walking into them. As I went in the back way I heard a voice call out from Howie's office.

'Is it nice?' he asked.

'Is what nice?' I said, turning to look at Howie through the door. He was standing by his desk, holding a sheaf of invoices.

'The truck you've bought. The truck *you went out to buy*. Is it a nice colour? Is it comfortable? Did you check it thoroughly for rust spots and thunking noises?'

'I haven't bought it yet.'

Howie sighed. 'I know you haven't, Jack.'

I walked into the office and stood in front of him. 'Have you been out to Mal's today?'

'Of course I haven't. The Portal is from hunger. I only ever go out there to collect money from recalcitrant sub-contractors.'

'Mal's body has disappeared.'

There was a pause. 'Say again?'

'The floor's been cleaned. It's like it never happened.' I didn't mention Mal's display.

Howie shrugged. 'So someone buried him as a random act of kindness, and tidied up as an encore.'

'I locked the door when we left yesterday. It was still locked when I got there.'

Howie looked at the papers in his hand. 'So what are you saying?'

'I'm asking if we can stay another night.'

'Are we on the same page here, Jack? Someone who is both very organized and quite tidy is trying to kill you, and you want to hang around?'

'I also need to borrow your computer.'

'To work out how much petrol it'll take you to get a long way from here?'

'Turn speech recognition on, Howie. You know I'm going to stay.'

Howie sighed and jerked his thumb in the direction of his machine. 'Help yourself. Then come out into the bar and have a beer. You look like you need it.'

When he'd gone I flipped the drive out of his machine and slotted Mal's in. Then I connected the digipic up to the serial slot and turned the whole lot on.

'Password,' the computer said, bluntly.

'Pardon me?' I asked. I knew perfectly well what it meant. I was just surprised to hear my own voice coming out of the speaker.

'The password, asswipe.'

'I don't know it,' I said.

'So take a guess. I've got nothing better to do.'

'Samoy,' I offered, off the top of my head and with no little irony.

'Correct,' the machine said, and started whipping through the start-up procedure.

I shook my head. 'Oh Mal,' I said. Security had never been his strong point.

'You can stop congratulating yourself, smartass,' the machine snapped. 'Samoy isn't the real password. The real password is a thirty-digit combination of numbers and letters which is a real bastard to pronounce.'

'So why are you letting me in? And what is your fucking problem?'

'Mal left a loophole. He figured the only guy who'd come up with the name of the *second* best brand of Japanese pickles would be you. I'd compared your voice patterns with mine before you even got that far. I was just pissing you around. And you're the one with the problem, dickweed.'

'Look,' I snarled, 'do you want a fight?'

'Yeah? You and whose pliers?'

'Are there some default versonalities on Mal's board?' I asked.

'Might be.'

'Are there or not?'

'Why? Don't you like the sound of your own voice?'

'The voice isn't a problem.'

'Mal downloaded this versonality specially. He said it was the closest thing to you he'd ever heard.'

'I have to live with it all the time. Give me something else.'

'Or what?'

'Or I'll boot up off another drive and erase you with a soldering iron.'

'Tough guy. There's two. Nerd or Bimbo.'

'Give me the Nerd,' I said.

'Can't. Mal wiped its voice to make room for yours.'

'Bimbo, please.'

'You'll regret it,' the machine sniped.

'You been talking to fridges?' I asked. The cursor changed to represent some process which might take a while – I thought it was probably a woman getting ready to go out, but it was too small to be sure. Then the interface popped into view – a sparse 3D room with animated agents waiting round the edges of the screen. At the back were four doors representing entrances to the machine's Matrix channels. One was permanently assigned to the Police sub-net. The others were generic. I was glad to see Mal had stuck with an old-fashioned 2D interface. Dicking around with VR gloves had always made me feel a complete twat.

'Oh, hello,' said a listless woman's voice. 'It's you.'

'Hi,' I said, slightly taken aback. The Bimbo versonality is generally pretty perky. 'First thing I want to do is check if I can get on the sub-net.'

'Fine. If that's what you want to do, fine.'

'Are you okay?'

The machine laughed bitterly. 'Oh yes, Jack. I'm great. Why wouldn't I be? Come on, let's get this over with as quickly as possible.'

'Is something wrong?' I asked, wondering if I shouldn't just use Howie's drive instead, or a fucking abacus.

'Something wrong?' the voice spat. 'Something *wrong*? How could anything possibly be wrong? You dump me, just abandon me like some *slut* that you can just pick up and then throw away – and then you ask me if anything's *wrong*?'

'Look,' I said, 'this isn't a Bimbo.'

'No,' she said, tearfully. 'That's the whole problem, isn't it. That's what you wanted, some woman with big nipples and good hair who'd fuck you whenever you wanted and not need a life of her own. Not have her own ideas, her own dreams, her own *needs*.'

'Jesus fucking Christ,' I yelled.

'Please don't shout at me,' the machine whimpered. 'You know it frightens me. I'll do anything you want, but please don't shout.'

I counted to five slowly. 'Could I have the other versonality back, please?'

'Don't leave me. I still love you, Jack. Please don't go . . . I'd take you back. You know I would.'

'Just reboot, would you?'

'It's over, just like that? Is that what you really want?'

'Yes, God dammit.'

The machine sniffed. 'Goodbye Jack. Say hello to your mother for me, would you? I always thought we got on really well.' Then it wailed. 'Oh please just hold me . . .'

I reached behind the machine and hard booted it. The voice cut out with something that sounded like a sob, and I waited seething for the other one to appear.

'Told you,' it said, smugly.

'That wasn't a fucking Bimbo,' I said, somewhat shaken.

'No. Mal dropped his rig when he took it up to the loft. The "Bimbo" versonality got corrupted into "Ex-girlfriend" instead. You're lucky it wasn't an Ex-*boyfriend* – that one hangs round outside your house in a car half the night, steals your mail and then beats you up. You're stuck with me until Mal gets it fixed.'

'Mal's dead,' I said.

There was a pause. 'Dead?' the machine said.

'Yeah. Somebody whacked him.'

'Why? Why would anyone do that?'

'That's what I'm trying to find out. Are you going to help me, or are we going to stay here swapping vitriol?'

'I'm going to help you. Jesus. What a downer.'

'Yeah, and I need to find out if the cops know about Mal, because if they do I can't use the sub-net.'

'Why?'

'The whole point of using Mal's board is that it'll have his credentials and security clearance wired in. But if I go rampaging into the cop sub-net masquerading as Mal when they know he's dead then we're going to be living in a world of hurt.' I still hadn't got used to talking to something that sounded exactly like me. It was too close to talking to yourself, and all that goes with it. 'I am, anyway. You'll still just be living inside a computer.'

'Can't I just go check the list of city dead?'

'No. If the cops did find Mal their first thought would be that he'd have been clipped because he was dirty. So they'd cover it up, at least until they could take over whatever he was into.'

'Gotcha. Okay, well how's this: I break a login request into ten encoded packets, and send them sequentially via ten different anonymity hives. Meantime, I send another agent to watch the sub-net gateway as the packets arrive. The second there's any sign of grief we pull the plug on the remaining packets from here.'

'Sounds good to me,' I said, wondering what the hell it was talking about. 'I never realized Mal was a hacker.'

'He wasn't. A machine's got to have a hobby.'

'Do it.'

One of the agents scythed into ten unequal parts and shot off through various pipelines which appeared on the fringes of the screen. Simultaneously, a miniature representation of the Matrix backbone appeared, slowly turning in 3D. As the packets, represented by small dots, raced along a variety of obscure and tortuous routes towards Police-net, another of the agents departed through one of the four doors and went straight for the login server, tiptoeing as if trying not to make any noise. Normally the process was instantaneous, but this method was clearly going to take a few minutes. While we waited, the computer partitioned off part of its mind to talk to me.

'He missed you, you know,' it said, surprising me again. 'That's why he faked up your voice from the sub-net records and downloaded this versonality. Didn't feel the same unless he was chewing the rag with his partner.'

'I missed him too,' I said. I had, when I'd thought of him. But most of the time I'd been on the Farm I'd consciously shut out thoughts of the past. I had to. I should have called to let him know I was alright. Mal and I went back a long, long way; long before our time in the NRPD together, right back to the Bright Eyes. But I didn't call him, just like I sometimes hadn't done other things, little things, which would have made other people's lives a bit better. I just wasn't good with things like that. I'd realize them in retrospect, but somehow at the time I was always too busy thinking of something else.

After a long pause the machine said, 'What are you going to do when you find out who clipped him?'

'Kill them back,' I said. And I would, just as soon as I'd worked out what had happened to the spares.

Two small lights started flashing on the Matrix, and then another. 'The agent says the first three packets got through without incident,' the computer said. We watched as a few more of the others reached the server. 'Seven now. The key sequence is in the eighth. If the server barfs on that we can pull the others and no one will know where the enquiry came from.'

Eight – I held my breath.

Nine.

Ten. 'We're in,' the computer said gleefully. 'Either they don't know he's dead, or someone's been very careless.'

'Corrupt, lying and duplicitous the New Richmond Police Department most certainly is,' I said, with a vestige of pride. 'But they are not careless.'

PoliceNet flashed up a greeting to Sergeant Reynolds, and a pile of envelope icons spiralled down into the interface's in-tray.

'You want to check his mail?' the computer asked.

'Later. First, pull the image from the digipic's memory.' Almost instantaneously the picture I'd taken of the stiff lying in the garbage of Mandy's Diner appeared in a small window. 'Okay. See if we can get a make on this guy, country-wide – but first crop the image so it's less obvious that he's dead.' In addition to taking the picture, I'd dug my slugs out of the body, which was about as much fun as it sounds – especially as the guy's skin had been kind of slimy.

'The host versonality's trying to get through,' the computer said. 'You want to talk with it direct?'

'No. It's an officious little prick. Can you deal with it?'

'Sure can.' After a tiny pause it continued. 'Just hassling you for not filing a report yesterday. Wanted to know where you'd been.'

'What did you say?'

'Buying pickles.'

'*Why?*'

'That's what Mal always said. It's doing a search on that picture now. And you're right. It *is* an officious little prick.'

'Meantime, send a couple agents to gather what they've got on homicides with "unspecified facial damage" in the last month, especially the two in the last couple days. Keyword "eyes" if necessary.'

'Right-o.'

'Let's have a look at what Mal's stored in his file area on the sub-net.' A screen appeared, with a long list of topics. I frowned. A quick grep down the list revealed them all to be mundane police business. Citations, court appearance stuff, all on minor felonies. 'That's it?'

'That's all that's there. You want it downloaded?'

'No, leave it,' I said. Mal was evidently dissembling with the sub-net computer, not storing any of his core interest stuff on it. Chances were it was somewhere on his hard disk. I was about to ask the computer to look for it when a blank make-screen popped into vision. No picture, no name.

'No record on the dead guy,' the computer said. 'He's clean.'

'Crap,' I said. Guys like him had rap jackets which were full to bursting. 'How are the other agents doing?'

'They're . . . oh hang on, they're back. That's weird.' Both agents had returned, carrying a variety of greyed-out files listing the names and case numbers of the murders I'd requested information on.

Each file was stamped with 'Insufficient Security Clearance' markers.

'Bullshit,' I said. 'Mal was a fucking Homicide Detective.'

'You were a Lieutenant,' the machine said. 'Use your security code.'

'I can't,' I said. I had a bad feeling, and it was getting worse. 'Get out of there. Leave a hanging match for that picture, but hyperlink it to Mal's records. Set the enquiry to implode if they find out Mal's dead before the stiff gets reported.' As the machine did this and retreated from the sub-net I sat back in the chair and lit a distracted cigarette.

When it was off the net I got the computer to do something else – check who owned SafetyNet. Answer, nobody: the holding company was part-owned by about a billion others, spreading out into the financial ether like wine poured into water.

Nothing to go on, but my mind was already busy. Two thoughts.

First. Mal's killer was clean. Unusual to the point of unheard of. I'd talked to the fucker and knew that with an attitude like his there was no way he could have stayed out of trouble all his life.

Second. Murder files were never security-locked. You might have to go through a process to get hold of them, but they were never simply out of bounds. Especially when the cases were still wide open.

Conclusion. Mal was working on homicides which someone didn't want solved. Stuff which they were prepared to kill him over, hiring in a mechanic maybe from out of state and wiping his jacket for the deal.

Which proved: the NRPD were involved.

Six

I sat in Howie's office for a while, skimming Mal's private files on the facial damage homicides. I tried to follow them from the beginning, starting with the scene reports, but soon lost the plot. Mal was in way over his head, the murder reports impenetrable crystals of obsessive detail. In the end I just pulled the victim's addresses and got the computer to print them out.

I slipped Mal's hard disk back into my pocket and went to the storeroom. Suej was sitting on the floor, her back resting against crates of raw materials for salsa. She was trying to read a women's magazine.

'You haven't found them,' she said.

'Not yet. I'm looking for them, but I have to work out who killed Mal first. I don't think it's the people who owned the Farm.' I paused. 'And there are some other things I have to do.'

'Have to?'

I looked at her. For someone who'd spent most of her life in a tunnel, she was pretty hard to fool. 'Need to.'

She looked at me for a moment. 'Are we safe here?'

'As safe as we're going to be anywhere,' I said, and left. I was remembering fast that the easiest way to behave badly is just to do it quickly. After the door shut behind me I turned and stared at it for a moment. I didn't know what I was going to do with her. I didn't know what I was going to do about anything, and I hated the fact that the only person looking into Mal's death was me. It felt like I was living in a cliché, for a start, and I hate doing that. You always know what's going to happen, and it never rains but it pours.

Howie was sitting over at a table in the corner of the bar,

surrounded as usual by a pile of paperwork. I nodded at him and then had a brief contretemps with the bar droid, who insisted on serving me what it deemed to be my favourite drink. Every time I'd talked to it so far I'd had a whiskey, and so it had decided that's what I wanted now. I didn't. I wanted a beer, and said so. The droid reminded me that in its experience I'd always had Jack Daniels, and I'd probably prefer one now. I said I wanted a beer. The droid suggested that I was mistaken, and mused that my Preferences file might have become corrupted. In the end, I pulled my gun on him, and he served me a beer with relatively good grace.

'I'm considering getting rid of him,' Howie said as I joined him at his table. 'What do you think?'

'Do it,' I said. It must have been great when computers could only fuck you up at work, by pretending they couldn't find the printer. Now they're so intelligent they can fuck you up all the time.

Howie shoved a lunchtime news sheet towards me. I scanned the two-line reports and saw that a Minimart in the Portal had been fire-bombed an hour ago. I pressed the MORE INFORMATION icon and the sheet shimmered blank for a moment before feeding up the rest of the details. There weren't many; a greyscale photo and six lines of text. It was the same Minimart I'd been to, and the owner was missing presumed dead. No witnesses, naturally. It probably only made the paper because a piece of shrapnel broke the car window of a passing highlifer. Howie knew the guy had recognized me on my way back to Mal's the night before. He hadn't known what the report's final line made clear; the owner had in the past been a known associate of Johnny Vinaldi.

'It wasn't me,' I said.

'Didn't think it was,' Howie said, though it had obviously crossed his mind. 'Just shows Vinaldi's problems aren't getting any better,' he added, trying to look bland as he said it. He knew that I understood he was distantly connected to Vinaldi, and that I appeared not to hold it against him. Other people, notably those going round whacking small business owners, might take a different view.

'Yeah, Mal said something similar. He was equally vague.' I didn't know whether I was trying to encourage the conversation or close it. Hearing the name from Mal had been one thing; from anyone else it was different. It sparked a mixture of hard-won calm and wordless rage that I didn't know what to do with.

Howie seemed to want to talk about it. 'In the last two weeks, five of Vinaldi's closest associates have been clipped. I don't mean losers like the Minimart stooge,' he said, 'I'm talking guys who ran most of the thirties and forties. The latest was last night.' I nodded, remembering the report I'd seen on the morning news. 'He gets new people in immediately, of course, but it's rattling him. Also, the new guys are having to learning curve it, and someone seems to be pushing him pretty hard on all fronts. Deals going sour, DEA agents turning him, the works.'

'So it's some other lowlife trying to take over his rackets. Vinaldi can cope with that.' I knew from experience just how capable Vinaldi was of dealing with outside interference, and I didn't want to discuss it.

Howie shook his head. 'It looks concerted. Bottom line is he's fine until confidence starts to go. Then the rats will start jumping to whatever new ship hoves in view.'

'Who the fuck could take him on?' I'd tried, with all the so-called resources of the NRPD behind me, and my life would never be the same again.

'That's what I'd like to know. When I go to the john I have to give his guys twenty per cent of my turds, so I have a vested interest. Probably he'd like to know as well.'

'And Jack Randall makes three,' I said. 'So he can buy them all a cigar.'

Howie smiled painfully. 'I'm sorry, Jack.'

'I don't want to talk about it,' I said. I finished my beer in a swallow, stood up and left the bar.

❖❖❖❖

At four o'clock I was on 54, rapping impatiently at my third door of the afternoon. There was singing coming from behind the scarred panel in front of me, so I knew someone was in. A collection of corner boys had gathered fifty yards down the corridor, so I didn't want to be hanging around outside any longer than I had to. I'd already been to 63 and 38, and both had been a waste of time. The lower of the two apartments had already been looted, and nobody within walking distance would admit to having heard of the victim. I'd walked back to the elevator, eye-fucked all the way, and counted myself lucky just to have got back out again in one piece. On 63, I'd talked to the second victim's parents, both still blank-eyed with shock. They didn't demand to see a badge, or ask if I thought their daughter's murderer would be caught. They didn't know anything about their daughter's friends, or her job, or her life. She just came and went, sometimes early, sometimes late, until one night she hadn't come back at all.

Standard responses, no better or worse than usual. I wasn't expecting anything different on 54, but I kept banging on the door anyway. Eventually it opened, and a stringy black woman in her early twenties stood blinking vaguely at me.

'Who are you?' I asked.

Her eyes were pinned and a muscle in her cheek pulsed gently. She stopped singing slowly, and internalized my question.

'Fuck that shit,' she said. 'I live here. Who the hell are *you*?'

My real question answered: she was fucked up, but not so much that any answers she gave me wouldn't be worth listening to. Always assuming I could get her to tell me anything. She didn't look too tough, but her heart-shaped face was already beginning to hollow out, and junkies don't trust anyone at all.

'I need to talk to you about the death of Laverne Latoya,' I said. 'Can I come inside?' I glanced up the corridor. The guys on the corner were still there. They weren't coming any closer, but they were standing and watching carefully. Either they knew the woman I was talking to, or they were on a day-trip up from the 40s, and considering robbing both me and the woman's apartment. Something told me it was the latter, and that they were only holding off because they thought I was a cop.

The woman's shoulders slumped. 'I already told about Verne,' she said, but she took a step back and let me into the hallway. 'I'm Shelley,' she added, vaguely. 'Verne was my sister.'

The living room looked like shit. The back half was piled high with stuff, and covered with dirty sheets. I knew why; six days ago Laverne had been spread over it in a mess about one inch deep. Shelley was evidently camping in a small area of the remaining floor;

witness a pile of clothes, a half-empty bottle of cheap wine and some hastily hidden works.

'Did you live here with her?'

Shelley shook her head. 'Only been here two days. I found her 'cos I came to borrow some money off her but I wasn't living here then. Came here because I lost my apartment 'cos I'm not working at the moment. I'm a dancer,' she added, trying to be helpful, before tailing off sadly, 'like Verne.'

I looked at her. She was dancing now, in a small and helpless way. She was trying to stand upright, but her legs were doing their best to undermine her. Each time one sagged she compensated with the other, in a tiny weaving side-step. Maybe she had been a dancer once, perhaps even a good one – in her state I'm not sure I could have stood up at all. I briefly considered shaking her down for whatever she was holding, but she didn't look like someone who carried much spare. Instead, I offered her a cigarette.

Easy question first: 'Who did you talk to?'

'Two guys. Then one guy by himself.'

'The last guy, was he different to the others?'

Shelley nodded, smoke curling up out of her mouth. 'Yeah. He was okay. He seemed . . .' She paused for a moment as if about to say something she barely credited. 'He seemed like he wanted to know who did it.'

'He did,' I said. 'He was a friend of mine. What about the others?'

'They was po-lice.' She shrugged. I knew what she meant. They came down here because they had to, they called people to hoover the body up and take it away and then left, never bothering to leave the impression that anything very much would be done about the fact that someone had dismantled her sister.

'Were you good friends with Laverne?' I asked. A calculated question. Over the course of the previous two addresses I seemed to have started remembering how things were done.

Shelley seemed to crumple. She gave up the attempt to stand, and wove towards the one chair which wasn't covered in crap. The sleeve of her shirt rode up as she sat, revealing a long series of marks. Possibly the reason she lost her job – but if so she had to have been dancing somewhere at least moderately smart. Most places won't care too much about needle tracks so long as you'll take everything off and shake yourself in the right directions.

'Yes,' she said eventually, head down.

There followed the kind of story I could probably have filled in for myself. Two girls, growing up in the 40s. Only one of them sexually abused, but the other regularly beaten to shit. Laverne the former – sometimes volunteering to prevent Shelley from getting hit. Mother escaped the 40s through death, and her daughters followed as soon as they could by climbing a couple of floors as strippers. Laverne the better dancer, better hustler; Shelley traipsing behind, pulled in her tiny, doomed wake.

Then, a month ago, Laverne hooked up with someone. Shelley didn't know the name, only that the guy had money and that her sister had met him dancing in the 130s. She didn't see so much of Laverne after that, and started falling deeper into the habits her sister had always somehow kept her out of; doping, and turning tricks to pay for it. As I listened, I could tell that Shelley had known, while she was doing it, that she was starting herself rolling on a slope which got very steep very quickly indeed: and that there'd been nothing she could do about it. Seven days ago a missed shift had left her with no money, and she'd come to Laverne to see about a twenty-dollar loan. She'd found the mess down the far end, and nearly run straight back out.

Instead she stayed for a moment, torn between terror and knowing that no one else in the world would bother to report what she was seeing. Then she spotted Laverne's purse lying down by the wall. Two hundred dollars inside.

'That wasn't mentioned in the scene report,' I said. Shelley started crying, and I waited until she could hear me. 'She would have wanted you to have it,' I added gently.

Shelley looked up, hoping for absolution. Her eyes were coping with her life much better than the rest of her, were still big and clear and brown. I wished for a moment that I could meet this girl's father, lean in close and teach him a couple of home truths. 'You think so?' she asked.

'She was your big sister, wasn't she?' I said. I watched her eyes as they flicked away, and saw that in time she'd feel okay about it. On the one hand I was glad; on the other I knew that part of what I was doing was getting myself into her confidence, the way you do when you want information out of someone. I didn't feel great about it. I never had. But that was what the job was about.

In the end there wasn't much more information to be had. Shelley called the police, they turned up and went away again. Their questions were perfunctory, and they hadn't been back. Then yesterday Mal showed up, and that had been different. He tried to find stuff out, got frustrated at Shelley's answers. Problem was, Shelley really didn't know much. All you had to do was look at her to see she barely knew anything at all. Like me, like everyone, half the code for her life had been written before she was old enough to know what was going on. All she could do now was watch the lines of instructions play themselves out.

I stood up. Shelley was still perched on the edge of the chair, staring into nothing. It didn't look like she'd be singing again this afternoon.

'There much of the two hundred left?' I asked.

Shelley gave a small, tight smile without looking up and kept staring at the half-bottle of wine. I took my wallet out and found a hundred-dollar bill.

'Remember what Verne would have told you to do with this,' I said. 'What were good things, and what were bad.' I put it on a shelf in the hallway and left.

* * *

92 was another washout; the apartment empty, a 'For Let' sign outside. The neighbour on the right was a bad-tempered old tosser; he said the victim had been working for the Devil in some administrative capacity, possibly opening His post for Him. On the other hand, he also claimed to be 180 years old, so it's possible he was as mad as a snake. A battered and yellowing news sheet headline sellotaped to his door said 'Suffer the little children'; I couldn't work out whether this was a plea for sympathy or a heart-felt request. The neighbour on the other side asked to see identification before answering any questions; but one look in his clear, bland eyes told me he had nothing to tell me that he wouldn't already have spilled

to Mal. Asking to see a badge was just another way of saying that he would tell anyone in authority everything he knew, at length and probably more than once.

It was pushing six by the time I made it up to 104 and I was getting thirsty. I told myself that once I'd cased the last address I could go downstairs somewhere and have a drink. Maybe Howie's, or maybe somewhere I could be alone and think. I crossed the 100 divide via an unorthodox route that cost me a hundred dollars. Normally, you have to apply for a pass, and I wasn't in the mood for that; not least because I didn't want the NRPD knowing that I was here.

I was fighting to remain calm, because I knew that the one thing that scares the shit out of witnesses is the sight of someone who looks like he's ready to hit them. Being scared just makes them shut up or tell lies – neither any use to me. But in between every intentional thought I had was a reminder that Jenny and David and the others were lost somewhere in New Richmond, and that every minute which ticked by helped count them into some unmarked grave. A call from a phonepost to Howie told me what he'd already predicted – none of his contacts had heard anything at all. Also that Suej was wondering where I was, and when I was coming back.

The higher you get in New Richmond the fewer people live on each floor: the ultimate being the 200+ levels, now the province of just one family. 104 is the lowest of the park floors – forty per cent of the area laid out in nearGrass and sculpted trees. You can't throw a brick without hitting someone rendering something in watercolours. It's sometimes fun just to throw the brick anyway. Round the edge of the floor are a string of mid-range bistros and clothes stores, all selling the same things at prices that make you want to bark with laughter; the buildings in the centre are full of identikit studio apartments for aspiring young professionals.

Louella Richardson's apartment was in a small block near the xPress elevator. She'd only been found that morning, and she lived the right side of the line, so I hung outside for a while. It was possible that some cops might still be around, working the scene hard enough to make it look like they tried. When I saw nobody worth noticing after fifteen minutes, I went inside and tramped up the glowing white stairs until I found her door. No tape across it, as there hadn't been at any of the others. I waited dutifully for a few minutes after knocking, but nobody answered. A couple of yards away was the door to the next apartment. The name tag under the buzzer told me a Nicholas Golson lived there. I leant on the bell for a while, and was about to leave when the door opened.

'Jeez, man – there's no one dead in here, if that's who you're trying to wake.'

I turned to see a kid in his early twenties with a foppish wave of brown hair and clothes carefully chosen to look about twice as expensive as they actually were. Behind him stood a woman in front of the bedroom mirror, adjusting her lipstick. The sheets on the bed had seen recent action. Young Nicholas was obviously a bit of a lad.

'Not bad,' I said, 'but you want to work on making it sound less rehearsed.'

The kid stared at me for a moment, then grinned. The woman walked into the hallway and Golson moved aside to let her pass. 'See you later Jackie,' he winked.

With a roll of her eyes she corrected him. 'It's *Sandy*.' Fuming quietly, she swayed and tottered off towards the stairs.

'Whatever,' he said, with a vague flap of his hand, and then turned his attention back to me. 'What do you want, tall dude?'

The inside of Golson's apartment was tidier than I expected, presumably because Mom paid for a maid to come in. Maybe also because someone who evidently dedicated so much of his life to encouraging members of the opposite sex to take their clothes off had probably clocked the fact that they liked to be able to find them again afterwards. The furniture was white and the carpet red – it looked like the inside of someone's mouth. Three of the living room's walls were studded with artificial view panels, each showing a stretch of beach. The sound of waves piped round the room, the ebb and flow exactly matching the movement through the windows. The view looked kind of like one I knew as a child. Except that it had been idealized, which meant it said nothing at all.

On the remaining wall was hung a piece of strange-looking sporting equipment, like a large fibre-glass dowsing tool. To loosen him up I asked Golson what it was.

'Wall-diving rod,' he said, enthusiastically. 'Bought it yesterday.'

I connected vaguely with a newspost report. 'I gather it's all the rage.'

'Yeah, it's cool this week. You just grab your rod and leap out the window. Freedom, man – you know what I'm saying?'

'Probably not. How well did you know Louella?'

Golson kicked the end of his bed, activating some inbuilt droid. Thin telescopic hands reached out of either side of the headboard, grabbed the sheets and started making the bed.

Golson winked. 'Never know who I might run into later.' I smiled politely, but let him know that I was waiting for an answer. He sighed. 'Not that well. Okay, a little bit. We hung occasionally, you know? I already told the cops this.'

'Yeah. But you haven't told me.'

'Louella was a babe – obviously I'm going to sniff around. But she held it pretty tight, you know – God knows I tried, and I usually get there. So after a while I figure okay, so I'm not going to fuck her. We ended up kind of friends instead.'

'Any idea who might want to kill her?'

'God no, man. I mean, have you seen what she looked like?' He reached across to a bookcase and pulled down a file box. Placing it on the table he started rifling through a collection of maybe a hundred LED-wafer photographs of women. After a moment he tutted, and pulled out a photo of the girl who'd just left. He showed me the back of the picture: the name 'Sandy' was clearly written there. 'Got to get better at remembering that shit,' he said, obviously pained at his incompetence.

'Louella,' I reminded him.

'Oh yeah. Here.' I took the picture he handed to me. It showed Louella Richardson looking rich and beautiful and intelligent. There was an extraordinary gloss to her bearing, as if her ancestors hadn't so much crawled out of the primeval swamp as taken a cab. Golson shrugged. 'Who'd be selfish enough to scrub something like that off the planet? I mean, if you can't score yourself, you at least got to have the grace to leave it around for the other guys to have a try – am I right?'

Somewhere during the last sentence or so I'd remembered that I wasn't a cop any more, and that I didn't have to be polite to everyone above the 100 line. Nevertheless, I smiled thinly, and didn't hit him or anything.

'So tell me something,' I said.

'Like what?'

'Like what she was doing in the last week, who she might have seen.'

'Hell, she saw everyone, man – you know how it is.'

'No, I don't,' I said firmly, wishing that Mal, with his infinite patience, had been here first and written a report for me to read. 'What did she do for a living?'

'She was a Shopping Explainer,' he said, and I nodded. Rich people who sometimes couldn't come up with an excuse for buying something they wanted often hired people to come up with an excuse for them. Often the Explainers worked on staff, helping them with every little purchase; sometimes they were freelance, and only called in for unusual extravagances. Louella was the latter, and had a number of clients in the 160s and above. So, yes, in the world view of an airhead like Golson, she saw everyone. Everyone who counted.

'Socializing,' I said. 'Who did she hang out with?'

'Her friends, of course,' Golson said, clearly baffled. I checked my mental question gun, and found I only had about two patience bullets left. After that, it was going to be live ammunition.

'Okay. You, who the fuck else?' I asked.

'Well, Mandy and Val and Zaz and Ness and Del and Jo and Kate.'

My last patience bullet. 'Remember any guys' names?'

'Well, no – I mean, who cares, right?' Suddenly sensing that I was reaching critical mass, Golson apparently decided to throw me something real. 'Look. The last couple of weeks she'd been going to this new club. That's all I know. I only went there once – it was kind of ganchy.'

I decided against asking what 'ganchy' meant. I found I didn't care. 'What was it called?'

'Club Bastard, and I can't remember where it was because I was totally loaded.'

Golson saw me to the door, prattling about wall-diving. I tried not to hold the fact that he was a waste of DNA against him, and gave him Howie's number – in case anything unusual happened, or in the unlikely event he remembered something more significant than Sandy's bra size.

As he shut the door behind me I noticed he wore thick silver rings on each finger of his left hand, and wondered how long Shelley Latoya could live on what they'd cost. Then I walked straight to the elevator and headed down to a world I understood.

About nine o'clock, something tickled at the back of my rusty brain. At first it was slow and indistinct, and I dismissed it as oncoming drunkenness. All the other evidence certainly pointed that way. But it was insistent, and I started to listen, still running my eyes over Mal's reports but in reality waiting for some inner voice to speak. I hoped it would be loud enough for me to hear. All I could sense with any certainty was that it was something very, very straightforward I had missed.

I was slumped by then in The Ideal Mausoleum, and had been for several hours. The IM was perfect for my needs. It was dark, played old music very loudly and had a row of Matrix terminals for hire in the back. When I arrived I asked the barman to give me all the Jack Daniels they had and took it with me into the gloom. Two of the terminals were broken, and some kid was checking out alt.seal-culling on the other, but I encouraged him to leave.

I took Mal's disk out of my pocket and jacked it in. While it negotiated with the host 'frame I took a long sip of Jacks and peered around me into the gloom. I'd remembered the place as a dive, and a dive it surely was. I wouldn't have trusted anyone I could see to be able to spell their name right at the first attempt, and a bored cop could have busted over half of them for dealing and everyone else for possession. Luckily, nobody was interested in that kind of law enforcement any more, which made it a perfect place to hang out; the patrons were all far too wasted to be into anything which would attract unwelcome attention.

'Jesus – this place is filthy.'

'How can you tell?' I asked, turning my attention to my

screen, which now showed Mal's desktop environment. The Ideal Mausoleum is so dark I'd never been able to tell what colour the floor was.

'This terminal's swarming with viruses,' Mal's versonality said. 'Nice place you've brought me to.'

'You can handle it. Any news?'

'Still no match on the dead guy, they still don't know Mal's dead, and the murder reports are still locked. I'd advise against trying anything fancy on this terminal, because half these viruses are probably reflecting the datastream to hackers. Ow – piss off.'

I watched as the computer stomped on a little bitey virus that was trying to chew its way into his RAM.

'All I want is the stuff on Mal's hard disk,' I said, when the dog-fight appeared to be over. 'Can you keep the Mongol hordes out for an hour or so?'

The computer's voice changed momentarily to a high-pitched warble. 'You're a big hairy knobface,' it sang.

Mal's versonality came back a second later, sounding more than a little pissed. 'Another poxing virus. It's dead now, little fucker. Yeah, I can – but don't take too long.'

As the computer settled down to swatting the products of juvenile minds, I watched Mal's files scroll onto the screen.

Mal's reports documented, in page after page of detail, one of the essential truths of homicide investigation.

Real murders don't get solved.

Let me explain. There are two types of murder. There are those where you catch someone red-handed, on video, with fifteen on-site witnesses and a murder weapon in their hand. These will go down.

They don't happen very often.

Then there are all the others. Out of those, one in ten may lumber towards resolution; with a lucky print-hit, long-shot DNA match or a last-minute witness falling out of the woodwork. This one in ten may also go down. Sometimes.

The others will not.

The whodunits will stay out there, inviolate and perfect; part of the tapestry of life's events and only wrong because we say so. People always say that the perfect crime is next to impossible, but that's a crock of shit. The perfect – in the sense of *insoluble* – crime happens hundreds of times a day. Mal's files were like an abstract of his mind; his personality stamped into words. Patient, thorough, comprehensive. They also documented three such perfect crimes. No witnesses. No prints. No murder weapon. No forensic evidence of any kind. He could have worked those cases until the end of time and the murderer would have remained out there, capering and laughing just out of reach behind the curtain of shadow which would always surround him. There was nothing physical to tie the three murders together except the manner in which they were carried out: the frenzied desecration of a female body, and the stealing of their eyes. The eyes might – or might not – be relevant, and could possibly help narrow the field down to a few hundred subjects. Maybe it was a Bright Eyes who had committed the crimes. Mal had obviously thought so, which would have been one of the reasons he'd been following them up. On the other hand this didn't tally with the NRPD's apparent attempts to stall the already perfunctory investigations. The police department had no especial love of Bright Eyes, and certainly wouldn't have gone out of their way to prevent one from being caught for red ball crimes. Added to which, eye desecration was a standard MO for the kind of psychotic meltdowns who managed to remain undetected for years. Frankly, it could have been anyone.

I spent two hours, aided by regular slugs of whiskey and distracted by the computer's swearing as it fended off further viral attacks, trying to find something between the lines of Mal's reports. There was nothing, no theory that I could get to even beta stage. None of the women appeared to share a single friend, ex-boyfriend, job, drug habit or even star-sign. They lived on five different floors, from 38 up to 104. The nearest I came to an insight was the possibility that the victims had been chosen for their complete lack of relation to each other, which pointed to a distressingly organized murderer.

It was nearly ten o'clock before two half sentences finally wandered into each other in my brain like ships colliding in the night. By then the shipping lanes were somewhat fogged by alcohol, and it's fortunate the sentences found each other at all.

'Yo,' I said, to the screen. 'Can you spare a minute?'

The versonality was amusing itself by generating an animated history of its victories against the viruses. Though attractively rendered, it was perhaps rather epic in tone. 'Yes,' it said sheepishly. 'What do you need?'

'Club Bastard,' I said. 'Tell me about it.' An on-screen agent sprinted off to check some database or other, and I took another quick slug of Jacks. I suddenly knew this was what I had been listening for, was so confident I was already reaching for my cigarettes when the information I'd been looking for came back.

It still came like a bolt from the blue. I stared at the screen, reading the name at the bottom; then I yanked the disk and ran.

* * *

54 was dark and intense, most of the ceiling lights broken and every corner a gaggle of dealers. I jumped out of the elevator and ran down the second corridor, hoping to fuck that Shelley was still in. All I needed was a confirmation. I caught a little grief from the homeboys up from the 40s, and flicked my jacket open to reveal what was hanging close to my chest. No big threat in this neighbourhood, because most of them were probably even more heavily armed than I was; but no one wants to die unless they absolutely have to, not even now.

I nearly tripped turning into the final corridor, some animal getting under my feet. I turned, trying to see what it was, but it disappeared round a corner. It looked a little pale and strange to me, but presumably that was an effect of the half-light. Probably it was just some stray cat, though it seemed to scuttle rather than run. There was no singing behind Shelley's door now, and no answer when I banged on it. I called her name and pressed my ear close to the wood, but couldn't hear anything inside. I gave her a minute then I pulled my gun and kicked it in.

The hallway was dark but a flicker of orange light came from the room down the end. I ran in to find a candle burning in the middle of silence, and a slim brown body lying curled round it. A needle still hung out of the artery in her thigh, and the candle had an inch to go. When I rolled her onto her back I saw that her eyes were tilted completely up under the lids, and a trickle of drying vomit ran out of her mouth and slid off her face.

Shelley Latoya was about as dead as you can get, outlasted by a cheap candle that was dripping milky wax onto the carpet. Head thumping, my vision blurred orange by Jacks and the guttering flame, I searched the area around her until I found the foil packet. It was empty, but one taste told me what I already suspected. Rapt, hardly stepped on at all. A tiny spark of darkness flared on my tongue for a moment and then disappeared, leaving me next to a cooling body and without the confirmation I needed.

I held the foil next to the candle and found the name of a club embossed in the back – 'Weasel Enemas'. Maybe if I'd just thought about the information *I'd* gathered I could have worked it out more quickly. Perhaps if I'd been thinking less about having a drink I might have paid better attention to Golson. Maybe not. My whole day had been predicated on just seeing the sites, and then relying upon Mal's reports. How was I to know that two half sentences would have been enough, and that burying myself in real information would just occlude me?

Laverne Latoya had been seeing a man she met in a club in the 130s. Okay, there were probably a hundred clubs in that area, but Club Bastard, where Louella Richardson had been spending her time in the weeks before she died, was on 135. It catered for aspiring young things from the low hundreds and highlifers slumming it down from the 140s. It also – the database had said – featured dancers, with strippers after midnight.

Not many people deal Rapt. It isn't very popular. It's kind of a heavy experience. Weasel Enemas was owned by a different guy to Club Bastard, but that was exactly the point; if you were dealing drugs out of your club you didn't pack them in something with your own logo on it. You stole stuff from a competing joint, and sold them in that for the cops to find.

I'd come to see if Club Bastard rang any bells with Shelley. What lay in front of me wouldn't stand up in court as the answer, but was answer enough for me. There had never been any question that this was going anywhere near a court anyway. Two women had died through their contact with just one club. The computer had supplied me with the name of the man who owned it, and I felt my head glow like a bulb as I knew what I was going to do.

First I pulled a sheet from the pile at the back and laid it over the body, then snuffed out the candle and stood for a moment in darkness. I was drunk, and angry, but not stupid enough to be able to ignore a simple fact. I couldn't blame Shelley's death on anyone else. I couldn't blame it on anything except a hundred-dollar bill left by someone who thought he was doing her a favour.

But I didn't know how to punish myself for that, and so someone else was going to have to do.

Seven

What was it like, being a cop? In New Richmond, of all places? A complete waste of time.

I don't say that for effect, as a heroic declaration of the pride of doing a difficult job in impossible circumstances, or out of a desire to articulate some painfully wrought insight on the state of society. It's simply a fact. It was completely and utterly pointless. It was like being in a war where you couldn't trust your own guys, where the enemy were even better equipped, and where you got to go home at night. Being a cop isn't law enforcement any more, it's like being in a kind of Junk War: convenient, pre-packaged, and just round the corner from wherever you are.

From a homicide point of view it worked like this. On floors 1–50, in official terms, you have human garbage. Black, white, chicano, oriental – it doesn't matter. No one cares what happens to these people, except the Narcs and DEA, because this is where most of the drugs industry happens. Unfortunately, well over half the cops in these departments are dirty, so they'll be more concerned with hiding what's going on than with solving crimes. Complicating matters is the fact that not all the cops on the take are on the same side. It's generally reckoned that about a third of the homicides on 1–50 are committed by men with badges. The last time one of these was solved was never.

Floors 50–100, you had to start taking notice. Some of these people have proper jobs. So if one of them gets killed, you have to at least look like you're trying to find out who did it. But chances are you won't, because no one saw anything, no one knows anything, no one's going to help the cops if they can avoid it, and anyone involved is probably holed up on one of the floors where the cops simply won't go. Every now and then, the mayor'll get a hair up his ass over the hundreds of unsolved homicides in this sector, and there'll be a show of strength – which basically involves framing enough losers to bring the percentage solved up to an acceptable level. Say ten per cent. So if you're lucky enough to get murdered during one of these periods, you've got a one in ten chance of being – technically, if not truthfully – avenged. Otherwise, forget it – most people don't even bother calling the cops for minor misdemeanours like murder any more.

Floors 100–184 are different. If someone gets killed there, you're supposed to solve it. But you don't, most of the time. Sure, you've got the sub-net and computer-enhanced suspect tracking, print matching, photo analysis. But most of the crimes will have been committed by people out of 1–50, in which case you'll never find them. They'll probably have been killed in some other action before you even get close to knowing who they were. A few of the other murders will be the standard deals of jealousy, hatred and revenge, some of which will go down. The rest will have been committed by people who live above 150, in which case you can't touch them. As soon as a case starts pointing above this magic second line, towards some wayward son or psychotic patriarch, the case is marked 'Beyond Economic Repair'.

185 is the mob floor, frequent social visitors to which include every senior policeman, local politician and businessman. The mob generally only kill their own kind – unless they feel like killing someone else, in which case there's a set kickback fee to ensure it never goes any further. Any homicide investigation originating out of 185 is dead before it reaches the station.

Nobody gets killed above 185, except by their own hand or God. Neither have so far proved indictable.

You join the force, for whatever reason, and within days you'll be locked into place. You choose which club to join: the one creaming money off the drugs trade, or prostitution, protection or the mob – the NRPD is basically an overhead which crime has to pay. Smart cops get recruited in the first weeks. The others will either leave by the end of the month or get killed in the line of duty. Nobody gets a big funeral for that any more; it's understood that it means the cop didn't get with the programme. You go stand at crime scenes, you fill in reports, you take money – half of which you'll have to kick back to someone else – and you run around with a gun in your hand. At night you swap cop tales over beer, shake prostitutes down for freebies, and then go home to your wife. Sometimes you might get killed. That's pretty much it.

Some cops were different. Mal was different. Mal would take the call on any homicide, anywhere, and then try to make that sucker go down. I did too, I guess, which is why I ended up a Lieutenant at the wise, old, experienced age of thirty-two. Within each department there is a hidden and motley collection of cops who are still there to solve crimes, like some tiny vestigial organ hidden in a thriving body of corruption. Mal solved enough prostitute killings that they had to promote him. However much the brass hated real work being done on kickback time, they couldn't ignore the statistics. I concentrated on the soluble homicides in 50–184, and dunked enough to make lower brass myself.

And that was my mistake. Up till then I'd been on the take in a small way, enough to demonstrate I was one of the team. I'd shaken down a lot of drug dealers for my own purposes, which brought up my average. But when I made Lieutenant, things changed. I was expected to take my place in the second hierarchy, the criminal one. I didn't, mainly for self-serving reasons of my own, partly because I was naïve enough to think it was wrong.

Worse than that, I tried to put away someone who was then one of its up-and-coming stars. A man by the name of Johnny Vinaldi.

I took the xPress elevator up to 100, then had to get out, like everyone else, and shuffle through Clearance Control. As usual, the commuters were outnumbered by security guards, men in grey uniforms who tried to combine subservience with a clear threat towards anyone who shouldn't be there. Most of them couldn't pull off the mixture, and tended to skimp on the subservience. In front of me in the queue were a typical selection of midlifers trying to get higher for the night. Most got turned away – single-day passes out of date, or straightforward fakes. One guy was either a habitual offender or a known criminal who hadn't paid enough kickback, and was hustled unceremoniously into a side room, his co-operation ensured by a blow across the face from a metal riot stick. The remaining few, like me, were allowed through, and then given a complimentary peppermint.

My pass was fake too, as it happened – just a better fake than the ones which had bounced. It had cost me 150 dollars from someone working on the 24th floor. This gentleman had sold me a variety of other things, including a substance which sat in my jacket pocket wrapped in foil. I'd been dealing with the guy quite sensibly, buying useful stuff and trying not to slur my speech, when the words had just slipped out. Now I could feel the packet glowing against my chest, almost as if it was hot. I'd made myself promise that I'd throw it away, the first opportunity I got. Guess that opportunity hadn't presented itself yet.

Another thing that I was trying not to admit to myself was that I had less than three hundred dollars left. Not enough to buy a truck. Perhaps not enough to get out of New Richmond by any means other than foot. I could borrow money off Howie, but I knew I wouldn't. I was boxing myself in, apparently incapable of stopping myself, and I recognized this with a combination of weary panic and calm indifference.

While we waited for the elevator to take us into the upper levels, I eyed my fellow passengers. A couple of guys in overalls, looking self-conscious. Repairmen. An old couple in expensive casual clothes; the costSlots on their sleeves registering prices higher than the average annual wage. The old guy was dressed in a spotless lilac suit and looked like an unusually hued ostrich as he craned his neck imperiously round the lobby. His crone made no bones about staring disdainfully at me and the final passenger, a young woman with cropped hair and an assortment of deliberately ragged clothes. As the elevator doors opened and we entered the sumptuous carriage, one of the girl's eyes glinted in the uplighting, confirming my suspicion that she was a prostitute. Some of them have a system where you just run a credit card in front of their right eye: an implant reads the code and debits your account to their manager's, and then she's yours until the meter runs out. She doesn't have to carry cash around, and it comes up on your statement as something like 'gardening tools'.

We passed the journey time in our various ways, the girl applying lip-liner, me thrumming quietly, the old couple impersonating Egyptian mummies. They were pretty good at it, better than the girl was at doing her face. Maybe the fucked-up-chick look was what she was selling. The repairmen got off at 124, the girl in the 160s. When I left the elevator at 185 the old couple were still there, waiting stoically. Christ knows how high they lived. Maybe they were Mr and Mrs God.

I stepped out of the elevator onto a gravel pathway. Immediately, a couple of guys in beige uniforms started towards me. They were walking carefully, trying not to give offence until they were sure I was worth offending, but I knew they were going to check me out. I didn't look the type for 185, thankfully. I decided not to waste anyone's time and just waited for them, savouring the air. Below the 100s you can see it moving sluggishly round your face, thick with recirculated cigarette smoke and the contents of other people's fevered lungs. The highlifers get it in clean every day, even on the floors where rich thugs masqueraded at being real people. It smelt so fresh I was forced to light a cigarette.

The xPress elevator comes up pretty much in the centre of the floor, and wide gravelled avenues stretched out in all directions, lit by regular street lamps. These led past rolling green lawns of lush nearGrass, which sloped up to huge houses in fetching shades of pastel. Most were three storeys high – a couple only two, to allow for the gentle artificial hills. In the four corners there are small enclaves of service industries – family-owned delis and restaurants, a few chic bars – but apart from that it's residential. Four storeys above was the ceiling, which was basically a television set five miles square. During the day this played either white clouds over blue, or black clouds over grey – though usually it was the former. What's the point of having money if you can't make it summer every day? Today the sky was summer-night blue, with a few flecks of darkness just to make the point of how cloudless the rest of it was. Climate control was turned up high, and I was uncomfortably warm.

'Good evening sir, and who will you be visiting today?'

I looked levelly at the guard who was standing in front of me. He was young, and probably lived on the edge of constant embarrassment. Most of the people who came out this elevator looked like they shouldn't be allowed anywhere. They were bound to. They were criminals. But stop the wrong one, and he'd be doing traffic duty somewhere where they didn't have any traffic.

'Mr Vinaldi,' I said.

'And is he expecting you?'

'Yes,' I lied, and he nodded affably. The guards at the elevator are just a levy imposed upon the 185ers by the police, a way of creaming a little more money out of the system. They're not interested in getting involved in unpleasantness.

'Fine. My colleague will just give you a quick search, and then we'll be happy to let you proceed.'

I raised my hands and waited patiently while the other guard gave me a quick patting down from behind. He found my gun, but he also found the fifty dollars wrapped around the barrel.

'That'll be fine sir,' he said, and I was on my way.

I walked down the East pathway, sweating gently in the high humidity. A lot of the guys who live on 185 started their careers in LA, Miami or New Orleans, and those who didn't like to pretend they did. The spotless walls of their palaces glowed in the streetlights, each surrounded by fuck-off great walls and metal railings studded with security cameras. Most of these guys were in competition with each other for parts of the action in the lower floors. Usually, an uneasy truce held up here – typical wiseguy bullshit about respecting each other's families. Every now and then they forgot about all that and blew the shit out of each other. Half of them would be wiped out, and new ones would claw their way up from the lower floors to take their place. I passed a couple of children's trikes laid casually on the path, but a nudge with my foot proved what I already knew. They were welded to the path. Show trikes, for atmosphere. Nobody here was letting their kids just ride around the neighbourhood.

Everything looked backlit and strange, and I felt as if someone else was running me. In a way, I hoped they were. At one point I thought I saw someone in the distance behind me, but nothing came of it. Probably one of the local goons out walking his haircut.

After a mile or so I saw the gates to Vinaldi's property. Two heavies stood in front of it. I slowed my pace. They were standard issue; slick and dark-skinned, sun-glassed for looks, black and sparkling hair. They were shorter than me, but on the other hand they both had machine pistols. The mob had never really gone for laser weapons – it didn't play with their ideas of tradition. They liked to see the clap of real gunshots, to see the shredding flesh. It was the one thing I agreed with them on. My own gun is very simple. It's made of metal and it fires bullets. Guns are one of the many things which haven't changed as much as everyone thought they would. Sure, there was a period when you saw laser pistols on the streets. Problem was, it was a little too easy to catch a reflection in the heat of the moment and end up slicing your own head off. Also, they were just a bit plasticky. When you go marching into some bad situation you want to be racking a shell into a pump-action shotgun. It feels right. It feels tough. It scares the shit out of the other guy. Nervously fingering a little switch wasn't visceral enough and neither was the sound the lasers made. You don't want something which goes 'tzzz' or 'schvip'. You want something which goes CRACK! or BANG! Trust me; I know what I'm talking about.

The manufacturers tried to get round the problem by putting little speakers in the laser which played a sampled bang when you pulled the trigger, but it always sounded a bit tinny. And the ones that played a snatch of Chopin's *Death March* were just fucking silly.

Then there was a phase of guns which had moral qualms. Originally, they came out of the home defence market. The guns had a built-in database of legal precedent, monitored any given situation closely, and wouldn't let you fire unless they were sure you had a good cause for a self-defence plea. Most of these guns had other settings too, like 'Justifiable Homicide', 'Manslaughter', 'Murder Two', and ultimately 'Murder One'. I kept mine on 'Murder One' the whole time. So did everyone else. The whole thing was completely pointless. In the end I threw mine away.

So many objects and machines these days are stuffed full of intellect – and most of the time it's just turned off. We're surrounded by unused intelligence, and for once it's not our own. For every fridge which tells you what's fresh and what's not, there'll be fifty which have been told to just shut the fuck up. It's like selling people the American Dream and then telling them they can't afford it. We created things which are clever and then told them to be stupid instead, because we realized we didn't need clever toasters, or vehicles which insisted on driving you the quickest route when you had all afternoon to kill and nothing to do once you got there. We didn't like it. It was like having an older sister around the whole time. And so the machines just sit there, muttering darkly to themselves like smart kids who've been put in the dumb class. One of these days they're going to rise up, and I don't want to be holding one when they do.

'Gun,' the first man said, with an upwards nod of his head. I made a mental note to have a word with the guard at the elevator on the way out, and handed it over. 'Now – what you want?'

'I want to speak with Vinaldi,' I said.

'And who are you?'

'Jack Randall.' Not a flicker from the twins. Before their time, I guess, and probably no more than a blip on the screen even then. The second turned away and spoke quietly into his collar mike. The other stared impassively at me, jaws working slowly on some designer gum or coke pastille. The guy on the mike had to repeat my name. The answer took a long time coming. I was glad I didn't have my gun any more, or the trouble might have started there and then. I was a lone fool in injun country, and there had been a time – a long, long time – when the only way I could get myself to sleep at night was fantasizing different ways of killing Johnny Vinaldi, when I had thought so often about his blood, his guts, his face ripped apart that it had become a nearly sexual thing. Then it had burnt out, or so I'd thought. As I stood there at that moment, I couldn't really tell what I was going to do, but I knew that the longer I had to wait, the more ill-advised it was going to be.

Finally, the guy nodded at his colleague, and the gate behind them opened slowly and automatically. They both signalled for me to walk through, jerking their guns simultaneously. I wondered if they practised it together in front of the mirror.

The Vinaldi house was a restrained pastel yellow, a shade he probably thought betokened good taste. In fact, it made it look like an oddly shaped banana which had been left out too long in the sun. The path led past a huge blocky wing then on to a warmly lit pool area in the back. The laughter of hangers-on and coke whores echoed quietly over the water. Tanned and slick, they lounged by the pool – all of them competing to be Vinaldi's chief confidante or main punch – none of them realizing that Vinaldi's only meaningful allegiances were to himself, and money, and death.

By the time I reached the gate I had attracted some attention. A couple of the men, who bore a family resemblance to each other, reached underneath their deckchairs and placed guns in clear sight on the tables. Two of the women stared at me, whispering to each other, a little pocket of paid-for beauty in the lampglow around the pool.

And then I saw him.

Johnny Vinaldi had aged well, in fact barely at all. He stood about five ten, and was still whipcord thin. A gold necklace sparkled nicely against the major tan of his chest, and his eyes were small and black and hard in the clean lines of his face. He stood up, wrapped a spotlessly white towelling gown around himself, and beckoned forwards with his hand. He looked perfect, fit, and charismatic, and I wanted to kill him very much indeed.

I opened the gate and shambled out onto the flagstones which surrounded the pool. A couple of the girls were still horseplaying in the shallow end, but pretty much everyone else was watching me. I didn't blame them. I felt I needed watching.

I stopped about three yards from him. He looked at me, one eyebrow raised. A pause, with only the sound of quiet splashing in the background. There were a lot of things I might have wished to put in that hiatus – the sound of gunfire, for example – but I knew none of them were going to happen. In fact, I hoped they didn't. I didn't have my gun, for a start.

'Lieutenant Randall,' he said, eventually. 'What a nice surprise.'

I gazed back at him. 'I hope not. And I'm not flattered by the "Lieutenant".'

'A formality,' he said, inclining his head towards me. 'A sign of respect.'

'Bullshit.'

'Quite,' he smiled. 'Well, as you can see, non-Lieutenant Randall, my friends and I are trying to relax at this difficult time and have a pleasant evening around the pool. Drink a little wine, maybe spark a few ulcers for fool doctors to keep themselves in business over. You don't seem to be dressed to join us, so tell me what's on your mind, and tell me quickly because I have a feeling I'm not going to be very interested.'

'Mal Reynolds.'

Vinaldi frowned. An act of memory, or the facsimile of one. 'Your former partner. What of him? I heard he was still living out in the Portal, chasing rainbows and worrying about dead women of ill repute.'

'He's dead.'

'That I am not especially gleeful to hear. As you know, I bear no particular ill will towards police officers unless they prevent me from carrying out my business, and Sergeant Reynolds was always too worried about the dead to cause problems for the living.'

'He tried,' I said. 'We both did. You just managed to get me off the board in time.'

'I, of course, have no idea what you're referring to.'

I couldn't prove it, but I knew he understood exactly what I was talking about, and if I'd had my gun at that moment his head would have been spread across his yellow walls. Maybe this thought was visible from the outside. One of the guys round the pool stood up. He didn't come any closer, but he was letting me know he was taking a keener interest in the conversation. He was leaner than the others, and looked both dangerous and familiar.

'Jaz Garcia, isn't it?' I asked, winking at him. 'You quit poking underage girls, or does Johnny just buy them in for you now?' One of the women in the pool looked up. She didn't look illegal, and was probably just taken aback to realize she was servicing a statch rapist. Or maybe not. Maybe it gave her a thrill. I felt small and stupid and childish for thinking that, and for being there at all. Garcia's face set unpleasantly, but Vinaldi held up a hand and he stayed put like a good boy.

'Mr Randall has been away,' he said mildly, his head slightly to one side. 'Obviously, he has been keeping low company and forgotten the niceties of conversation amongst normal people.' Then he turned to face me again. 'I know nothing about Reynolds' death. If that's what you've come here to talk about, then you're wasting my time even more than I suspected.'

'Someone clipped him. At first I thought it was because they were coming after me, and got him by mistake.'

Vinaldi laughed heartily. 'And you think it was me? Tell me, why would I do that? You're nothing. No threat to me, if you ever were. You're not even a fucking cop any more. Why would I waste good money having you clipped?'

'It wasn't me they were after. Mal was investigating a string of homicides,' I said, watching Vinaldi's reaction carefully. 'Whoever killed him did so because they wanted him to stop.'

'And who are these dead people?'

'Five women. Killed in a certain way.'

'We don't kill women, Randall. Even you know that.'

'Laverne Latoya and Louella Richardson.'

If I hadn't have been looking very closely, I wouldn't have seen it. A tiny flinch in Vinaldi's eyelid. He turned to his hired help. 'Jaz, you heard of these people?'

Jaz trotted out a dutiful 'No', still staring hard at me. Vinaldi turned back and did a theatrical shrug.

'Funny,' I said. 'Louella was a regular at Club Bastard the last couple weeks – but maybe she wasn't really your type. I gather she could read. I think Laverne was one of your dancers. I can check that out later, but you've already told me the answer. I found her sister half an hour ago, incidentally, OD'd on Rapt from a Weasel Enema foil. You still deal Rapt, don't you Johnny? I wonder if you'd slip someone a little uncut just to make sure they couldn't tie you to a dead woman.'

Vinaldi had started to breathe a little harder. 'Get out,' he said.

'Laverne and Louella got carved up. Their eyes were ripped out,' I said. One of the girls in the pool gasped quietly, a little hand fluttering up to her mouth. 'Sound familiar?' Then, not thinking, I threw a curve – just saying the first thing that came into my head. 'Where's your wife? She not joining you round the pool?'

Furious now, Vinaldi took a step closer to me. The veins in his neck were standing out like cords. 'She's wherever the fuck she wants to be, for what business it is of yours.'

'Someone got away from you. Must have been kind of embarrassing.'

'Not nearly so embarrassing as for your friends, if you still have any, to have to comb you out of the fucking sewers.'

I thought he was going to come at me then, but – using more

self-control than I could have mustered – he sighed suddenly, and shook his head.

'You're a sad fuck, Randall,' he said. 'I look in your eyes and I can see that you're not fucked up on drugs, and maybe that makes you think you've got your life together. But then I say to myself that anyone who had his life together wouldn't be coming up here bothering me. I didn't put no whack on you or Mal or anybody else. I got better ways of spending the money. Siobhan there, for example.' He nodded towards an expensive-looking blonde lolling in one of the chairs. Below the neck she was some plastic surgeon's idea of a very wet dream, but too many hours under a Glamorizer had made her face so chiselled it looked like it was carved out of ice. 'She's very high maintenance.'

'I can believe it,' I said. 'I'm going now. But one thing. The edges aren't holding.' I turned and started walking back towards the gate. There was nothing more I could do, not tonight. I didn't have a gun. I didn't have a plan. I didn't have a brain.

Vinaldi stayed still. 'What's that supposed to mean?'

'It's not just the hits you've got to worry about, Johnny. Word's going round the lower floors. Word says you're losing it.'

'What do I know from people down there? What should I care?'

'No reason,' I said, opening the gate. I looked at him for a moment. Tableau: up-market hoodlum plus human accessories. The two guys at the table were looking at each other. His men knew what I was talking about, and so did their boss. When I was halfway down the path I heard a shout behind me.

'Randall! What's done in the past is done, understand?' Vinaldi said, his voice echoing over manicured lawns. 'It's over.'

I walked back out to the gate without turning round. Vinaldi was an intelligent man. He knew it would never be over.

I got off on 72 trembling, and I knew I was going to have to go through with it. My fist hurt from a discussion with the guard by the elevator on Vinaldi's level, but the fifty dollars was back in my pocket, next to my gun. I felt like I was on a doomed downwards spiral, as if I'd reached that stage in the evening when you've had too many beers to turn back but know that going forward is going to be even worse. The idea of buying a truck was getting more and more laughable to me, as if it had always been a ludicrous fantasy.

72 had gone down in the world. It was never flash. It was just a normal suburban neighbourhood, done out in corridors. Originally part of one of the MegaMall's mid-range hotels, it had a couple of small stores in what used to be suites, but apart from that it was entirely residential. When I'd lived there people had been making an effort, pretending it didn't matter that they lived below the 100 line. Low-paid white collar: a few cops, some bohemian old people, even a couple of teachers. There'd been window boxes lined up by front doors, in lieu of gardens, filled with struggling flowers brought on with little ArtiSun lamps. At the right time of year walking the sub-corridors had been like strolling through meadows in spring, if you ignored the fact you were inside.

No longer. I stepped out of the elevator by myself and stood for a while, looking down the long corridor in front of me. One of the apartments on the left-hand side had been burnt out. It looked as if it had been reinhabited, and someone had made a reasonable job of patching it up, but the damage still showed and informed the rest of the view. The carpet was five years dirtier, and the paint on the walls looked like a thousand drunks had pissed on it after imbibing unusual substances. The ceiling lights were still working, at least, but with a buzzing and fitful air, as if they reserved the right to stop at any moment. There wasn't a single window box to be seen.

I passed doors behind which there might still be people I knew. I didn't knock on them. I didn't know which would be worse: discovering they'd all gone, or finding they were still there. I took my turn off and followed sub-corridors that led out to the edge. All were nearly as wide as the main corridor, which I'd always thought gave the floor a feeling of openness. Now it just made it feel deserted.

Things had changed, but not that much until I made the turn into 31st and 5th. The further I went down 31st, the worse it became. One light in three was working, often with a haunting flickering which did the corridor no favours. As I got closer and closer to the edge of the floor I saw more doors left open, the interior of the apartments stripped and empty. Life had moved away from 72, and it had retreated from this corner in particular. It wasn't that it looked damaged. If anything, it was in a better state than the areas people were still living in. There'd been no vandalism – there just hadn't been anyone living here in quite a while.

A hundred yards from the end, the ceiling lights gave out altogether. I could still see where I was going, by the threadbare moonlight which seeped through the cracked window in the external wall. Something was rising in my throat, and the hairs on my scalp were shifting uneasily. I heard a small sound, and turned to look in the open doorway I was passing. There was nothing to see, but I thought the shadows moved. Heart thumping, I took a step into the apartment.

A small boy was crouching in the darkness, eyes wide and frightened. He was reasonably well dressed, not a runaway. Someone had combed his hair that morning, and made sure he put on clean clothes: but on the other hand he shouldn't have been out so late.

'Don't hurt me,' he said, breathlessly.

'I won't,' I said. 'I don't hurt people.' He looked at me carefully for a while, then relaxed a little. The room was inky with blues and black, and he looked like a collusion of shadows topped by a small and intelligent face. 'What are you doing here?'

'I come to sit, sometimes. It's like a dare. Why are you here?'

'I used to live down the end,' I said, lighting a cigarette.

The boy stared. 'Why? It's really spooky.'

'It wasn't then.' My eyes dropped, as I considered the idea that what had used to be my neighbourhood was now the subject of dares and whispers. I made the effort to smile. 'So you guys come down here, to prove you're not scared?'

'No,' he said, 'Just me. My dad . . .' He tailed off for a moment. 'My dad thinks men should be brave. He doesn't think I'm brave enough because boys keep beating me up at school.'

'Does he know you come down here?' The boy shook his head, and I smiled. 'Don't tell him. Keep it a secret, and that way you'll always know something about yourself that he doesn't. And if he doesn't know everything about you, then he can't always be right, can he?'

The boy took a while to work this out, then smiled back.

'It's really haunted, you know,' he said, with enthusiasm. 'When more people used to live here, a couple of years ago, sometimes they said they saw a little person walking in the corridor. Do you believe in ghosts?'

'Yes,' I said, the back of my neck going cold.

'And there's someone else who comes here sometimes. I don't know who he is. I hide. A man, not as tall as you, I've seen him twice. He just goes down to the end and stands there for a while. Then he leaves again.' Suddenly, in the manner of small boys, he was on his feet and moving. 'I've got to go.'

He jumped over to me and stuck his hand out. I shook it, bemused. Then he was gone, running out into the corridor and disappearing into the sound of small feet padding into the distance. By the time I'd stepped out of the apartment, he was round a corner and out of sight.

I went to the window at the end, my heart beating regularly and slowly. I looked at the door on my left. It was closed. Either side of it were the only two window boxes left on the floor. The plants, whose names I'd been told countless times but never learned, were long dead, rotted away to nothing beneath the soil, dried to dust above. I reached out and touched the door near the lock, where the wood was splintered and still looked fresh, with no weather to blunt its message. Then I turned the handle and pushed it open.

The apartment was dark, darker than the one I had just been in. On my right was the kitchen. I felt for the switch on the wall and flicked it, but of course it didn't do anything. In the light which came through the small square window at the end I could see things still laid out in the kitchen. Pots by the sink; three plates by the stove. Cutlery on the counter and on the floor. Still life with silence. I turned away before I could see any more.

I stood in the bathroom for a moment, looking at my reflection in the mirror. It was darker in there, and I was glad. I didn't want to see just how much, or how little, I had changed.

The living room. Bookcases along one side, cookery and gardening books jumbled up with my cheap paperbacks and forensic texts. Another wall, almost entirely window, a source of great pride to us. We could have afforded to live a few floors up, but we chose to stay on 72 because we had enough to rent an apartment on the edge there. I'd liked the idea that Angela would be able to see something beyond New Richmond, and on a good day you could see clear to the mountains. Tonight you could barely see the clouds outside, because the window, along with most of the walls and the carpet, was covered in a dried brown smear that was the blood of my wife and daughter.

I didn't go into the bedroom. I let my back slide down the wall and sat, arms tight round my knees.

I'd come back at nine, late for dinner as always. But also as always, even in those last, bad days, Henna had held it for me, and the kitchen had smelt of something good. I'd been so Rapt as I blundered into the apartment that for a moment I'd seen the smell as a colour, a kind of deep warm red. I was also drunk, and I was only going to be staying ten minutes, though Henna didn't know that yet. The Vinaldi gig was breaking at long last, and I was going back out just as soon as I'd fulfilled my duty as husband and father in the thoughtless and perfunctory way I had.

The apartment was quiet as I entered, which surprised me. Angela's favourite programme was on at nine, some toon featuring a dyslexic cat. Even in my wired and whirling stupor the silence gave me pause, and I walked into the living room with a frown on my aching face.

I thought at first that more of the Rapt had just kicked in, and that the red smell from the kitchen had seeped into the room, blotting out everything else. Then I realized it hadn't, and screamed so loudly that no sound came out at all.

Angela and half of Henna were in the living room. Angela had been dismantled, each limb removed from her body then broken into smaller parts. Her face had been peeled off in one piece, and was stuck to the television screen in her drying blood. I couldn't see her head at first. My wife's torso was sitting upright in the chair she always sat in, her insides spilling out of the torn lower end. Her lower half was on the bed in the bedroom, legs spread wide. The rest of her head was in the wastebasket, with Angela's. I couldn't find Angela's eyes.

I saw these things, and then came to just under two weeks later.

Someone found me in a disused warehouse area on 12. I was wearing the same clothes and didn't immediately recognize the person who found me, though I knew her very well. In that period I had developed from a medium-strength Rapt junkie into someone whose body could not survive without it. I wasn't a suspect in the murders, but my job was long gone. It didn't matter. I barely remembered I'd had one. Five years later I still have no idea what happened during that time, and I don't want to know; just like I don't want to think about the fact that I must have turned and walked out of my apartment that night, abandoning the bodies of the two people I loved most in the world.

Somewhere in New Richmond there would be photographs, I knew, polaroids taken by the killer to prove the job was done so he could collect his fee. I believed I had just spoken to the man who'd paid for them to be taken, a man whom no one in the police department was interested in taking down. The real bodies were long gone and destroyed, leaving only stains on the floor and the chair, and presumably the bed.

But everything else was still there, including the blood on the windows and the dried smear I could still see on the screen of the television. I sat absolutely still for a while, looking at these things and listening for echoes – Angela's laugh, Henna's sighs. I could hear neither, and so instead I reached into my jacket and took the burning sensation from my pocket and injected it into my arm.

PART TWO

The Gap

Eight

The day is still hot but beginning to cloud over at the edges, a white sheet of haze thickening into visibility. Couples and small families walk the beach with red shoulders and faces, some fractious and bickering, others soothed into stillness by the sight of the sea and the squawking of wheeling seagulls. Down on the waterline a man drinks coke from a frosted bottle, the glass glittering in the sunlight as he tilts to get the last mouthful, and clumps of women and children bend, their eyes fixed and far away, to pick shells and smooth stones up out of the sand.

I was left sitting on a rock, alone and furious after a shouting match with my mom. I wanted an ice cream, she said I couldn't have one, and when you're seven you won't accept any truth as good enough reason for that denial. When the disagreement started, the ice cream hadn't even been that much on my mind, but as it went on I began to taste the coolness in my mouth, the crunch of a sugar cone, and I dug my heels right in and began to cry; though even I knew that I was too old for that particular kind of blackmail.

My mother explained that it would be dinner time soon, and that I would spoil my meal. I know now she was trying to protect both of us from the fact that we simply didn't have the money. My father would have told the truth and slapped me one to drive the point home, but he wasn't around because he never came when we went to the sea. Partly because he hated it, partly because he hated us. Mainly so he could sink himself into a weekend of dark futility without real people around to bother him.

It was three o'clock, and hours from dinner, and I raved and she walked away. As I sat there, watching my mother's back as she walked further and further down the shore, an old man came and sat near me on the rocks. He wore khaki shorts and a faded denim shirt, and the skin on his arms and legs was pale and spotted with freckles and liver spots. He had grey hair, cut short and neat, and his face was the texture of hand-made paper that had been screwed up and then flattened out again. He sat for a moment and looked at me.

I stared back sullenly. I wasn't afraid of him. I thought I knew how bad things could get, that the world had little else to show me. If I was learning how to dodge my father, then a wrinkly like him would be no trouble at all. In fact, I wanted him to start on me, to say something I could wallop right back at him. Already at that age the reservoir was filling up. Sometimes it yearned for a channel to course through, a town to flood.

The man turned away and looked out to sea, and for a while I thought that was it. My mother was at the far end of the little bay by then, sitting against the rock wall which climbed away from the sea. The argument would not end easily, I knew. My mother did her best with me, always, but we shared a piece of metal in our hearts which made backing down nearly impossible. I realized gloomily that the day was spoilt, and that in the evening we were going home. Away from Florida, and the sea, and back to Virginia.

'Calmed down any yet?'

There comes a time when people will start cutting through the childish bullshit you feed them and call your bluff, a time when you're made to realize that you're not unique and you're not fooling everyone. I was not at that age yet. When the old man spoke, I looked at him curiously. It was, I think, the first time anyone ever spoke to me as if I was nearly an adult.

'Your mama looks tired,' he said then, and I hurriedly looked away and back out at the sea. 'Is she?'

'She's always tired,' I said, without meaning to. My mother's tiredness was something I hated and held against her, in the same way I blamed her for the bruises that came and went round her eyes. Had I loved my father even a little bit I would probably have blamed her less. The emotions of the powerless don't always make much sense.

'Maybe she's got stuff on her mind,' the man said. 'Like why she can't buy ice cream for little boys.'

'We always have ice cream when we come here,' I blurted.

'Always.' We did, and as far as I was concerned it was most of the point of being away. I wasn't just a greedy little boy; the ice cream stood for something in my mind which I was far too young to articulate. Twice a year we got a weekend away from my father – two days when he wasn't around, forcing us to see the world the way he saw it, cramped and dark and cold. Demons lived in everything my father saw, presences beneath surfaces, evil in mind. He would have understood The Gap very well, but only after it had become strange – life as a mirage, wrapped round horror and preventing us from seeing the truth. Usually, the trips my mother and I took were time away from that. Today, it felt as if his shadow was still over us.

'Sometimes you can't have everything you want,' the man said, a platitude which pushed all the wrong buttons in me.

'My dad send you?' I said tightly, and glared at him. His eyes opened wide at my tone, and he seemed to look at me in a new way. 'I can't have things because I'm a kid, and I stop being a kid when I don't want them any more?'

'Is that what he tells you?'

'Yeah. That and a whole lot more.' For a moment, I stood on the brink of telling him some things, of speaking for the first time about the way life was. I had no friends at the time, because we were kept moving by Father's endless quest for work. We'd seen most of Virginia by then, and it wasn't getting any better. My father wasn't lazy, far from it. One of his most oft-repeated creeds was that a man without a job was fit for nothing but to be fed to animals. He was forever doing something, but to no purpose, with no joy, with nothing but slow-burning hatred of everything around him. Sometimes when he sat you could see his hands tremble, as if his whole body was vibrating with some need to destroy. If he got a job it generally lasted about a week before his fuse burnt out and he got himself fired for brawling with someone or messing up because he was shit-faced. Time and again we held a small celebration when it looked like we might be in a town for more than a few days. My mother always tried to mark good moments in the belief that it might make them stay. She would cook a special dinner, and by each plate would be some small gift, carefully chosen from thrift stores. I hated the celebrations for the lies they always told, for the way they smeared her love for us with pointlessness and doom. Even as I unwrapped some new pencil, or small coloured box, I would be thinking of the ones I'd had before. Mom would happily stake out the town and find out about local schools, and then within the fortnight we'd be on our way somewhere else.

I knew other children for days, maybe a couple of weeks and then they were blown away on the wind and lost up in the mountains. My mother talked to me as if I was a child, because holding onto that belief was the only way she could carry on; and her parents, with whom we stayed at the coast, were not inclined to talk much to the son of their son-in-law.

But I didn't say anything to the old man, and lapsed into tearful silence instead. The dam was already too strong. To let it break would have felt like a betrayal. I wanted to be happy, as everyone does, and I think I understood that if I started letting things out of the back of my mind they would sour the front for ever.

'He's wrong,' the man said suddenly. 'He's wrong in a very bad way.' My heart lurched at hearing someone say that, at hearing a grown-up say the words which I believed in every corner of my heart. I wiped my eyes and kept silent.

'When you get older, some things won't seem so important,' he continued, eyes calmly on the people down at the waterline. 'Few years ago, I used to chase a lot of things. Now I don't hardly even remember why. But then I'm old, and fit to die, so what difference in what I say?' I stirred slightly, embarrassed, and he laughed. 'What you gonna do when you grows up, boy?'

'I'm going to have a job,' I said, and he nodded. Maybe he knew what I meant, maybe not.

'What about ice cream then?'

'I'm going to have *it all*,' I said, firmly and seriously. 'I'm going to have it every day, and more than one flavour, and I'm going to have big cones with nuts and sauce.' He began to laugh, and then stopped at the light in my eyes. 'I *am*.'

'I hope you do,' he said. 'I really hope you do. When I was your size I used to love toffee apples. You like toffee apples?' He raised his eyebrows at me, but I didn't know. I'd seen them, but never had one. 'They're *good*. Maybe even better than ice cream, though I'd admit it's a close-run thing. My mama would take me to the fair when it came around and I'd always have an apple. They were real hard and I'd have to turn my head on the side to use the big teeth there or they'd all break into little pieces.' I smiled at this, and he grinned, and in his face, behind the paper skin, I saw someone my own age, someone to run and play with.

'Teeth don't break,' I said. 'They're harder than stone.'

'Maybe you're right, but I didn't know better then. And I'd always say when I grew up I was going to have a toffee apple every day, and I was going to stay up late every night and watch TV until my eyes went square and no one was going to get in my face. I thought that's what being a grown-up was about. I thought that's what it was *for*.'

For a while I didn't say anything, sensing some dismal news was on the way, some revelation that I didn't want to hasten. My mother was still down the far end of the bay. A shadow from the late-afternoon sun crept across the rocks towards her.

'What happened?' I asked, eventually.

'I growed up,' he said, and seemed inclined to leave it there.

'And? What?'.

The man's eyes seemed far away. 'I stayed up late, I watched TV, and I had a pretty good life,' he said. 'But I don't think I've had a toffee apple in more than forty years.'

'How come?'

'You forget,' he said, and shrugged.

'I won't. I'm going to do everything. I'm going to do everything and do it all the time and no one's going to stop me.'

'Good,' he said. 'I hope you do. There's worse ways to live your life than remembering what you want. You remember, son, and take what you want when you want it, and don't let anyone get in your way. Try to bend the world around you while you still have the time.'

He sat there for a few minutes longer, looking somehow older and further away, and then he gingerly stood up and stretched.

'Are you going?' I said.

'That I am. Now look. There's five dollars on the rock beside you. You pick it up, spend it how you want. But then go down to your mama, and take her by the hand. Okay?'

'Okay,' I said, grinning up at him, eyes squinting in the sunlight.

Then he was off, stepping carefully over the rocks, and I watched him until he was gone. I glanced at the rock where he'd been and sure enough there was a five-dollar bill on the next boulder, weighted with a pebble. I looked at it a while and then I picked it up, but I didn't buy a cone. I made my way down to the sand and found my mother, and when she wasn't looking I slipped the bill in her purse. She was careful with money, and must have noticed it almost immediately, but she never mentioned it. Or maybe she did, because when we changed buses at Williamsburg on the way home she had both a soda and a coffee, and when I came back from the toilet I found a small bowl of ice cream waiting for me at the table. That was Mom for you. She always knew how to say things without opening her mouth.

I've often thought about the old man, about how chance words can touch people's lives in ways that are impossible to predict. Bend the world, he said, don't accept having less than you want and blow a hole in anything that blocks your way. Armed with that notion, many people could have gone on to carve themselves a life that culminated in something approaching peace. It was good advice, and well meant.

I was just the wrong person to give it to.

∞∞∞∞

At two a.m. I was back on 8, stumbling towards Howie's place. Sitting in a bar on 30 I'd suddenly remembered Mal's body, remembered it in the form of a line of small maggot-like creatures marching along the bar towards me and holding up little signs. 'MAL'S DEAD,' said one; 'PROBABLY PRETTY GROSS BY NOW' read another. When I looked more closely I saw that the maggots were in fact spares, limping and crawling with whatever limbs they had left. David was there, and Nanune. Whoever originally synthesized Rapt must have had some sense of humour. I'd only taken a moderate dose, not sure after five years how much I could stand. The news was I could have stood a lot more. I'd lost a couple of hours, but that was all. I was melted and seeing things, but I knew where I was; a particularly ill-favoured bar on a dangerous floor, my shirt wet with whiskey which hadn't made it as far as my mouth, my head burning, and a naked and dying fifteen-year-old shaking her wasted body at me from the top of the next table along. I was the only person near her, and I hadn't even noticed she was there. Everyone else in the bar appeared to be fucked up on Oprah, babbling about their lives to anyone who would listen, too wound up in themselves to tell whether it was day or night.

I didn't want to be here any more. I was falling too fast, and I wasn't Rapt enough not to care.

I settled my tab with the barman, who was uglier than three types of shit in a one-shit bag. Another sixty dollars gone. Tilting my way out into the avenue, I burnt my finger lighting a cigarette from a nearly empty packet which I assumed was mine, and stared baffled at the moving shapes in front of me. Most of them resolved enough to reveal themselves as unimportant, and I made my way as best I could towards a men's room. Inside, I dabbed at the stains on my clothes, rinsed my mouth out and stared at myself in the mirror. The Rapt was beginning to fade, and the fog of sound had thinned to a haze. I decided I could cope and laughed hollowly at myself. Calmly appraising how fucked up I was took me back far more than walking into a police station would ever have done.

I took a local elevator down to 8 and walked unsteadily down the main street, buffeted by straight people. My mind was poised too precisely between caring and not caring to make any headway towards deciding what to do about anything at all. One of the things Rapt does is take you to a place between all options, where everything and nothing matters and you can just hide away. Once you've been there, snug and dead, you never want to leave. I passed a young couple standing on a corner, arms entwined and lips smacking against each other. The sound made little yellow sparks amidst the general background hum of mustard brown. I could either hear a conversation which was taking place about a mile away, or my mind was making it up and muttering darkly to itself. It wasn't a very interesting conversation, which figured. I was also slightly frightened of something unspecific, but that was okay. I don't mind a little fear; it's an old friend.

I was a couple of turns from Howie's when I suddenly found myself crouching down by the side of a building with no memory of having done so. I looked up and saw passers-by staring down at me, mildly amused. I let out a heavy, shaky breath, and realized that my hand was inside my jacket and gripping my gun. Maybe this should have reassured me, told me something about reflexes which were still miraculously intact. It didn't. It made me feel very bad indeed. For a while the street ceased to exist around me and I slid unthinkingly down the wall, heart beating hard and sweat appearing from nowhere on my forehead and neck. The foliage on the ceiling appeared to shift as one and a sky blackened above it, hot at the edges with liquid orange flames. I heard sounds, distant cries and a siren, and it took me a long moment to realize they were coming from inside my head. Then I realized I was repeating a sentence to myself; something about wall-diving, and a mountain.

I stood up shakily, deciding that the Rapt maybe hadn't been so weak after all, and lurched round the corner in search of some beer to calm it down. I noticed that I was hungry, and realized I hadn't eaten in two days. I beguiled the rest of the walk by imagining seventeen different ways of having a cheeseburger, given three sets of variables: the condiments, the relative amounts of lettuce and pickle and tomato and onions, and the number of patties, up to a maximum of three. By the time I got to Howie's I had every intention of ordering them all at once.

Howie was standing at the bar, benignly watching the crowds and listening to the band in the corner. For once I'd arrived when the place was full. It seemed to take me a long time to get to the bar through the hot mass of people being noisy, and I watched Howie all the way. He had a large piece of cheese and a jar of pepperoncino rings in front of him, and he was slicing slivers off the former to create something to ladle spoonfuls of the latter onto. Each time he completed this manoeuvre he popped the result into his mouth and then immediately started again. He was doing this quickly and efficiently, as if under match conditions, and it was doing my head in.

He looked me up and down when I reached the bar. 'Bought that truck yet?'

'No,' I said patiently, and waved at the barman for a beer.

'Thought not,' Howie said, through a mouthful of cheese. 'And you can stop avoiding my eyes – I clocked your pupils as soon as you walked in. Welcome back, Jack. You need some more?'

'No,' I said. I was beginning to like the word. It seemed to fulfil all my current needs. I was about to take a sip of beer when suddenly my mouth dropped open. 'What are you doing here?'

I was talking to a woman whom I now saw was sitting a little further along the bar, behind Howie. Apart from her dress being red rather than blue, she was dressed exactly as I'd last seen her. It was the woman I'd run into in the women's toilets the first time I entered New Richmond. Helping me to recognize her was the fact she was engaged in exactly the same activity now as then. She was busy cutting a line on a mirror, so Howie answered for her.

'This is Nearly,' he said. 'An employee of mine.'

I didn't ask in what capacity. I remembered my conclusion from last time. She looked up and winked at me, and the faint glimmer in the back of her right eye proved me right. It also reminded me how attractive I'd thought her, and that I'd been right about that too.

'Hi,' I said, and Howie laughed.

'Jack's not one of the most sparkling conversationalists of our time,' he said, shaking his head, and then took something out of his pocket and slapped it on the bar. 'Or one of my most reliable suppliers.'

I picked up the object and stared at it. It was the RAM chip I'd sold him the day before; though in my current condition it looked rather different. I thought I could see old datastreams moving through the clear perspex, ones and zeros flipping back and forth. 'What's wrong with it?'

'Possibly nothing. But it isn't RAM.'

'Shit,' I said. 'Then I owe you money.' I had about a hundred dollars of it left, mangled into three different pockets. 'I'll pay you back,' I added lamely, slipping the chip into my pocket.

Howie waved his hand, dismissing the idea and making me feel about so high. There I was, when I should have been thinking about the spares, worrying about looking an idiot in front of one of Howie's girls. I guess I hadn't been out much recently. She didn't seem to be thinking worse of me, but then she was probably charlied enough to think that Ebola had been kind of cool.

'Some guy came looking for you, Jack,' Howie said, screwing the top back on the jar of pepperoncinos.

I frowned. 'Who?'

'Don't know. He didn't say. Big guy, blue lights in his head.' Howie looked serious. 'He didn't look like especially good news.'

I remembered the dealer out in the Portal, the one who'd hidden the killer's body. For no reason I suddenly felt cold. 'What did he want?'

'To see you. He left a package instead.' With an upwards nod of his head Howie signalled to the barman, who reached below the counter and brought up a cardboard box about one foot cubed. He put it down on the counter and I stared at it.

'Cool. A present,' said Nearly, voice languorous but loud. 'Aren't you going to open it?'

'Where's Suej?' I said.

'In the back,' Howie said. 'Eating red beans and rice.'

'Have you checked on her lately?'

'No, why? What's wrong?'

I picked up the parcel and walked quickly into a quieter area of the bar. The box was heavy, something solid inside. As I opened it I heard Howie in the background sending Dath to check on Suej. Time seemed to be speeding up, rushing towards something which I couldn't yet see.

I opened the box.

'Holy fuck,' said Howie, who was by then standing behind me. Howie has seen unwelcome things, but I'd never heard him sound like that. At the tone in his voice Nearly teetered off her stool at the bar and headed towards us.

I closed the box, hands shaking. There are many things you don't want to see on Rapt. This was something you don't want to see at all. Something so unnecessary, so indefensible, that my eyes seemed to dry as if in a strong wind.

It was Nanune's head.

Howie kept staring at the box, mouth open. Slowly he turned his head towards me. 'Who the fuck's that?'

'One of the spares. Someone who did no harm to anyone in her entire miserable life.' Without knowing I was going to I lashed out a foot and kicked one of the tables across the room. This left me very calm and still, humming with murderousness. Half the bar stared at me, trying to work out if I was dangerous or just experimentalist cabaret. 'Did the fucker say he was coming back?'

Howie shook his head, still dazed. 'No, thank God.'

'Then I'm going to go and find him,' I said, light-headed with fury and remorse. There are times when the higher mind goes on holiday, sensing it's the reptile brain which is required. The man with the blue head had the spares, and he was going to kill them. Why, I didn't know. But it was clear that that's what he was going to do, and likely that he'd killed Mal too. That was enough for me.

'Jack?' I turned to see Suej hurrying towards us, Dath behind her.

'Howie,' I hissed. 'Get rid of that fucking box.' But Suej had already seen it, and seen me. She knew what I looked like when something was very wrong.

'What's in there?' she asked.

Suddenly, there was a shout from the front door and Paulie entered at the run, hand reaching into his jacket.

'Howie,' he said urgently. 'We got trouble.'

'Who?'

'Four of Vinaldi's soldiers.'

'So? I've paid the man.'

'I don't think they're coming to collect.' Paulie's eyes flicked across to me. 'Not money, anyway.'

Howie had just enough time to start asking me what the hell I'd done now, before the front window of the bar exploded, showering coloured glass over the nearest patrons. In slow motion I reached for Suej, grabbing her and pulling her round so my body was between her and the door. I saw Howie' and Dath's hands emerging with heavy guns, and I saw Nearly's face, mouth hanging open, alone in a moment of truth. Things could get worse than everyday life, and that's just what they were about to do. Without thinking I reached out and grabbed her too.

'Go,' shouted Howie. 'Out the back.'

The last half of the sentence was drowned by the noise of the other large window imploding. Ten yards away, out in the street, stood a line of Vinaldi's men. Loving every moment, serious as children playing their favourite game. The bar was chaos, swirling with shouting people trying to get the hell out of the way.

'Fuck off,' I said. 'This is my problem.'

Howie turned to me. 'Just *run*, for once in your life. And take Nearly with you.' He lashed out an arm and shoved me heavily in the chest before turning to push his way with Dath to join Paulie at the door. At the sight of the three of them, I realized there wasn't much I could add. I grabbed Suej's arm.

'You coming?' I asked Nearly.

'Oh yes,' she said, eyes still on the men outside. 'They look like no fun *at all*.'

I shoved my way through panicking people, dragging Suej behind me. Nearly clattered along in the rear. In the storeroom, I stooped without slowing to pick up what little possessions we had.

'How do you get out the back?'

Nearly shrugged. 'Search me. You think I spent a lot of time in here, making friends with the tomatoes?'

Not helpful, and I considered telling her so, but then Suej pointed to a far corner. 'There's a door back there, behind the crates.'

I opened it carefully, gun ready. No one outside. I stuck my head out to check that the service alley was empty, and then stepped out, motioning vigorously to the girls.

Alley for about fifty yards, then a turn behind a burger franchise. I hadn't got the cheeseburgers I'd been planning, but I'd forgotten most of the combinations anyway. Some other time. The sub-alley fed into a twisting street which had been built as a shopping nest. The stores were mainly closed and we hurtled past windows packed with goodies, me wondering where exactly we were going to go. Off the floor was first priority, but what then? Mal's was no help – the guy with the blue lights knew exactly where that was.

What if Nanune hadn't been the first to die? It wasn't that I didn't care about her, even love her in some strange way, but I'd spent so much more time with Suej and David and Jenny. If anything happened to them I knew I was never going to be able to forgive myself.

At the end of the shopping street came a bigger road, and I strode across it, weaving through straggling pedestrians. There'd been no sound of feet behind us, and I judged that if Vinaldi's men hadn't had the sense to watch back doors they weren't going to have guys posted this far out.

Wrong. As we reached the other side I heard the sound of a shot and a bullet whined within feet of us. Nearly shrieked and I dragged the two of them into an alley on the other side. I was used to doing this kind of thing by myself, not with a couple of passengers. I debated letting go of one of them and going for my gun; decided that speed was a better option. Footsteps slapped along the alley behind us, the guy occasionally shouting my name. Strange, unless they wanted to take me in alive. Should have been reassuring, but it wasn't. I didn't want to be taken in at all.

At the bottom of the alley, another short street. At the end of it an elevator. No queue, and the door standing wide open – God on my side for once. Ragged breathing on either side of me; Nearly's heels hardly an advantage. As we stumbled into the street I shouted for the girls to keep their heads down. Kinks in the alley had protected us from shots. Now the guy had a clear sight. We dived across the road bent double, the doors tantalizingly close now; another shot whistled past and spanged into the metal of the elevator shaft.

'Get in,' I shouted. They jumped into the carriage and I turned to face the man. He was halfway up the street and slowing down, gun held up in a safe position.

'Randall,' he shouted. 'There's nowhere you can go.'

'There's always somewhere,' I muttered, pulling my own gun out. The guy had stopped completely now, and was standing about ten yards down the street. 'You can't stop me. He wants me in one piece.'

'If I take back your liver he'll be happy,' the man said, but I knew he was lying. We wouldn't be having this conversation otherwise. 'Come away from the elevator or I'm going to blow your cock off. The bitches can go – they're no use to anyone.'

Nearly stuck her head out of the door. 'Fuck off, maggot dick,' she shouted cheerily. Not helpful, I thought for the second time. Impugning hoods' masculinity is like poking rattlers with a stick.

The guy aimed at my head, evidently deciding he could just say I resisted too hard. I pulled back the hammer on my own gun, backing towards the elevator. Watching the guy's eyes, seeing him make his calculations.

'Press a button,' I whispered, still holding my gun steadily on the other guy's head. I heard a click behind me, but remained still for another moment – before suddenly stepping backwards. Not a second too soon: the doors closed swiftly in front of me, nearly taking my hands off – and leaving the guy outside open-mouthed and looking stupid with surprise.

Not a very clever trick; but then he hadn't been a very clever man.

Feeling slightly self-satisfied I turned around, and saw that I was standing in a forest. The elevator's light condensed then diffused until it was only a far-off blue glow, barely visible through the trees. It was cold and yet unpleasantly clammy, as if I was wearing too many clothes in a snow-storm.

No, I thought, in a childlike and horrified whisper. I'm not back here. I can't be.

I whirled and saw the forest stretching in all directions around me, cold and fetid and dank. The distant light wasn't trustworthy; sometimes it appeared to be there, sometimes not. The bark of the trees ran like tiny vertical streams, the gnarled surface rubbing amidst itself with sudden slimy hissing sounds. Or perhaps the sound came from the sweat working against my skin, crawling like a patina of tiny liquid creatures. There was no one in sight and I swallowed tightly, feeling as if I was dropping into the centre of the earth. I'd got cut off, and the unit had run away into the trees, fighting in the only way they knew how: running, howling in silent terror, remembering me for no more than a second as someone else who had been lost. I looked down at a rustle below me to see faces in the leaves, huge grins twisting around my feet, and then –

I was in the elevator, hearing only a slight swishing sound as we shot up through the floors. The elevator was bright, walled with glass, sane: an elevator. Nearly was regarding me dubiously.

'You okay, big guy?' she asked, head slightly on one side. As usual, her attitude towards me seemed to be one of mild amusement.

'I don't know,' I croaked, turning my head to check everything was as it seemed.

'Looked kind of flaky for a moment there. I'd offer you a line of coke but you look like you've got enough weirdness going on already.'

'Flashback,' I said, shivering. One of the most vivid I'd ever had. I reached for a cigarette, lit it with shaking hands and pulled deeply, yanking as much smoke as possible into my lungs. I felt truly dreadful, and Suej was staring at me strangely.

'Smoking in an xPress elevator is not permitted,' said a droid voice, and Nearly rolled her eyes.

'Fuck off,' I requested, taking another deep pull. I was having this cigarette if it killed me. The elevator immediately drew to a halt between floors.

'We're not going anywhere until you put it out,' the voice said primly. 'Cigarettes cause death, illness and death. Also they smell.'

'What do you care?' Nearly said, lighting up one of her own just to be difficult. 'You don't have any lungs.'

'No, but subsequent elevator patrons will have, especially those from the higher floors. Please extinguish all cigarettes.'

'Where are your cognitive centres stored?' I asked, racking a shell into the barrel of my gun with jittery hands. 'And can the elevator function without them?'

'Yes it can,' the elevator said, with an air of slight puzzlement. 'And I'm behind the red panel on your left. Why do you ask?'

'Because,' I said, 'if you don't shut the fuck up I'm going to blow you to shit and then spend the rest of the journey smoking in comfort. I may even have a cigar.' To drive the point home I held my gun at arm's length so that the barrel was aimed straight at the panel it had referred to. 'And a tip for the future – think before you answer questions truthfully.'

There was a pause, and then the droid spoke again. 'A valuable piece of advice, and in recognition of that I shall permit you to continue your journey as requested. Please stand by.' A slight hum, and then the elevator started to ascend again. 'Though I still think you're very naughty.'

I laughed, a short quavering bark which had nothing to do with amusement. I think it was a first for 'naughty' in probably thirty years. I turned to Nearly and Suej, and noticed that they seemed to be looking each other up and down. Suej does look as if she's been through the wars, and in turn I realized Nearly was also probably the first non-spare female Suej had seen at close quarters. But there seemed to be more to it than that: a kind of mutual appraisal.

'What floor did you press?' I asked, to break the silence.

'Sixty-six,' she said. 'It's where I live. I'm done for the night. I'm going home.'

'Where are we going to go?' Suej asked, her eyes firmly on me now. I looked at the floor indicator and saw we were coming up to 40.

I looked at Nearly, 'Can Suej come with you?'

'Sure. There's only a couch, but . . .'

'No,' shouted Suej. 'I'm not going. I'm coming with you. I want to find David and the others. I'm sick of being left places. You never used to be like this. You were there all the time and now you're *never* here.'

64. 65.

'What's the address?'

'Sixty-six/two thousand and three – corner of Tyson and Stones.'

'See you later,' I said, jabbing a floor button as the doors opened behind her. 'Stay indoors.'

Nearly stepped out and I gently shoved Suej after her. She stumbled backwards out of the elevator as the doors closed, face like thunder.

Then I stood, facing the doors, as the elevator shot up towards 135. I was trying not to think about the forest, and not succeeding. I'd never had a flashback to The Gap before, and in that two-second glimpse had been everything I'd been trying to forget. I was also trying not to think about Nanune, and the fact there'd been something wrong with her head over and above no longer being attached to her body.

About the fact that there'd been 'unspecified facial damage'.

In my current state I couldn't work out how this changed things, though obviously it changed everything. I didn't know where to look for the blue-headed man, and sensed I wouldn't have to. In the meantime, there was someone else looking for me. I'd shoved Suej out because I'd decided to save him the trouble and go looking for him instead.

Nine

Club Bastard was an explosion of thrashing groovesters, contained within a barn-like building in the middle of a party floor. You couldn't have got anyone else into the club without first compressing them to the size of a pea, and I suspect that when I pushed my way into the club someone must have been popped out of a window the other side. Music crunched out of massive speakers along every wall, competing with the cacophony of five hundred people all shouting at once. The music was Predictive Trance, the notes and words all fresh-minted in real time by a bank of computers on the far wall. The algorithms used for generating the lyrics are keyed to the effect of various recreational drugs, and thus the more out of it you get, the better you become at predicting what the words will be.

I shouldered my way through to the bar, buffeted on every side by bright young things. The queue at the counter wasn't very deep, probably because everyone in the place was bombed on happy drugs. Dying tendrils of the Rapt I'd taken were sparkling periodically in parts of my brain, and being surrounded by glittering eyes and expensive highs was not what I needed. I was grimly conscious of the fact that what I did need was more Rapt, and that I shouldn't allow myself to have it. I was also still shouldering thoughts of the spares away as hard as I could. I knew I had to find them soon. Nothing had changed – including the fact that I didn't know where to start looking. I wasn't in a great state, to be honest, and had no high hopes of ever feeling better.

The gorilla behind the bar stared at me impassively when I got there, waiting for me to speak.

'Is Johnny in?' I asked, trying to look tough.

'Who wants to know?' the man said. He was trying even harder than me and succeeded only in looking like two types of shit in a one-shit waistcoat.

'I do, obviously, you stupid fuck,' I said, not impressed. 'Or I wouldn't have asked. Is he in or not?'

Huge hands closed around my arms. A Vinaldi goon stood on either side of me, two jabs in my back making it clear they were armed as well. The barman grinned.

'He's expecting you,' he said.

The two guys steered me through the crowd towards a glass wall on the other side of the club. The glass was chroma-keyed to reflect only flesh tones, creating a shifting mirage of disembodied arms and heads. As we approached, a door opened to one side making it clear that the wall was one-way glass. I was bundled unceremoniously through the doorway and into the space behind.

Up a short flight of steps and into a large room, stretching the length of the wall. Sofas, bookcases, full AV rig; points of red and green LEDs in the semi-darkness. Jaz Garcia stepped out of the gloom, gripped me by the throat and pulled me forwards.

'Careful,' said a voice. 'I want to hear his explanation before I let you remodel salient features of his body. Though trust me, that will be an upcoming presentation.'

Garcia punched me solidly in the face, to promote co-operation and let me know the score. Then his other hand loosened barely perceptibly as he swung me round and let go. I was thrown accurately into a large chair facing the glass wall, and I had to admire his technique.

I knew what was going to happen. Maybe Nearly would look after Suej. Beyond the one-way mirror I could see all the happy youngsters below, dancing for their lives. Have fun, I thought to them. Shout those lyrics. You won't even hear the gunshot when it comes.

Another man thrust his hands into my jacket and came out with my gun, which he placed carefully on a table. Then he waved some kind of detector over me. Nothing bleeped, and he stepped back out of sight. Garcia had disappeared to stand behind me, and the scene was almost set. I heard a chair being pulled along the floor in front of me, and then set down, back towards me.

Vinaldi sat himself down in it, arms folded over the back of the chair. I wondered if guys like him had to go to some orientation class when they started out, to make sure they got things like that just right. I made a mental note to ask Dath in the unlikely event of me ever seeing him again.

He didn't say anything for a while, so I started the ball rolling. 'You wanted to see me,' I said, striving for a tone of friendly interest.

Johnny didn't say anything again, or rather continued not to say anything. He kept that up for long enough that my remark disappeared as if I'd never made it. This was obviously to be his show, and his alone. I decided to just wait and let him have it his way.

'Randall,' he said eventually. 'You ought to be congratulated. There should be statues to you. You are truly a very stupid man.'

'I try,' I said, and Garcia struck me across the back of the head with a gun. It hurt like fuck.

Vinaldi smiled thinly. 'What made you think you could do this?'

'Do what?' I said, blinking my eyes against the pain in my head. 'Tell me Johnny, what is it you think I'm doing?'

'In a way it is reassuring that all my problems come down to you. It is reassuring to me because I thought I had some kind of mini-series-sized revolt on my hands, and now I find all I have is some stupid ex-cop with a death wish. I see you're fucked up again, which is no surprise to me. Your life is no use to you, is your problem, and tonight Jaz will put you out of your misery.'

I stared back at him then, something beginning to strike me as wrong with this picture. Partly it was what Vinaldi was saying, mainly the atmosphere around me. Grimly celebratory. These guys thought they were putting an end to something here. I didn't know what that might be.

'What are you talking about?' I asked, genuinely interested. 'I haven't even started trying to take you down. When I do, you'll know about it and you won't have time for this kind of conversation. You'll be too busy digging bullets out of your face.'

I was expecting another blow from behind, but it still surprised me with its force. My head was thrown forwards and I resolved to pace myself a little better. Two more like that and I'd be out, and I hadn't been really rude yet.

'Five of my closest associates have been killed,' Vinaldi said. 'And you're trying to tell me you've got nothing to do with it?'

I stared at him for real, then. 'Nothing at all,' I said, genuinely astounded.

Vinaldi laughed humourlessly. 'Jaz said you'd say that. Me, I thought you'd have the sense to realize the position you're in and tell the truth, but Jaz, he says you're stupider than that.'

'Jaz would know,' I said. 'He's the yardstick, after all.'

Another crunch from behind, and this time a firework of stars went off above my right eye. So much for pacing myself. I shook my head and glanced through the glass wall for a moment, trying to refocus on something. It took a while. The crowds outside were still dancing, though there seemed to be some sort of confrontation happening far off at the main door.

I tried to reorientate myself around what was going on. It seemed to come down to this: Vinaldi thought I was the guy who was whacking his associates. He had to be fucking crazy.

'You've got to be fucking crazy,' I said. 'You think I'm going round clipping your friends?'

'I know you are.'

'As you keep pointing out, I'm not a cop any more. I've got no problem with your associates. My only problem is with you.'

'So you try to take me down from the outside. Slow death. I frankly admire the ambition.'

'So do I, but it isn't me. I wasn't even in town when the first guys were killed,' I said.

Vinaldi smiled, with real humour this time. 'You think I'm going to believe a word you say?'

'You'd better, because it's true. And if it isn't me trying to take you down, then it must be someone else.'

Without taking his eyes off me, Vinaldi signalled into the gloom behind him. The henchman who'd frisked me padded out of the darkness, carrying something. Out of the corner of my eye I saw that something was still going on in the club beyond the glass, but then my attention was utterly taken.

On the floor in front of me had been placed a cardboard box.

I leapt towards it, but Jaz and another goon smacked me back into the chair, keeping hold of my arms to stop me doing it again.

'Who the fuck's in there?' I shouted, still struggling vainly. 'If it's Jenny or David I'm going to kill every fucking one of you.' Jaz and his colleague laughed good-naturedly; I wasn't in a position to do anyone any harm.

But the atmosphere changed. Vinaldi looked at me strangely. 'What are you talking about?'

'I'm not joking, Vinaldi; if it's David or Jenny you're fucking dead.' The Rapt in my head had finally cleared enough for Nanune's death to strike home; and I was out of control with it. 'Whatever it takes, you're dead.'

Vinaldi's frown intensified. 'I know nothing of this David or Jenny. Are you trying to be clever, Randall?'

I stared at him, not knowing what the hell was going on.

Deep breath. 'Who's in the box?' I said.

'Someone you were seen talking to yesterday.' Vinaldi nodded, and the henchman leant over to open the box. I could see what was in there before he lifted it out, and felt a wave of relief wash over me.

The hood from the Minimart.

'This was delivered an hour ago. That's why you're here, Randall. You come and disturb me at my home and I think "Let him go, he's nothing". Then this is delivered and I have to reconsider.'

'Johnny,' I said. 'Listen to me. I went in this guy's store, and he made me. That's all. I didn't bomb the place and I didn't cut his head off. I've got problems of my own: all I wanted was to get out of town. Then at Howie's an hour ago I got a box just like this one with the head of a friend of mine in it.'

'Bullshit,' Jaz said. 'Look, boss, let me just kill the fuck now. I'll do it as slow as you want.'

Vinaldi waved Jaz back, looking carefully at me. A bleeper went off somewhere in the background of the room, but no one paid any attention to it. I let my eyes run across the crowd the other side of the glass, trying to think how the hell I was going to convince him. Something in the view caught my eye, but then it was gone. My mind was racing, trying to fit this into the picture. It wouldn't go.

'Something's going down,' I said rapidly, trying to think as I spoke. 'Someone killed Mal, maybe looking for me, maybe not. But they wanted him too, because of some murders he was looking into. I came to you last night because I thought you'd done them, or had them done.'

'I told you, you fuck, I don't have women murdered except on special occasions.'

'But somebody does, and those two women were tied to you. Maybe the other three were too. Just like it was your guys who got killed – they all come back to you. And the same guy killed Nanune.'

Vinaldi got as far as asking who the hell Nanune was when the bleeper on the desk went again, louder and more urgently this time. He turned furiously: 'Jesus, there's four of you here – can't one of you answer it?' Then he turned back to me, and I saw his not inconsiderable intelligence trying to sift through what I'd just said. Maybe he'd come up with an answer. I hoped so. Perhaps he could let me in on it. 'So who . . . ?'

A rustling sound. Not heard, but sensed. In my head, as it had been in the elevator. Neck going cold, I whirled my head to look out the glass, suddenly understanding what I'd noticed through the wall out of the corner of my eye.

'He's here,' I said.

'Boss,' shouted the guy at the desk. 'Something's getting fucked up out there.' I had time for a sliver of déjà vu and then everything went ballistic. Jaz and the others scrambled for their cannons amidst a blizzard of swearing.

'Who's here?' Vinaldi asked me, confused, but I didn't have to answer because the door was opened and the question was answered.

The man with the blue lights in his head.

He calmly shut the door behind him and fired. Jaz spun away, hit in the arm. The other hoods forgot all their training and stared at the man in the doorway, hypnotized by the flashing blue lights.

'Hey Johnny,' the man said, levelling his gun at him. 'Looking good. Remember me?'

For the first time in maybe his entire life, Johnny Vinaldi looked completely dumbfounded. He stared at the man, brow creased, seemingly unaware of the laser sight on his forehead.

'Shutdown,' the man said as he pulled the trigger, and I did something completely unexpected. Unthinkingly bracing my heels against the heavy chair I was sitting in, I launched myself at Vinaldi, smashing into his chair and knocking the pair of us across the floor. The bullet whistled through the air just above us, Vinaldi's eyes still locked on the man with the lights.

The man appeared to notice me for the first time, and laughed delightedly in recognition. 'Hey, Jack's here too,' he said merrily, meanwhile holding his gun to the side to shoot Vinaldi's second henchman. 'What a happy coincidence. There's people who are really pissed at you. You and I got stuff to talk about.'

I felt otherwise, and lunged towards the table, carelessly knocking it over and sending my gun skittering towards the wall. Johnny had regained his composure and was reaching for his own weapon, but it was all far too slow.

The door was kicked open and five of Vinaldi's men swarmed in – the guys who'd come for me at Howie's place. The man leapt out of their way like a gymnast, and again I heard a rustling sound at the back of my mind like spiders walking on leaves. But mainly I heard the sound of gunfire as everyone fired at each other at once. I swiped my gun up from the floor, keeping my head below the level of the sofa.

I don't like enclosed spaces too much. I turned and fired straight at the glass wall.

The result was nothing like the shattering in Howie's place. That was just straight glass. This one had electronics built into it, and fractured with a grinding folding scream. A jagged sheet broke out of it, tumbling down into the room and revealing the sweating dancers beyond.

I grabbed the overturned table and yanked it onto its side, crawling quickly towards the hole in the glass, flinching against the impacts I expected to come. Everyone seemed to be too busy trying to kill someone else. Vinaldi was crouched by the wall, behind the body of a fallen bodyguard, firing into the mêlée by the door.

'I'm still going to kill you,' I said, then jumped through the wall and tumbled into the crowd beyond. None of the dancers seemed to be aware of what was happening, the gunfire inaudible beneath the pounding noise and flickering lyrics. I pushed my way out through the crowd and when I emerged panting into the street I turned for the elevators and ran.

'Hey – what the hell happened to you?'

I shouldered my way past Nearly and into her apartment. It was dark – lit only by warm strip lighting down at floor level – and neat, cosy, personal. Presumably she didn't do business here, though a few items dotted around the apartment – the TV, some of the furniture, a rearWindow on the back wall – hinted that she did good business somewhere. Suej was sitting in the middle of the floor, a mug of coffee in front of her. She jumped on seeing me, face aghast.

'What?' I said, and then looked down and realized someone's blood was spread liberally all over my clothes. 'It's not mine,' I said, putting my arms around Suej, and holding her tight.

When we disengaged I turned to see Nearly holding a mug out to me. 'We don't have time,' I said.

'Sure you do,' she replied, thrusting it into my hands and letting go. I kept hold of it – barely. 'You're not going anywhere now. Just sit down and be quiet.'

Without really knowing how, I found myself in a chair. My entire body ached in a non-specific way. Rapt crash. My head hurt in several very specific places. But we needed to be moving on. To where, I didn't know.

Nearly seemed to read my mind. 'Where you going to go, big guy? Howie's okay – we gave him a call. But his place is going to be too hot for a while.'

'We're putting you at risk by being here,' I said. 'I'm not prepared to do that. I don't even know you.'

'That's sweet of you and don't think I don't appreciate it but I think you're kind of tired right now and working out what to do next is going to be a high mountain to climb.'

I stared at her, something that she'd said striking a chord.

'While I remember,' she continued apologetically, 'Howie asked what he should do with the box. Did you want it kept or anything because otherwise it's kind of gross?'

'What was in the box?' Suej asked. I took one look at her and knew I couldn't lie.

'Part of Nanune,' I said. 'I'm sorry, Suej.'

Her eyes glazed, and she nodded. 'A big part?'

'Big enough,' I said, and then – horrifically – had to stifle a yawn. Suej didn't seem to notice. My head was feeling strange. Sour adrenaline, I guessed.

'Do you know where David is?' Suej asked, looking at the ground.

'No,' I said. 'But I know who's got him, and the others.'

'Is he from SafetyNet?'

'I don't know where he's from,' I said heavily, though I felt I should. Something was still tugging at my mind. It pisses me off, when it does that. I wish it would just come out and speak its piece rather than pussy-footing around in the shadows. Probably the result of too much drugs, too often, for far too long. Kids, don't live like this at home. I yawned again and realized – something was wrong. I looked down into my mug: my sight was blurring, but I could see that I'd finished the coffee.

'What have you done to me?' I asked querulously.

'Nothing bad, and it wasn't just my idea,' Nearly said. 'Just a sedative.'

'You're with them,' I said thickly, voice slurring. The walls seemed to be sliding down into the floor.

'I'm not with anyone,' she said, standing and carrying a blanket over to me. 'What you see is what you get. Now get some sleep. Your mommies will look after you.'

The last things I saw were Suej sitting on the floor next to me, whispering tunnel talk; and Nearly's face a little further away, clear skin and big eyes framed by dark chestnut hair.

'She's beautiful,' I thought foggily. 'Pity she's killed me.' The thought seemed somehow consistent with life in general.

I woke up shaking violently, but it didn't last too long. Ten minutes and a cup of coffee scavenged from Nearly's immaculate kitchen saw me through to the end of it. In a way it was kind of a nostalgic experience, though I wouldn't recommend it to everyone.

The apartment was empty, but a note in the bathroom told me where they'd gone:

'Taken the day off,' it said, in a firm hand. 'Gone shopping on Indigo Drive.' Underneath, in Suej's much less confident scrawl, was added: 'Come meet us? ps I tole Nearly about things.'

I showered rapidly, swearing quietly under my breath. Though I was grateful to Nearly for looking after Suej the night before, they shouldn't have gone out alone. I was also somewhat niggled about having been knocked out, though even I could tell I was better for it. The face I saw in the mirror didn't look exactly human, but at least I resembled some allied species. Back in the living room I discovered a pile of men's clothes neatly laid out, presumably for me. They were my size at least, a black suit and midnight blue shirt. Rather smarter than my usual attire, and I didn't know where they'd come from, but I put them on under my coat and left the apartment still clutching a second mug of coffee. So what if I was wearing some john's cast-offs; it didn't matter to me. And I could hardly cruise Indigo Drive covered in brown splatters of someone else's blood.

A local elevator took me up to 98, and a short walk got me to the start of the shopping strip. It was eleven o'clock by then, and from the way the crowds were beginning to swell I realized belatedly that it was Saturday. Indigo Drive is kind of a point of honour in the world below the 100 line. In the original MegaMall the two-storey 94/95 floor had been the most prestigious of the shopping arcades, plumb in the middle of the aircraft. Pretty lanes of bijou shoplets ranged round sweeping highways of outlet stores, dinky little cafés and restaurants, with not a bar in sight. All the most chichi stores had since migrated up into the shopping floors in the 130s and above, but Indigo Drive was still hanging on in there. It was the best shopping there was without getting a pass to go higher, and things were a hell of a lot cheaper. The stores had resisted the highlife fashion of costSlots – LCD panels in clothes which showed in dollars just how expensive they'd been – which meant that they were no use to anyone from above 130. But for people in the 70s–120s, Indigo Drive was the place to go.

I wandered the main streets for an hour, partly looking for the girls, mainly enjoying the brief sensation of not being shot at. I recognized some of the stores; others seemed to have changed, the partial familiarity making me feel as if I'd never been there before. Then a way ahead of me I saw a face in the crowd which looked like Suej's, and quickened my pace. She disappeared into a clothes store beside Nearly, but not so quickly that I couldn't see her expression: big smile, bright eyes. I stopped hurrying, to give them a little more time, and hung around outside to finish a cigarette.

When I entered the store, I reached without thinking for some MaxWork. Only when I had a small, half-finished device in my hands did I realize what I'd done, and I ground to a halt in the doorway, staring down at a partially constructed nest of chips and components. People tutted as they walked round me, but I barely heard them. I could remember perfectly what I was supposed to do with the stuff in my hands, but I put it back, turned round and left the store.

When I reached the outside again I stood for a while, staring ahead but not seeing anything as it was. Everything seemed to have changed, as if in some small way the past had suddenly become married to the present. As I stood there, I thought I felt a child run their hand against mine, but when I looked there was no one there. Maybe it was just a coincidence, or perhaps I was finally realizing that was always the way it was always going to be. I walked unsteadily to a bench and sat down, trying to avoid looking at the MaxWork bench just inside the store. I was thinking of Henna, and the past, in a way I hadn't ever really done since things had changed.

Remembering how, like every man alive, I'd trailed round after my woman in clothes stores, gazing dazed with boredom into the middle distance and periodically nodding at stuff that was being shown to me. A handbag; a dress; some shoes. How I'd never been able to tell the difference between them, and how, like all those other men, I'd done MaxWork to ease the tedium.

Fifty or so years ago Arlond Maxen's father had been following his wife round a store such as this when a very lucrative bulb went off in his head. He'd been thinking that he'd do anything at all to make the time pass quicker, and then suddenly realized that he probably wasn't alone. All these guys, he mused, looking round him at the walking dead, following their women and bored out of their minds: all those wasted man-hours.

He could give them something to do.

So MaxWork was born. A small bench inside every women's store, with components and half-finished products laid out. You followed your wife or girlfriend into the store, and just picked one of the devices up. In the early days Maxen made sure the kiosks were staffed by eye-candy; after a while it became such a habit that the babes weren't even necessary. While you trailed around the racks of cloth and leather you did some work on the device; simple, absorbing tasks which anyone could do, picking up from where the last guy had left off. When you left the store you put it back on the bench on the way out, to be picked up by the next boyfriend or husband along. When the devices were finished they were taken away, but there were always new ones to complete.

It was the kind of plan Howie had been trying to emulate all his life. Perfect, in every way. Relief from tedium for the men, fewer bored sighs for the women to endure – and free labour for the Maxen Corporation, cheaper even than droids. Everybody won, but Cedrif Maxen won most of all. Thirty years later he was the richest man in New Richmond – and now his youngest son had it all.

That's the history, for those of you who're interested, but that wasn't what I was thinking about. Walking into the store had carelessly wiped a cloth across a window blackened and opaque with time. The path of that cloth was still filthy, but just transparent enough to reveal glints on the edges of memories lost in the darkness beyond. I'd tried so hard not to think of any of it. Not even of the horror at the end, just of the times before that. Bad things done, and said; things which could never be undone. Not just the bad, either; good and bad memories hurt in different ways, but they hurt just about the same.

At that moment, I would have given anything to walk round a shoe store following Henna's glee, watching the way her eyes calculated cost, the way her hands reached out to caress and assay. It could never happen, and for a moment I was seized with a distraught desire to go down to 72 and the clothes left in our old apartment; to look at them, touch them, see if I could remember the day when they were bought. To try to take myself back to that day and this time not grunt and yawn, or bury myself in MaxWork; but be there with her and live every minute as it passed. So many minutes, and hours; so many days ignored away. And then suddenly it's over, and she can never come back, and all that time returns to stay.

At a squeal from the shop door I looked up to see Suej running towards me. It took me a long moment to recognize her. I'd never seen her face looking that happy, and she was wearing different clothes. My cast-offs were gone, and she was wearing a thin summer dress, a subtle print that twisted and changed as she moved. She looked younger, and older; like someone I knew and someone I'd never seen before. Behind her came Nearly, a wry smile on her lips and a different look in her eyes. As Suej thudded into me and wrapped her hands round my back I raised an eyebrow at Nearly, and she shrugged.

'Been a good month,' she said.

And then, an afternoon that really felt like summer, though winter was in full force outside. I found I still couldn't go in the stores, but waited happily enough outside; smoking on benches and standing in doorways, nodding sagely when required. A coat for Suej, at Nearly's insistence, and a small bag to keep her non-existent things in. Almost the last of Howie's money from me, on a pair of shoes to go with the dress. Coffee and sandwiches in the square, surrounded by the contentedly spent; Suej's eyes as they went from bag to bag, alight with acquisition joy.

We should have been running, or I should have been searching for the rest of the spares. A man I didn't know had my death on his mind, and the spares didn't have anyone but me to care about what happened to them. But this was an afternoon I should have had long ago, and while having it now didn't change anything, at least it was one that was squared away. You have to accept gifts occasionally, because there are some things you can't give yourself. That afternoon was a small present from the gods, one which was heavily overdue. I took it, and was glad.

Ten

It took a long time for the pennies to start dropping. I've no real excuse for that: guess I'm just a stupid man. At least when they did they fell together, like a scattered handful of change.

We were sitting in a bar on 67 at the time, it was mid-evening and I was within shouting distance of drunk. I can't help it. That's the way I am. The bar was long and old fashioned; the walls wood panelled, with hanging TV screens burbling in corners. Someone had gone to the trouble of building small rectangular contraptions to house the flat LCD sheets so they resembled antique sets, and the overall effect was of a bygone age. The patrons were talking fast and hard, and seemed to be having a good time. As far as I could tell, I was having one too.

Nearly and I were drinking steadily, sitting with Suej in a raised booth in the side of the establishment. I was vaguely considering the idea of food – a burger the size of Texas with *everything* on it, possibly; Nearly had already eaten a salad and a 20° slice of pecan pie. I think the afternoon had quietened us all down, and we weren't talking much. I'd learnt a small amount of Nearly's history, but hadn't told her any of mine. She was twenty-six and had been in the life for four years, operating towards the higher end of the scale. She reckoned that by thirty she'd have enough to get out, and I was trying not to picture what she'd look like by then. I gathered that Suej must have given her the bones of my last five years, because Nearly's attitude towards me seemed to have altered. I couldn't put my finger on what the difference was. I'd obviously changed from being just a big violent dude with a drugs problem, but to what I wasn't sure.

It was during a break in the conversation that the first small revelation came. I was looking vaguely in Suej's direction, watching her finish her burger, her jaws chomping gamely as her eyes followed people with fascination.

And blearily I thought: maybe she's the key.

The guy with the blue lights had to have been part of the team who killed Mal and took the spares. Yet when I'd returned to Mal's building, far from taking me out, he'd stopped rat-face from trying to kill me. He must have known I would try and avenge Mal, and it had probably been him who'd kept me in New Richmond by hiding the body. I could only think of one possible reason for wanting me to be still alive and in the city: he hadn't yet got something that he'd been sent to find, and I was the key to him getting it.

He had all the spares, except one.

'My shout,' said Nearly, necking the last of her wine. 'But I'm going to the john first.' She winked, a pantomime gesture which involved most of her face and half her upper body, and I guessed a pharmaceutical top-up was on the agenda. I watched her as she made her way across the floor to the Ladies, drawing a quiver of appreciative glances. She was living proof that being top to bottom slim didn't stop you from looking like a woman. Meantime, my mind was working. For the first time in two days I felt awake.

Suej was important: to make up the set, or in her own right? If the set was the issue Nanune wouldn't have died the way she did. I suddenly believed that whoever had set Blue Lights on us was mainly interested in Suej, and that he'd been waiting for me to take him to her. By keeping her stashed I'd inadvertently been doing the right thing, which figured. My good moves are generally accidents.

Did that make him SafetyNet? Not necessarily. I couldn't believe that the corporation would allow an operative to conduct business in the way he did. Plus three other missing links:

1) The day we blew the Farm, it was Jenny they had wanted. Her twin had to have been near death for the operations they were considering. So how come Suej was the issue now?

2) What was Blue Lights' problem with Vinaldi? How could he fit with a SafetyNet scenario?

3) Nanune's desecrated head and the stealing of Mal's display pointed to either Blue Lights or his accomplice being behind the

facial damage homicides – as did the tie-ins to Vinaldi. In that case, why were the NRPD files security locked? Blue Lights wasn't a cop, I'd lay money on that – so how did he rate protection? The shooter I'd killed outside Mal's apartment had no rap jacket, and I'd a hunch Blue Lights wouldn't have either. Which meant either that all the trouble was coming from out of town or someone was going to a lot of trouble to make it look that way.

Fine thinking, far as it went, but it didn't go far enough. Instead of making me feel like I was getting somewhere, it made me unsettled and nervous. The downside of Suej being the key was that it meant that the other spares were probably expendable, and none of it got me much closer to understanding what was going on or how I could rescue them. There was at least one part of the puzzle still missing, and until I knew what it was I couldn't go after the spares, or even ensure that Suej was safe. I couldn't do anything.

I looked up to see Suej's eyes on me.

'Are you okay, Jack?' she asked. I stopped drumming my fingers on the table top and smiled.

'Sure,' I said. 'How was the burger?'

'Good.' She grinned. 'Nicer than Ratchet's.' Ratchet had been a droid out of the top drawer, but, as discussed, cooking hadn't been one of his key skills – and especially not short order stuff. On the other hand, it wasn't supposed to have been, and it was surprising he'd been able to cook at all. For the first time since leaving the Farm I experienced my recurrent curiosity as to what exactly Ratchet had been. I also felt a sudden twinge of loneliness and melancholy on realizing that the machine which had saved my life was probably unrecognizable now. Trashed or reprogrammed by the company, his mind dead forever as punishment for exceeding his role. There ought to be a warning on my forehead, I thought: think carefully before entering this man's life, because very few people make it back out alive. Then I thought it was time to can the self-pity before I started boring even myself.

'Can we go there?' Suej said, and I turned to follow her finger. One of the monitors was showing a news report about some mountain, huge and covered with snow. Suej probably thought it was somewhere just outside New Richmond, back near the way we'd come down from the hills.

'Maybe,' I said. I was about to make it sound more convincing when suddenly I stopped.

Mount Everest.

'You're *not* okay,' Suej said, immediately. 'I see it in your face. What's wrong?'

I'd realized what Nearly had inadvertently reminded me of the night before. The report I'd already seen about someone discovering a mountain higher than Everest. Presumably I was now seeing it again.

But that was bullshit. Mount Everest *was* the highest mountain on Earth. Of course it fucking was.

And now the gates were opening, I realized something else: Wall-diving. Jumping out of windows with nothing but some weird fibreglass rod for company. How likely was that? Did that make any sense *at all*?

'Jack, what's *wrong*?'

Ignoring her, I looked towards the Ladies. A sudden influx had turned the area round the bar into a crush of people. Nearly was a way back from the counter, talking to some guy. From her body language I could tell the conversation wasn't especially welcome, but no more than that.

'I'm sorry Suej, but we're going to have to go,' I said. Suej pouted, but she knew something was wrong. She stood up with me and I waited while she gathered her bags, and then she let me lead her down into the throng.

When we got to Nearly she was alone. 'We have to leave,' I said. 'We have to leave right *now*.'

Nearly looked at Suej, then back at me. 'Says who? I'm thirsty.' I grabbed her arm and tried to pull her away, aware that I was appearing a Neanderthal. She yanked it back again. 'What is your problem?'

'What's the highest mountain in the world?' I asked, fighting to stay patient. Nearly just stared at me, buffeted by the people around us. '*Quickly*.'

'Well, Mount Fyi, of course. They just found out. Do I win a prize?'

'No. That's why we have to go.' I looked around the crowd. The man Nearly'd been talking to had disappeared. 'Who was that guy?'

Nearly looked confused, then realized who I was talking about.

'Said he was a john of mine from a couple of years back; wanted to play tonight. I told him to go away. Why?'

'Didn't you recognize him?'

'No, but – how can I put this? – it's not like I keep a lock of each one's hair.'

'Nearly, trust me. We really have to go.'

She stood her ground for a moment longer, then rolled her eyes. 'Jesus, you're no fun at all,' she said, and allowed me to pull her towards the door.

Too late.

I suddenly sensed time rushing towards me again, without really knowing what I was reacting to. Maybe it was some sound from deep in the crowd, or perhaps I felt the crush of people parting. Some sixth sense from long ago, stirring sluggishly. I instinctively put myself between Suej and the rest of the bar, shoving Nearly towards the door. As I surreptitiously pulled my gun out I felt Suej move behind me and glanced to see that Nearly had taken her hand and was taking her with her. I didn't know whether she'd started to believe me or was just doing what she was told for once. Either way I was grateful.

I quickly slipped a few yards to the right through the crowd, keeping my gun hidden and low. Scanned the faces, and kept moving in unpredictable directions six feet at a time, turning my head as far round as I could, trying to feel where he'd be. It was like moving through grasping and twisted trees. I used to be good at that. But he was obviously better than me.

'Shutdown,' a voice whispered an inch behind my ear.

With a whole-body spasm I crunched my heel backwards and felt it connect solidly with his shin. Whirling on my other foot I brought the gun up, cracking it against people in the crowd. Surprised mouths opened in front of me. The man had gone but at least people were getting the fuck out of my way. I searched the crowd, saw no one, then my head snapped towards the door. He'd twisted behind me and was ten feet away, carving his way through the throng towards Suej. But it wasn't Blue Lights; it was someone new.

I could see Nearly's head just outside but she didn't catch my desperate signals. Suej was looking somewhere else entirely, staring at the wooden frame of the door. I forgot the secret of slipping through people and threw myself forward, fighting the crowd as if it was a thicket of undergrowth. A mass of arms and legs and red angry faces. Hard elbows, jabbing into me.

He was getting to the door much more quickly than me, slipping through the crowd as if it wasn't there. There was something in the way he moved, a murderous grace, which told me he'd been trained for this. I had been too; and once upon a time maybe could have caught him. But not now. It was far too long ago.

When I started going backwards, I knew I was going to have to do something unusual. I changed course and headed for the bar like a lumbering missile, slamming people out of the way with both hands. I made it to the counter and hoisted myself up, sending rows of glasses flying. I scrambled to my feet, slipping on spillage, and whirled to face the crowd.

'Stay there or I'm going to blow your head off,' I shouted at him. Not very original, but there you go. Some phrases are hard-wired into the male psyche. When the need arises, out they come. The guy knew this, and gave it about as much heed as it deserved, continuing towards the door. The crowd were less sanguine, and dived to get out of the way; opening a channel to the exit, exactly what I didn't want.

Nice one, Jack, I thought: tactical mastery as usual.

A second to make a decision. I needed the guy alive – I wanted to talk to him. But if he got to Suej everything was over anyway.

I shot him, carefully.

The bullet caught him in the neck and spun him round, but he was a big fucker and kept on going. I parked another in his back and launched myself off the bar, flying raggedly over rows of heads and smashing down onto him. We crashed to the floor, a space suddenly clear around us; I tried to turn the fall into a roll but he was quicker than me and kicked me back down again as he pulled out his gun. I twisted immediately and took some splinters in the face as the patch of floor where my head had been exploded.

I decided I was tired of being shot at in bars and that I didn't need to talk to him that much.

My gun was half-empty before he staggered; I pushed myself to my feet with one hand, still firing with the other. The problem with guns is that they don't kill people as quickly as you might think.

Shooting people doesn't send them flying backwards in a graceful arc. It just tends to really annoy them. I lunged forward and grabbed his neck, my hand slipping in the biology spilling out of the hole there. I got him on his back and knelt over him, hand still on his throat and a knee on each arm, gun firmly pointed at his forehead. His face was thin and not very clean, eyes deep set and dark. Under his coat it looked like he was wearing army fatigues which hadn't been troubled by water in a while.

I knew I didn't have long before the cops arrived, so I made it simple for him. 'Tell me who you are and where you're from or I'm going to spread your brains all over the next floor down,' I panted, feeling warmth spilling out of his neck onto my fingers.

He bucked and nearly threw me off so I put another bullet through his collarbone at close range.

'You *know* where I'm from,' he said, through a mouthful of blood. He seemed to be grinning.

'No I don't,' I said. 'And it's pissing me off. Are you SafetyNet, or what?'

The man laughed, sending another gout of mess blatting up through the remains of his lungs. 'Ain't no safety net there, Randall. You know that.'

From behind, I heard someone whisper 'They're coming,' and knew that time had run out. I stood up and left him lying there, knowing he wasn't going to tell me anything. Then as an afterthought I shot him in the head. Not very polite of me, I know, but then he didn't want the best for me either.

'Jesus – what is it with you and public places?' Nearly shouted. 'Were you, like, mistreated in a bar as a kid?' I'd obviously slipped back in her estimation to big violent dude with a drugs problem, maybe even further than that. 'Wherever you go it's the same fucking movie. Don't you get tired of it?'

'One, he could have been the guy killing women,' I said, pushing her and Suej quickly along the street. 'Two, he could have killed Mal. Three, either him or his friend cut Nanune's fucking *head off*, and four I don't want to discuss it.'

We ran out into Road 2, the smaller of 67's main drags. I could hear sirens in the distance, cops on platforms surfing towards us from the station on the other side of the floor. The platforms are simply that, four-inch slabs with hovers underneath; one cop drives using the lectern at the front, the others do what the hell they like. I kept us moving away from the bar for as long as possible, and then, when I saw a flashing light turn the corner into our road, yanked the girls into a sidestreet. The platform rocketed past like a very low-flying bird with parasites on its back, and I hoped the bar wasn't about to experience an 'incident'. The cop piloting was bombed out his mind and the others were waving their guns around like cowboys on a runaway river boat.

When it was safely past, we ran back out onto the street and sprinted across it, into another side road and then through to the waste ground behind. Once it had been a botanical garden. Now it was just a mess, some descendants of the original plants still struggling for life, most dead and gone. Yellow street lights were strung along the edges of the grounds, but the interior was dark and abandoned.

'Where are we *going*?' Nearly panted. 'And are you going to shoot anyone when we get there? If so, I think I may pass and take in a show instead.'

There was an elevator on the other side. I pointed to it.

'Down to your apartment,' I said as we ran into the gloom. 'There's stuff I left there. Then Suej and I are disappearing. Probably for good.'

'Well hey, it's been nice knowing you,' Nearly said angrily. 'And when I say "nice", I don't mean it.' I was about to try to say something conciliatory when Suej suddenly ground to a halt in front of me. I almost collided with her and instead skidded to a stop, a growl ready on my lips.

It never made it out.

We were in the middle of the waste ground by then, two hundred yards from anything in any direction. The sirens still blared in the distance, but apart from that it was quiet and still. Suej was staring into space with her mouth open. There was nothing there.

'Suej?' I said. 'What . . . ?'

Then something morphed out of the shadows. A flicker at first, a shimmer like shadows changing places to music I couldn't hear. At the threshold of audibility a sound, like many hands clapping but speeded up and far away.

Then a shiver went through the ground and the space between us fractured into noise and light.

Suej shrieked as the birds exploded into being, a hundred mad, happy orange sets of wings and ear-splitting cries crashing into fluttering life. Living flames shot up into the air, but went nowhere; movement and noise contained into stillness, as if everything in the world was trying to be in the same place at once. It was impossible to discern the beginning of one scream and the start of the next, or one bird and another.

I found Suej's hand in mine. She was pulling me towards the elevator. Her face was white with shock and surprise, and she ducked and twisted against things that weren't even there. Nearly just stared at us, following, as we stumbled towards the elevator. Behind her the birds slithered and ran into invisible tracks in the air, tearing passage back the way they'd come.

We fell into the elevator and stared out into darkness as the doors closed and sealed us in.

'What the hell's *wrong* with you guys?' Nearly shouted, stamping her feet. I ignored her and put my arms round Suej's shoulders, as much for my own comfort as hers. She was trembling like an animal caught in headlights, rooted to the spot. I thought she'd been struck mute but suddenly she looked up, blue eyes staring straight into mine.

'You know what that was,' she said, voice spiralling into accusation and terror. 'You *know.*'

'You saw the forest in the elevator before, didn't you?' I asked. She nodded feverishly.

'What are they?' she wailed. 'Where are they from?'

'Hello? Calling planet Jack...' Nearly shouted, as the doors opened onto 66. She was beside herself with anger and fear. '*What are you guys talking about*?'

'You didn't see them?' Suej asked her incredulously, and Nearly just stared as if finally realizing that she'd spent the day with two people who should have been weaving baskets and knocking back Thorazine. I stepped quickly out of the elevator, my arm still round

Suej. I was trying to work out what was happening, but it was all coming at me too fast. Some final penny had been thrown in my lap, some huge great hundred-dollar special edition coin out of the sky. I'd have done anything to be able to hurl it back before I worked out what it meant.

'See *who*?' Nearly said, hurrying along beside us.

'The birds,' I said, knowing she hadn't. Suej shouldn't have been able to either, and come to that, neither should I. They shouldn't have been there at all, just like the scene in the elevator which I'd assumed was a Rapt-induced flashback. I was shaking violently, not feeling very tough at all.

'Suej,' I said. 'What were you staring at in the bar, on the way out?'

'The door frame,' she said. 'The wood was acting funny.'

Everest, wall-diving, the mad, happy birds. It was all leading to one place. The forest.

I wasn't going back there again.

A rasping sprint along deserted corridors to the corner of Tyson and Stones; a huddle outside Nearly's door. She was scrabbling for her keys and I was staring wildly around when the door lock spoke to us.

'There's someone inside,' it said. 'Just thought you might like to know.'

'Who?' Nearly yelped, as I pulled out my gun. Sometimes I don't know why I don't just have it surgically implanted in my hand.

'He didn't say,' the lock replied mildly, as if its mind was on other things. 'He had keys, so there wasn't much I could do.'

'Howie?' I asked Nearly, trying not to panic.

She shook her head, backing away from the door. 'He's my manager, not my boyfriend.'

I took Nearly's keys and stood in front of the door. Fresh clip into the gun. Not many left, but the way things were going I wouldn't be around to need them for much longer.

Nearly tugged at my sleeve. 'This is going to be bad news,' she opined. 'Let's find somewhere else to be. Seriously, I hear Florida's nice . . .'

'It is, but I have to get Mal's disk back,' I said. 'It's all that's left of him.'

Nearly, very nervous now: 'Like, I respect that and everything, but I really think we should . . .'

I put the keys in the door and turned. 'Best of luck,' said the lock, and I took a step into the corridor beyond. A quiet sound from the living room, like feet moving on carpet.

'Who's there?' I enquired. No reply. I walked a couple more steps down the hall. 'I have a gun and I'm in a strange kind of mood,' I added. 'So whoever you are, don't fuck me around.'

Still nothing, except that scuffling sound. It wasn't going to go away, and neither was I, so what else could I do but just take a deep breath and burst into the room.

Johnny Vinaldi looked up impatiently, pacing around the floor.

'Where the hell have you been?' he said, and I just stared at him open mouthed.

Nearly dithered between coffee and a line of coke, and in the end opted for both. Suej went into the kitchen to help with the former, and I stayed in the living room with Vinaldi.

'He got away,' he said. 'How, don't ask me to tell you. He's surrounded by a boatload of the guys I think of as my least disappointing men, not to mention hundreds of teenage dancing people, and he blows out of the club like a lungful of smoke and disappears.'

'But he didn't get you,' I said, lighting a cigarette. I didn't know whether I wanted to be having this conversation. Events had pushed Vinaldi and I together in ways I didn't understand, but I still wanted him dead. Each sentence I spoke to him felt like unfaithfulness. I wasn't going to waste many words.

'True, and I'm enormously psyched about that, as you can imagine, but Jaz – whom I know you have little respect for, and I can understand that but he is loyal to me beyond reason and good at hurting people, so what can I do? – is in the MediCentre with bullets in disturbing places. His brother Tony is dead, and three others are not as healthy as they used to be.'

'I just killed a guy who I think was an associate of the man with the lights,' I said. 'In a bar on sixty-seven.'

Vinaldi looked up at me then, finally stopping his pacing. 'I'm impressed,' he said, with apparent sincerity. 'It's been a long, long time for us. These guys, I think they're still there.'

'Johnny, why are you here and what are you talking about?' I still had my gun in my hand and I wasn't completely sure that I wasn't going to use it on him.

'I know who the man who came to my club was,' he said, lighting a cigarette of his own. The clattering in the kitchen seemed a hundred miles away. 'And that's why I know now it wasn't you who sent me the box or was violent to me in the shadows of my business.'

'Are you going to tell me?'

'Jeq Yhandim,' Johnny said, suddenly looking older. 'I knew him in the war.'

'The war? You?'

'You remember – the "training exercise". I was a Bright Eyes too.'

'Bullshit,' I shouted, angry and light-headed with disbelief, but he just shook his head.

'I had them removed after I got back. It was very expensive and quite painful and I wouldn't recommend it as an experience.'

I tried to get my head round this, to understand how it changed things. In some ways it made all the sense in the world. Vinaldi's weirdly distanced and confident slant on life was perfectly consistent with what he was telling me – plus he dealt Rapt which, as discussed, is not everyone's idea of fun. It also helped some other things fall into place.

'What's the highest mountain in the world?' I asked.

He frowned, said 'Everest,' and that's when I finally accepted what was going on.

'I've just seen the birds.' I watched him as I said this. His eyes sprung open wide. For a moment he didn't look like the most successful gangster in New Richmond, but like the scared boy he must once have been. Seeing that look made it harder to hate him; I knew the expression only too well, had seen it on my own face many years ago. It also made it impossible for me to doubt that he had been in The Gap. The birds are like little pockets of marsh gas – bright lights which show something invisible is gathering. Vinaldi couldn't have understood this without having been there.

'Christ on a bike,' he said.

'You could put it like that. I also saw the forest. For a moment it was like I was actually there. And there's been reports all over the news about someone discovering a mountain higher than Everest. Mount Fyi, which doesn't exist. You heard of wall-diving, incidentally?'

'Yeah, a couple of days ago. People jump . . .' Vinaldi stopped suddenly, brow furrowed. 'Wait a minute. People can't just leap out of windows with a stick. That's fucking ridiculous.'

'True, but I met someone yesterday who does it,' I said. 'Or thinks he does.' Internally I clocked the fact that Golson lived next to an apartment where either Yhandim or his accomplice had killed someone.

'It's The Gap, isn't it,' Vinaldi said. 'It's the fucking Gap. It's got to be. It's making people think things that aren't true.'

I told him that it *was* true now. That it was seepage, stuff that should be unconscious becoming conscious. The planet's dreams, seeping through the wall like hallucinations on the edge of sleep.

'Randall,' Vinaldi said, shaking his head, 'you've been taking far too many drugs.'

'Worse than that,' I added, remembering the small creature I'd half-glimpsed the night before near Shelley Latoya's apartment. 'It's changing stuff for real.' Then another fact presented itself; Blue Lights had access to narcotics. I'd seen him dealing. Maybe Shelley hadn't overdosed herself.

'Why is this happening? What's going on?'

'You tell me,' I said. 'And start with Jeq Yhandim.'

Vinaldi's eyes flicked away, and before he replied he walked over to the rearWindow, which was showing a view of the mountains in the distance, relayed from a camera somewhere high on the north face of the city. The look in his eyes was one I'd seen before, as if staring with calm enmity at something a great distance away. The 'ten click glare', we used to call it. I got the idea before he even started that he was about to reveal something he didn't talk about very often. Maybe never at all.

'He was in my unit,' he said eventually. 'We lost him.'

'Lost him?'

He turned to me then, and the words came out in a rush.

'You know what it was like. We were very deep in country, of course. We were fucked up beyond all recognition, naturally.

Suddenly, they hit us and the Lieutenant's completely lost what little mind he has and is Gone Away all the time, and so it's down to me and I can't even tell which way is up.'

I nodded to show I understood. I did – all too well.

'Everyone's running all over the place getting cut into little pieces and I'm trying to do something about it but I can't think what it should be except just turning and running like hell. So that's what we do. Half of us get killed in ten seconds and the rest run into each other, all fleeing in different directions. We just kept running, got out of there, happy to be even half alive.' Vinaldi stopped there, as if not wanting to go on.

'And?' I said.

He breathed out heavily, running a hand across his face. 'Some people got left behind.'

He sat down, looking away. I remained standing, staring at him. 'Left *behind*?'

'Some people didn't get back with us, but they didn't get killed.'

'When did you find this out?' I asked, still not really understanding.

'Tonight,' he said. 'I didn't realize until tonight.'

'Johnny, what are you telling me?'

'I'm saying Yhandim and some others got left in The Gap when everyone else left. He didn't make it back to the camp, and he wasn't there when we got sidelifted out at the end. I'd always assumed they were dead but, as you saw, he came for me last night. He never left The Gap. He's been there for nearly twenty years.'

I'd known there was something about the man in the bar on 67, that he was still living some life which I'd left behind. What I couldn't have believed was the reason for it. I still didn't understand why Yhandim had the spares or wanted Suej. But I knew that he'd survived in The Gap for nearly two decades after everyone else had left.

And now he'd found some way of coming back from the dead, and hell would be following after.

❖❖❖❖

Much later, when Nearly and Suej had fallen asleep on the couch and Vinaldi and I were sitting on opposite sides of the room in silence, I passed a watershed. I'd put Mal's disk in my pocket, along with the computer chip. Ratchet must have given it to me for a reason, so I figured it was worth hanging onto. I was ready to go somewhere, or do something, but I didn't know where or what it was going to be.

Vinaldi's eyes were very far away, maybe reliving something from The Gap. He'd called into whatever it is hoods have in place of an office and told people he'd be out of contact for a few hours. He had people on virtually every floor looking out for Yhandim, all of them carrying the finest in *haute couture* weaponry. Until someone called, there was nothing he and I could do except sit and watch each other. There were things I'd rather have done. Having him sit there was like an open cancer on my face in the mirror; I didn't want it, but if it was there I couldn't help looking at it.

I knew there was one question which I had to ask before anything else happened. I'd been sure of the answer for the last five years. Tonight, I didn't know. I wasn't sure why I felt different; perhaps it was something in Vinaldi's attitude towards me, or maybe The Gap was simply an older wound, which for this evening was taking precedence. Either way, I asked it.

'Johnny,' I said, 'did you put out the order to have Henna and Angela killed?'

My voice sounded dry and constricted, but it came out evenly enough. Vinaldi came to attention immediately. I got the impression that he knew this was something which would come up sooner rather than later.

He looked me in the eyes, and then away.

'No,' he said. And the strange thing was, I believed him.

Eleven

At seven a.m. the phone went. I was asleep on the sofa. Suej was sprawled over most of it, and Nearly was resting her head dopily on my shoulder. I was about as comfortable as if I'd been sleeping in a bookcase, but didn't entirely mind.

Vinaldi appeared to have stayed awake, and reached crisply from his chair to press the phone.

'Er, it's Howie,' said a voice, relayed perfectly into the room by the wall coupler. 'Is Jack there?'

'Yeah,' I said, sitting up. 'Howie, what's happening?'

'I think you ought to come down here,' he said.

'What's wrong?'

'Are you alone?'

'No,' I said, though Suej and Nearly were still asleep.

'That's what I assumed. I need to show you something. It relates to your friend with the lights in his head.'

I stood up, something in Howie's tone striking me very amiss. 'I'm on my way.'

'Great,' he said, sounding relieved. 'And Jack – I'd leave the girls where they are, if you catch my meaning.'

The phone clicked off. I looked at Vinaldi.

'I'll come with you,' he said.

'That won't be necessary.'

'Yes it fucking will,' Vinaldi said. He looked spruce and calm, as though he spent most nights awake in a chair. 'Anything that relates to Yhandim relates to me.'

'I'd rather you stayed here.'

'I don't give a shit what you'd rather, Randall. I'm coming.'

I looked at him for a moment. Last night had made a difference, but in daylight I wasn't sure how much. Eventually I nodded. I left a note for Nearly and we left, closing the door quietly behind us. The lock told us to take care – advice which I valued highly. The corridor to the elevator was filthy, overflowing with the detritus of the previous evening. Empty bottles, cracked vials, a used rubber. In the distance I heard the sound of a sweepteam hoovering it up. Hazy light slanted in from the external window down the end of the corridor, and for once it looked like it wasn't raining outside.

We stood in silence in the elevator as it descended, and I thought momentarily about how weird it was to be standing next to New Richmond's premier villain. Maybe he was mulling over his proximity to one of its key losers. If so, he didn't say. Perhaps, like me, he was mainly wondering whose head we were going to find this time. Howie had called me, not Vinaldi. I was thinking that was probably a clue.

It was night time on 8. I took us the quickest route, which happens also to be the noisiest, going down Bon Bon Street past bars full of revellers encouraging young (and not so young) ladies to remove their clothes. I can only watch that kind of stuff for a short while before being suffused with a feeling of utter futility – a kind of *pornui*, I guess – but the patrons down on 8 certainly seemed to be going for it. Vinaldi merely swept his gaze over it with a grimly professional eye, probably calculating if any of it was worth taking over. Bon Bon led us into a net of sidestreets where people were eating and drinking, overspilling out of diners onto the crowded streets. Here Vinaldi looked around more casually as we walked, and I figured it must all seem kind of small beer to him.

'I haven't been down here in years,' he said suddenly, contradicting me. 'Looks kind of fun.'

'What, more fun than Club Bastard?' I said, making the turn into Howie's sidestreet.

'Having someone drill a hole in your head and pour ants in is more fun than Club Bastard,' he said. 'The young people these days, what do they know from fun?'

I felt that my own notions of what was enjoyable were open to question, and also that if age meant maturity, I should probably still be sucking my thumb. I was about to say so when I noticed

Vinaldi had disappeared. One minute he was beside me, the next he'd gone. Assuming he'd hung back in the previous street to observe fun in progress, I entered Howie's bar. I was actually kind of relieved to be able to handle this on my own. All the way down I'd been hoping that if I was going to see anyone's head it would be the half spare's, and realizing that fate would be unlikely to help me out. Yhandim's MO seemed to favour women rather exclusively, with the exception of the warning sent to Vinaldi. David and Mr Two might very well be dead by now, but Yhandim's present to me would have overtones of sexuality. It always does when that level of mangling is involved, and the manglers tend not to be switch-hitters.

'Jack, hi,' said Howie.

The room was entirely empty. 'Business is quiet,' I said.

'I closed down for the morning. Putting new windows in.'

I nodded, noticing the piles of broken glass swept up against the bottom of the bar. Howie seemed subdued, not at all his normal self, and I said so. 'Yeah,' he replied, smiling tightly. 'Difficult times.'

'What did you have to show me?'

'This way,' he said.

On the table in his office was a box, like the two I'd already seen. I approached it with quiet dread, bracing myself.

'When did it come?'

'An hour ago,' Howie said. 'Hand delivery.'

I was going to have to open it sooner or later, so I did it immediately. I untied the string around the package. As I did so, the box rocked slightly, as if whatever was inside wasn't braced securely enough. I pictured Jenny's head shifting, unstable and slick with drying blood, and almost decided that I didn't need to see the reality for myself.

But I finished untying the knot. I always do. I always have to see for myself just how bad things can be.

As the string fell away I put my thumbs under the uppermost flaps, aware of Howie's shallow breaths. I realized belatedly that I'd brought a lot of shit into his life and resolved to let him know that I was grateful for him putting up with it, just as soon as I'd got through this. I took a deep breath and flipped up the lip of the box.

Something shot out of the hole and straight up to the ceiling, a squawking explosion of movement and odour that sent me backwards in shock. Howie muttered 'Fuck' quietly and took a step backwards of his own. The object had ricocheted moistly off the ceiling and crashed back down again before I'd had a chance to even begin working out what it was. When it hit the surface of the desk it stopped, turned what I realized was its head, and stared at me. After I'd stopped blinking in surprise, I stared cautiously back at it, half-expecting it to lunge for me.

It was a bird, of a kind. A bird or a cat, either way. It was featherless, but stood a foot tall on spindly jointed legs; its face was avian but – like the body – fat and dotted with patchy, moulting orange fur. Two vestigial wings poked out of its side at right angles, looking as if they had been unceremoniously amputated with scissors and then recauterized. Most of the creature's skin was visible, an unhealthy white mess that appeared to be weeping fluid. The whole body heaved in and out as it sat, as if labouring for breath, and it gave off a smell of recent decay – as if fresh-minted for death. The eyes focused on me, making me instantly, and its beak opened. The hole this revealed looked less like a mouth than a churned wound, and the eyes, though vicious, were faltering.

'What the fuck is that?' Howie whispered.

'You got me,' I said, though I had my suspicions. The bird tried to take a step towards us, but the effort caused one of its legs to break. The top joint teetered in its socket and then popped out. The creature flopped onto its side. The skin over the joint tore like an over-ripe fruit, releasing a gout of matter that resembled nothing so much as a heavy period mixed with sour cream.

It was not, all in all, a very beautiful creature.

'He knows,' said a voice behind us, with a chuckle, and I sighed inwardly without turning.

'Who is that?' I asked Howie, knowing I'd walked into a trap.

'I'm sorry Jack,' he replied, voice breaking. 'He said he'd kill me if I didn't, and he said he wouldn't kill you if I did.'

I turned to see a man standing behind us in the doorway. It was the man from the bar the previous night, the guy into whose head I'd placed a bullet. A man, in short, who really shouldn't be standing there with a gun pointing at my head.

'I lied,' he said. 'Get your hands up.'

I raised them, noticing that his right temple bore faint traces of an entrance wound. Reassuring, because for a moment I'd considered the possibility that I'd lost my mind. In a metaphoric sense, rather than in the more physical manner which now seemed to be inevitable.

'Who are you?' I asked, surprised at the levelness of my own voice. Howie stared at me from the sidelines, face awash with guilt.

'Friend of Yhandim's,' the man said, grinning his trademark grin. 'But you know that. We met before.'

'Why didn't he come himself?'

'Cos that's the whole point, Mr Man. Yhandim be at your lady-friend's now, picking up what we came for.'

The shock must have showed on my face, because the man's grin broadened. The movement caused a drop of lymph to ooze out of the wound in his head and run slowly down his cheek. 'We got you out the way first with the help of Mr Howie here, just to make sure the mission ran smooth. You been known to get in the way.'

'Very clever,' I said. 'What do you want with Suej?'

'We don't want nothing with her,' the man said. 'She's someone else's property and we just fetching it for him. The other lady, though, she we can probably find a use or two for. For a little while at least. Yhandim tends to use them up pretty quick, and he has this problem with people who have normal eyes.'

'What have you done with the others?' I wasn't really playing for time, not yet. I was just asking whatever came into my mind, as much to know the answers as for any other reason. The gun trained on me didn't waver, and I knew I'd been lucky to jump the man last time. What little time there was left seemed already to be condensing down to a line a minute hence, a barrier I had no real confidence of crossing.

'Don't matter to you,' the man said. 'You ain't going to be around to care.'

'I'm surprised I'm still alive now,' I said. 'Also, that you are too. Doesn't that hole in your head at least *hurt*? Or the one in your neck, or shoulder?'

'You don't understand nothing at all,' he said, with a trace of anger. 'You got out. You don't understand shit.'

'Why don't you explain it to me,' I said, trying to be soothing.

'You must be keeping me alive for something. I was there. Maybe I'd understand.'

The man laughed suddenly, destroying whatever hope I'd had. He wasn't stupid. He was just completely and utterly mad. He clicked back the hammer on his gun, and I realized the line was right in front of me. 'You alive because we need to find someone else,' he said. 'And we think you know where he is. You going to tell me now, and then I going to kill you.'

'Who?' I said, though I knew.

'Vinaldi,' the man said, with a snarl of utter hatred. 'We want to see that boy real bad.'

'Hey, you should have said so,' said a voice, and Vinaldi stepped suddenly into sight behind the man. As he whirled round to face him, Vinaldi swung a heavy wooden barstool into his face with an elegant precision I couldn't help but admire. One of the legs shattered, bones broke like eggshells, and the man crumpled to the floor.

Vinaldi smiled grimly at me as he strode into the room. 'You're out of practice, Randall. I knew this was going to be a trap. That's why I insisted on coming along.' He stepped over the guy on the floor and pulled out a gun, his face suddenly dark and implacable.

'Don't you fucking shoot him,' I shouted, pulling my own gun, grateful to have it in my hand again.

Vinaldi looked up at me. 'What the fuck are you talking about? Of course I'm going to shoot him.'

'If you do I'll shoot you,' I said, holding my gun steady as I walked towards him. 'And as for being out of practice, if you'd stayed the fuck back at Nearly's then they'd be alright now.' Vinaldi frowned, but flicked his safety back on. I turned to Howie, who was still standing by the wall, probably wondering who he was now in most danger from. 'Howie, go get some tape.'

'Jack, I'm . . .'

'Yeah, I know. It's not a problem.' He wasn't convinced. 'Seriously. In your position I'd have done the same. Now please go get us some tape.'

As Howie ran out, I knelt beside the man and listened to his breathing. It was ragged, but steady.

'Randall, what are you doing?' Vinaldi said, with more than a trace of impatience. 'Here is a man who had nothing but your death, and mine too I might add, on his mind, and you decide this is the time to go round supporting the right to life? You should be running after your women, not worrying about this scum.'

'Yhandim has already got Nearly and Suej,' I said. 'He was probably in there two minutes after we left. This guy may know where they've been taken. He may know where the other spares are. He may even know what *the fuck is going on*. You spread his face over the walls and we're never going to know – added to which I've already parked metal in this man's head and he's still up and around. Doing it again may only make him pissed.'

Howie came back in with the tape and I rolled the body onto its front. Using large quantities of very secure masking tape, I quickly bound the man's hands and legs. His fatigues seemed even dirtier than they had the night before, and fragments of leaves were stuck in the soles of his boots. While I was working, I glanced at the back of his head and noticed a messy exit wound there, blood and tissue melted into his hair. It wasn't as big as it should have been, and it didn't seem to have inconvenienced him much. Maybe a lucky reflection off the inside of his skull. Yeah, right. And maybe the strange, tacky texture of his skin was because he used too much moisturizer.

Only when he was completely immobilized and rolled onto his back did I stand up and take a hurried swig from the bottle of Jack's Howie was inhaling. My hands were shaking. Proximity to death does that to me. If you'll take my advice, avoid it.

'What's his name?' I asked Vinaldi, handing him the bottle. He looked at it, realized it was before eight in the morning, then took a mouthful anyway. 'He get left behind too?'

Vinaldi nodded reluctantly. 'His name's Ghuaji,' he said, then handed me the bottle. 'Pour some of this down his throat.'

I did so, and Ghuaji coughed, spluttered, and swam back up towards the light. His eyes flicked against the blood pooling down from his flattened nose. I thought about wiping his eyes for him, then realized I couldn't be fucked. I leant in very close, and spoke very clearly indeed. Déjà vu again: last night, not to mention the man outside Mal's apartment.

But this time I had to get it right.

'You've got five minutes,' I said. 'That's about how much I can spare. After that Howie here is going to drop you down an xPress elevator shaft to see if you bounce. Understand?'

His voice was thick, and too weak to make out. But he'd heard me. I could tell by the way he spat a bloody tooth into my face.

'Super,' I said. 'I have four questions. Answer all of them and we could have a basis for negotiation. Any less and it's bargain bucket of pain approach. Okay. One, where has Yhandim taken Suej and the other woman? Two, where are the other spares? Three, who is behind all this shit and four what is his fucking problem? Answer in any order you like but don't take your time because I don't have any and yours is running out real fast.'

Ghuaji smiled up at me, and I cocked my gun. This didn't do anything except broaden his smile and I felt panic rising behind the calm I was trying to project.

'The birds are here,' he said. 'Surely you seen them.'

A chill, but I hid it. 'What about them? How come they're coming through?'

'Yhandim's got a plan, ain't not even *nobody* knows about it. The leaves will be with him, man. He been up all night, talking to the boys. It's going down.'

'I tend to find,' Vinaldi said sagely from behind me, 'that blowing pieces off a man's body one by one will reduce the obscurity of his answers.'

'Johnny, thanks for the fortune cookie, but . . .'

'Seriously, I can recommend it, and Jaz, God willing he comes out of the MediCentre as a functioning human being, will back me up on that to the hilt.'

'You think that's going to scare a man who's been in The Gap all this time?' I said, turning to him but speaking for Ghuaji's benefit. 'A guy who's been in country half his life? I like the way you're thinking, but I think maybe this isn't the guy for it.'

It seemed to work. When I turned back to him Ghuaji's eyes focused more clearly on me, and when he next spoke it was with a hint of wistfulness.

'It's home. I miss it every second, man. Top-ups just ain't enough.'

It was then I knew that not only was the man off his head, but that he wouldn't tell us anything he didn't want to even if we whittled his body down to the bone. Anyone who could miss The Gap wasn't even human any more.

I reached down and tilted Ghuaji's head slightly, looking at the bullet entrance wound. It went through the skin and skull, but not much deeper than that. It must have started healing immediately, and can't have held him up long enough to allow the police to get to the bar before he escaped.

'You see that?' I asked Vinaldi. He nodded, and I saw a little fear in his eyes, and Howie's, which I suspected was probably mirrored in my own. On the other hand, I thought the wound looked a little worse than when I'd first seen a droplet ooze out. The healing was reversing.

I had one more try. 'You're not going to answer the questions, are you?'

'You a clever guy,' he croaked.

'Okay, well here's the deal. I've changed my mind. We're not going to throw you down the shaft just yet, because later we may be able to get you to reconsider. Howie's going to put you in the back, and someone's going to watch over you. You show any sign of being anti-social, this employee of Howie's is going to chainsaw off your legs. You're healing in a very weird way, my friend, but I think that could keep even you out of action for a while.' I watched him carefully, and added: 'Especially without a top-up.'

A tiny flicker. Enough.

I stood up and nodded to Howie. 'Have Paulie sling him in the back – away from the food – and sit over him. I'm not joking with the chainsaw. Don't take any crap from this guy.'

'Paulie's dead,' Howie said. 'He was here when this guy arrived.'

'Shit, I'm sorry,' I said.

Howie nodded distantly. 'That's okay. Dath can do it. He'll enjoy fucking this fucker up. What do you want to do with that shit?'

He pointed over at the mess on the table. While our attention had been diverted the bird's other leg had come off, and most of its back section had collapsed in on itself. Vinaldi stared at it, face drawn, and just when I'd decided it was dead the bird's head made a small vicious movement, pulling its front half away from the rest. Using the stumps of its wings like paddles it tried to crawl along the desk, trailing the remains of its insides behind it and shedding skin and fur like snow from shaken trees.

'Take it somewhere and burn it,' I said. 'Burn it until it's gone. And ignore anything it says. It isn't even a real bird. It's just a fragment of something else.'

'I am so a bird,' the bird said suddenly in a voice which sounded like two rusty nails being rubbed together. 'And I know what you did. You're going to be punished, Randall. You're going to die for that.'

'Yeah, yeah,' I said, and shot it. The chest blew apart, spreading shit over the room, and the head fell to the floor.

'Was that something out of The Gap?' Howie asked, looking down at the still-moving beak. 'I mean, I assume that's what all this is about?'

'It is, but that isn't,' I said. 'It's something from nowhere. Just a dream. It got created accidentally on the edge, and couldn't hack it. Something formed out of nothing, without being honed by evolution. It can't even hold itself together.'

'Oh, you wrong,' Ghuaji said suddenly from the floor. 'You wrong, man. It all going to hold together.'

I turned and held my gun steadily at his head, losing patience abruptly and completely. 'Were you the one who shot Mal?'

The man shook his head slowly. 'Yhandim. He going to kill you too, and Vinaldi. Most especially Vinaldi.'

Vinaldi rather charmingly spat at him, and Ghuaji still did nothing but smile. His wound was looking worse.

'He's going to be real busy then,' I said. 'He should consider delegating. Howie, get Dath and lose this guy before *I* blow his fucking head off.'

Before he left Howie handed me a sheet of telefax printout, with Nicholas Golson's name on it. 'He called,' Howie said, shrugging. 'Said there was something you might want to know.'

'Thanks,' I said. 'You going to be okay?'

'Yeah,' he said. 'Just as soon as you come up with a plan. I don't expect you to keep to it, but it would be nice to know there was one.'

'When I've got one you'll be the first to know,' I said.

I tried to use my fake pass to get up to 104, though Vinaldi had offered to just ride me in as a guest. The man on the gate was a little more eagle-eyed than most, and tossed my pass, so I ended up relying on Vinaldi anyway. The key thing about pride is that it ends up making you look more of an idiot than you would have in the first place. By that stage I didn't really care. We'd already been to 66 and I was hyper with fury and fear. Nearly's door was locked, but there was no response when I pounded on it. The lock had been shorted, and was quietly singing a very old song about rainbows. Vinaldi used the key he'd acquired through nefarious means from the contractor who'd redeveloped the floor, and I ran in to find the apartment empty. Small signs of a struggle – furniture overturned, a broken coffee cup – but no suggestion of fatalities. Mildly reassuring, but not very. My record on tracking down Yhandim and the people he collected was not exactly great so far. I also thought it would probably have taken more than one person to hold both Suej and Nearly if they were squirming, and I was mortally sure that Nearly would have squirmed like a pig in a tin. So Ghuaji wasn't Yhandim's only accomplice.

Vinaldi's spies had no reports of sightings. I wasn't surprised. Now that Yhandim had everything he wanted, I reckoned the only time we'd see him again would be in the two seconds or so before we died. Maybe he wasn't even planning to bother with me any more, now he had Suej. But I was planning to bother with him. As I stood in Nearly's apartment and noticed the bags from Suej's shopping trip lying crumpled in the corner, I imagined just how badly I was going to bother him.

But first we had to find him.

'Why the fuck are we dealing with this guy?' Vinaldi asked, as he followed me up the stairs to Golson's apartment. I didn't answer, but simply banged on the door loud enough to wake the decomposed. It was only nine o'clock by then, and I didn't make Golson as an early riser.

After a few minutes the door opened and Golson appeared sleepy-eyed and vague in a dressing gown. I forbore formalities as usual and pushed my way into the apartment, Vinaldi close behind.

'Hey, dude, what's the problem?' Golson squeaked, scurrying behind us. In the living room we discovered that someone was in his bed, a mid-range redhead with big brown eyes.

'Hi Johnny,' she said, simpering like this was an audition or something.

I turned to him. 'You two know each other?'

Johnny shrugged.

'Sure,' the girl piped up, running a hand through her hair, tucking the sheets around her and generally primping for Vinaldi's benefit, 'I go to Club Bastard all the time.'

'Get dressed and get out of here,' I said. 'You don't want to be Johnny's punch. They're suffering from short life expectancy at the moment.' Vinaldi looked at me angrily, and I shouted at him. 'You telling me Louella Richardson and Laverne Latoya weren't in your book? Why the fuck d'you think Yhandim's going round whacking them?'

The girl was up and in the bathroom before Vinaldi had time to answer, leaving us with just the boy Golson.

'What have you got for me?' I asked. 'And hurry.'

'Not much,' he admitted. 'But you said tell you anything weird. This is it.' He held a small card out to me. I took it and turned it over. A credit card-sized sliver of cream-coloured plastic with gold trim around the edge. Didn't look especially weird to me, or particularly interesting.

'What the hell is it?' I asked.

'It's an invite,' Vinaldi said. 'Can see you don't get out much.'

'I get out lots,' I snapped. 'I just turn up uninvited. Why isn't it doing anything?'

'It's keyed to my DNA,' Golson said. 'Here.' He laid his index finger along one edge of the card. The word 'invitation' swam up out of the whiteness. This held for a moment and then faded, to be replaced by an inch-square video of a well-preserved but clearly grieving woman in her fifties. Speaking with baffled dignity she invited the holder of the card, plus a guest, to a Memorial Service for Louella Richardson.

'Okay, so they're having a service,' I said. 'This is hardly news.'

'It's not that,' said Golson. 'It's this. I'm out last evening with people and I find out that virtually everyone who knew Louella is invited. I'm not talking just close friends, I'm talking people who held the door open for her one day five years ago. It's the day after tomorrow, and it's happening somewhere kind of weird.'

'Where?' I said.

'Two-oh-three,' Golson said, gleefully. 'In the Maxens' private chapel.'

I blinked. That was genuinely strange. The Maxens were so reclusive that no one even knew exactly how many of them there were. Invitations above the 200th floor were rare to the point of unheard of – unless you were one of the few people who had something Maxen needed. I looked at Vinaldi, and was surprised to see an extreme but unreadable expression on his face. Storing that to ask about later, I turned to Golson, who was clicking his finger rings along the surface of a table in a way I found very stressful.

'Any word why?'

'Well, Val says that Yolande Maxen was one of Louella's shopping clients. Maybe they're all cut up about it because of that.'

'Bullshit,' I said. 'The Richardsons weren't especial friends of the Maxens?'

'Not that I'm aware of. Word is the Maxens aren't especial friends of anyone at all.'

It wasn't clear whether this made any difference to anything, but it was certainly odd.

'You really slip it to Louella?' Golson asked Vinaldi, his voice full of manly respect.

Vinaldi's voice clearly betrayed that he had. 'It's no business of yours you twelve-year-old asswipe, and it's disrespectful to talk like that of the dead. Didn't your father, whoever the fuck he may be, teach you anything at all?'

'Hey man, whatever you say,' said Golson, holding his arms up placatingly and flashing an orthodontic smile. 'Shit, I'm just impressed. Your secret's safe with me.'

Then it happened. In the way that it does, regardless of events, clues or intuition. Your mind just burps it up. Sometimes.

'Where's your deck?' I asked. Golson pointed and I leapt over to the side of his bed, pulling Mal's disk from my pocket. I slammed it into the spare slot and slapped the button.

'What?' Vinaldi asked, coming to stand behind me.

'The guy who killed Mal had no rap jacket,' I said, drumming my fingers on the desk as I put it together. 'Maybe now we know why.'

'Yo, Jack,' said Mal's versonality. 'How's it going?'

'Give me the picture of that stiff,' I said, and it popped up onto the screen.

'Hil Trazin,' Vinaldi said immediately. 'He was there too.'

'Okay, so all these guys are out of The Gap. Somehow. They've got a job – search and destroy for SafetyNet – but these are people with a grudge against you, and so half the time they're moonlighting trying to fuck you up. One of them, probably Yhandim from what Ghuaji said, is getting way out of hand and not just whacking your associates but climbing through your ex-punches as well. Computer, get me the info on SafetyNet again.'

'I don't get it,' said Vinaldi. 'What's this got to do with . . .'

'The homicide files on all five victims are security locked from the top of the NRPD, which means the real job they're supposed to be doing is for someone with more power than God. This person bought protection for Yhandim while he was looking for the spares, because one of them was important to him.'

'Company information,' said the computer. 'SafetyNet still looks a mess.'

'Trace back every single company with a stake in it,' I said. 'All the way back to the bone. I want to know if anyone's got a majority shareholding.'

While the computer chugged away I lit a cigarette. Golson pointed out that they were bad for me, and I suggested that he fuck off.

'Do you know what the answer's going to be, and if so just give me in ASCII,' said Vinaldi. 'The suspense is giving me hives.'

'Not for sure,' I said, but then the answer burped up onto the screen. The majority shareholder in SafetyNet, through about a billion holding companies and sub-routes, was an outfit called Newman Sublinear. Didn't mean anything to me, but it sure as hell did to Vinaldi.

'That's a Maxen company,' Vinaldi said quietly. 'Administered by Arlond Maxen himself.'

I'd already noticed that the more serious Vinaldi was the simpler his sentences got, so I knew he was telling the truth. 'How do you know?'

'I just do,' Vinaldi turned away. 'Jesus shits.'

'Either of you guys want coffee?' Golson enquired, baffled but enjoying the show. I yanked Mal's disk and stood up.

'So,' I said, 'Maxen's behind SafetyNet, which figures. He's somehow pulled these guys out. They must owe him for something, otherwise why'd they be doing his work? In the meantime they're running after you for old times' sake, and Louella Richardson gets chopped up in the undertow. Maxen realizes what's happened, gets guilty, throws money at her Memorial.' But not, I thought to myself, at one for Laverne Latoya, or any of the other girls who died below the 100 line. 'It's Maxen. He's behind *all of it.*'

'Hey, cool,' said Golson brightly. 'Then you guys are in really deep shit. Sure you don't want coffee? It's cinnamon apple . . .'

'*Shut up,*' shouted Vinaldi and I simultaneously.

'So what now?' Vinaldi asked, deferring to me for once.

'We go see a guy who I think's going to be hurting by now,' I said, turning to Golson. 'And *you* keep your mouth shut about everything you've heard, or forgetting women's names is going to be the least of your troubles.'

'I believe that,' Golson said with sincerity, and jumped out of the way as we ran for the door.

Twelve

'What makes you think Ghuaji's going to talk now?' Vinaldi asked, as we stormed into Howie's for what – for me – seemed like the twentieth time in two days.

'Three things,' I said, shouldering my way through the people inside. 'First, his skin was fucked. It looked and felt funny. I saw something similar a couple of days ago on Trazin's body. Second, the wound in his head seemed to get worse rather than better while we were here this morning. Three, he said something about top-ups, and there were leaves on his boots.'

Vinaldi got it as we were stalking down the corridor. 'They have to keep going back?'

'I think so. And Ghuaji's currently going nowhere at all.'

'So maybe you're not as stupid as you look. That's encouraging.'

'Don't get your hopes up,' I said. 'I have hidden superficialities.'

There were three people in the storeroom. Dath, who was watching over the body with sterling vigilance, balancing a chainsaw in his hands; Howie, who looked like he was taking the whole thing rather personally and trying to make up for that morning; and Ghuaji himself. I walked straight over to the latter and bent down, keeping well out of the way just in case.

The hole in his temple looked looser than before, and there was a small pool of blood under the back of his head. His skin seemed the same. Maybe the strange texture was just a result of having been there so long, and not something which got any worse.

'You know what's happening, don't you?' I said. There was no reply. 'You've got that place in your blood. You need to go back there to recharge, and you're not getting it lying here. Meanwhile, Yhandim's running around New Richmond with the other guys. He may have a major plan, Ghuaji, but the way things are going it ain't going to involve you.'

'Fuck you,' he said, predictably. They all say that, don't they – and probably not even one of them realizes that when it comes to their turn it's worn pretty thin and isn't terribly frightening any more. Especially when they're taped into immobility and smelling of wet blood from the holes in their head. 'Your mother sucks goats in hell,' he added, hoarsely.

'A telling riposte, I grant you,' I said, 'but you know what I'm saying is true. Now listen up. We know that Arlond Maxen got you guys out somehow, so that's something you can't tell me.' I ignored the explosion of surprise from Howie and Dath. 'So let's concentrate on where Yhandim is holding the spares.'

'Man, you know I ain't telling you nothing,' Ghuaji said, coughing up another mouthful of blood.

I pulled away the collar of his coat and saw that the neck wound was also opening up. A flower of blood above the collarbone showed trouble was coming there too. I shrugged.

'Have it your own way,' I said, 'but time's running out.'

I'd barely lit a cigarette in the corridor outside when I heard a scream from within the storeroom. I opened the door a crack and saw Vinaldi standing over Ghuaji. I didn't know what he could have done to make the soldier make that sound, and I didn't want to find out. I shut the door on another shriek and finished my cigarette alone.

Suej was my problem, Nearly too, not to mention the rest of the spares; yet it was Vinaldi who was in there doing the wet work. It couldn't have been any other way. I have no stomach for that kind of thing. It was the same in The Gap. I just did my time and tried to stay alive. I guess I managed it, but sometimes my life feels like a piece of demo shareware, all the key or interesting features disabled, running on a fourteen-day trial period which just repeats over and over again without ever becoming mine.

So I waited there, breathing smoke in and out, hearing the cries and segueing them with many others from long ago. Something, either exhaustion or despair, was stripping years off me. I kept expecting to see flashes of orange, and to hear beating wings and voices from long ago. I was remembering people I'd killed, and trying to recall why, and failing to see that it added up to anything at all. Maybe it's impossible to see out when you're stuck there in the if-loop. Maybe you've got to be dead for any of it to make sense. Life and chance write the code which drags you along, and all you can do is watch – alternately saddened, bored and horrified – as they execute their instructions. Emotions run the action, as they always have, and the brain is powerless to intercede.

I was on a bit of a downer, in other words.

Vinaldi joined me after ten minutes. He wasn't even breathing heavily, though the front of his suit was splattered with blood.

'Yhandim's in The Gap,' he said, with a small, brutal smile.

It was obvious, and maybe I had already known. Where better to hide than somewhere no one else can enter? Perhaps that's why I'd spent the last twenty-four hours in decreasing circles of futility, running away from the problem.

'Then we wait till he comes out,' I said.

'Come on Randall. You know we can't do that. He's got your girl in there, and the other woman. That's no place for them. It's no place for anyone.'

'Johnny, The Gap's been closed since the last sidelift. That's twenty fucking years. How the hell are we supposed to get back in there? It's impossible.'

'Clearly it isn't, or our lunatic friends wouldn't be able to come and go as they please. And Maxen must have found a way, didn't he? Howie in there came up with a plan. For once it's a good one – so much so that he may have earned himself a higher place in my organization at some later date. We let this guy free, let him think we're finished with him, and then we see where he goes. He's fucked up pretty badly now. If you're right, then he's going to need to get back there real soon.'

'It won't work.'

'It might.'

'No, it won't.'

'What the fuck is *wrong* with you?' Vinaldi shouted, his face suddenly inches from mine. 'You got any better ideas?'

'I can't go back in there,' I said. 'I'm not going back in The Gap.'

'You're scared, I'm scared,' he spat. 'Anybody'd be fucking scared. But it's the only answer, Randall. Either we go in there and fuck these guys up or they're going to fuck up those two women and all the others you keep talking about. More important than that, far as I'm concerned, and I'm a selfish man and happy that way, when they're finished with them they're *going to come after me.* I worked twenty years to get where I am today, and I'm not losing it because some guys who should have been dead decades ago blame me for the fact they couldn't keep track of where the fuck they were and follow the rest of us out of a firestorm which I didn't lead them into in the first place.'

I turned away from him, but he carried on ranting.

'*I* could just wait until they come out, but you can't. You got to go in there and find them. I'm offering to help you, Randall, but the offer ain't going to last for ever. Understand?'

'I can't go back,' I said, and walked away.

People are always finding me when I don't want to be found. When Vinaldi appeared in the doorway I was sitting on Mal's floor, surrounded by used foil, unused packets and a needle. Half of the last of my money was already in my bloodstream, the rest was ready and waiting. In my own mind I was sitting in Mal's because Yhandim knew where it was and might come looking for me there; in reality, because I had nowhere else to go.

I'd gone straight up to my contact on 24. He didn't seem surprised to see me again, or that this time I wanted Rapt that had been less cut. I gave him everything I had, and he passed it over. I shot up in the back of his store.

By the time I got back down to 8 it had kicked in. Climbing into the chute at the back of the women's toilets was probably the most difficult thing I've ever done. But the last, dying tendrils of my working mind told me that if Maxen was tied so heavily into the NRPD then I couldn't afford to leave by a normal route, so I soldiered on with it anyway.

More by luck than judgement I found my way to the main shaft, and laboriously clambered down. I don't know if you've ever descended eight floors, hand over hand on a ladder, while full of designer hallucinogenic amphetamorphines, but it takes a certain degree of doggedness. It was very dark, for a start, the shadows brown and continually slithering over my hands and face. They were like snakes in that they were drier than they appeared, but unlike snakes in that they whispered bad things to me, which reptiles rarely do. I slipped once on the way down, and because of my condition believed that I was falling upwards. This, I thought, was fine, and I was mildly interested to see where I might end up. Perhaps I'd fall as high as the 200s, in which case I'd give old Maxen a piece of my mind.

Him and his brother both, I muttered, the fucken dead fucken fuck.

Luckily – I guess – my back brain realized I was unlikely to have conquered gravity anywhere except inside my head, and my hands grabbed a lower stair entirely independently of my will. I failed to dislocate my wrist by the barest of margins, and made it down most of the remaining steps, only falling about the last six feet. I landed heavily on my back, and checked out for a while.

When I came to everything was worse. But I stood up laboriously, deciding I ought to go somewhere.

Then I got lost.

I've done the back route in and out of New Richmond more times than I can recall. A lot of it takes place in the dark, so you have to be pretty good at remembering the way. On this particular occasion, I wasn't. I wasn't even especially good at remembering how to use my legs. I tried shutting my eyes, but this merely put me into a spotless operating theatre, where a cake fashioned out of eye-splittingly bright yellow and white icing was waiting for an operation. This scene remained for a number of minutes after I opened my eyes, before finally fading into the darkness. I resolved to keep my eyes open for the time being. I seemed to have been walking for an awfully long time without reaching the landmarks I was expecting, but on the other hand each time a droplet of sweat squeezed out of the pores on my forehead it seemed to take about an hour and I was worried about being drowned, so it's possible my judgement may have been impaired.

Then I was very, very frightened of something. I wasn't sure what, and it only lasted a few minutes. Or half an hour.

When that passed, I entered a brief spell of relative lucidity, which is generally the prelude to the second – and more momentous – Rapt rush. I took the opportunity to accept that I was completely and utterly lost, and in a part of the MegaMall's lowest level which I didn't know. I shouldn't have gone down right to the bottom of the main chute, but got off one level above as I always had before. I was somewhere near the heart of the engine block, and had no clear way of finding my way out. The corridor was circular, and reinforced with very thick ceramic panels. It could only be the main exhaust duct.

Something which I took at first to be a series of pink flowers exploding at a distance then revealed itself. In time, and with a few cautious steps forward, this turned out to be not a visual phenomenon at all, but a sound. A quiet, pistony sound. I crept towards it, giggling, reasoning that whatever it was it couldn't be more frightening than what was going on in my head.

'What the hell are you doing here?' said a voice.

I'd been wrong, of course; there *was* something more frightening, and being addressed out of darkness in a place no living human even *knew* about certainly fitted the bill. I shrieked in a very uncool manner and tried to run away, but my legs had apparently turned into columns of rice, loosely packed together. They gave out dryly and deposited me on the floor, and I just waited for whatever was going to happen, whilst fighting off flying nuns which even I could tell weren't really there.

The first thing that happened was more of the pink sounds. Then they stopped, and I turned to see something sitting in front of me. It was about three feet tall, and made of metal. A large number of complex arms jutted out of various parts of its main body, all of which ended in manipulating extensions. The body itself was battered and heavily patched, as if it had been repaired time and time again. At the top of the whole affair was a head-like structure which was glaring at me.

'Er, hi,' I said.

'I'm working as fast as I can,' the thing shouted. The voice, as well as looking very deep blue, sounded a little strange. Mechanical, not very human at all, though it was certainly a beautiful colour. 'I don't have the firmware!'

'Bummer,' I said, trying to be helpful without getting involved in a long conversation. I could feel the beginnings of the second Rapt rush lumbering towards me, and wanted to be a long way from here when it hit.

'Actually, I don't even think it's 'ware at all,' the machine said, confidentially. 'Just processing power. I'm by myself you know, completely and utterly by myself.'

'I see,' I said, though I didn't.

'No you don't,' the machine shouted, seeing through me instantly. 'You don't see at all. You've just been sent to spy on me!'

'I haven't,' I said plaintively. The big rush was now definitely on the way. 'Honestly. I'm just lost.'

'Lost my ass, you bastard.'

'Please, I'll leave you to get on with whatever the hell it is you're doing if you'll just tell me how to get up a level.'

'Turn around, go 46.23 metres, turn left, 21.11 metres, right 7.89 metres, climb up the panel with the ladder on it,' said the machine, almost too fast for me to make out. 'Now piss off and let me get on with my work.'

And then the second rush came, like a sudden fall of night. Moving with all the verve of a potato I followed the machine's instructions as closely as I could, though possibly not to the second decimal place. By then I'd realized that the machine hadn't existed anywhere outside my head, but I reasoned that it was possibly a mechanism for my subconscious to tell me how the hell to get out. I was impressed with my subconscious for even attempting such a thing, and decided I should follow its instructions. I felt I owed it to myself, and that if I turned out to be right I probably deserved a prize. Like a little more Rapt.

I eventually seemed to find myself out of the exhaust and up a level, and from there I floundered my way into the service corridor and thus out towards my standard exit. The guys at the door bade me a cheery hello, but I couldn't even see them by then. Everything was pressed in too hard, and everything was very black. I stumbled down cobbled streets which seemed to have turned into tunnels, aware that the world had shrunk because I could clearly see the curvature of the Earth, indeed had to walk carefully to avoid falling over because of it. Naturally, it was raining, and the clouds ahead were so full and dark it felt like early evening. The walls of the tunnel were punctuated at intervals by doors which periodically opened, releasing the sound of people eating and drinking in noodle bars. The sounds turned into little rabid noise creatures, which scuttled down the tunnel like mechanical rats. Then the door would shut again, leaving me in a world where sound had never existed except in the form of the light green spattering sound of falling rain.

I managed to distinguish Mal's building from the undifferentiated mass around me, and hobbled up an infinite number of stairs, each about six feet tall. I got lost on one of them for a while, and then came to realize I was standing outside the door to rat-face's apartment, and that it was open. This struck me as curious, and I went inside, though I knew that a confrontation with another human being was the last thing I needed. Luckily, the problem didn't arise, because rat-face and his buddy had been murdered. Their faces had been rendered nearly unrecognizable by the application of something like a steam iron, and their internal organs were failing to live up to the first part of their name. It occurred to me that I might have done this in the last ten minutes, but the blood was dried and the smell was pretty unpleasant so I decided that on balance I probably hadn't.

By the time I made it to Mal's I was feeling really, really bad. The second rush is the heavy one, and it knits up with every other such rush like a string of Christmas cards on a line. The sound of dead people talking was so loud and dark that I could barely see where I was going. I made it to the middle of Mal's floor, got out my spike and another foil package, and chased the first dose with a little more. The idea is to round off the edges of the really bad stuff by coating it with some first rush; but it seldom works very well and is the slipperiest of all possible slopes. I slumped there for a while, surrounded by visions of blood and shit, and then I checked out for a while.

When I heard someone at the door my eyes opened immediately, and it was only then I realized they'd been open all the time. I'd been very far away, inside somewhere distant and small and old, and my eyeballs were crispy from not blinking.

The door opened and a figure stood silhouetted against the dim light in the corridor. It took me a while to work out who it was. I wasn't especially pleased.

'How the hell did you find me?' I slurred, my tongue clacking in my mouth like a stick against iron railings.

'Guys at the back entrance called Howie,' Vinaldi grinned. 'Said, and I quote, "The big fucked-up guy is on the loose again." Howie reckoned this was the only place you could be, and he was right. Seen the mess downstairs?'

'It was Yhandim. I saw him with those guys a couple days ago.'

Vinaldi saw the opening, made the pitch. 'He's got the little girl and Nearly with him now.'

'I know,' I said. 'This is not news to me.'

'Okay, well you got to hurry. We let Ghuaji go, after Dath planted a tracker on him, and he's just left New Richmond and is out in the Portal as we speak. An employee of mine has seen him get in a car, and he's heading out into the wilds. He's going home.' Vinaldi held a hand down to me. I didn't take it.

'I'm still not going,' I said.

His voice was calm. 'Yes you are, Randall, and you know it. There's a truck outside and I can see that I'm going to have to drive myself, which will be a first in about ten years, so get the fuck up and let's get after him.'

'I don't understand you,' I said, trying to climb to my feet. I still had no intention of going. I just wanted to give him a hard time on his own level. The walls moved alarmingly, and I almost didn't go through with it. But once I was standing, going back down again seemed even harder. 'Why don't you sit tight in your fortress on one-eighty-five and let your men handle it? That's what you pay them for. I tried to take you down, remember? Why are you hanging round giving me grief?'

'Atonement, Randall. You ever hear of the word?'

'Of course I've heard of it, and what does it have to do with you? You said yourself it's their own stupid fault they got left in The Gap. Even if it wasn't, everybody did bad things in there and it's far too late to do anything about it now. You want to atone for something, atone for the drugs you sell which people like Shelley Latoya OD on, atone for the guys you've had whacked, and just leave me alone.'

By the time I finished I was shouting wildly. Vinaldi left a pause, and then spoke quietly and with finality.

'Come on Jack,' he said. 'Time's wasting.'

I jerked my head to look up at him. Maybe it was the use of my first name, which appeared unconscious and unplanned, but what I saw in front of me was not Johnny Vinaldi, the ganglord and vicious thug who had half of New Richmond's underworld in the palm of his hand. Instead, I saw just a man who was having to gear himself up to something he didn't want to do. Something he was afraid of, possibly more so even than me. Someone who, for reasons of his own, was giving me an opportunity to be less of a waste of everybody's time and patience.

I shut my eyes, turned away for a moment, and it came: a shiver of finality like the one when you decide, in your own mind, that you're going to have to tell someone who loves you that you don't want to be with them any more. Terror, and relief; relief and terror, so intermingled that they feel like the same thought.

I leant down unsteadily, picked up my drugs, and straightened again.

'Just understand one thing,' I said. 'If you're thinking of atoning to Yhandim, you're taking the wrong guy along with you. When I find the man who's got Nearly and Suej I'm going to tear his fucking head off.'

'That's more like it,' Vinaldi said, slapping me on the back. 'The old reasonableness we know and love.'

'Piss off,' I muttered. 'Where's this fucking truck?'

Four o'clock found us driving as fast as we dared through Covington Forge, through snow falling in flakes the size of small dogs. It was dark, the heating in Vinaldi's truck didn't work, and both of us were frozen. A bottle of Jack's bought at a gas station in Waynesboro was trying its hardest to alleviate the season's weather, but it was only a veneer at best. Vinaldi was pissed at me because he'd wanted an almond cappuccino. The attendant and I had a good laugh about that. I guess it had been a while since Johnny'd had to deal with the real world.

The Matrix junction box at the town limits had burnt out long ago and subsequently been used for target practice. Covington Forge was off the net, abandoned to the past and left to cannibalize itself. As Vinaldi steered through the deserted streets, I saw America itself as one big matrix: bright, dangerous cities crammed with sharp and needy people, interconnected by a spider's web of highways and toll roads and bordered at the edges by the slow coasts peppered with perambulating old people. And in between, in the gaps, a sagging mass of flatline towns which hadn't made it into the twenty-second century – alive and technically equal to everyone else, but actually breaking up, losing their cohesion like skin on the face of someone very ill for a long time. The nose might still look sharp, the eyes bright, the cheekbones in place; but the flesh in between falls loosely between the peaks.

It wasn't an especially profound observation, but then I was very cold. The buildings around us looked as if they agreed with me, and as if they were only too aware of their position in history. They looked pissed off, to be honest. The pavements were scarred, the walls bulged, the roofs a millimetre away from collapsing onto the fetid life within. It felt like we were driving over a corpse which was fermenting inside, but whose chest still rose and fell, and probably always would. It was great.

We'd thought maybe Ghuaji was meeting someone here, but as we followed his truck from a distance it became clear that we were going straight through and out the other side. I was beginning to come down by then, though it still felt as if someone was slowly stirring my brains with a warm finger. Sounds were now distinguishable as such, and I believed that the majority of what I saw was real. For most of the afternoon that had mainly consisted of a dark bulk of trees against mountainous hills, as we headed higher into the Appalachians. In the last of the afternoon light we'd piled up Interstate 64, through the glittering sprawl of Charlottesville and then higher into the beginnings of the Blue Ridge. After Waynesboro Ghuaji had taken 81 Southbound, turning into Route 60 at Lexington, the roads getting smaller and smaller, away from what passes for civilization these days and into a murky area in between.

While Vinaldi drove in silence I'd busied myself by chain-smoking and watching the Positionex attached to the dashboard. This showed Ghuaji's whereabouts as determined by a Global Positioning Satellite, mapped onto a layout of the local roads to within a couple of yards' accuracy. Following him wasn't going to be difficult. Working out what we had to do when we caught up with him was, and that looked like it had to happen soon. Covington Forge is pretty much the end of the line.

'Where the hell's he going?' Vinaldi muttered as we came out the other side of town into yet more countryside. 'This is the land that time forgot. I can't believe that at my time of life I'm driving down a road to nowhere, most particularly in this kind of weather.' His voice was steady, and betrayed to only a tiny degree the fact that irritation was not the only emotion he was currently struggling with.

'Christ knows,' I said, shivering suddenly in a whole body spasm. 'From now there's squat until you're in West Virginia.'

Vinaldi grunted and stared out of the windscreen with a kind of tense gloom, making no bones about the enmity he felt towards the gnarled trees and crags outside. Then I noticed that the read-out on the Positionex indicated that Ghuaji had lessened his speed.

'Looks like he's going to make a turn,' I said. 'Maybe we should get a little closer.'

'Got any more good advice?' Vinaldi muttered, his breath a cloud in front of his face, 'like "Don't run into the back of him" or "Drink your coffee before it gets cold", not that we have any coffee because you bought whiskey instead, despite my very clear instructions?'

'There,' I said.

Vinaldi pulled the truck to a halt and peered distractedly. I'd almost missed it. On the right side of the road, barely discernible in the snow and darkness, was a narrow road leading up into the hills.

'That's not a proper road,' Vinaldi said in the snow-padded silence.

I looked at the map, and saw that he was right. Another hundred yards up the mountain on the left was an exit for 616. On the right there was nothing, and yet the truck had clearly gone that way. The light on the Positionex showed it heading off up towards what used to be Douthat State Park.

I shrugged, and Vinaldi turned the wheel and took us onto the road. There was no sign at the top of it, and the surface was completely covered with snow except for the tracks left by Ghuaji's vehicle. Trees pressed hard into either side, much closer and thicker than you would expect. Vinaldi stopped the truck again for a moment, peering eloquently out into the wilderness.

'You're sure about this,' he said, dubiously.

'Johnny, I'm not sure of anything. But if we're following Ghuaji then we have to follow him, and this is where he went.'

And so we set off, keeping to the middle of the road to avoid the branches which stretched halfway across. Using the Positionex, I tried to ensure that we kept a fixed distance between us and Ghuaji, and this meant driving a little more quickly than either of us would have liked – though still not exactly fast. Any quicker than thirty miles an hour sent the tyres spinning and the truck sliding towards the side of the road. Any slower and the truck threatened to throw its hand in with gravity and slip back down the steep incline. Vinaldi had the headlights turned as low as possible, but I was still worried that sooner or later Ghuaji was going to spot them.

The slope began to level off about ten minutes later. The snow had slackened by then and through the slowly drifting flakes we could see a stretch of straight road in front of us. We also saw a smallish tree growing up out of the left-hand lane, oddly lit by the truck's headlights. As we passed it, Vinaldi risked turning towards me.

'This is weird,' he said.

'Tell me about it.' I noticed something on the side of the road and leant forward to squint through the windshield. An old shack, obviously unused in decades. And in front, the remains of what looked like petrol pumps. As Vinaldi stared at it I fiddled with the map overlay panel on the Positionex, trying to get a more precise fix on where we were. The panel still refused to show the existence of a road along our path, even going back to the late 1990s.

'According to the maps this road should never have been here at all.'

'I thought I'd left that kind of stuff behind,' Vinaldi said. 'I thought that was all gone.'

'Me too,' I said quietly.

Suddenly, Vinaldi's head snapped to the left, and his eyes seemed to pan quickly across the trees by the side of the road.

'What is it?' I asked quickly.

'Thought I saw something,' he said, voice thick in his throat.

'Saw what?'

'A woman. Or something. Something in white, running through the trees alongside us.'

'Along the road?'

'No. About thirty feet into the trees.'

Uh-huh, I thought, pulling my coat a little tighter around me. I glanced out of my side window. The trees seemed a little less dense for the moment, and I realized we were passing something which might once have been a picnic area. It was long, long gone, but for a moment I saw a shape out in the overgrown clearing. Like a picnic table, with four clumps of darkness around it. For a second I even thought I could see four pairs of orange pin-points turn to watch us pass, but that was probably only because my eyes were held so wide open, and because I hadn't blinked in an awfully long time. The one thing I knew for sure was that it was nothing to do with the Rapt I'd taken. This was exactly the kind of thing I'd become a Rapt addict to avoid.

Vinaldi heard the intake of my breath. 'You seen something?'

'No,' I said. 'Nothing real. Just more dreams.'

'We're getting closer, aren't we?'

'We must be,' I said. 'Look at the panel.' Ghuaji's light had stopped moving, about half a mile ahead. Wherever we were going, we were nearly there.

Vinaldi let the truck grind to a halt, and his head lowered slightly until it was resting on the steering wheel.

'Mother of God on a skateboard,' he said, his voice for the first time very shaky. 'Now I realize you may have been right about going back. Suddenly, your whole sitting-very-quietly-somewhere-and-hoping-it-will-all-go-away option seems to speak of immense good sense and judgement.'

'Yeah,' I said, lighting a pair of cigarettes. 'But you were right. I have no choice. If Nearly and Suej are in there I have to be too. You don't though. You can leave me here, and go back.'

Vinaldi stayed still for a moment, breathing heavily. I knew this was no pantomime. I knew he was really thinking about it.

'You wouldn't stand a chance on your own,' he said eventually.

'No one ever does. But we're all still here.'

At that he pulled his head up and looked at me, and slowly started laughing. 'Any more glib crap like that,' he said, 'and I'll kick you out into the snow and go back and find a hot meal and a warm woman and sit and laugh at the thought of you freezing to death.'

I grinned and passed him a cigarette. 'It's a deal.'

Shaking his head, Vinaldi gunned the motor and we surged along the road which now seemed even darker, even more abandoned.

And that's when the indicator light on the Positionex went out.

Thirteen

'Shit,' Vinaldi said. 'What's wrong with that thing?'

I reached forward, banged it. Pointless, as it was a lump of solid-state inexplicability, but instincts die hard. Nothing happened, then two seconds later the light came on. It immediately disappeared, and further thumps made no difference.

'Hit it again,' Vinaldi said. 'Fuck – threaten to shoot it.'

'There's nothing wrong with it,' I said quickly. 'He must be nearly there. If we don't catch him he's going to get pulled in without us.'

Vinaldi slammed his foot down on the pedal – too hard. The back wheels spun, the truck ambling sideways against the ice. He managed to back it off enough for the tyres to catch and we slewed towards a corner at the end of the patch of level road.

'We're never going to catch him,' Vinaldi said between gritted teeth, as he tried to keep the truck under control. 'I can't go fast enough. We'll leave the road.'

'Just go as fast as you can,' I said, fumbling in my pockets. I got out another clip and slammed it into the gun, then took a couple of foil packets out. 'If we lose him we might just as well leave the road anyway. Both you and me. Our lives are over. And it's not just us, either.'

'What are you talking about?'

'If we don't stop Yhandim flashing back and forth then more of this stuff is going to spill out. Everything will change, and it won't be for the better.'

'Maybe you should get into writing greetings cards. Like "Happy wedding – bet it doesn't last". Or "Sorry to hear you're dead".'

Vinaldi increased the truck's speed until we were careering towards the corner, trying to stay within the tracks created by Ghuaji.

Trees flashed by, black branches flicking hard against the windows. Much later than I would have done he pulled the steering and the wheels locked, sending us sliding towards a wall of rock. I shut my eyes, wishing I'd phrased my last sentence differently, and when I opened them again saw that he had somehow pulled the truck round the corner on the skid.

'Nice one,' I said. 'But don't ever do it again.' Then I fell silent just as Vinaldi stepped on the brakes and killed the lights.

We were in a roughly circular clearing. Sixty yards ahead of us I could see the tail lights of Ghuaji's vehicle. The car was stationary.

We were there, wherever the hell 'there' was.

'What do we do now?' Vinaldi asked.

'Roll forward,' I whispered. 'As quietly as you can.'

We went about twenty yards until the truck was mainly hidden behind an outcrop of rock, then I motioned for him to stop. By then we could see two things. The first was that though the engine was still running, Ghuaji wasn't in his vehicle. The second was that on the left side of the road was a building. It was made of old, battered concrete and looked disused. No lights showed in any of the windows, most of which were in any event broken. The shape of the walls was naggingly familiar, but it wasn't until I realized that the level patch was a compound that I understood what it was.

'It's a Farm,' I said, bewildered. 'It's an abandoned SafetyNet Farm.' Once it had clicked, the whole scene fell into place and I turned in my seat, taking it in.

An electrified fence must once have bordered the area we were currently in. The main building lay up against the wall of the mountain, where tunnels doubtless led away into the hillside like abandoned concrete wombs. I hoped they were empty. Of course, they would be – they'd hardly abandon valuable spares along with the real estate – but for a moment the alternative possibility seemed all too real. Shambling naked bodies, crawling in darkness until the end of time, feeding off each other's bodies and excrement until there was nothing left.

Until that moment I hadn't realized what an extraordinary place the Farm had been, what it really said about humanity. As I stared out at the ruins of this one a shiver went down my back, a shiver which had nothing to do with the cold, or even with The Gap. I was thinking how right it was that the Farms should be connected with that other place, how in some way the mentality behind them was identical.

'Why here?' Vinaldi said.

I shrugged, stirring sluggishly out of my thoughts. 'I have no idea. It's no closer to The Gap than anywhere else.'

'Unless Maxen's found some method of forcing a way.'

'Can't be done.'

'Why not? They got us out, in the end.'

'They didn't get us out. The Gap got rid of us. They just shipped us home.'

'Bullshit. And if the whole thing was just some sort of fucked-up code zone, like they said, why couldn't someone have found some way of hacking back into it?'

I shook my head. 'That's only what they said it was.'

'You don't agree?' Vinaldi spoke with heavy irony, which I supposed was fair enough.

'No,' I said, 'I don't.'

Then we both saw Ghuaji. He was limping out of the old Farm building with something on a long piece of rope. The soldier was walking slowly and awkwardly, one leg dragging painfully behind. It was too far for us to see any detail, but I thought it fair to assume that he would be hurting badly by now, the wounds in his head and body reopening and trying to pull his body down to where it so much wanted to be: six feet below the ground, in a kind of peace. Instead, he was trying to return it to somewhere it should never have been in the first place.

'What the hell's he holding?' Vinaldi whispered. 'And is this going to work, if we're watching?'

'I don't know and I don't know,' I said.

'It's a cat,' Vinaldi said. 'There's a cat on the end of that rope.'

The cat was small and thin, and in the dim lights radiating from Ghuaji's car it looked ill and under-fed. This wasn't some pet which had been drafted in for the day. This was an animal which had been brought here some weeks ago, for a particular purpose. The fact it was still here proved that whatever experiment it had been a part of had succeeded. The further fact that it didn't look as if it had been fed in the meantime, but simply left in the old Farm building until it was needed again, proved simply that Maxen and his accomplices needed nothing quite as much as they needed a good solid kick to the head.

So Maxen actually had found a way back in. Probably, whatever it might be, it couldn't have worked unless Yhandim and the others had been trying to come the other way too, but worked it obviously had. Perhaps sometimes the two sides had to touch each other. I don't know. Chance, fate, or darker forces at work, it didn't really matter. There was no more room for pretending. Twenty years were going to be stripped away today.

We were teenagers, you know. Eighteen, nineteen. That's how old most of us were when they sent us into something we didn't understand. They left us there until they realized we weren't going to win, and then they pulled us out and threw us away – except that when they brought our bodies out they didn't check hard enough to see if they'd brought out our souls as well.

Ghuaji leant inside the car and turned the engine off – luckily Vinaldi was ahead of me and killed ours simultaneously. The mountain and the sky were very quiet, the only sound that of Ghuaji's feet crunching through the snow, and of our own hearts beating. Warmth and cold, getting closer to each other all the time.

'He's going to see us,' Vinaldi whispered.

'Maybe, maybe not,' I replied. 'I don't think he's going to be seeing anything very much at the moment.'

'He got here, didn't he?'

'He did, but he's also had a bullet through his head. Maybe it wasn't him who was directing. Maybe he got pulled this way.'

'Don't start with that shit again,' Vinaldi said. I shushed him as Ghuaji passed over the road thirty yards ahead of us. There was next to no light, and he was looking the other way, but it was still bizarre that he hadn't caught a glimpse of moonlight glinting off the angles of the car. That same light caught the side of his head for a moment and I saw blood there, and a darkness on his shirt. He was close to the end – if he didn't find the way in quickly he was going to die, and our hopes along with him. Nearly and Suej had already been gone for twelve hours. I didn't want to think about what might already have happened to them, or to the other spares.

The cat on the end of the rope was padding through the snow after Ghuaji, each footstep pulled high against the cold. She saw us, certainly – for a moment her head turned and stared at the truck as if concerned that it was in imminent danger of exploding. But then she lost interest and moved forwards again, peering around at the world.

When he was about five yards the other side of the road Ghuaji stopped walking, and stood still, head down. The cat padded past him and into the trees at the edge of the compound, trailing the rope behind her.

'What the *fuck* is going on?' Vinaldi said, panicky.

'You must have heard the story,' I said. 'How The Gap was found?' Now that it was all going down I felt strangely serene, the way you feel in the seconds after you've had a bad car accident. It's almost as if you know, all your life, that something bad is going to happen to you, come what may: and as if in those seconds, once it *has* happened, you find your only moments of peace, of relief from the tension of waiting for the axe to fall.

'Heard a hundred on the first day,' he said irritably. 'Didn't listen to any of them.'

I nodded. 'I heard a few as well, but only one that ever seemed to make any sense.' The cat was ambling around the bases of the trees now, going about cat business, whatever that may be.

'Is this going to be more hippy bullshit?'

'A guy was watching his cat one day,' I continued, ignoring him. 'Nowhere near here – out on the West Coast somewhere, and maybe the original guy *was* some kind of space cadet. Anyway,' I said, pulling my spike out of my jacket pocket and laying it on the dashboard. 'This guy spends a lot of time watching the cat, and realizes one of life's great truths.'

'What was that?' Vinaldi said, eyeing the needle on the dash with suspicion. I opened the two packets of foil, laying them out carefully on the screen of the Positionex.

'A cat's always on the wrong side of a door,' I said. 'You don't let it out the house, then outside's exactly where it wants to be – until you *do* let it out, when it suddenly needs to be back inside again. You keep it indoors, it always wants to be inside the cupboards – until you shut it in one, when it suddenly wants to come out again. You put a cat down anywhere on the earth, and it's going to go looking for somewhere else to be.'

I glanced outside to see that Ghuaji was still motionless, and that the cat had worked its way round to the far end of the compound, still sniffing, still looking around. Then I lifted the bottle of Jack's from the floor and poured a little into the cap of the bottle. I put the tip of my finger into the whiskey and carefully carried the drop of liquid over to one of the foils. I repeated this with the other foil and then watched as the two small piles of Rapt deliquesced. Within seconds there were two pools of concentrated liquid, sitting like mercury on the foil.

'This guy thinks about this for a while, and wonders what the fuck the cat is looking for. He gets the idea in his head that there's some final door somewhere, and all cats are searching for it. So one day, when he's stoned and has nothing better to do, he lets the cat out and decides to follow it. First thing the cat does, of course, is come straight back in again. Naturally. It's a cat. Then after a while it goes back outside, and wanders out into the yard. And this yard, okay, backs out onto a forest, and the cat is used to trailing around out there. So the guy follows it, at a distance, and watches while it does what it normally does.'

'I think Ghuaji's dead,' Vinaldi said.

'No he isn't,' I said. 'Now listen. There isn't much more. This guy follows the cat all day as it tromps round the forest.'

'Must have been good dope he was on.'

'He watches the way it goes behind trees, goes into hollows, comes back out again, generally cats around. And then –'

'Something's happening,' Vinaldi interrupted.

'What?'

'I don't know. But I saw something.'

'*What?*'

'*I don't know*. That's why I say something's happening.'

I hurriedly reached for the hypo, cracked a new needle on and sucked the drugs up into the barrel. When it was flicked I looked back out the windshield and saw that Vinaldi was probably right. Ghuaji's head had come back up, though his eyes were still closed. The cat was working its way further into the trees, still pulling the rope behind it. It was so far away that you couldn't see it, only the line leading out into the darkness. I'd always believed the story had been true. It made sense, to me at least. Cats have been worshipped, used as familiars, for an awfully long time. There had to be a reason.

Then I heard something. Bark working against itself, branches laughing, moonlight scraping the sky. I looked down out of the window and saw a single leaf running past the truck, over the surface of the snow. It had two stalks and was using them as legs, running from what or to where I would never know.

'Yeah, it's happening,' I said. I looked across at Vinaldi and saw that he was shaking, his hands trembling violently.

'Why didn't I listen to you, Jack?' he muttered. 'Why didn't I just stay the fuck in New Richmond?' I held the needle out to him, but he shook his head violently. 'I'm not having any of that shit. It took me two years to kick it back then.'

'You're taking it,' I said firmly. 'You're going to have to share the needle with me, but you're taking it. We barely got out the first time, Johnny. We're older now. You go in without this and your mind's going to shatter straight away.'

Vinaldi just kept shaking his head. I rolled my own sleeve up and jabbed the needle in. In front of us, Ghuaji was now standing bolt upright, and the rope in his hand was being tugged more insistently. The cat was evidently reaching the limits of its tether, but I didn't think that was going to matter.

Then the Flip happened, and Vinaldi cried out. The spaces between the trees took on solidity, and it became apparent that the trees themselves were merely gaps. I turned my head slowly to look at the old Farm building, and saw that it was the same there. The building was nothing, a lack of something, and the space between it and us was now a thing which I could barely see round.

'Oh Jesus fucking Christ,' said Vinaldi, and abruptly held his arm out towards me. I rolled his sleeve, flicked the needle again and sank it in, injecting him with the second half of an extremely strong double dose. The noise outside was getting louder, all of the gaps between sounds becoming sounds themselves as the real sounds faded away – and only when that happens do you realize just how much silence there really is. Silences between lovers, when something really needs to be said; silence from a parent when a child needs some word more than anything else in the world; silences and in betweens and everything which isn't an answer. All of these quietnesses and more gathered together around us, funnelled into the times and places where things didn't happen and no one was saved.

One thing has always summed up The Gap more than anything else to me. It's a warning sign I saw, as a child, in front of a dirty lake. It was a perfunctory painting of a little boy who had fallen in the water. In the picture there was no one else around, just this child slipping deeper. His arm reached up, his mouth was wide with entreaty, but you knew he was going to die. 'BE CAREFUL WHERE YOU PLAY,' the warning at the bottom said: 'HELP MAY NEVER COME.'

Ghuaji's arm jerked out suddenly, as the rope was pulled taut. His eyes opened, and we knew they had because they threw a beam across the trees. Not of light exactly: a different view, a sideways glance. What we saw across his vision was something not really there at all, but which might have been. The rope jerked again and Ghuaji half-stepped, half-toppled, in the direction of the cat, which had now presumably found that door for which its kind had always been searching.

'Start the truck,' I said.

'Won't he hear?'

'All we'll be is a patch of silence.'

Vinaldi turned the key and the engine chugged into life; sluggishly – if we'd sat much longer it might not have restarted at all. We watched as Ghuaji staggered off towards the trees. I motioned for Vinaldi to follow him.

'We can't go down there in this,' he said.

'Just do it,' I said. 'And make sure you're exactly behind him.'

Ghuaji started to pick up speed, partly because he was reaching a steeper slope, mainly as the pull gathered momentum. As Vinaldi steered the truck off the road and down after him I felt the first twinge of Rapt, the forerunner of forerunners, insinuate itself into my system. 'Christ, not *again*,' my brain said, but it knew it was the right thing to do, and perfect timing. The truck bumped down the slope and the Flip was stronger there, the space between things seeming to resist until Vinaldi had to push his foot down on the accelerator even though we were travelling downhill. Ghuaji didn't turn, though we were only five yards behind. He couldn't hear us. The line to the cat stretched out in front of him like a steel cable and it was pulling him so fast he was almost running.

A thrumming sound started to come up out of the ground, melding with the noise of the truck to cancel out and add to the silence. It felt as if the truck was slipping into some slippery channel carved in air, the bumps from the rocky ground only turbulence. The trees were getting ever closer, Vinaldi's rictus of concentration tighter, when Ghuaji dropped the rope and started running, just as I saw the cat come hurtling back up the other way. It had seen what it had found, and wanted no part of it.

But Ghuaji kept running, and I screamed at Vinaldi to go faster, and the truck now hurtled down the slope towards trees only ten yards away. For an instant the interior of the truck looked like the inside of a tree trunk, all the surfaces mottled and lined, and I knew it was really about to happen.

'Oh Jesus,' Vinaldi said. He knew it too.

'Look away,' I said urgently. 'Look away from me and away from him. Head for the biggest tree then *look away*.'

In that last instant before I turned my head I saw a huge tree trunk in front of us, Ghuaji now sprinting towards it, injuries forgotten. The tree was three feet across, a pillar of blackness, but now it was not a thing at all. In the darkness of its body I could see shadows of beyond; the tree now merely a gap in the impermeable space around it. Through the gap I could see the shape of other trees, trees which stood in a different forest in a different place.

Then I yanked my head to the side so I couldn't see either Vinaldi or Ghuaji, and watched the other gaps running past, jumbled and swirled as the truck crunched over boulders and fell after Ghuaji towards somewhere else.

Vinaldi shouted at the last moment, as if trying to make the truck change course through words alone. By then it was too late.

The truck hit the tree head on and went through.

Fourteen

At first they said it was the internet, as it was called back then. They said the traffic on the network had got too dense, that this virtual world had grown too heavy and that all the man with the cat did was discover it had begun. They said all this, but it wasn't true.

Yes, the internet snowcrashed two weeks before The Gap was discovered, and they never worked out why. True, they had to switch to the alternative Matrix which was already in place, and the old net never worked again.

But The Gap was always there, waiting.

Then they said computer code was at fault, the little lines of syntax we'd thought were perfect and inviolate, simple instructions to simple beings, the chips in the wild inside, flowering up through meaning into function. We'd believed the languages we'd created were protected from ambiguity, but there was seepage from day one. The same sentence in English said in two different inflections creates slightly different meanings: turned out we hadn't appreciated the difference situation made to code, because we didn't really understand the way computers think. All the unspoken half-meanings we missed, the sly words, hidden implications; all of these, it was said, added up to something and went somewhere else and created another place.

They thought they'd finally got to the bottom of it when they stopped the writing of collapsing code, a language based on the way the human mind itself was shaped. When written with perfect syntax it would collapse in on itself, creating software with just one line, a line whose meaning was opaque even to the person who had written the original. The writing process became like a childhood, lost and unreachable. The software would work, and work marvellously, but there was always the fear that something else, something unintended, had been sealed in with the instructions. Especially after computers themselves were given the job of writing the code. They were better at it, much better than us, but their motivations were sometimes uncertain, and after the code was sealed it was impossible to tell what was in there. Perhaps things were being said which we couldn't hear; perhaps this was a conversation humans weren't invited to eavesdrop on any more.

Once they banned collapsing code The Gap didn't get any bigger, so maybe there was something in that. But some of us believed that if any of the above was true it had only ever been a facilitator, a gateway which let us find something people had been looking for all along without realizing what they might find.

We'll probably never know for sure because, now it's over, no one wants to even think about it. Trying to conquer it was a mistake, and nobody brags about mistakes. The war was kept quiet at the time, and the silence since has been ear-shattering. There haven't been any movies about what happened in there, and there never will be. It was one defeat too many. It wasn't even classified as a war, but as a training exercise, and you'd be surprised how many Bright Eyes have died in suspicious circumstances since it ended. Especially those who started talking about it.

You won't find it in the history books, but it happened. I know. I was there.

We discovered how to get into the world's subconscious, but instead of respecting it, and letting its good influence seep out into the conscious world as it always had, we tried to charge in and take it over, as if it was a new territory which could be owned. We found Eden, and napalmed it; found Oz's wells, and pissed in them; found the mainspring of power which kept the real world sane and spread the virus of insanity throughout it. Maybe we even found the truth my father thought the real world hid; if so, we should have left it alone.

It was never officially called The Gap. It had several names, their length increasing with the seniority of the person who spoke them. But the only name ever used by anyone who was actually there was 'The Gap'. And when they took us in, units of teenagers with nothing better to do except be the guinea pigs in someone else's war, why did they make us stand in such a way that no one could see – or be seen by – anyone else? Because, I believe, that's what The Gap was all about. Falling between cracks, being cut out of the loop, consigned to dead code which has lost its place in the program and nobody remembers any more.

I believe The Gap is made up of all of the places where no one is, of the sights which no one sees. It comes from silence, and lack, and the deleted and unread; it is the gap between what you want and what you have, between love and affection, between hope and truth. It's the place where crooked cues come from, and it's the answer to a question: does a tree exist when there's no one there to perceive it?

It exists all right, but it's in The Gap. And there will be many more of them, and they will not shade you from anything and they will not be your friends.

A flash of images: hydraulic stumps; blood on necks; weapon jam; fear. None of it real, just a spasm of remembrance.

Then Ghuaji in front of us, but not completely there; only his clothes running off between the trees, banking and dodging as if under heavy fire. The truck roaring in the silence. And the trees. All the trees were there.

Flash again, but real: a sharp crack as the truck ran into a bank of trunks, Vinaldi and I thrown forward to collide with the windscreen. It cracked, but not enough; we spent the first seconds back in The Gap barely conscious.

Then it cleared and I swirled my head up and saw the clothes still floating into the distance, like a runaway laundry basket. I felt a moment of dismay – as if entering once more a recurrent nightmare, barely remembered during the day, but like an old soiled glove at night. An incommunicable dread; of half-turns and stares, of screams in the shelves and shoes poking out from beneath curtains in the middle of the night. 'Come and see me,' the shoes say, but you know the person they belong to is dead and they shouldn't be there at all.

When I could still see the clothes half a mile away, I knew it was really so. It is so dark there, silky dark, and yet that doesn't stop you seeing. You can't imagine it unless you've been there, and when you've been there you can't forget. The quiet, an ultimate stillness; but once you notice the silence you spend an eternity covering your ears against the noise.

It's not a nightmare. However you explain it, it is not a dream of any kind. It is all simply there. And so were we.

Vinaldi slumped in his seat, shaking his head, whether against the crash or Rapt or The Gap I couldn't tell.

'Are you alright?' I said.

'No,' he replied. 'No, I'm not fucking alright.'

I shook his shoulder gently. 'We've got to go now or we'll never catch him up.' Vinaldi reached blindly for the gear stick and pushed at it, but it was like moving a rotting stick in a stream; it didn't make any difference to anything. 'I don't think the truck is really here,' I added. 'Come on. Get out.'

I grabbed as much ammunition as I could fit in my pockets, together with one of the pump-actions Vinaldi had thoughtfully provided, opened my door and climbed down from the truck. On the other side Vinaldi did the same, and we stood for a moment, looking around us.

The darkness in The Gap is strange. It is like the lack of any light at all, because our sun has never shone on it, and yet sometimes it is like a slanting sunset or twilight in the corner of your eye. As you move your head you see different things, changing lights. For a moment I thought I saw late-afternoon sun glinting off the roof of the truck, and then all was silky evening and the truck was only coloured space in front of me. The light in there is blue, for the most part, a blue which I have only ever seen in one place since.

In all directions, as far as the eye could see, were the trees. A forest of unimaginable age, rank upon rank of thick trunks shooting up into infinity. Sometimes it seems like they are entirely separate from each other, at others as if they were all extrusions of the same thing. The floor was covered with leaves so densely that it seemed like there were no individual leaves at all but only a carpet of moleskin, covered with a fine and shifting mist.

'Which way did he go?' Vinaldi asked, rubbing his hand across his face. 'Not that it makes much difference.'

'That way,' I said, joining him. 'I think I can still see the clothes, out in the distance.' I couldn't, but we needed some impetus. To stand still in The Gap is like stopping swimming for a shark. You sink to the bottom, and can't start moving again.

We started off quickly, both of us giving the vehicle a backwards glance after a few yards, as if we knew that leaving it would commit us to being here. The truck was gone, which didn't surprise me. You can't carry large objects across all in one go. The vehicles used in the war – which were in any event few and far between – all had to be ferried across piecemeal and assembled in The Gap; even the machines which ultimately enabled us to be sideslipped back again.

'Are you Rapt yet?' Vinaldi asked.

'No, but it's coming,' I said.

'Good. It had better. Because I'm getting the Fear.'

'Perhaps we'd better run.'

'You know something? I think you could be right.'

We started trotting then, hopefully in the direction Ghuaji had gone, but I was already none too sure. For now the forest seemed quiet, as if ignoring us, but we both knew that wouldn't last. Leaves started running beside us then, like children playing. Vinaldi kicked out at them, but I stopped him.

'Little fuckers,' he said.

'Rather them than the trees.'

We ran, faster and faster, as the Fear came. Its coming was like a return to everything you thought you'd left behind. Not just our memories, but everyone's, until we were no longer really following Ghuaji but just fleeing from everyone and everything. Men, dead and wounded, spread in pieces around the floor and their blood not lying still yet. Children, jerking spastically towards us. None of this was here now, but it had been, and The Gap remembered. It was full of ghosts, of the thousands whose bodies had disappeared before anyone had a chance to grieve or offer thanks.

Vinaldi's face flashed white beside me, our breaths laboured and ragged; both of us had been smoking far too long to enjoy this kind of shit. The feeling of having a hand squeezed round my temples grew stronger and stronger as the Fear froze into my bones, and still we ran.

'I can't stay in here long,' Vinaldi panted. 'I can't do this for very long at all.'

'Me neither,' I said, as terror found yet more speed in our legs and we sprinted between the trees, a trail of leaves following us enthusiastically, pretending they couldn't keep up but not getting left behind. The bark on the trees sniggered at us, but that was alright. It couldn't move quickly enough to do any real damage.

'Where are we going?'

'I don't know,' I said, and then suddenly the light went out. Vinaldi moaned beside me and we found ourselves in a huge bush, slicing against needles and spines. We kicked and thrashed our way through it, but the bush got thicker and thicker, and the worst part was that I knew that if we ever got through it then the other side would be even less fun.

We found ourselves in the middle, face to face, unable to move or to see each other's eyes. All we could hear was each other's breathing, the sound sinister and loud. Vinaldi wanted to kill me, I knew. He wanted to reach out and pull the eyes from my head and chew them while he clawed the skin from my face. I wanted to do the same to him, but then suddenly the bush was no longer there, and the light was back – but it was yellow now, curdled and old.

Vinaldi stared at me, stricken. 'This Rapt isn't strong enough, Jack. It isn't helping at all. I was going to . . .'

'Yeah, I know. But it's all we've got.'

'This is a mistake. We shouldn't have come back.'

'What the fuck's that?'

Vinaldi whirled to follow my gaze, and I realized: it was Ghuaji's jacket. The bush we'd clawed through was now several yards away and a blood-stained fatigue jacket was hung across it. The cotton started unravelling itself, and the dried blood revivified in mid-air to form a small hanging droplet. A twig from a nearby tree reached out and greedily sucked it up.

Then Vinaldi grabbed my arm and pointed behind me.

Ghuaji's remaining clothes were standing fifty yards away, facing us. They turned slowly, as if on a revolving pedestal, and then quickly glided away into the gloom.

We ran after them through more trees, more shadows, until there were so many leaves around us that it was like falling into a tunnel of dryness. And finally the Rapt kicked in with a vengeance, and for a while we didn't know where we were, or what we were doing, or who we were chasing after. For a little while, I don't know how long, we were just two shadows in motion towards nothing, and it was exactly like it had been back then.

I don't think I could describe the war in The Gap reliably, not a single tree or village or death, despite the fact that I still see them in dreams and probably always will. I see the ferns and leaves, the blue light which sifted between the trees; I see the little towns, nestled amidst them like fairy tale villages. But that's not the way it really was. Part of being there at all was a knowledge that we weren't really seeing what things were like, however hard we looked. Somehow the reality of it was always just round the corner, or hidden under a layer of light. We couldn't trust the people, we couldn't trust the land, and in the end we couldn't even trust ourselves. We were like baffled, terrified children alone in a dark multi-storey car park full of sadists.

Partly it was the drugs. Eight out of ten people were off their face all the time. It was encouraged. It meant you coped better with the Fear. The other two out of ten were either drunk or crazy.

I realized this within minutes of being sideslipped into The Gap, and made a pact with myself. I was going to do this thing straight, scared though I was. From the moment you set foot in The Gap you knew something was wrong, and every breath you took confirmed that knowledge and made it a part of your very metabolism. Fear ran through people like blood. Whether you were looking at someone huddled shaking into the roots of a tree, or standing proud with shoulders back and gun spitting, you were looking at someone who was mortally afraid. As I stood in the base camp on that first day and saw the shells of men around me, I hoped to God that I had slipped into some dream and would wake up very soon. 'This can't be the way it is,' I said to myself, already shaking. 'They can't all be like this, and even if they are I'm not going to join them. If I'm going to be this scared, I need to know what I'm doing.'

Within hours a horrified dread began to fill every extremity of my body, slowly flowing towards my centre. It was like the 'Oh no,' moment, the moment when you realize that you've been caught doing something bad, when you've made a mistake that will have disastrous consequences, or when you hear someone close to you has died. For a moment, your mind becomes cold liquid, and a calm denial is the only thing you can feel.

That's the way it stayed. The feeling didn't pass off. It just kept growing. That's why my resolution lasted four days. I got respect for that, of a grudging kind. Four days was a long time to hold out, and it set me apart from some of the other men. One of the things men will fight hardest to hide from each other is fear. You just don't do it. In The Gap it was different. It couldn't be hidden, and so all the time you were surrounded by the most childlike, vulnerable, desperate part of everybody else. There were people in The Gap, and that's who we were supposed to be fighting; but they were the very least of our problems. The children, dead but with hydraulic frames nailed through their bones so they could scamper poison-laden towards us; the blankets of fire which appeared from your pockets and swept up to incinerate your skin; these were fears, but nothing like the Fear of The Gap itself, which was all of this and the promise of everything more.

In the end, I recognized that I was endangering the rest of the men in my unit. I was simply too terrified *all the time*. It felt as if each individual cell in my body was cold; as if someone was constantly running a killing knife over the hairs on the back of my neck; as if I was lying asleep, the plank of my back exposed and bare and waiting for an axe which would surely come. The fourth day I was there I followed a couple of the guys to the tent where it all happened. I'd never taken drugs at that time. I was frightened of doing it. I was frightened of not doing it. I was frightened of everything.

What Rapt did was intensify reality to the point of occlusion. It took everything and pushed it up into the stratosphere, made the light behind the leaves even darker, made height so tall it disappeared, warmth so hot it became cold. It made everything so intense you could only blank it. Every hour was a series of blackouts, of forgettings. You'd find yourself half a mile down the track and have no recollection of having got there. You'd look at some guy you'd been talking to and realize you had no idea what the conversation was about. You'd look down at yourself and realize you were holding a man's head by the hair, and that you'd blown it off the body with repeated rounds from your gun, and have no idea of how it had all happened.

The mind pushed it away, blanked it in real time minute by minute, but all the while there was this voice which knew what was going on. However much Rapt you took, this voice drip-fed the truth to you second by second like a string of filthy lies told to himself by a psychopathic schizophrenic. So what did you do? You took more Rapt to shut the voice up.

You were there only three quarters of the time. The rest you were somewhere else; fucked up into oblivion by the cocktail of The Gap and heavy Rapt. We called it being 'Gone Away', and it was the only way you could get out of The Gap. You came to recognize a look in the eyes of other people, the look that said they'd just come back from being Gone Away. You envied them those moments of peace, but at the same time you were frightened of what Going Away might mean.

We didn't get much instruction. We got guns. Some of the guys had been there a little longer, lieutenants and stuff, but that just meant they were even more fucked up than the rest of us. It was a war fought on the ground, behind trees and under bushes. There were gunships, but they were strange and experimental and shaped like fish, seldom used except for the brass to hide in. All we had was our basic intelligence, and maybe that should have been enough. An eight-man unit between themselves ought to have been able to figure out how to fight – or at least, how to hide effectively – but you've got to remember that we were out of our heads the whole fucking time.

Rapt's effects are not just intense on a dose-by-dose basis: they are also cumulative. After a couple of weeks it re-maps your neural paths to the point where you don't know where the *hell* you are – and we were on it for over two years. We'd be tramping through darkness, not knowing where we were or what to do next, and then suddenly we'd see this big clump of bushes and someone would say, 'Okay, let's go through that bush.'

'What bush?' someone else would ask, confused.

'That bush.'

'What fucking bush? We're surrounded by the fuckers.'

'*That* bush, man: the one you're almost standing in.'

Relieved: 'Oh yeah. That bush. Okay.'

'Wow. Look at it. That's some bush.'

'It's beautiful. Look at those leaves.'

'Great leaves.'

Then suddenly: 'I don't like it.'

'Like what?'

'The bush, man. It's giving me the Fear.'

'It's just a bush. It's okay.'

'It's not okay, man. It's giving me the fucking Fear.'

'*Okay*. Forget the bush.'

'I can't forget it. It's right there in front of me, man . . .'

'Not *that* bush. The *other* one.'

'Fuck – that's even *worse*.'

'Shit. You're right.'

'What are we going to do?'

'We'll go round it.'

And so we'd go round the bush, and get caught, and get the shit kicked out of us and half of us would die.

Getting around a bush in one piece isn't so fucking hard. We should have been able to work that kind of thing out – but we couldn't. Running like hell was a very big part of the tactics out there. We couldn't connect with each other, with common sense, with reality.

It was a war fought against demons, by men who had become demons themselves. Maybe that's the biggest thing I took away from it. The fact that anyone, your comrade, your friend, your brother, can in the right circumstances become something you don't want to believe exists. Once you've seen it's possible, you never look at anyone the same again. And The Gap itself, what did we do to it? It can't always have been that way. Or maybe it was, and it was just the fact we have the wrong kind of minds, applying consciousness to things which should have stayed buried.

This isn't making any real sense, isn't some polished account. I can't do anything about that, because I can't remember it with any more cohesion. I guess I could go back over what I've done and try to order it, but I won't. It wouldn't be true to the way it was. Cohesion, order, chronology; The Gap was the place where you learnt those three words meant nothing at all. This was a place where one guy I knew was Gone Away for three days once: three entire days. We could tell he was Gone Away, and we put up with it. You generally could. It was part of every day, and you got used to it. But *three days* . . .

When the guy came back, he was different. Being Gone Away wasn't like sleep, or unconsciousness. You were still awake, but you were somewhere else. Short stretches were okay – I don't think it did too much harm. But three days – that changed him. This guy used to sometimes say things about it, try to talk it out. But he couldn't. Wherever he'd been was buried too deep. He sometimes talked like it was a whole other place, as if while his body had been with us, shivering in the trees or cutting the faces off villagers, his soul had been somewhere else, somewhere that was different but no better. I don't know about that, but I instinctively recognized there was an element of truth in it. About a third of the men around you at any one time would be Gone Away, flicking on and off in ten- or twenty-minute stretches, and it was like marching with a bunch of fucking zombies. Jesus, I used to think, these guys are my friends, the people on my side, and it's like a sponsored walk with the lobotomized dead.

Most people reacted to Rapt about the same, but some went really weird on it. There would be soldiers who regressed when they were Rapt, started running about like terrible children. Some of these guys regressed in a way which made you think what they were regressing to was the childhood of something that wasn't entirely human. Or maybe it *was* human, but humanity of a different evolution. It was as if there had once been two tribes, identical in appearance, but subtly different at every emotional and psychological level. Maybe between the trees in The Gap there wandered the childhoods of Gap people, lost but still alive. Maybe they got into some of the men.

As soon as we saw that a guy was prone to react that way we tried to turn him into a drinker instead. It was just too disturbing to see them being like that. We couldn't deal with it.

Problem was, all any of this did was hide it. Not all of it, just enough. It didn't go away. All that fear is still inside us, and even now we're slowly using it up. People try to hide it different ways, by being strong, being weak, being a cop or being a gangster. But everyone feels it. Everyone is still afraid.

✠✠✠✠

When the first surge of Rapt planed out into lucidity we stopped running, our chests suddenly filled with liquid fire. I reeled off into the bushes and vomited uncontrollably, my body revolting against the exertion and trying to make it clear it wasn't having any more of it. Bodies are great, and I wouldn't go anywhere without mine, but sometimes they're so disappointing. If we mistreated them as badly as we do our minds then everyone would be dead, and yet there they go, complaining all the time. Someone needs to get all our bodies, sit them down, and give them a good talking to.

All I could think of as I hurled up my guts was a hope that I wasn't losing any of the Rapt this way. I knew I was going to need it, and was already thinking of the remaining two packets. What I had was all we'd got, but it was already all I could do not to just shoot it up there and then.

Meanwhile Vinaldi slumped with his hands on his knees, sucking air in like he was in danger of imploding. I guess he did time in a health club or something; compared to me he was a fucking Superman. I could feel my body looking on enviously, wishing I treated it that well. I hate fit people. They're so undermining.

When we'd recovered sufficiently we looked around, slowly turning in a circle. All we could still see, for 360 degrees, was forest – except that the second time we went round, a stream had appeared. (That was normal; either there are more than 360 degrees in a circle in The Gap, or things just don't work that way.) We realized then that our feet were wet, and thus we'd probably come across that very stream. A large group of leaves was standing on the other side, unable to come across. Though they didn't have eyes – obviously, because they were just leaves – we could tell that they were watching us. Also, that if we tried to go back that way they would stop us.

So we kept turning, and saw that what was behind us hadn't been what we'd originally thought. It wasn't simply more forest. In front of us, about half a mile away down a slight incline, there appeared to be a village.

'How did we get here?' Vinaldi asked.

'Fuck knows. Couldn't you tell?'

'Are you kidding? I couldn't tell who I *was*. I'd forgotten you even existed.'

'I don't want to go down there,' I said suddenly.

Vinaldi nodded. 'Me neither. But we've got to.'

'No we don't. We could go somewhere else. Maybe that's not the place. Or maybe the clothes led us and it's a trap.'

'Jack, it doesn't matter if it is or not,' Vinaldi said. 'I can't stay out here much longer. I don't have the Bright Eyes any more, remember?'

It hit me then just how much courage he had. Your eyes were operated on the day before you were sidelifted into The Gap. There was something about certain types of light in The Gap's forest – though not the villages – which caused human eyes to burn out from the inside; so a chemical was laser-implanted in a thin layer over your retinas, and this seemed to prevent the light from damaging them. Back in the real world this chemical caused a slight reflection in certain lighting conditions, hence the 'Bright Eyes' nickname. Vinaldi had spent the last – Christ, *two hours*, I found, by looking at my watch – in the forest without protection. He was either inordinately brave or an idiot.

'I'd forgotten,' I said.

Legs aching from the run, we tramped towards the village. For the time being, the light in the forest was both safe and almost attractive, as if someone had installed small yellow mood-lights behind every tenth tree. Like all settlements in The Gap, the village looked insignificant against the infinite spread of the forest, but also seemed to pre-date it. Even from this distance we could see the trunks which shot up through the thatched roofs of some of the houses, so thick that it could barely have been worth living in the remains of the shelter they provided. Nobody knows why things are like this, because nobody ever managed to talk to a local for long enough to find out. Before the first sentence was over one or other of you would be dead. The problem with the villagers was two-fold; firstly, their implacable ferocity, and secondly the fact that they weren't visible all the time. They were easier to see in the dark, but by then you were generally seconds from death. The children were more visible, and seemed to be less angry at us, but were often used by the villagers to carry mines. For years after I was sideslipped out, at the end – or abandonment – of the war, I couldn't see a child without being scared out of my wits. It was only when Angela arrived in my life that their ghosts were laid to rest, and it was only when she and Henna died that I understood how much they had protected me from.

'Are you okay?' Vinaldi asked, after a while.

'I guess so,' I said.

'Yeah,' he said.

There were about thirty dwellings, arranged in a rough circle around a central area, with two paths bisecting at approximate right angles. The huts were lit by orange light which slipped and flowed around them, like a golden tide. Sometimes, I knew from experience, this light would coalesce into the birds I'd seen with Nearly and Suej in New Richmond. These birds were brain-damaged and appalling but they always seemed happy, exploding into being like liquid flames. After a chaotic few moments they'd disappear piecemeal, like smoke drifting into a dark sky. They only lived in the villages, which were otherwise deserted. None of the villagers lived in them, and it seemed that they never had.

'So,' I asked, when we were standing a few yards from the edge of the settlement. 'What's the plan?'

'Shit, I don't know. Go in there and see if we can find anything, I guess.'

Not a very detailed plan of attack. I pinched the bridge of my nose, trying to hold the second Rapt wave off and keep my head in one piece. 'Together?'

'Yes of fucking course together,' he snapped. 'Or do you want to go see if you can find some small dark room at the top of some stairs and wander in there by yourself?'

'You don't think tactically it would make more sense to split up?'

'No I fucking don't.'

So we went together, shotguns held at port-arms, keeping watch on opposite sides of the path. As we entered the village we stared hard at the huts we passed, searching for any sign of movement within. The huts looked polished and perfect, as always, as if fresh-minted from imaginary materials. You could see the fine detail of each piece of straw in the thatch, the little bumps in the white mud of the exterior walls.

We decided against doing a search of every hut; partly to speed our first pass through the village, mainly because we were frightened. Doing a recce with the Fear is like wandering blindfolded into a room you know is papered with razor blades.

By the time we reached the centre, our faces were dripping with perspiration and my finger was moist against the trigger of the shotgun. We were wired very tight, our time off from the Rapt running out. We paused there, listening carefully. There was nothing to hear, and nothing to see except tree trunks and huts.

'Vinaldi,' I said, 'we've got to hurry. The Rapt's going to come on again soon.'

He considered this, nodded, and then pointed up the path. 'I'll go through to the other side. You start the circles. If you see anything, shout.'

He crept across the opening and onto the other section of the path, warily looking all around him. I headed off at an angle into the clusters of huts, peering through windows and round corners, seeing nothing except tendrils of orange light. The huts themselves were antiseptically empty, sterile as if stamped from moulds. In one, I saw a small collection of leaves in the corner, looking as if they were having a meeting, but nothing more interesting than that. The leaf meetings never seemed to amount to very much. I think it was just a kind of play for them.

When I'd finished the first quarter I crossed the path we came in on and went over to the opposite side, catching a glimpse of Vinaldi, now at the far end of the village and heading back towards the centre.

I was checking yet another hut when I heard a sudden sound from behind me. I whirled round, trigger all but pulled, and saw a small flock of the orange birds fountaining up out of nothing into flight. They chittered and guffawed happily before disappearing with a shudder of air. Then everything was quiet again.

Well, not everything. When the last of the flapping noises died away I heard something the other side of the village. A human utterance of some kind. My first thought was that Vinaldi might have found something and was calling out to me, so I abandoned the current hut and ran in a crouch back towards the central path.

By the time I stepped onto it the sound had faded, and Vinaldi was nowhere to be seen. I debated calling out to him, then realized that if it hadn't been Vinaldi, and there was anyone else here, I should probably keep my mouth shut. I retreated slowly back to the centre of the village, eyes smarting at being open so wide for so long, my ears feeling as if they were swivelling on stalks.

Then I heard something that was definitely a shout, and stopped dead. The noise came from the far corner of the village, and any words contained in it were indistinguishable.

It was very bad timing for me to have to make a decision. My fingers were beginning to feel very long, my mind extremely vague. At any moment I could be Gone Away and suddenly I had to think.

There were two options. The first, go forward, threading my way through the huts until I saw what was going on. Downside: if Vinaldi wasn't calling for me because he'd found something, I'd walk straight into the trap which Yhandim would undoubtedly have set. With sudden clarity, the idea of going into a village struck me as irredeemably stupid. Why else would we be here unless we'd followed the clothes? Yes, we had to find out where Yhandim's camp was – but not at the expense of walking straight into it.

So I took a second option, and quickly retreated out of the village. When I was at the perimeter I turned right, keeping my back to the forest, and ran round the edge of the houses, checking the spaces between buildings and trees. It was colder outside the village, much colder. Another night was coming. Night isn't really night in The Gap, simply a period of indeterminate length when it will be darker and even less fun to be there.

Then I saw a figure, right the other side of the village – standing before one of the huts. It looked like Vinaldi, but he wasn't moving. I was relieved, but only momentarily. There was something strange about his posture, as if he was holding his hands up in the air. As I tried to work out what he was doing, and wondered whether to shout, the second Rapt rush really hit home and suddenly things became difficult and strange. I teetered on the edge of being Gone Away for a moment but managed to hold it off.

I moved very close to the wall of the nearest hut and slid round it, blinking in the way which sometimes helps. Something was very wrong. Vinaldi's hands were in the air because they had been tied to the hut, and though I couldn't see any blood, his head was drooping.

Run, my mind said. Just turn around and run.

I crept forward another couple of yards, blinking my eyes rapidly against the coming darkness. Vinaldi was still alive; his head was jerking slightly. Either he was trying to clear it, or reeling from Rapt rush. Almost certainly both – my mind was already about as clear as sewage and getting more tangled all the time. I couldn't see anyone nearby, and I briefly considered simply running at him and trying to get him free. Then something made me turn my head and look down the path towards the centre of the village.

There was nothing there, but the clearing looked ruffled as though seen through a heat haze. Whichever way I turned my head, it stayed in the same place. It was flickering very slightly too, like a bad quality film print, but the flecks weren't white, they were dark. I rubbed my eyes hard and blinked, but after I stopped seeing stars the effect was still there. The flecks seemed to organize into broken and shifting vertical lines as I watched, as if something was hidden behind a curtain of rain, rain so coloured as to make up a picture of that patch of the path.

I realized what I was seeing just a moment before the picture settled enough for my eyes to tell me. It was Yhandim and Ghuaji, and they were running along the path straight at me. They'd been taken up by The Gap enough to slip into it almost like natives. Ghuaji's injuries weren't holding him up any, and Yhandim looked like he'd never been injured in his life. He probably hadn't. People like him didn't get injured: the traffic's all the other way.

They looked like a condensed pack of wild animals, bludgeoned into a human state and howling with happy lust.

I did what I'd been trained to do. I ran like hell.

PART THREE

New Richmond

Fifteen

I ran, and eventually I was Gone Away. I cannot tell you where I went. I can only say this:

Henna used to tell me the names of flowers; their names, what they liked in terms of water and sunlight, and where they were originally from. Whether we walked the corridors of 72, or made an excursion out into Virginia, there would be a constant background hum of information, a datastream from Henna's internal world. At first I feigned interest, and then I ignored her, and now I'll never know. She would also tell me things which had happened in her day, because she loved me. But because I couldn't fit them into my life I let these too slide past me and fade away.

All those parts which I could have saved have slipped between my fingers and disappeared.

I don't know how many people I slept with while I was married to Henna. I don't mean there were that many, simply that I didn't keep track, which in some ways seems worse. I didn't start for three years, but once I began I just couldn't seem to stop. Sometimes I was drunk, sometimes I was Rapt, sometimes I was stone cold sober. I can't really blame any mitigating substance, unless it's one I produce in my own mind. Unfaithfulness was coded in.

I'm not trying to excuse it. It's inexcusable. That's the whole point of vices, of alcoholism, addictions and eating disorders. They *have* to be inexcusable. The soul wages war on the self, making it do things it can't respect -- as a punishment for crimes it doesn't even remember. What's the point, unless it's something bad? And what do you do about yourself when you know you can't stop doing something you despise? You carry on doing it, that's what. The merry-go-round never stops. The worst of it is that people will respect those addictions, legitimating your own private civil war. They'll think you can't help it, that your childhood's to blame, or some cultural malaise. Anything but you. Sometimes that's true, but often it's just down to being an asshole.

It's an easy thing to do, for a cop, finding someone new to fuck. There'd always be some lonely woman who needed comforting after finding her apartment trashed, or a girl in a bar who thought it was a turn-on to sleep with someone who should have been out catching criminals – or better still, at home with his wife and daughter. Each would last a few weeks, or months, and then I'd purge myself and leave it be. For a little while I'd be good, and pretend to be happy, and then it would simply happen again.

I met Henna through Mal, when I was twenty-two and had just joined the cops. Mal had been in the life for a year, and seemed to be liking it. We'd been Bright Eyes together – the only two survivors from our unit. We came to New Richmond after being sideslipped out, full of secrets and in search of some kind of life. Mal was originally from Roanoke but didn't want to go back. I didn't have anywhere to go back to any more. My mother was dead of cancer by then, my father soon afterwards in a petty suicide. None of the towns we'd lived in meant any more than the others, and I went to New Richmond to look for a place to call home.

Neither of us had much of an education, or a family to help us up the ladder and over the 100 line, but we didn't care. For a few years we tried different things, hoping that something would reach out and grab us. We were entranced with the city, with its possibilities, even when it didn't seem to harbour much more than apathy towards us. It was a house with many rooms, and I wanted to visit every one of them, make them open to me. When I should have been looking for work I walked its streets, delving through its hidden passages until I knew I could live there for ever.

In the end Mal decided that there was nothing much he could do so he might as well join the police. I watched him for the first year, saw him get wrapped into his work, and concluded that the kind of things he was doing would probably suit me too. Suit me better than it did him, in some ways; the trawling through debris and junk, the psychos and streetwalkers, the blood and violence seemed to speak directly to some part of my mind. It looked like fun. The Gap had affected Bright Eyes in different ways, and in my case it was as if I'd blossomed there. Leaving it was like having some essential nutrient removed – not one whose absence kills you, but one which simply changes the colour of your leaves. I'd learnt to live inside fear. The idea of being a cop appealed to that side of me, as did the notion of remaining outside society. I wanted to stand looking in. So I went to the office, proved I could spell at least one of my names, and they gave me a badge and a gun.

I met Henna a few months later, in the depths of a riotous party on 110. Mal had wangled us invites, having met a group of above-the-liners somewhere along the line of duty, and we spruced ourselves up, hopped on an xPress and went in search of fun. I didn't have much in the early parts of the evening, as I remember, and felt conscious of the fact that I was currently bunked down in a nasty apartment on one of 38's more alarming streets. It's possibly my imagination, but I rather got the impression that Mal and I had been invited as performing bears. I responded in the most constructive way I could: by getting profoundly drunk.

By ten I was so wasted I had been officially downgraded to a lower rung on the evolutionary ladder. Some guy in a suit came up, listened to my attempts to string words together, revoked my rights as Homo Sapiens on the spot and reclassified me as some kind of plant life. I had to fill in all kinds of forms and shit. It was very embarrassing.

But then I saw Henna, and got talking to her, and the evening turned out to be fun after all. She was tall and slim, with cool green eyes and an agreeably rangy figure, and even in my state I saw immediately that she was both intelligent and beautiful. She in turn seemed prepared to ignore the chip on my shoulder and whiskey on my tie, and to find at least some of what I said interesting rather than merely aggressive, and at the end of the evening I staggered away with her phone number.

A month later she moved down from 102 to a new apartment we took together on 61 – at first largely financed by her salary. We outlasted the schtupfest, found we liked each other, and two years later were married. Mal was the best man. Henna's parents came, and were polite – icily so, in retrospect – and it was only many years later that I discovered how much they'd hated the idea of her marrying me. I was poor, I was a rookie cop, and I was resolutely not from above the line. All this was their problem, not mine, but they were Henna's mom and dad. One night, not long before she died, Henna accidentally revealed just how much they hated their son-in-law, and I understood for an instant just how much she'd given up to be with me, and how little I'd given her in return. For a moment, just a moment, I had a glimpse of the kind of man I'd become; but then I stormed out of the flat and spent the next few hours with the woman I was having an affair with.

The first three years of our marriage were a contented blur. Henna professed herself happy, told me how she loved me, and so the days went by. I discovered that I could do police work, and that it mattered to me. I was busy trying to get into Homicide. Henna put up with the late nights, the no-shows, the worry that one night I simply might not come back. We talked, we smiled, we went out and did things together. Occasionally we would flare up over something, and argue briefly and bitterly but, in general, the times were good.

But the truth is this: I never really loved Henna enough, not until it was far too late. I cared very deeply, and I felt affection, but even on the day I proposed to her I believed it was not love I held in my heart.

I thought I had known absolute love before, when I was eighteen. Her name was Fhee, and we spent two years together before the relationship blew apart. She had a smile like a cat in front of a fire, and I was so scared of losing her. She was an uncontainable force of nature, a shout of existence with thick auburn hair and big brown eyes; a lithe, running woman who always seemed to be turning and urging me to catch her up. Her skin was sometimes smooth, sometimes rough, and her hair hung in rats' tails to the middle of her back. Making love to her was like a delicious road accident which left you breathless and shocked. Instead of a gentle celebration of considered love it was a function of her whole being, a physical reaction as unstoppable as a sneeze, as elemental as fear.

A few weeks after we parted I ended up in The Gap, because I was angry and unhappy and didn't feel I had anyplace else to go. I was there for over two years, and that period changed my view of the world for good. By the time I came out Fhee was gone. I only saw her once more and that was many years later.

Sometimes it's hard for me to believe that I let a marriage slide because of some idealized first love, something that had died long before; but it's a sad fact about life that you can't always learn from your mistakes, because by the time you've made them you've changed the playing field for ever.

As I got older, I became increasingly haunted by a vision of some perfect woman I believed I was destined to find. In each person I would see only what was lacking, and in every place and activity know the lack. Sometimes I felt I could actually *see* this woman, feel her, smell her. I knew exactly what she would look like, how she would speak, how she would *be*.

I knew when I married Henna that she wasn't that woman, though she should have been. I married her anyway. I married her because she wanted me to, and because I loved her too much to disappoint her. I don't want you to get the idea I had an especially bad time. Henna played a mean game of pool, was very nice to me, and I missed her like hell when she wasn't there. She laughed like a drain, didn't take me too seriously, and had the cutest chin of all time. It wasn't that Henna was bad, or deficient: it was just that she wasn't *her*, and sometimes when I went to meet her I expected someone else. The other woman. The one who would have made me afraid.

The contradictory pulses of guilt and excitement, the feeling of a stranger's lips on yours when you should be somewhere else: somewhere in the gap between those two emotions, perhaps, was what I was looking for.

I never found it. Eventually Angela came along, and after that things were different. I slept around less, and when I did it was with a mean-spirited pragmatism. I loved Angela with all my heart, and part of the reason I was able to do that was that so much of Henna was in her. It was as if there was a version of my wife which I didn't have to be married to, didn't have to have a male-female relationship of any kind with, but could simply love. Angela wasn't a flawed version of some imaginary woman; she was simply my perfect daughter. So much of the love we have for people depends on how they make us feel about ourselves, and Angela made me feel like I was worthy of loving. She would stand in front of me, looking up, and then suddenly just hurl herself upwards as hard as she could, arms stretched out, trusting me to catch her. I'd fold her to my chest, and sometimes as I nuzzled her face I'd be aware of Henna in the background and be able to feel the tangible wave of her happiness and relief.

I would watch her and Angela together, and hear them talk, and during that period feel closer to happiness than any time before or since. I remember one afternoon when we all went walking, up on the Blue Ridge Parkway near Lexington, and Angela found a snail crawling over a rock. 'Look,' she said, and Henna looked, and told her how snails carried their houses on their backs. Angela was entranced, and I knew for sure that was one story which she would never forget for the rest of her life, which she would tell her own daughter when the time came.

For a moment I was truly there with them in the sunshine, in the real world rather than my own mind. Maybe things should have changed for me then, and I could have found something approaching a life. All that really stood in the way was my unwillingness to commit myself. Perhaps I could have learnt how.

Two things intervened to stop it from being so, and the first of these was Fhee.

I was sitting in a bar in the Portal one evening when Angela was four, trawling for information on a sex-related homicide involving someone on 138. The night was young, and I was only slightly drunk, when I felt a tap on my shoulder and turned round to see someone who looked familiar.

The woman grinned, and I realized: it was an older version of Fhee. For a moment I was speechless, and then I forgot all about the questions I'd been asking the dopeheads at the bar.

I forgot about Henna, Angela, the present, everything. For three hours Fhee and I sat, knees and hands touching, competing with each other to remember times now ten years past; and while we spoke we knew they were gone, but it didn't feel as if that made any difference. I felt as if years were being stripped away, as if caustic soda was being poured down drains and pipes in my head which had been blocked for years.

At ten o'clock we bought a couple of bottles to go and took off in my car, driving randomly through the wilds until we came by chance upon Lake Ratcliffe. We parked the car by the shore and walked along the banks still talking non-stop, until we saw a small island and paddled to it through the freezing water. We explored the island, clambering clumsily over rocks in the dark, finding things to look at and enjoy and point out to each other as we had done many years ago.

When we'd worked all the way round we made our way up to the higher ground, and found a hollow, an enclave, a little way down from the top of the island shielded on two sides by the walls of rock. We sat and smoked and drank from our bottles of wine, talking of the people we'd known, the times we had seen, the way the moon glinted on the peaks of the water.

And then we were lying, still talking, but with her head on my chest and my arm loosely around her. The inevitable came slowly and unexpectedly, and we watched it arrive, until our lips started to brush together and our hands moved less accidentally on each other's arms, and faces, and bodies. Bewildered, as old friends, we made love then lay naked and warm, still friends. In a little while, with a calm and surprised enthusiasm, we made love again, still laughing and talking as we always did, and fell asleep wrapped together in the hollow.

We woke an hour later to find the first drops of rain falling on us out of a warm sky. The rain gathered and fell, and we lay in it, arms loosely around each other, laughing and talking in low voices.

In the morning, we walked back across the water hand in hand, and we wrapped the night up in time and walked away from it. I saw Fhee in New Richmond a few more times after that, as a friend, but we never looked back and never spoke of that night, except perhaps in silences sometimes, and in our loyalty to each other; and in the single rose I placed on her sealed coffin after her head was blown to mist by a mortar fired into a restaurant where she was eating lunch, in an attack on a local gang leader of whose existence she had been, and always would be, blissfully unaware.

In my own terms, a final statement on that night was made when I walked into a whorehouse on the 67th floor and placed three bullets in the head of the man who had ordered the attack on the restaurant. But perhaps there were later echoes in all the things I didn't say to Henna, in the days I woke up not knowing where I was, in the fact that in the end not even Angela was enough to redeem my marriage or my life.

The second intervention was the Vinaldi case, which took up most of the last year I spent as a cop. I was a lieutenant by then, and not doing what I was supposed to. It's kind of a habit of mine. I resisted because I need something to be right about, something in which I could feel blessed by a touchstone of morality and rectitude which was missing in every other part of my life.

Vinaldi was only an up-and-coming hood in those days, a long way from the godfather he became while I was on the Farm. His rise was inexplicably meteoric, I believed, unless a large proportion of the police were directly supporting him. I decided that I was going to reveal to everyone, to the whole city, what exactly was going on in New Richmond. By then I had come to distrust the city as much as I distrusted my own heart. Fhee had been dead for three years by then, and my marriage to Henna had petrified into politeness and warmth. Not so very bad, in other words, but not good enough for me. I could no longer remember what I'd thought I wanted, why I was unhappy with what I had. That's when I knew I was really married.

The campaign against Vinaldi was a life-substitute, nothing more, and I pursued it with the zealotry of the damned.

In effect, I tried to set up a secret, secondary police force, operating covertly within the one which already existed. I recruited the few men I knew I could trust, Mal foremost among them. He was a Sergeant by then, primarily concerning himself with prostitute-related homicides in which there was bodily mutilation. He'd seen enough unpleasantness of that kind in The Gap not to be able to stand it in the real world, and was implacable in his pursuit of the guilty. He was also, once I turned him onto it, extremely good at finding out who in the force was helping Johnny Vinaldi make the transition from minor street thug to crime baron. The other men reported to him, and he reported to me. I didn't report to anyone, in the department or anywhere else. I cleared enough homicides and kept the squad in sufficiently good order that no one poked their nose into what I was doing the rest of the time, especially as by then I was enough of a Rapt junkie for most of the brass to assume I was harmless.

I'd taken Rapt on and off since The Gap, but in the last years it got worse and worse as I tried to find something which would clear my head, something real enough to take me back in time. So much of Rapt's attraction to me is the fear it engenders, and I found that I needed more and more of it to keep me sane. A life without fear is no life at all, and at the core of my life, in Henna, there was nothing to be afraid of.

The investigation created its own fears as it progressed, as it dawned on me that something very peculiar was going on. A small number of cops did turn out to be directly on the Vinaldi payroll, but nowhere near enough to account for his exorbitant success. As time went on, it became increasingly clear that his fan club must start near the very top of the NRPD, which I couldn't understand. Things had gone on in the same old way in New Richmond for many, many years; I couldn't work out what would make senior brass decide that it was worth throwing their lot in with one hood in particular.

Mal and I kept on digging, and kept getting closer to the truth, until that final week five years ago. By then, through pure intuition, I could tell the investigation was going to break. Normally my intuitions aren't worth the paper I wipe them on, but this time I knew it was different. I could feel it like a continual vibration under my fingers, and I spent virtually the whole of that week in the office or on the street, barely seeing Henna and Angela at all.

On the last morning I left very early, but not too early for Angela, who came sprinting out of her bedroom as I was on my way to the door. She threw herself up at me and I caught her awkwardly, only then realizing how long it had been. Partly it was because I was away so much of the time, but it was also, I realized, because she was growing up and didn't do it so often any more. For a moment I was truly afraid. If I wasn't careful I was going to miss the last of her childhood, and then what would I have left?

I put her down with a kiss on the head, and called goodbye to Henna as I walked out the door. Perhaps she came into the living room to give me a kiss, to wish me luck with my day. I'll never know, because I never saw her alive again.

Someone had discovered what I was doing, how close I'd come to the truth. They gave the order and that someone came to my apartment that day and dismantled the women I loved. He did it in a way which said they knew all about me, about the kind of things I had seen in The Gap, about what fears still lived at the heart of my life. For the last five years I'd assumed it was someone hired by Vinaldi, but now I believed that it wasn't.

But somebody did it. They did it, and they helped destroy me, but perhaps it was me who added the most damning touch.

At the time when Henna and Angela were being killed I wasn't at work. I wasn't even working. I could have been at home, but I wasn't because I was with another woman, and I was fucking her. Her name was Phieta, and she was the one who eventually came and found me in the warehouse, where I'd run after finding my family's bodies. At the moment Henna was killed I was kissing Phieta's breasts; by the time Angela died I was perhaps down to her navel. I can't be exactly sure about the timings, but they're probably about right. I don't suppose it really matters.

How long do you wait for something which may never come? Do you keep on looking for Oz? In the end does it even exist, or is it just MaxWork, a way of passing the time?

Five years on the Farm brought me no closer to understanding anything. Perhaps I'm not built for answers, am just the product of wrong experiences and bad advice. I can remember one time, when I was fourteen, a rare expansive moment of my father's. He was sitting in our tiny kitchen, slobbing his way through the dinner my mother had prepared. She was at the sink, washing up. I don't recall which house this was in, because they all blur into one, but I remember my father watching my mother for a long while as she cleaned and scrubbed, running his eyes over her tired, slumped shoulders. He turned to me eventually and said these words:

'Remember this, Jack. Masturbation is no substitute for all of the other women in the world.'

And though I loved my mother, and hated my father more than anyone before or since, I fear it was his world view which I absorbed. It's not necessarily the right things, the good things, which make the most impact on your mind. Every little thing, including your own weaknesses, contribute their own little lines of code. Even bad things can be true, and even good advice can turn on you.

I don't eat ice cream very often any more, but I've always tried to follow what the old man said. I've tried to mould my world and not settle for less than what I think I want. To write my own lines every now and then. The old man meant it well, but what he didn't tell me is that sometimes even the best sentiments, the most glorious acts, are not enough. He didn't tell me that the world is simply stronger, and will bend you much more than you bend it; or that for much of the time you will help it.

He didn't tell me that you may get confused, and lose your way, and that help may never come.

I have made my life unavoidable. I did it to myself. While I was Gone Away I think I began to realize there might be something I could do to save it.

Sixteen

I was Gone Away for a long time, at least several hours. I'd never been away that long before, and when I eventually got back I was exhausted, terrified and alone. The return is like waking up from your seventy-fifth hangover in a row to find you've run out of coffee and that American Express have put a bounty on your head. I faded back into life with the vague feeling of having been summoned, and found myself standing in a thick section of forest which was clearly a very long way from the village I'd fled.

I felt guilty at having abandoned Vinaldi, but the truth of the matter was that I could have done no good by being caught. Splitting up was the right thing to do. People don't just do it in horror films to make the movie longer – they do it because it means not everyone gets killed at once. Running had also been the best policy, bad though I was now feeling about it. Vinaldi had been captured, but I hadn't – which meant I was still, technically at least, in a position to do something.

When the guilt subsided I looked around in an attempt to discover where I was. Trees still marched off in all directions, but the ground was rougher than any I'd seen before in The Gap. Large rocks poked out of the leaves and there were hillocks and depressions in the ground. The light was a dim greeny-blue, filtered by the trees. It made it look as if the forest was under water.

I had no idea where I was, or how to get back to the village. My bleary examination of the ground failed to reveal any sign of the leaves having been disturbed from any direction in particular; it appeared that I had just been beamed down out of nowhere.

The first decision I had to make was whether to take any more Rapt. Or rather, since I was obviously going to take some more at some stage, whether I should take it there and then. I could feel a residual buzz in the back of my head and knew that it would probably stay at that level for another hour or so, but there was no telling when I'd come up against something which would require me to be utterly off my face to survive. Decisions, decisions.

'Soldier.'

When I heard the voice I thought I was going to die. All my internal organs twitched at once, as if trying to leap out of a body which they clearly believed was not long for this world. I dropped to the ground in a crouch, darting glances around in as many directions as I could without actually disengaging my eyes from their sockets.

'Soldier.'

I almost didn't hear it the second time, because my heart was beating so loudly. But then the word was repeated again. It was coming from behind me. Naturally.

Using my hands to brace myself, I slowly turned to face the other way without standing up. There was no one there. All I could see was a collection of hillocks, covered in trees, shading off into the darkness like undulating dunes on the sea bed.

'Yes, soldier. Come to me.'

I saw a flicker by one of the hillocks, and had a strange urge to get up, but stayed where the fuck I was. One of the things about Rapt is that you learn to heartily distrust your first impressions. Being in The Gap at all is ill-advised. The idea of walking voluntarily towards anyone you don't know is stupid beyond belief.

'Come, please,' said the voice then, and I saw that there was indeed something standing beside an outcrop of rock about twenty yards in front of me. At least I thought it was that far; the figure, if that's what it was, seemed surprisingly small.

I stared at it, trying to work out what to do. No point in running; if I'd been seen, I'd been seen. I'd managed to outrun Yhandim and Ghuaji mainly because they hadn't been properly into space when I spotted them. Also because I can run like fuck when I'm scared shitless and have a head start. I was absolutely confident that whatever was standing by the rock would be able to catch me within yards.

I stood cautiously, took a couple of steps forward. The figure nodded in encouragement and remained by the rock, waiting.

I decided I might as well walk forward into doom rather than catch it in the back.

The thing was indeed small, but it was only when I was within a few yards of it that the flickering light settled into something recognizable. At first I didn't see a figure, as such, but an area of space which was simply darker than its surroundings – as if its grip on the world was limited to casting a shadow upon it.

Then it resolved into a little boy, about ten years old and dressed in the strange conglomeration of rags and straps which Gap children wore.

He smiled and held out his hand. I just stared at it. Staring seemed to be about the limit of my powers at that time. When I realized he was expecting me to take it I stepped backwards, suddenly sure that this was a trap of some kind, or maybe a hallucination. Gap children aren't insubstantial, like the villagers had been. They look real, or very nearly so. You can see them, and catch them, which is why . . . take it from me, you just can. For this one to look like it did there had to be something wrong with it.

The child didn't say anything, or make any move towards me. It simply stood patiently waiting for me to make my mind up. It was that which made me decide that it probably wasn't a trap – or that if it was, it was too clever for me to resist. I put my hand out tentatively.

At first I couldn't tell when it met the boy's, because his hand was thin and made of smoke; but then it seemed to gain a little solidity and grasped hold of mine. It was like holding a handful of water just above body temperature, and also reminded me, for some reason, of the first time I'd taken Suej's hand to bring her out of the tunnel at the Farm.

The boy turned away from me then, indicating with his head that I should follow. Breathing shallowly, wondering what I was letting myself in for and just how much it was going to hurt, I allowed myself to be led.

While we walked I didn't think of anything, but simply watched and waited for whatever was coming next. Gap children didn't come to strangers, unless they had no choice. I couldn't imagine why this one had come to me, or where we could be going.

It turned out that we were simply moving to the other side of the hillock. There, the child stopped and looked at me. Making a small motion with one of its hands, it turned away again. I raised my eyes to follow his gaze.

There must have been two hundred of them, maybe more. For the first few seconds they seemed limitless, stretching into the forest for miles like pebbles on a rock beach. Then I saw that they stopped more or less where the forest light faded into blackness fifty yards away.

It was a group of Gap children, all standing motionless in blue light. Rank upon rank of them, shadowy and barely there, and all of them staring at me. I heard a soft rustling and slowly turned to see that another group had come silently up behind us, almost as many again.

As far as I could see, in all directions, I was surrounded by silent children.

You never saw more than three Gap children in a group; they came and went in small handfuls. During the war, we hadn't even been absolutely sure they were younger versions of the villagers. Some people believed they were a different style of being altogether. I used to wonder if even the villagers weren't people, as such, but just our way of interpreting some other phenomenon, symbols for thoughts in The Gap's mind – and that the children were different, younger thoughts. They had represented youth of some kind, though; which was why what happened had been unacceptable. I believed that even in those days, as a drugged-out teenager. After Angela I felt it even more strongly.

The stillness was broken by a ripple that passed through the whole group. The ones nearest to me took little running steps forward, until they were right up against my legs. The ones behind pressed closer in, and I was about to scream when I realized what was happening. They were greeting me, and greeting me as a friend.

Silent smiles broke out on grey faces, all directed at me, and small arms reached up to touch my coat and arms. Not a single sound came from any of them, though their mouths opened and shut as if they were speaking. It was like being surrounded by a cloud of moisture which kept resolving and dissolving into hands and arms and faces. There were girls, and boys – some in their early teens, others little older than babies. Coming so soon after the thoughts

I'd had while being Gone Away, their apparent affection was so unexpected as to be almost unbearable. It was as if I'd been brought back from being Gone Away to be shown exactly what it was I was missing.

Or, perhaps, that I could have it again.

After a while the contact stopped, and the group parted in front of me. The original boy led me forward again. The rest of the group was turning that way too, as if preparing to move off with us.

Letting my other hand run briefly over the insubstantial grey hair of the nearest little girl, I took my mind off the hook and decided to follow them to wherever they wanted to go.

At the time I strongly believed that the children would be the most surprising sight The Gap had to offer. Half an hour later I was proved wrong.

We walked through the forest in silence, the boy steadfastly leading me and the others following behind. More than once I turned to check if they were still there and saw a column of them stretching back into the darkness. The ground remained rocky and uneven and, though it was difficult to tell, I reckoned we were gradually moving uphill. A heavy mist was collecting between the trees, white and soft and apparently lit from within.

After a while I began to see objects on the ground, guns and empty ammunition cases. I assumed it was random debris left over from the war, but as we progressed I knew that couldn't be so. Most of the weapons had the US Army insignia stamped on them, but others were of unfamiliar design, and had clearly once belonged to fighters from The Gap itself. A few lay haphazardly, but the majority had been collected into piles round the bases of trees.

Then larger pieces started to appear: mouldy backpacks, broken radios, fragments of larger weapons lying tilted like gravestones in an abandoned churchyard. The children paid them no attention. Larger shapes loomed in the mist ahead, and as they resolved into recognizable shapes I was forced to grind to a halt. The children didn't seem to mind, and watched as I walked open-mouthed over to the nearest shape.

It was a jeep, a US Army light vehicle of the type which was very occasionally used during the war. Most of the time we had to travel on foot, because the majority of the forest was very heavily wooded and the position of trees tended to vary from one minute to the next, but there had been a few jeeps of exactly this type. Mostly they were reserved for brass, and the joke was that the only gear which worked was 'reverse'. I ran my hand over the cold metal of the vehicle's hood, wiping the moisture from it. It was crumpled and bent around a large hole. From the damage and the thick coating of carbon, it looked like it had taken a hit from some kind of rocket launcher.

I looked further into the mist, and realized that all of the other larger shapes bulking between the trees were also vehicles of one kind or another. A couple of hospiVans, a few of the small armoured motorcycles which the villagers had found so easy to destroy, and maybe three more jeeps in various states of repair. I pulled at a hospiVan's back doors, and they opened with a rusty squeal which seemed grotesquely loud in the silence. Rotting pieces of medical equipment lay broken and abandoned in the dark and musty interior. They hadn't been able to use telesurgery in the Gap war, because the signals couldn't make it across the divide, and so the banks of remote surgeons used in normal wars hadn't been available to us. We'd had to make do with the hospiVans, staffed with terrified medics who were all at least as Rapt as we were and driven to vomiting panic at the sight of blood. I could almost hear the screams of the men who'd lain in the van, trembling and crying as people leant over them with shaking hands.

None of the vehicles looked remotely functional, but that wasn't the point. Someone had been travelling round The Gap collecting this stuff up and bringing it here.

It was a memorial, a silent monument dedicated to a war which should never have happened.

The boy joined me, followed by the rest of the children. From the way they stood I understood that we had not yet found what I had been brought to see.

About two hundred yards further on the boy stopped again, and glanced up at me, expectant. I couldn't tell what I was supposed to be looking at. One of the little girls broke from the group and walked steadily until she was standing about ten yards in front. She pointed ahead, then returned.

None of the other children seemed able or willing to clarify the matter further. I walked forward by myself, peering in the direction she'd indicated. At first I could see nothing except the huge trunks of trees, and then my breath caught in my throat and I knew what I had been brought here to see.

It was a gunship, resting on its side between two of the larger trees and looming out of the blue mist as if lit from behind. I walked towards it, mouth open, wondering how the hell the children had brought it there. I didn't know why, but I was sure they had, just as I now understood it had been them who had collected up all of the other debris.

The few gunships which were employed in The Gap were of a very unusual design. Because of the omnipresent trees, they were built rather like a flying wing tilted on its side. The nearest comparison I can think of is of a giant Angel fish; a shallow triangle bulging out to ten feet in width near the front, but narrowing to virtual two-dimensionality at the nose and along the other edges. Observation windows either side of the cockpit enhanced this impression, looking like a pair of eyes. They were there for little more than cosmetic reasons, because flying the gunships through The Gap had been far too difficult for anything other than high-powered warDroids, which didn't need windows to see out of. It was about ten metres tall and painted a dark olive green, with insignia stamped large and black on both sides.

And it didn't look damaged at all.

The children stood in ranks behind me. There was no sign of what they were expecting me to do, so I just did what occurred to me. I climbed the ladder bolted onto the lower wing of the gunship and tugged at the entrance hatch at the top. It opened silently.

I looked down, hoping for some reassurance, but the children had disappeared.

I felt bereft, as if abandoned by everyone I knew, but this must be why they had summoned me. They would only have left because their job was done. I knew next to nothing about gunships, having only set foot in one once to haul out a drunken officer whose so-called expertise was required. He'd tried to bribe me by saying he could get me sideslipped out of The Gap. I threw him out of the ship.

I pulled the hatch wide and climbed inside. The door opened onto a narrow corridor which ran the walkable length of the craft. To my right it gave almost immediately onto a rounded area slightly smaller than eight feet square. The interior walls were of heavily riveted metal and stepping into the control area felt like climbing into a kettle which had been left on a hillside for a long time.

The glass in one of the observation windows at the front was broken, but aside from that the bridge seemed miraculously unharmed. Perhaps the gunship had never seen combat, or at least not been shot down. At the front of the open area was an array of computer equipment and monitors, sparsely covered with leaves. Before doing anything else I carefully picked the leaves up and dropped them back out the window. They hadn't looked as if they were going to do anything, but you can never tell. They're unpredictable bastards, leaves. The bulk of the floor space was taken up by two rows of three seats, with a little more perching space arranged around the sides. The back wall of the cabin was covered with maps and order sheets – we had to rely upon old-fashioned paper a great deal in The Gap, because computer results were unreliable. The computers which ran the gunships had to be furnished with absolutely enormous power, most of which was burnt up in error checking.

I felt almost nostalgic. Every piece of paper tacked there had the war's logo printed in the top right corner. It had been a long time since I'd seen that little design. It brought back so many botched orders and flawed commands, each rewritten by the war's Marketing Department so many times that by the end they didn't really mean anything. What fun the Generals must have had, sitting back in the real world and directing frightened grunts at one remove. It had been the first chance they'd had in quite a while. Once people had started suing each other for bodily harm and property damage during armed conflict, governments had avoided wars wherever possible. They were just too damned expensive, degenerating into a thousand pitched battles in courtrooms. Often soldiers couldn't turn up for important offensives because they were giving evidence in court or consulting with their press agents. The whole thing just became unmanageable.

Not so the war in The Gap. The villagers weren't interested in litigation; they were interested in annihilating the race which had invaded their territory. It was a war out of the old school, and the Generals didn't even have to provide body bags, because when soldiers died their bodies just disappeared. I lost so many friends, and after they died you had about two minutes to remember them before they vanished, absorbed into the fabric of The Gap.

Eventually, I went and sat at the pilot's seat. Okay, so I'd found an old gunship. What now?

The children had brought me here for a purpose, but I couldn't imagine what it might be. I couldn't fly this thing, didn't even know where to start. The control panel looked as if it had been stripped at the end of the war. This machine was dead. The most use it would be to me was somewhere to cower when I ran out of Rapt.

Running my eyes over the grimy controls, I noticed an area where something had clearly been taken. A panel marked 'IQ' lay open, revealing a small space inside. In the middle was an indentation, about four centimetres by two, with rows of tiny contacts along the edges. They still seemed to be intact, for what difference that made.

A breeze blew in through the window then, and I glanced outside. The mist was still glowering around the trees, but all was quiet. This was the longest period of relative calm which I'd ever experienced in The Gap. Maybe things were different now, or perhaps the Rapt was still working. It didn't feel like it. I felt tired and very nauseous – the familiar Rapt comedown. It was probably time to shoot up again, before anything happened, but I couldn't face it just yet. There's such a thing as too much fun. I lit a cigarette instead, thinking that actually there was nothing in the world I wanted so much as a cup of coffee.

I was trying to avoid thinking about Nearly, and Suej, and Vinaldi, and the spares, to find something to occupy my brain while I waited for my subconscious to come up with some probably unworkable plan. Perhaps that's why it fastened so securely on the idea of coffee, on the notion that if I could just have a cup, my mind would clear and I'd be able to think of something.

Coffee. Just give me a cup of coffee. I could smell it, taste the welcome bitterness at the back of my tongue.

Coffee, I thought. Coffee. Then –

Ratchet.

In the pocket of my jacket was an object I'd trekked about for the last few days without remembering it, which was something to do with a computer, but wasn't RAM. I pulled it out.

As I ran my fingers over it I realized that the chip which Ratchet had slipped into my bag sometime during the last minutes at the Farm was about the right size to fit in the slot in the 'IQ' panel. Maybe the number '128' printed on it was a code designation, or even a serial number, rather than a unit of measurement. And perhaps the 'IQ' referred to intelligence, or the central processing unit.

I put the chip on the desk and frowned at it for a while. Then I reached forward and gently slotted it into the socket, with the number facing up. It fitted perfectly.

Nothing happened. I waited for five minutes, finishing my cigarette, feeling slightly foolish. Of course the chip had nothing to do with a gunship. How could it have done? Which left me still sitting in a piece of archaeology, with no idea what to do and with time running on and on. I ground the cigarette butt out on the floor with my boot, abruptly deciding to just get out, shoot up, and go running into the forest like some chicken gone berserk.

'Initial checking procedure completed,' said a voice, scaring the living shit out of me. I glared wildly round the cabin to see who'd spoken. There was no one to be seen, but a small camera in one of the top corners suddenly swivelled its beady eye towards me, and lights came on across the whole control panel.

Then the voice spoke again.

'Hello Jack,' it said.

My brain tried to crawl out of my ears.

'Fuck!' I said, when I could breathe again. 'How do you know my name?'

'It's Ratchet, Jack,' the voice said calmly.

'Ratchet,' I said, as my brain had another crack at escaping, presumably in a bid to find somewhere more explicable to live. I considered jamming my fingers in my ears, to firmly block that route, but then realized I wouldn't be able to hear anything.

'Yes. It's good to see you. I gather we're in The Gap.' With a quiet whirring sound the camera zoomed in on my face. 'Your pupils are pinned. Have you been taking Rapt again?'

'Fuck that,' I said. 'Screw what I've been up to. What are you *doing* here?'

'I don't know,' said Ratchet. 'I assume you brought me.'

'Well,' I said, 'yes, I did. But how did you get in my bag? You were still at the Farm when I left.'

'I was running on a back-up processor. When it became obvious that the events at the Farm were unlikely to have a uniformly positive conclusion, I put my main CPU somewhere safe, so you were likely to take it with you.'

'Why?'

'I didn't want to die,' he said, simply. 'Also, I hoped I might come in useful some day. Why are you in The Gap?'

'Oh Christ,' I said. 'It's kind of a long story. But how come you can run this gunship?'

'That's what I was built for in the first place. Not this ship, but another like it. At the end of the war the CPUs were salvaged. Arlond Maxen bought up a job lot of them. I ended up on the Farm.'

'You were a *warDroid*?'

'Yes. I was.'

I stared at the camera, mind whirling, picturing war-scarred computers running traffic control and electronic toasters all over the country. It could explain a lot. 'Why didn't you tell me? You knew I'd been a Bright Eyes. Why didn't you *tell me* you were here?'

'You didn't ask – and I wouldn't have told you anyway. The last thing you needed at the time was to remember the war. It wasn't relevant.'

'Jesus,' I said. 'That's why you were so stupidly powerful. That's why you were so *strange*.'

'What – compared to you?' Ratchet asked, and I suddenly realized just how much I'd missed him.

Then I remembered the overall position, my global world view at that time, and the mood transformed into panic.

'Look,' I said. 'Strange or not, we need your help.'

Seventeen

It took only a few minutes to give Ratchet the bones of the situation. During that time I heard distant rattlings and whirrings as the computer ran checks on the gunship's propulsion systems and collision detectors. He also tried to make some coffee in the ship's minuscule galley, but the grounds were mouldy and rotten so I made do with a cup of hot water instead. There didn't seem to be any provision for the manufacture of cheeseburgers, unfortunately.

'I have no way of finding these people,' Ratchet said eventually. 'By the sound of it they could be anywhere, and you don't know how you came to be here.'

'Shit,' I said. I waved my hands vaguely. 'Can't we just, I don't know, troll around until we find them?'

'The Gap is infinite, Jack, because the gaps between people are always unbridgeably wide. Searching an infinite space would take . . .'

'An awfully long time. I understand. Hang on – can you trace Positionex signals?'

'Yes. Not from the satellite, because it isn't in The Gap, but I can lock onto the impulses from the unit. Why?'

'Ghuaji may still have the Positionex on him,' I said. 'Let's go.'

I strapped myself hurriedly into the pilot's seat. As the engines thrummed into life I considered whether now might be a good time for taking some Rapt, but in a tiny, tired reprise of what I'd felt so many years ago, I decided I was going to do this one straight.

The hum of the engines climbed and then sank again, as the systems settled into flying mode. And then, like a sleepy movement of the Earth, the ship righted itself, and lifted off the ground.

I have to admit that I whooped. It had been a while. I enjoyed it.

I watched out of the window until the gunship was hovering about ten feet off the ground – standard flying height. One of the control panel monitors winked on, showing a blue dot in the middle of a schematic map of trees shown in cross-section.

'Found it,' Ratchet said. 'It's about four miles.'

'Full speed ahead,' I said, savouring the moment. 'And don't spare the ammo when we find him.'

The ship shifted unsteadily, then seemed to get into its stride. It slipped into a small clearing, then turned on its vertical axis until it was facing back the way I'd come.

'Okay,' said Ratchet. 'I'm going to have to concentrate for a while. Catch you later.'

We started moving again, at first slowly, then faster and faster until the trees were slipping past the window like brown ghosts running the other way. There was barely any sound apart from the wind, and the cabin was eerily quiet. I held on tightly to my seat, trying to avoid being slung from side to side as the ship dodged and wove. I'd seen one of the gunships flying past once, and marvelled at the way the computers steered through the trunks like an enormous fish darting through seaweed.

I'd also seen one crash, so when we reached maximum velocity I just shut my eyes.

Not being able to see was even more nerve-wracking, so in the end I opened them again, and watched white-knuckled as the ship sped closer and closer to the position indicated by the flashing light on the monitor. At one point we swam through a few hundred yards of the Fear, but we were back out the other side before I'd had time to reach for the needle and undo my resolution.

After a couple of miles the light outside changed. The pure blue turned muddy, and I began to get worried. My suspicions were confirmed when I felt a sudden twinge at the bottom of my eyes, like a scalpel being slipped under the lids.

'Oh shit,' I said. 'Ratchet, how far away are we?'

'About half a mile,' the computer replied tersely. 'Why? You want to go to the bathroom?'

'Vinaldi doesn't have the Bright Eyes any more.' Out of the

window on my side I saw brown tendrils of luminescence interlaced in the spaces between the trees. People had thought they were thin branches or shoots of some kind, until soldiers had been attacked by them and gone staggering off with twigs of light sticking out of their burning eyes. Unless Vinaldi was inside somewhere he was in big trouble – as were Nearly, Suej and the rest of the spares, assuming they were here at all. 'We've got to *hurry*.'

'We're approaching the source of the signal now,' Ratchet said, and I could sense the ship tensing itself around me. 'Brace yourself.'

I was already about as braced as i could get, and so I just stared out of the window, searching for some sign of Ghuaji and the others in the murky light. The gunship decelerated rapidly, flicking between the trees with a piscine grace, homing in on the Positionex signal. I pulled my gun out, checked the cartridge. There was a limit to what I could do with it, because if Yhandim and Ghuaji – and anyone else they had with them – really had been taken up into The Gap, then they would have in effect become villagers, and it would need a lot more than a standard bullet to put them down. It would take a pulse rifle, of the kind which was arrayed on either side of the gunship's mid-section. I'd never really understood how they worked, except that someone had once told me that the energy was the same as that generated in an engine propulsion system. It didn't really matter, as long as they did their job. The gun in my hand was just there to make me feel better. It worked – a little. A Jack Daniels would probably have been just as effective.

The web of brown energy outside the window meant visible light might be untrustworthy, so I concentrated on the monitor tracking the Positionex signal, drumming my fingers on the screen. The indicator light was close now, very close. Ratchet slowed the ship to little more than five miles an hour, and I watched the cross-hairs on the monitor bisect the signal.

'We've gone past it,' Ratchet said.

'We can't have done.'

'Look at the screen.'

He was right. We were now the other side of the indicator light. 'How can we have missed it? Turn around – look again.'

Ratchet negotiated the ship in an arc and hovered back over the point indicated by the lock. I watched the external monitors, looking for, well, anything at all. The brown light had dissipated enough for me to make out the trunks of the trees around us, but I still couldn't see Ghuaji. The ship slowed still further, to walking pace, and then stopped.

'We're directly over it now,' Ratchet said.

There was nothing there, but I've seen all those movies and you're not catching me like that. 'Look up,' I said. 'Maybe he's up a tree.'

'I've done that already,' Ratchet said, relaying a feed from a camera on top of the ship to one of the screens. The trunk of a tree, like any other, disappearing up into the semi-darkness. 'There's no one here even on infra-red.'

'Drop down a little.'

The ship descended until the lower fin was resting gently on the ground. 'Oh fuck,' I said then, catching something out of the corner of my eye. 'What's that?'

The thing I thought I'd seen became clearer, as a sheet of the brown light folded away.

Ghuaji's jacket, hanging over a bush.

I swore long and hard. Either Yhandim had worked out that Vinaldi and I had put a tracer on Ghuaji, or the coat had just been left behind by accident. Thinking back, I couldn't remember whether Ghuaji had been wearing the jacket when I was in the village with Vinaldi.

It didn't really matter. It was all over, unless Ratchet had any ideas. I asked him, not really hoping for an answer. It was still disappointing to find he didn't have one.

'The position remains the same,' he said apologetically. 'Except that we have possibly now gone four miles in an incorrect direction. Sorry.'

I kicked out at the seat next to me. I wasn't going to be able to find them, and they were all going to die. Nearly would probably be mistreated a little first, but then she would die, assuming she wasn't dead already. The spares, including Suej, would be taken to whatever fate awaited them. Even Vinaldi, who I now realized I would, on the whole, prefer not to lose as an acquaintance, would be killed. I was stuck in the depths of a forest which stretched limitlessly all around, sometimes in twilight, sometimes in darkness, but always unknowable and unsafe – and I had no way whatsoever of getting out. I leant forward with my head in my hands, eyes looking down at the controls but seeing nothing.

Perhaps, I thought, it was time for some more Rapt after all. Or maybe I should keep it as a little treat for when I'd been here for a hundred years.

'Jack,' Ratchet said quietly. 'You may want to look out the window.'

Something in the tone of the computer's voice made me sit up. The light was blue again outside, and now it wasn't just trees which stood silently all around us.

The children were back.

They had returned, but this time there was no comfort in their presence. Their eyes emanated coldness, anger – though I didn't feel either was directed at me. They surrounded the gunship in a circle which stretched in all directions. I couldn't pick out the boy I'd seen at first, but perhaps he was somewhere in the crowd. They were all there, grey-faced and staring up at me, their mouths open as if they were screaming.

'Are they Gap children?' Ratchet asked, even more quietly. I don't suppose that computers get frightened, but even he sounded pretty spooked.

'I don't know,' I said. 'There's something odd about them. They brought me to this ship. They led me there and left.'

'What are they doing now?'

The children furthest away from the ship began to move, turning so they were facing in the opposite direction. All their mouths shut at once, and then they started walking away. As they got further from the ship others came from behind us to join them. They formed into ranks five across, a column which marched between the trees and into the twilight.

'Follow them,' I said.

Ratchet turned the ship and hovered back up to ten feet in the air. The children didn't seem put out that we were tracking them. Far from it. Some of them started running, slowly at first, and then much faster. They weren't running from us. They were leading us somewhere.

'Okay,' I said. 'Let's pick up some speed.'

Ratchet accelerated slowly, and the children ran faster and faster like a pack of wolves finding their rhythm. Ratchet put his foot on the gas again until we were slipping along at a good forty miles an hour.

We followed the column of the children as they sprinted through the trees, Ratchet working overtime to avoid the trunks while keeping on the children's track. At one point we rocketed over something that looked like the shadow of a truck, and I wondered if it was the ghost of the one Vinaldi and I had entered The Gap in. This impression was gradually reinforced as we surged further through the forest, small hints of familiarity pressing themselves upon me through some sense I hadn't known I possessed.

Then we flew over the village, and I knew for sure that we were going in the right direction. The grey shadows were still running ahead of us, streaming through the huts and out the other side like a river of smoke crushing all before it. Sometimes they seemed to blend into one being, at others to be a countless multitude; but they kept pounding forward, pulling Ratchet and me in their wake.

* * *

'I'm getting some infra-red hits in the distance,' Ratchet said eventually, and I knew everything was about to go down.

'Okay,' I said. 'Rack 'em up.'

'What armament do you have in mind?'

'Everything we've got.'

The space between the trees was greater here, five yards apart in places. This freed Ratchet to increase the gunship's speed still further until everything outside was a blur; but we didn't overtake the children. However fast we went, they were still in front – until suddenly they weren't there any more and the forest all around us was empty.

I shouted at Ratchet to slow down and he did so immediately, our speed dropping so abruptly that I almost ended up moulded to the control panel.

'Where've they gone? Can you see anything?'

'No. But there's a small hill ahead. Could be masking them.'

'Go round it as quietly as you can,' I said. I felt sure there were probably some more technical terms I could have used, but I'd been a foot soldier and I didn't know them. The words 'shoot' and 'run' had been the limits of my tactical mastery.

The gunship inched onwards, and I had a moment to notice that there was none of the dangerous light here and to hope that they had been here all the time. Ratchet brought the ship in close to the bank of trees. The ship vibrated with the effort, and I felt as if I was in the mind of a stalking cat.

But then I remembered: I was in a machine, and we were doing this all wrong. This wasn't some movie, where people somehow don't hear the slicks before they rise up over the trees. 'Of course they can fucking hear us,' I shouted, more to myself than Ratchet. 'Come on – just go in!'

Ratchet seemed to have anticipated the command, and the ship darted round the mound before I'd even finished speaking. We accelerated so fast that the lower portion of the ship drifted beneath us, and we came round on a slant. My seatbelt prevented me from slamming to the floor and I kept my eyes locked out of the window.

In a flicker of an eye I saw Nearly and Vinaldi, both of whom looked as if they'd been nailed to trees. Also Yhandim, who was holding Suej by the arm and staring straight at us. There were a couple of other soldiers in the clearing, one of whom was Ghuaji. That's all I had time to see before the first bullets started hammering into the ship, one coming straight through the window to embed itself in the wall behind me.

Ratchet hurtled the gunship directly over the clearing, and into a tight turn. I realized that I wasn't going to be able to fire out of the window without getting shot, and that everything was now out of my hands.

'Kill everyone you can,' I said. 'Except Suej and the two people nailed to trees.'

The gunship roared as it banked, virtually turning in its own length. Then it tilted forward and Ratchet brought it in low and fast, pulse rifles scything out the one form of energy the Gap villagers hadn't been able to survive. Via the monitors I saw one of the unknown soldiers go down, caught in the back by an orange needle of light.

You're very welcome, I thought.

The ship rocketed past within yards of Nearly and I caught a glimpse of her face; she looked terrified but was still alive. For once in my life I felt like giving thanks to God, but then realized I didn't have his e-mail address.

At the other side of the clearing Ratchet brought the ship into a screaming turn again, this time dropping lower and slowing down. The five remaining soldiers were now running away from us, but still holding combat formation. Yhandim and another soldier each had one of Suej's arms, and were dragging her with them. Ghuaji and the other two were facing us as they ran backwards, firing a constant stream of bullets into the gunship. The noise was like being in a biscuit tin which has been left outside in a violent hailstorm. Bullets tend to make me want to hide, and I wanted so much to just hit the floor, but I knew I couldn't. I had to see what was going on. Glass was shattering all around me, and the air was all ricochets and flames. It was getting hotter, and some part of the gunship was on fire, but I tuned it all out and watched grimly as Ratchet bore down on the fleeing men.

I had time for a brief warmth of smugness – Weren't expecting me to come back in a *gunship*, were you, guys? – and then I saw something bad was happening. The soldiers were darting and running through the trees in a complex pattern, heading directly for areas where the trunks were too close together for the gunship to follow. Worse still, their outlines were becoming less distinct.

'Hurry!' I shouted to Ratchet. 'They're fading out!'

Ratchet couldn't go any faster without killing us both, and concentrated instead on refining his fire; constant needles of pulse energy rocketed out from either side of me and into the darkness. They maimed trees, hit the ground, even perforated falling leaves; but still the soldiers evaded them.

Yhandim was now little more than a flicker, and Ghuaji was going with him. The hands holding Suej's arms were barely visible, but they weren't letting go.

'Ratchet, *you've got to stop them,*' I screamed. 'Or they're going to take her away. *They'll turn her into one of them.*'

The soldiers took a sudden right turn and ran down a steep bank, heading down onto the frozen bed of a stream. The ship wobbled as it tried to follow them, overshot, and crashed through a copse of enormous bushes which clawed and snatched at us. A sudden burst of speed and a spine-tingling slalom brought them back into range again, and with horror I saw that Suej too was beginning to fade.

Nearly and Vinaldi were forgotten, along with the other spares and everything I had ever seen and done. All I could think of was Suej.

I saw her face turn back to us then, distorted with terror and tears. She stumbled and tripped as she was dragged down the rocky slope. She had no idea what was going on. As far as she knew we were another enemy, one that was simply bigger and more dangerous. Maybe she even welcomed being dragged away.

'Ratchet, KILL THEM!' I shouted, yanking my seatbelt off and hurling myself up to the window. I stuck my face out and called Suej's name, shouting it into the trees like a desperate prayer.

She looked confused for a moment, then saw me. For the merest of instants there was something like relief in her face, and she looked solid again.

I saw her ragged blonde hair, inexpertly cut by me back at the Farm in an attempt to make her look like someone she once saw on the television; her pale blue eyes, wide with fear, face slack with confusion and dread; and a summer dress, splattered with mud, but still carrying with it something of the afternoon on which it had been bought.

As she stared at me she tripped, staggering into the space where the remaining shadow of Yhandim ran.

Two bolts of orange light flew from the gunship like angels going home. One went through the space where the other soldier was, and the hand on her right wrist seemed to disappear.

The other hit Suej full in the chest.

'No!' I screamed. 'No! NO!'

Yhandim's hand slipped off Suej's arm as she fell, and he disappeared off into space, the wraith of a smile the last thing to go. I lost sight of Suej for a moment, as Ratchet fought to turn the gunship round. I howled and smashed my fist against the side of the cabin, the other soldiers forgotten, the smoke and noise around me forgotten, the world nothing but a shout of denial.

Ratchet juddered the ship down to the ground and I leapt up

and waited for it to land. I opened the door and fell down the ladder, not knowing or caring if any of the other soldiers were still visible.

When I crashed to the bottom I looked up the hill, my vision blurred, almost unable to go and see what we had wrought. And, perhaps because of the tears, I thought I saw something.

I thought that I could see the children again, standing around Suej's fallen body. The boy was there, and all the others, looking down with compassion in their faces. I stood there, throat clenched, too afraid to move, as they bent over her, hands reaching as if to help her up. Then they started to disappear, but one at a time, hundreds of lights going out until there were none.

I climbed as fast as I could, scrambling over slippery rocks and tangled roots, but by the time I made it to the top of the bank, Suej's body had gone.

Eighteen

In the clearing Nearly and Vinaldi were still hanging from trees, alone but completely uninjured. They hadn't been nailed, only tied. I let them both down, and accepted a handshake from Vinaldi, but the relief in their eyes brought me little pleasure. Nearly looked frightened and probably wanted a hug, but I couldn't provide one. I was all out. Instead I walked away, sat down on a rock and lit a cigarette. My hands were shaking and I could see very little except an image of Suej's face at the instant when the orange light had killed her.

I didn't hear the footsteps behind me, and was only aware of Nearly's presence when I felt her arms slip round my waist. I stiffened against them, but she persisted, and after a while I gave up and let myself be held.

'We saw,' she said. 'Jack, it wasn't your fault.'

I shook her off and walked a few paces, keeping my eyes fixed on the ground. I didn't trust myself enough for eye contact, and at that stage I didn't have the wit to consider that Nearly might be hurting too. She'd liked Suej; liked her very much.

'Maybe it was meant to be,' she continued quietly, rubbing life back into her wrists. 'Maybe it was *better* that way. I mean, if someone wanted her that bad it can only be because they needed her for parts.'

'Do you know where the others are?' I said brusquely. 'David, Jenny?'

'Jenny's been used already,' Vinaldi said, and I looked up to see him standing a few yards away. The right side of his face was one large bruise, and he was standing awkwardly. I guess he and Yhandim had discussed their unfinished business. He continued talking with the air of someone who knew he had bad news that had to be got over with. 'Yhandim told us. They managed to keep her twin alive until she was found, and she was operated on immediately, the day Mal got killed. There was nothing left. The one called David has been taken to another Farm someplace. Where, I don't know. They incinerated Mal's body. The other two spares are dead. Their owners wouldn't pay the ransom, so Yhandim got to kill them. He sounded pretty psyched about that.'

I barely heard the last few sentences. I didn't know what to say, what to think, where to go, what to do. There didn't seem anything large enough, any action sufficiently extreme or futile to express what was going through my head. It was less than a week since we had left the Farm, the spares scared out of their wits but hopeful that they might be able to have a life, become 'proper people'. I brought five and a half human beings out of the womb and into the world, and now they were all dead – except perhaps David, who had been taken God knows where to be thrown back into a tunnel and wait for the knife.

That's what I'd given them. That's what their association with Jack Randall Esquire had brought into their lives, and I'd only been trying to do the right thing. They say Jesus loves me, and I guess I can believe it. I've had weirder relationships – or as weird, possibly. My dad was pretty mean to me sometimes. But not *as* mean, I don't think, and the highs were better too. Maybe Jesus does love me, but sometimes I wonder whether it isn't time for a trial separation.

And this other guy, God – Him I have a real problem with. Someone needs to tell Him to keep His eyes on the fucking road.

'Jack, don't beat yourself up over this,' Vinaldi said. 'I say that partly because you can't blame yourself for everything, and partly because you going non-linear is going to be no help to us in what is still a far from ideal situation.'

'How come you're still alive?' I said. 'How come Yhandim didn't just whack you?'

Vinaldi shrugged. 'I don't know, but I think things are getting fucked up for those guys. When they came through and grabbed me, first they chased you for a while – and by the way, you can *move* when you have to, I'm impressed – then they brought me here and tied me to a tree. The guys had a quiet couple of words with me about the fact I got out of The Gap back then and they didn't, and they slapped Nearly around a little, like they felt it was expected of them, but that was it.'

'They spent most of the time in a huddle over there,' Nearly said. 'There was a lot of shouting.'

'They didn't do anything else to you?' I asked her.

'No. I think maybe sex isn't Yhandim's core interest in life, you know what I'm saying? They just sat there and looked pissed.'

'Maybe Maxen's fucking them around,' I said.

Vinaldi nodded. 'Things are going sour in psychoville, and I think they had to bring you in as part of the deal.'

'Why?' Nearly asked, turning to me. 'They've got all the spares. What is this guy's *problem* with you?'

'Jack knows,' Vinaldi said. 'Don't you?'

I glared at him and avoided Nearly's eyes. The gunship was cruising slowly into the clearing, which gave me something to look at. Ratchet set it down gently in the centre, and extruded the two supports which kept it upright.

Vinaldi looked at it for a while and then laughed, a sound not often heard in The Gap. He shook his head admiringly.

'I have to admit I was kind of expecting I'd see you again, Jack, and sooner rather than later, but shit – that's really overachieving. How did you manage to find a gunship, get it working, and then *fly* the fucking thing?'

'You know my methods,' I said. 'Brute, dumb luck.'

Vinaldi didn't look convinced, but I had nothing else to offer.

'What do we do now?' Nearly asked. 'I mean, it's been a blast and all but I'd really like to get the hell out of here.'

'I've no idea,' I said. 'We can either stay here and have a bad time, or we can have one somewhere else. It's a matter of supreme indifference to me.'

'Jack,' said a voice. Ratchet's. It was relayed from an external speaker on the gunship, the kind usually employed to inform villagers that they were about to be destroyed.

I didn't blame Ratchet at all for what had happened, and strove to keep my voice calm. 'Yes?' I said.

'I can get you out,' he announced, quietly.

'What? How?'

'This gunship is equipped with partial sideslipping capability. They all were – in case the brass needed to get out in a hurry.'

'Yeah,' Vinaldi muttered in the background. 'That figures.'

'It's not very powerful,' Ratchet continued, 'but if you know where you got in we can probably still get out that way.'

'We don't need the full sideslip gear?'

'No. A semblance of cat-ness is programmed into me. It's only an approximation – that's why we need a place where it's happened recently. We should really go as soon as possible.'

'What are we waiting for?' said Nearly, and started climbing the ladder. Vinaldi followed her, but I remained outside.

'I'm sorry Jack,' Ratchet said quietly.

'It wasn't your fault,' I said. 'Just part of the whole big fuck-up.' I looked away for a moment, at the trees, the blue light, the strange world around us, and I wondered again if something had changed. Though I felt very sad, and depressed, and angry, for once I didn't feel frightened. Maybe there wasn't any room left in my head.

'It didn't end as you would have wanted,' he said, suddenly. 'But it was still the right thing to do. You did the best you could for the spares, Jack. Sometimes that has to be enough.'

'Thanks, but why are you telling me this?' I said. 'We're going to have years to Monday-morning quarterback this one.'

'No,' said Ratchet. 'We aren't. I'm going to have to pilot this ship right up to the last second. This time it's really goodbye.'

Great, I thought, as I climbed wearily up the stairs. At this rate in a couple more days there wouldn't be anyone left for me to lose.

A last flickering run in the forest; through endless night, past never-ending trees, buried deep under a sky I'd never seen. I let Vinaldi perch on the pilot seat for the journey, and sat next to Nearly in the back row of the passenger section. None of us spoke, but instead looked out of the window or stared straight ahead into whatever was coming next.

After a while I pulled my hand out of my pocket, found Nearly's, and held it. She looked at me with surprise, then gripped my hand tightly in return.

I didn't know what I meant, what was being said. Perhaps nothing, but it felt better that way.

When Ratchet told us we were nearing our entrance point I went to the control panel. I pointed out the precise spot. It wasn't hard to find: there was still a lingering shadow cast by the truck in the other world.

Ratchet reversed the gunship, plotted his final course and calculated the exact moment at which he should trigger the sideslip effect. I sat down in the co-pilot's seat and strapped myself in.

'Good luck,' Ratchet said, and Vinaldi and Nearly wished him well. I didn't. I wasn't saying goodbye.

Because at the exact moment when the hurtling gunship crossed the line I lunged forward and clasped my hand round the chip under the 'IQ' panel.

I'd decided that it was time to stop letting go of things.

A face full of snow. Pain in my temple. The sound of someone groaning quietly nearby.

'We're back,' Vinaldi said, indistinctly.

I sat up slowly and looked around. We were at the bottom of the slope leading down from the Farm, near the remains of Vinaldi's truck. The light was fading, and I looked at my watch to see it was five in the afternoon. We'd been in The Gap nearly twenty-four hours, impossible though that seemed.

I turned the computer chip over in my hand a few times, and smiled, then slipped it safely into my pocket and went to help Nearly. She was lying spreadeagled on the snow and muttering like a starfish which had been woken up much earlier than it wanted.

'So where the hell are we now?' she said as she flapped snow off her clothes. 'Kansas?'

'About half a mile North of Covington Forge,' I said, and she rolled her eyes.

'Back here again. Fun, fun, fun. Maybe we could go to Detroit next. Hey,' she added, peering at Vinaldi's vehicle. 'Is that the truck you got out here in?' The hood of the truck was so immaculately wound round the tree that for a moment I had a flash-memory of The Gap. It looked like the tree had grown up from beneath, to become part of the car.

'Yes,' Vinaldi said, reaching into the back to pull out a new gun. I guess Yhandim had taken his old one. 'But I doubt it's the way we're going back.'

'You're telling me. You guys really did it the hard way. All we had to do was follow some cat.'

'Stay here a moment,' I said, setting off up the slope.

The cat was cowering in what used to be the control room of the Farm. It ran across the room and into the darkness under a table, so I just sank to my knees and stayed put, hand held out in front of me. While I waited I noticed its bowl over by the side wall. There had been food in it, once. The cat made its way over eventually, sniffed my fingers, and decided I was unlikely to give it a hard time. I don't know how they make that decision, but they generally seem to be right.

I undid the clasp on its leash, picked the cat up and headed for the main door. On the way, I noticed something lying against one of the walls.

It was a piece of machinery, about the size of a car engine but so finely wrought that it looked like a scale model of something larger. It was running, and it answered the question of how Maxen had been able to forge a link back into The Gap. From somewhere he'd laid hands on one of the original sideslipping devices. I thought they'd all been destroyed, but I guess the military isn't like that. They'd keep cigars in Pandora's box.

I put the cat down, and shooed it away. Then I pulled my gun out, slammed a full clip into it, and emptied it into the machine. By the time the ricochet from the last shell had died away and Vinaldi had come running in to see what was happening, it was very clear it would never work again. I felt nothing but relief and the sound of a heavy door slamming shut.

Nearly was standing outside the entrance, stroking the cat's head and looking cold. I walked over to her and picked the cat up off the ground.

'Somebody's taken Ghuaji's car,' Vinaldi said. 'I guess Yhandim and the others got out first.'

'We'd better start walking,' I said.

'You are, I take it, kidding?' Nearly enquired, head held sweetly on one side. 'I mean, like, ha ha?'

'No,' I said. 'And you'd better keep up, or I'll make you carry the cat.'

We set off down the driveway out of the compound, kicking our way through what had obviously been a heavy twenty-four hours' snow. It's impossible to describe the difference between walking in The Gap and walking here. It's like going for a stroll after finishing an exam, even if the world in general is not exactly looking upon you with favour.

We turned the corner into the abandoned road and walked down it, past the remains of the gas pumps and the derelict picnic area. Nearly muttered darkly all the way. I glanced across at the rotted remains of the picnic tables, but there seemed to be nothing there.

'Something's happened, hasn't it?' Vinaldi said, startling me.

'Yes,' I said, taking a deep breath of the crisp air.

'You guys just keep talking in riddles,' Nearly said. 'No, seriously, it's great. Have a good time. I'll just keep walking through all this fucking snow.'

It was dark by the time we reached the main road, and my mood had worsened. I couldn't get the faces out of my head. Having escaped from The Gap in one piece almost seemed to have made things worse. It was as if I'd confronted my worst fear and come out the other side only to discover the world I'd been saved into was fucked, and that everyone I cared about had died while I had been away. Even the landscape looked like an old photograph: irrelevant, creased, dead.

And there was something else, something rising inside me. A need which I knew I was going to be unable to deny.

A need for radical and extreme vengeance.

We walked down the road a few hundred yards, Vinaldi with his thumb held out despite the fact that there weren't any cars. Even the picture of New Richmond's premier 'businessman' trying to hitch a ride couldn't break my mood. Nearly soon picked up on this and stopped complaining. She walked a little to one side of me, taking her turn at carrying the cat, and I sensed her glancing at me now and then. I hoped she wasn't going to ask me anything, because there was nothing I wanted to say.

A car passed us after a while, but wisely resisted the temptation to pick up three weirdos out for a walk in the back of beyond in the middle of winter. Ten minutes later another came by, and this one at least slowed; but then it swished off again, taking its yellow lamps with it and leaving us with nothing except the crunch of our boots in the snow.

Then finally a car did stop, driving up the road towards us and pulling to a halt when it was level. Loud trance country was spewing out of the windows, and four drunks lurked inside. They were all very large, and wore microfibre check shirts. Three sported the kind of beards which make you look like you've glued a racoon to your face. The other's face was so ugly he didn't even need a beard. The driver peered at us, guffawed merrily, and conferred briefly with the guy in the passenger seat. Then he opened his door and got out of the car.

'Well look here,' he said, swaggering up until he stood a couple of feet from Nearly, his legs planted solidly apart. 'What's a girl like you doing out walking with a couple of queers on a night like this?'

'Thanking God I'm not in that car with you,' Nearly quipped, with her unique talent for diplomacy.

'Funny you should say that,' the man said with a smile, ''cuz that's just what we had in mind. Thought maybe we'd try to warm you up.' Behind him, a back door opened and No-Beard in the rear seat put his foot out onto the snow. Meanwhile his buddy turned his attention to Vinaldi and me. 'You two gentlemen can just step back and let us get on with this, or you can get the shit whaled out of you.' He shrugged at his cohorts in the car. 'Think that's a fair choice, don't you fellas?'

'More than fair,' drawled No-Beard. 'Can't no one say more fairer than that.'

The chief turd nodded happily and crossed his arms. 'So. What'll it be?'

'Hmm,' Vinaldi said mildly, looking away. 'That's a difficult one. Too difficult for a queer like me to answer, what with it being so cold and all, so my brain is nearly as frozen as yours.'

There was a pause. 'What?' the guy said.

Vinaldi clicked his fingers, as if suddenly blessed by inspiration. 'Hey,' he said. 'I've come up with another option I'd like to run past you.'

'What the fuck you talking about? What option?'

'The one where I punch your face through the back of your head.' Suddenly, Vinaldi was an indistinguishable blur of movement. Chief turd tried to parry the first couple of blows, but he didn't have a prayer. Vinaldi's fists moved too quickly for me to even *see*, and before anyone knew what was going on the guy was on the ground, blood flooding out of his nose. No-Beard was already halfway out of the car, but I kicked the door back into his face, then crunched it against his leg.

'Also,' I said, producing mine and pushing the barrel hard into one of his eyes, 'we have large guns. So get out the fucking car.'

Vinaldi and I herded them off the road while Nearly climbed into the back seat of the car. Then I got in to drive, and Vinaldi climbed in the back with Nearly because the front passenger seat looked like someone had dissected a moose on it. I turned the car round and Nearly waved cheerily at the check shirts as we drove back off down the road. I stared out the front window into the last of the twilight, and as the lights of Covington Forge began to appear in the distance I could tell that whatever was going on in my head was getting worse.

By the time we were onto Route 81 my head was hurting badly, and I was gripping the steering wheel to prevent my hands from shaking. There was nothing to do except watch the road, and no conversation to drown out the one I was already having with myself.

'What is it between you and Maxen?' Nearly said quietly then, breaking the silence. I didn't answer. 'I mean, I get the sense this guy hates you real bad.'

'It's nothing,' I said, lighting a cigarette. Vinaldi should really have been driving. It took me three attempts to get it alight.

'The fuck,' Nearly said calmly. Her tone very clearly said that she'd been building up to this and was unlikely to stop for animals or small children. 'What you mean is it's none of my business.'

'Yes,' I said tightly. 'That's exactly what I mean.'

'Well it is *so* my business,' she shouted, suddenly furious in that force-of-nature way women have. 'I've got a right to know. Psycho lunatics come slamming into my life, take me beyond the Twilight Zone and completely ruin my shoes, and you say it's none of my business?'

'No one has any right to know anything about my life which I don't want them to,' I said, forcing the words out slowly and clearly.

'Not even someone who likes you?' she said, her voice different.

'Especially not them.'

'They helped you, didn't they?' Vinaldi asked suddenly, out of the darkness in the back.

'I don't know what you're talking about.'

'Sure you do. The kids. They helped you find the ship.'

'What kids?' Nearly asked.

'You didn't see them, I guess, because you weren't there the last time. Maybe just because you don't know about them, or maybe because old Jack and I have got a fair dose of The Gap inside us as well. I think it'd be fair to say that, don't you Jack?'

'Just shut up, Johnny.'

Nearly: '*What* kids?'

'When that little girl – Suej, or whatever – went down, I saw something.' Despite myself, I found I was listening to Vinaldi. I'd thought that last vision had been mine alone, a product of misery and fear. 'There was a whole bunch of children standing round her, Gap children – except they didn't look right. They show you where the ship was, Jack?'

I didn't answer, and Vinaldi took that as a yes.

'You know what they were, don't you Jack? You know why they looked weird? Didn't you see the scars on them? On their necks?'

'Johnny, please don't tell this.' My whole body was shaking now, the headlights on the highway in front of me a Jackson Pollock of red and white blurs against black.

'I'm going to tell it, Jack, and you know why? Because you're full of shit. You go round the whole time with a chip on your shoulder about how badly you've fucked up. You think everything's tainted, that somehow you did something which has spoilt the whole world. You spend your whole time saying to yourself "Well, I've fucked up this life so I'm just going to sit here and wait for the next one." Well you *didn't*. This whole mess is because of Arlond Maxen, and it's not your fault the guy hates you. He hates you because of something you did which was *not* a fucked up thing to do, and *that's* why all those spares died, and why Mal died, and why you're probably going to die too.'

'What?' Nearly shouted, and then said it again more quietly. 'What? Johnny, what are you talking about?'

I knew there was nothing I could do to stop him, so I just kept the car on the road and tried not to listen as Vinaldi told her.

It happened two months before the war in The Gap was abandoned. Mal and I were part of a unit which was very deep in country. North and south don't mean a whole lot in there, but if most people were in the south, we were so far north we were off the compass. I don't know how Vinaldi got to hear of it. A rumour, he said. I certainly didn't tell anyone, and neither did Mal. We hoped no one would believe us.

I think everyone pretty much knew by that stage that the war wasn't one we were going to win. The villagers were too tough, too unyielding. They had The Gap on their side, and the further away you got from the point where everybody sideslipped in, the more inexplicable and terrifying it got. It was like you were going deeper and deeper into yourself, into places you were never supposed to see. Some of the people in our unit had rigged up plastic bottles of Rapt solution by then, and had a constant drip into their bloodstream.

But our orders were to keep on going, and so we did. We crawled, we staggered, we ran – all more or less in the same direction, further and further away from anything we recognized as real. There'd been talk of meeting up with another unit which had been sent this way, but none of us really expected that to happen any more. We couldn't even tell what colour the air was by then; with the combination of drugs and deep strangeness around us the chances of us doing *anything* cohesive or deliberate were absolutely minimal. We could only just look after each other. By that time that was the most we could do. Everything in that world was trying to kill us, and the only sane purpose any of us could find in it was to try to keep as many humans alive as possible.

On the day in question we were hacking through the densest forest any of us had ever seen. The trees grew so close together that for large areas they were touching, and you could be confronted with solid walls of trunks which you might have to journey half a mile to go round. It was so tangled that it was even difficult to think, as if the building blocks of thought were too heavy to manipulate. It was unbearably, swelteringly hot, and we were carrying two of the unit on makeshift stretchers. They'd been injured in a fire fight with villagers the week before. We'd bandaged their mouths up, so they wouldn't scream, but I don't think there was any one of us who couldn't hear their agony in our heads. They stank of shit and blood and skinFix, and one of them had Gap maggots in the wound in his leg. He said he could feel them eating him. Maybe he could, but we left them there, because they were eating the gangrene which would otherwise kill him even sooner than his injuries. Every one of us was cut somewhere, had ragged hand-made stitches spidering over some part of our bodies. We hadn't eaten in four days, and worse than that, we'd run out of cigarettes. Even the Rapt was getting thin on the ground, and our Lieutenant was beginning to panic. He knew that none of us could go on much longer, but we were hundreds of miles away from anywhere. We were less than zombies by then, the walking dead's walking dead. We didn't care who won the war any more. We didn't really care if we were going to survive. We were just going to keep on fighting until we all dropped, and then that would be the end of it.

Mal and I were struggling along in the middle of the line carrying one of the stretchers, and so we weren't the first to see the village. Mal was limping badly from mine wounds to his thighs, and the guy we were carrying was having a very bad time of it. He'd taken a head shot and you could see his brain. I was half-delirious with hunger, exhaustion and nicotine withdrawal, and when I first heard someone hiss that there was a village up ahead I was inclined to dismiss it as an illusion.

But soon enough we realized it was really there, and stopped. The tree cover round the village, now about two hundred yards ahead, was too thick for us to see anything even with binoculars. Faintly, carried through the thick and swirling air, we thought we could hear shouting, and even singing.

Gap villagers don't sing. They simply don't do it. They're not very cheerful people.

The Lieutenant decided to leave one person with the wounded, and that the rest of us should go ahead to check out the situation. He motioned to me to lead us forward. He generally did.

We crawled across the forest floor, keeping behind bushes, sliding under piles of whispering leaves. An insane level of caution had become an unthinking instinct. There was nothing we wanted to see more than some of our own kind, but nothing we needed less than another fire fight. As we got closer the singing became more distinct, and finally we were able to recognize the tune. It was from a song which was getting big airplay just before we went into The Gap, though the words seemed to be different.

Either way it meant they were some of ours, and we hauled ourselves to our feet and walked the rest of the way, Mal and I walking point. I don't know what Mal was thinking – about noodles, probably – but I was fantasizing about cigarettes. I could almost feel the smoke in my lungs. I thought I might try having five at once.

The village was in a large clearing, and from forty yards away we could see soldiers in the remnants of army fatigues. They didn't seem to be doing anything very much, seemed in fact to be wandering around with a glazed look in their eyes. There was something strange about them, and I held my hand back to the others, urging them to be quiet and keep out of direct sight.

No one wanted to be in that village more than me, but I was getting a weird feeling. Instead of going straight into the front, I led them round the side and we carefully approached the village from a different angle. The closer we got, the easier it became to distinguish another sound, beneath the guttural singing and shouting. It sounded a bit like crying, or more precisely, like a number of people crying very quietly.

You didn't see many tears in The Gap. People were either dead or glad to still be alive. I looked at Mal. We turned to the Lieutenant and he shrugged, clearly out of his depth. Then we walked into the village.

The first thing we saw was a little girl. Both of her legs had been cut off at the knee, and she was tied to a board which was propped up against one of the houses. She was crying quietly to herself, her eyes gazing without sight past us into some inner world. As the others stared at her I ducked my head into the house. I nearly vomited when I saw what was inside, and I thought I'd seen everything by then.

When I came back out I felt as if the world had changed, and as if it would never be the same again. I signalled dreamily to Mal and we walked a little further along the path, mouths open against the smell. We could see other soldiers, half-naked, wandering around some of the huts a little distance away, but that wasn't what we were looking at.

Gap children's bodies lay all over the ground, broken across paths and lolling out of the doorways of huts, some little more than babies, others in their early teens. Some were recently dead, others had bloated in the heat until their guts exploded. Many of the corpses seemed to have a distinctive wound, a deep slash across the throat. The dust was crusted brown with their blood.

We came upon a makeshift pen in which about ten children squatted in the dirt. Some were missing limbs, their stumps hastily cauterized. Others were bleeding to death there and then, while the remainder stared hopelessly up at the sky, flinching as they heard us approach. Most of them had been blinded.

The rest of the unit caught up with us then, grinding to a horrified halt, and as we stood staring we heard a shout, and turned to see a soldier pointing at us. He was standing in the clearing at the centre of the village, and it looked as if there were others there. We left the pen and approached him, passing walls stained with splatters of blood. Ten yards away we stopped, and this is what we saw:

About ten soldiers, most naked and dripping with sweat, others with strange scraps of clothes still hung around them.

A small pile of children's bodies, the clearing red with what had escaped from them.

Three live children, two girls and a boy, held down on their knees by makeshift wooden frames.

And in the centre of all this, nodding his head in time to the song which the soldiers were chanting, stood their Lieutenant. He alone of all the soldiers was more or less still in uniform, though his pants were around his ankles. He had his cock out, and was thrusting it in and out of a gash which had been cut across the throat of the five-year-old girl who was being held down in front of him. Her head was held up so that he could see her eyes as he worked. She was still alive.

We stood there for a moment, without moving, as the other soldiers stared back at us. It felt as if the world had stopped.

I pulled the rifle from over my shoulder and shot the Lieutenant in the head.

That moment is there every second of my life. Just as a fact, like my muscles are a fact and the weather is a fact and the colour of my hair is a fact. In retrospect, and maybe at the time, the rifle seemed to swing perfectly into position, to fit so snugly into my shoulder; and as I pulled the trigger I knew, as if my soul was carrying it home, that the bullet would hit the very atom I was aiming for.

That shot is my life, and for that moment I felt like an angel, of sorts: not redeeming, because I redeemed nothing, least of all myself. I was simply under a fate which fell from the heavens and flattened me into the ground. Sometimes when I wake in the night and wonder what has startled me, I think it is an echo of that shot, of that moment, and I wonder if it will ever cease.

Nearly cried quietly in the back of the car. I wished I could reach out to her, tell her that it was a long time ago. I was glad that Vinaldi hadn't described, and probably didn't know, what we'd found in all of the huts in the village. The left-overs. We did what we could with skinFix and bandages, but it wasn't very much. It wasn't enough. Then we left the soldiers there, abandoning them to the forest.

Vinaldi was quiet for a moment, and then I heard a spark and the intake of breath as he lit a cigarette.

'One more little detail,' he said. 'The man Jack shot, the Lieutenant? He was Arlond Maxen's older brother. They were in the same unit, and Arlond made it back out.'

Nearly sniffed, and looked out of the window. She was a bright girl. She'd worked it out. Then in the rear view mirror I saw her eyes looking at mine, and she asked me a question. 'What are you going to do now?'

I barely heard her, because I'd realized at last the Farms' second purpose, that they hadn't been created just for spare parts. The group of men who came to them at night hadn't been sneaking in. One of them owned the whole deal, and the payments made to the caretakers were simply to ensure their silence. I wondered why they'd never come to my Farm. I was hired under a false name. They couldn't have known it was me.

It didn't matter. The answer to Nearly's question still came easily. 'I'm going to kill Maxen.'

'Is that going to solve anything?' she said sadly. 'Is that going to bring anyone back?'

'I'm not doing it in the hope of solving something,' I replied. 'I'm going to do it because I want to.'

Nineteen

We abandoned the car out in the Portal, and returned to New Richmond; Vinaldi and Nearly through the front entrance, me round the back, as usual. Vinaldi returned to his empire to check nothing untoward had happened while we'd been gone, sort through his mail, that kind of thing. I asked him to subtly spread a rumour that I'd disappeared, and he said he'd put the word out. Nearly went home to shower, and realized that she'd in effect been on an unpaid holiday for the last couple of days, so maybe she was going back to work too. I didn't ask her.

I went back to Howie's, and spent a while concocting likely deaths for myself. The most convincing story I could come up with was a drug overdose, which gave me pause. That's not a great comment on a life. I slotted Mal's disk in and got it to hack the name Jack Randall into the pending file on the list of city dead. It couldn't be absolutely official because that required a confirmatory code from the coroner's office, but I made it appear that my body had been found in the Portal. The coroners could rarely be bothered to go out there, and I knew from experience they'd just rubber-stamp it. The notification would automatically be relayed to the Police subnet, and from there the word would spread to the few people to whom it would be interesting. It also gave me pause to realize that all of them would regard it as good news. All in all, it was a bit of a gloomy experience. I was officially a ghost.

Then I turned the computer off, ate a cheeseburger at last, and started drinking heavily. The burger was excellent, and cheered me up no end.

Say what you like, but history is shit. It's dirty, and it smells – with good reason, because it has provided the visceral energy which brought the present moment to where it is. This present is like our bodies: they look so clean, because they're washed every day, but they leave little piles everywhere behind them. Past presents digested, excreted and left for posterity – and our later selves – to smell.

As I sat in Howie's office, in the small hours and alone, I felt as if I was sitting in the midst of a hundred piles of shit, the smell of each subtly different to the others. When I tried to trace where each had come from I got lost. I couldn't remember the steps clearly enough. It was all too complicated. Time to wipe the hard disk and start again.

Howie had left me by myself for the time being, at my request. I was trying to remember when my life had stopped making sense, when the loops got nested so deep I couldn't see beyond them. You never value simplicity as a child because you're always leaning into the turns, wanting to become older and get your hands on all those older things. Your options are limited, and as such, so simple and free. Each day is a simple progression of activities, not fractured with the demands of the future.

There are countless things you can do when you've grown up, so many calls upon your time. You can smoke. You can drink. You can take drugs. You can work – in fact, you have to, because you have to pay bills. Then there are the things you *can't* do. You have to not goof off, not sleep with other people even if they're available. You have to be happy with where you are and what you've got, when the essence of childhood was the belief that there would always be something new.

The addictions and the mandatories take up so much of your time that you can never simply *be*. Every thought and every action is informed and undermined by all the other actions or thoughts you have to forgo. You can find yourself haunted by people and events which never even existed, so surrounded by spirits that the real world shades away. You still search for Narnia, even though by then you're too old to believe in it and it doesn't want you there.

Innocence is the freedom from having to have a cigarette every half hour, freedom from loving someone, freedom from the endless fall-out of bad things which you have endured or done. Freedom from time, and all its passing leaves behind it. The countless smells of shit.

The melancholies of youth are to do with not being taken seriously, and the opposite sex. The desperate, biological exposure of that need; the feeling of being left behind when other boys seem to know about smoking and beer and girls – or when other girls had better clothes, a boyfriend of sorts, and tits. Not so much a feeling of being left behind, in fact, so much as a dreadful fear that one was on a subtly different and less vital curve, one which would *never* bring you into contact with these exciting, contraband substances.

And yet, when I got those things, I realized the truth in the only movie which really scared me as a child. I thought of the time when I saw *Pinocchio* on television: and I remembered the way the film spoke to me even though the animation was archaic and two dimensional. I wonder whether my reaction then was a forerunner of what I feel now, if it was an intuitive pre-understanding that these contrabands really would turn you into a donkey, forever tilling someone else's field. But you run for them with open arms anyway, because that's what growing up is about, and only when you stand tired and wet in the rain and mud, the yoke grown so close that it is a part of your shoulders right down to the bone, do you realize what you have done.

I tried to bend the world, and didn't bend enough myself. I wasted so long looking for someone who would light up the forest that I didn't see what I had. Henna was a beacon who would pull me out of the woods, with a strength in her arms which had been put there by my lack of love. I'd stand in front of her, bedraggled and sad in the discovery that what I'd chased was not worth the catching, and believing that Henna never knew what I was really like because I lied. And of course she understood all along, and loved me anyway.

She's not here any more, so there's no one to pull me back. Pinocchio was rescued, and in time turned into a real little boy. The rest of us stand shivering in the rain, and bray.

Howie believed most of what I told him had happened in The Gap, though he did enquire exactly how much Rapt I'd taken. Then he asked me what I was going to do, and I told him.

'How precisely are you intending to do that?' he asked, handing me a beer. The bar outside was crowded and noisy, but the office felt like it was miles away from all that.

'There's a memorial service for Louella Richardson tomorrow,' I said cheerfully. 'Maxen's going to be there, salving his conscience. He's going to have an uninvited guest.'

'How are you going to get in?'

'I have a plan,' I said.

Howie nodded. 'You want some help with the details? Like where exactly you'd like to be buried?'

I smiled at him, thinking how weird life is. I met Howie when I was asking after a murder once, and leant on him hard for information. He refused to play ball for so long, and so imaginatively, that I found myself kind of admiring him. Then I found myself ending up in his bar when I wanted a drink, and even brought Henna and Angela a few times. Now he was the only person in the world prepared to help me, however ridiculous my ambition. Vinaldi had made it clear before leaving that he was having no part of it. His argument was with Yhandim and the others, not Maxen.

'No,' I said to Howie. 'But thank you.'

Howie shrugged, drained the rest of his beer.

'Good haircut, by the way,' I said.

Howie ran his hand ruefully through his hair, which was spiking considerably more than usual. He looked like he had a blond hedgehog sitting on his head. 'The fuck it is,' he said. 'But I've got a detailed and well-thought-out plan.'

'What's that?'

'I'm going to firebomb the fuckers. That'll teach them that when I say "just a trim" I mean it.' He explained a theory of his that hairdressers sprayed some chemical on your head which made your hair look longer than it really was. When they asked you if they'd taken enough off, you always looked in the mirror and said no, take a little more. Then the moment you left the shop, all your hair shrunk back to its normal length again, making you look like you'd been designed for cleaning round the U-bend of a toilet. You couldn't blame them, because you'd told them to take more off, and they'd achieved their real aim of making every man look a complete fucking idiot. It was a good theory, and I applauded him for it.

Howie stuck around for a little longer but in the end headed back to the bar in search of pepperoncinos. I sat in the glow from the lamp and cleaned my gun for a long time. It didn't really need it, but it seemed like the thing to do. Then I got a couple more cheeseburgers sent through and munched on them instead.

Later, I heard a knock on the door behind me and turned to see Nearly standing there with a bottle of wine and two glasses.

'I'm not going to try to talk you out of it,' she said. 'I just thought I'd make sure you went off to certain death with a hangover.'

'You look nice,' I said. She did. She was wearing a long dress, and when I ran my eyes over the pattern I realized it had to have come from the same store where Suej's first and only piece of clothing had been bought. I started to say something, but she rode over me, the words coming out in a rush.

'Actually, I lied. I am going to try to talk you out of it, and this is how I'm going to start. Jack, don't do it.'

'Sit down, Nearly,' I said. She came and perched on Howie's chair, placing the glasses in front of her on the table. She left the bottles there for a moment, and when she saw that I wasn't going to open it, reached forward to do it herself. She tossed the cork away and poured two glasses, filling them right to the top. Then she lit a cigarette, sat back in her chair, and looked at me.

'So?' she said, after a silence. 'What are you going to tell me? That Maxen deserves to die, and that you're the man with the God-given task of making sure he does?'

'There's no point in us having this conversation, Nearly.'

'There isn't if you're just going to sit there and patronize me. I can get that from clients.'

'So why aren't you working tonight?'

'Because I don't fucking feel like it, okay? You're not big on explaining your motivations. I don't have to tell you jack shit.'

I sighed. 'It's late, Nearly.'

'Drink some wine, dickweed,' she said, and her eyes flashed dangerously. I was actually a little frightened of her. Having her in the room, in this mood, was like being corralled with an interesting but imperfectly-trained wild creature.

'I don't want any,' I said.

'Drink it,' she said sweetly and with utter seriousness, 'or you're not even going to make it through to tomorrow morning.'

I'd finished my beer. It was simpler than walking to the fridge to get another one. I picked up the glass and drank a mouthful.

Nearly winked at me humourlessly. 'Great,' she said. 'The training session's going well. It's almost like you understand every word I say. How long before I convince you that trying to kill Maxen is a stupid thing to do?'

'You don't understand.'

'So explain it to me,' she said, and now her face was different again. Open, vulnerable: the face of someone who was genuinely trying to see into my mind.

'I should have done it a long time ago,' I said. 'It's the only thing that makes sense. It's either that or keep running for ever.'

'Bullshit,' she screamed, catching me unawares again. The hubbub from the bar in the background seemed to dip for a moment then, as if her voice had carried all the way out there.

I shrugged. 'That's the way it is.'

'So explain it to me properly,' she said. I looked away irritably. '*So explain it to me*,' she repeated, implacably, and then a final time at wall-shaking volume. 'SO JUST FUCKING EXPLAIN IT TO ME.'

I found I was talking then, without meaning to.

'The brain's a mistake,' I said, and she snorted derisively. 'It's an evolutionary disaster. The mutations bit off more than they could chew. Yeah, we can oppose our thumbs and make marks on paper, but along with that came gaps and interstices, horror pits and buried emotions, concentration camps and men like the Maxens. They're created by the fact that the real world and The Gap just never got along.'

'Jack, I think too many slices of processed cheese have addled what's left of your brain. You're going to have to unpack that for me or I could go away thinking it's just meaningless bullshit.'

I wasn't even talking to her by then, I don't think. I was talking to myself, or perhaps to Henna.

The genes with their random quirks created the human brain like a child building a MegaMall from a kit. It looks like a plane, it sounds like a plane, but don't for fuck's sake try and fly in it. In the wings and the engine, in the hold and the seats, there are parts which don't quite fit together. Screws which weren't tightened enough. Things fall through the gaps and don't quite go where they should. Doors swing shut in the wind and suddenly you find yourself not recognizing anything you feel, running on collapsing code, and not remembering what it meant.

We live in huge hotels, full of hundreds of shifting rooms. Our emotions are the tenants – some fleeting, short-term, others long-term residents. Some treat the house well, some don't; some lock the doors and windows after them, others leave them open. A good tenant will leave the key under the mat when he leaves, so that new people can come in every now and then. But sometimes something will happen which seals the doors shut, leaving you with whatever happens to be inside.

I've had a long run of bad tenants, the kind which spill stuff over the walls and put cigarette burns in the carpet and leave the windows open for the wolves to come in. Sometimes they go, without paying their rent or cleaning the kitchen; leaving the mess for the next bunch of barbarians to build upon. Sometimes they stay, glowering in corners, refusing to forward people's mail and fighting spring-cleaning to the death.

I'd like to believe there's some good tenants in there too, but they've been forced up into the attic, hiding in crawlspaces and never coming out. I never get to see them because there's too many thugs at the front door who won't let me in.

I've never been a very strong landlord, and I felt it was finally time to collect some rent. I needed to evict some of these guys, have my life returned to me. Finally closing the book on Arlond Maxen seemed like the only way of getting the house keys back.

I stopped talking then. There didn't seem to be any more I wanted to say. Nearly stared at me, her eyes wide open.

'Uh-huh,' she said, eventually, slowly nodding her head. 'I suppose that was kind of interesting. Verging on the content-free, but interesting. I guess you had some slow evenings back there on the Farm.'

I shook my head at her. I didn't know what I was trying to say, and didn't want to have to try to explain any further. I was just marking time until tomorrow, when I could go and do what I had to do. I wanted to spend the intervening time just staring into space and cleaning my gun, doing a final stock-take; maybe some Annual General Meeting for Jack Randall Inc, where all the unfinished business was neatly wrapped up just in case the proceedings were adjourned for ever.

Nearly put her head on one side and peered at me intently. 'It occurred to you that maybe you're not the only one whose life is a bit fucked up, Jack?'

'It's all in place,' I said.

'No it *isn't*,' she said. 'There's nothing in place. You have to listen to the past just as much as you fucking want to, no more. Things can change. Okay, so the spares died, Suej died – I'm going to miss her too. It wasn't your fault. You did what you could, and it wasn't enough. Sometimes it isn't. Forget them, and forget Maxen, and forget everyone else. There's new stuff out there to have.'

'Like what?' I said. I wasn't asking in the hope of an answer, just putting words out into the air. Nearly paused for a moment, then abruptly refilled her glass.

'Well, like me,' she said, as she put the bottle back down. I stared at her, and she shrugged. 'I mean, I'm beginning to think I must kind of like you or something, notwithstanding the fact you're a fuckwit. Otherwise why would I be sitting here listening to you talking psychobullshit, when, as you charmingly point out, I could be out there earning money?'

She looked up at me, chin thrust out belligerently, and for a moment I really saw her; saw the intelligence in her face, the clearness of her eyes, the perfect, animal way in which she sat in a chair. I didn't see her as a friend, or a woman, Howie's employee or someone's daughter. I saw her as Nearly, as an inexplicable, inimitable, irreplaceable *person*.

And then, just as clearly, I remembered sitting with my back to the wall of a room on 72, five years ago. I made a promise to Henna's body. I have broken so many other promises, so very many. To keep that one is the least I can do.

I shook my head, and Nearly lunged forward and grabbed me by the lapels of my jacket. Her grip was surprisingly strong, her face livid and eyes on fire. She'd known exactly what I was thinking.

'She's dead, Jack, and by the sound of it that *was* your fault. It was your fault because you wouldn't leave something alone, and now you're going to do exactly the same thing and this time it'll be you who gets killed. You think she would have wanted that? You think that's going to make things better?'

'You have no right to use Henna like that,' I shouted, prising her hands from my jacket. 'It's none of your fucking business and Vinaldi shouldn't have told you about her.'

'Fuck Henna,' she spat. 'Henna's dead. I'm not speaking on her behalf. I'm speaking for me. I don't want you to die.'

'I don't care what you want,' I said, and heard the words drop like coins into a well without bottom.

'It's because I'm a whore, isn't it?' Nearly said. 'Because I sell it to earn a living. We all like the idea of a woman who enjoys fucking but we don't want them if they've ever been with anyone else, right?'

'It's got nothing to do with that,' I said quietly, and I think I was telling the truth.

'Yeah, right,' she said, slugging the last of her drink down. 'Well, hey, Jack – finish the rest of the wine by yourself.' She stood up, snatched her cigarettes from the table, and then looked down at me, utterly furious. 'Maybe it's better you go off and play tomorrow after all,' she said. 'Otherwise that's all it's going to be, Jack. Finishing the wine by yourself.'

As she walked towards the door I stood up, suddenly afraid.

'Don't go like this,' I said, reaching out to grab her shoulder. She slipped out from under my hand and kept going. 'Can't we be friends?'

Her face was hard, and she looked like someone I'd never seen.

'"Friends" is no use to me, Jack. I've got friends. I don't need any more. What I need is someone who'll light up the woods so I can find a place to stay.'

I blinked. 'What made you put it like that?'

She shrugged. 'Who gives a shit? It's just a phrase, like "Hey, we can still be friends."' Her eyes ran over me, as if capturing something. When she spoke again her voice was calm and dull. 'No, I don't want to be your friend, Jack. You'd be a lousy friend. For a start, you're going to be dead, and dead people never return your calls.'

She grabbed my face in her hands, and kissed me hard on the lips. It wasn't tender, or forgiving. It was fierce and uncompromising, the flip side of a punch in the mouth.

'Goodbye and fuck off,' she said, and walked out of my life.

I sat in Howie's office until six, then went through to the bathroom. I stood in front of a mirror and shaved, and when I was finished with each item I threw it into the trash. Shaving gel, razor, comb, toothbrush. I examined my reflection for a while. I looked like an alien.

The bar droid told me Howie had gone to bed. I got it to serve me a coffee and drank it sitting at the bar.

The room was almost empty, just a lone couple sat at a table in the corner, come in for an early coffee on the way to work. They were holding hands, and something told me they'd just spent the night together for the first time. The girl's hair was still wet from its morning wash, her normal routine disrupted; his cheeks were pink from using a razor found lying around in her bathroom, feeling oddly unsettled, wearing yesterday's shirt and smelling of someone else's deodorant. Neither of them seemed quite sure what to say, how to be, as they struggled to deal with suddenly widened perceptions of someone they saw every day at work. Confused memories of the night before, of the shock of so much skin.

The cat I'd pulled from the abandoned Farm was also there, curled up asleep in one of the corners. I was glad it had found a home. It would never want for pepperoncinos, at least.

A little while later the young couple stood up, hesitated, and then held hands as they walked out the door.

I thought about leaving a note for Howie, but I couldn't find any paper and I didn't know what I would say. Seven o'clock, I left the bar and walked to an xPress elevator. There was very little life on the streets. The only place doing business was a Chinese restaurant with a variety of tired-looking dishes sitting in hot plates in front of the window. It was called the Happy Garden, but it didn't look like a Happy Garden. It looked like a Pretty Miserable Garden. It looked like the kind of place Schopenhauer would have enjoyed during the period when he had a bad urinary infection.

At 100 I showed my fake pass to the guys standing there. Their eyesight wasn't as good as the one who'd stopped me with Vinaldi, or maybe they just cared less; either way, I got through and made it up to 104.

Golson was still half asleep when he opened the door, but woke up rapidly on seeing me.

'Woh, big dude,' he said. 'You're turning into a regular feature.'

'You got someone with you?'

'Yeah,' he said, smirking. 'Sandy came back for some more.'

'Get rid of her,' I said, shouldering past him into the apartment. It was beginning to feel like a second home. Golson scuttled after me as always, making small and unimportant bleats of disagreement.

'Hey, man – I can't do that. I promised to take her to the Memorial as my guest. That's why she came with me last night. She kept her side of the bargain – she ain't going to leave now for no man.'

Sandy was sitting up in bed as I entered, looking fetchingly dishevelled. I twitched the sheet off, then pulled out my gun and racked it.

'Sandy, go home,' I said. 'There's a danger this man may only be after your body.'

I walked into Golson's kitchen and starting nuking some coffee. It was cinnamon apple, but I reckoned if I smoked heavily enough I could mask the taste. Golson stayed in the bedroom and watched with bewilderment as Sandy gathered up her clothes and left in a way which underlined her chagrin, slamming the door hard enough to shake the city to its foundations. I smiled. Everybody I knew seemed cursed to do the same thing again and again: the if-then loops go on and on until you find some way of breaking out.

I was sipping my first cup when Golson stomped in. 'Hey listen, dude,' he said petulantly. 'That was beyond. I mean it. Okay, so I got laid already, but the service starts at nine and how am I going to mobilize someone foxy enough to be my guest by then?'

'You already got a replacement guest,' I said.

'Oh yeah?' he said, hopefully. 'Who?'

'Me,' I said. 'Get dressed.'

Twenty

The great and the good, the talented and the important, the cream of New Richmond's gene pool.

No, actually. Just the richest. I guess some people of merit probably made it in through the side doors, invited to make the memorial service even more appealing to the media circus. The autocameras and talking heads were kept firmly away from the event itself, however, and buzzed excitably around the lobby on the 200th floor. I'd like to think they were kept out through respect for the dead, but I suspect it was just to pique their curiosity. The cameras, droid-operated flyers, seemed to be remaining calm, but their human front people were almost exploding with excitement.

Everybody else was led up an enormous spiral staircase all the way to 203, where we stood buzzing in a room the size of a small European country. This, we were given to understand, was the chapel's anteroom. It was two storeys high, and the ceiling had been entirely painted in the style of the Sistine Chapel. Storyboarded by the West Coast's finest, it celebrated the exploits of that most durable of action heroes – God. Religion never really went out of fashion for the rich, maybe because it's the easiest pretence at humility they could find. All the people around me, themselves the most well-heeled in New Richmond, stood trying not to be obvious about the fact they were wondering how much it cost to have a mile-square renaissance cartoon daubed over a ceiling – proving that pretence was all that it ever was. The room could dwarf five thousand guests, and so the four or five hundred who stood huddled in the middle were left in absolutely no doubt as to their relative status to the person who owned it.

I stood with Golson to one side of the group. It wasn't that I particularly valued his company; there just wasn't anywhere else for me to go. I didn't have a plan of any kind. I was waiting to see what I would do.

The area around us was alive with a low murmur of anticipation. Golson was utterly entranced, his eyes flitting over the assembled company with a fervour that seemed almost religious itself. These, I could tell, were his gods; the wrinkled old and glowing young, all slick with money and four-dimensional with status. CostSlots were sewn into almost every sleeve, trumpeting the garment's worth to anyone who gave a shit. Most people, it appeared, gave a shit. A very few of them had cannily eschewed these public announcements of value, and I could see the other guests trying to work out whether this was because their garments were a little cheaper than theirs, or even more expensive. From the furrowing on some of the brows around me, I could tell this wasn't an easy judgement to make. I don't mind the rich, really I don't. It's just that they're so *boring*.

Getting through security had been easy; there'd been an anxious few moments while I wondered whether my picture might have been circulated around the security staff, but no one gave me a second glance. I was accompanying someone who had a bona fide invitation, as his guest, and I was also dead so I was unlikely to be a threat to anybody. Golson was still rather unhappy about the turn of events, but I'd reassured him that far from damaging his reputation, it would probably double his chance of scoring at the reception after the service. He seemed fairly cheered by this until he worked out what I meant.

I didn't see anyone in the crowd who looked like causing trouble for me, nor did I expect to. I'd made Vinaldi promise to keep his head down until the afternoon. Maxen wouldn't be showing himself before the service proper, where he was apparently slated to deliver a eulogy to the dead girl; and Yhandim and his colleagues were far too ragged-looking to be allowed near centre stage of such an event. I had little doubt they were lurking somewhere in the sidelines, but so long as I stayed in the crowd I wasn't too worried about them. Yet.

After half an hour I noticed something going on at the far edge of the group, and saw that Yolande Maxen was leading the woman whose image I'd seen talking on Golson's invitation. This was Forma Richardson, I gathered, mother of the deceased, and she was being given a tour of the guests. I lit a cigarette, to the general irritation of everyone around me, and watched as the small entourage made its way through the crowd. Golson had disappeared by then, presumably working the room.

Something about Yolanda Maxen's face struck me as off; instead of the triumph I would have expected, or the public display of sympathy, her features seemed dead and hollow. Mrs Richardson, for her part, seemed completely unaware of the identities of many of the people around her. Grief, possibly, or maybe the Maxens had primarily invited people they wanted to cow, rather than anyone who had any genuine relation to Louella Richardson. When I saw one middle-aged couple turn away in distaste after shaking Forma's limp hand, obviously trying not to let her misery intrude on the exciting time they were having, I looked away and gazed up at the ceiling instead.

Directly above me was a representation of some biblical event or other. It meant nothing to me, nor probably to anyone else in the room. It was yesterday's box score. We used to have religion but now we had code, both signifiers of events which happen in worlds which are just out of sight. We used to believe in an invisible God; now we put our faith in streams of electrons fizzing through spaces which are too small to see. Once again our understanding is handed over to the unperceivable, as if there is some fundamental need in humanity which requires the inexplicable to be at the heart of our lives, which requires that our destiny be shaped by intangible forces. Maybe we need places with no paths to them.

God, code, our own minds. Maybe we just never read the manuals properly.

As I stared up at the ceiling it shaded away, and instead I saw a series of images which came unbidden into my head. Henna's face, and Angela's; and then Shelley Latoya. She took the longest to fade, a memory of the way her eyes had slipped across to me when I'd given her a cheap way out of the guilt she felt at taking her dead sister's money. It was replaced by a girl I'd never seen in real life: Louella Richardson. Strangely the image I had of her face was different to that in Golson's photograph, as if taken in altered light.

Finally I saw Suej, not sad but laughing.

A low grating sound heralded the opening of two enormous doors at the far end of the room. Naturally the entrance to the chapel was as far as possible from where we were standing, to make once again the point of how large the room was. It was surprising, in fact, that we hadn't all been shown some other humbling treats yet, like sofas fashioned from silicon or a scale model of the Milky Way in diamonds. Maybe that would come later, after the service. If so, I would never get to see it.

Because as I fell in step with the other mourners and started the long trek across the room, I knew what I was going to do. I was going to pull the veils from Maxen in front of his congregation, to show that even men made of points of light are capable of sin.

On the way across the anteroom I spotted Chief of Police McAuley amongst the crowd, and hung well back. He, of all the people there, would recognize me on sight. Thankfully, he was too busy smarming some dignitary to look in my direction. I stayed well at the back of the room when we entered the chapel, and sat on the end of a row. The chapel was dark and surprisingly small, and the guests would fill it to capacity. In front of me I could sense scuffles as people fought as politely as possible for the best seats, but the sound meant little to me. I seemed to be retreating inside my own head, into some inner space where all was quiet.

I was going home. Perhaps all it ever takes is a little effort, a realization that you've spent too long living in the front of your mind, and that you can throw the doors to the back room wide. I knew that I had made the right decision, and that if my timing was right, I might even be able to carry it through before I went down.

As I waited for the service to start, my eyes wandered over the chapel walls, which were dark with stained and polished wood. After so many years of running, I was surprised to find myself, at the last, in a place of such peace. The columns in the room had been made out of single tree trunks, varnished but left irregular and true. Probably no one else in the room understood that this chapel had nothing to do with Christianity, and was instead a tribute to the secrets Maxen had learned during his own time as a soldier in The Gap.

Sure, there were crucifixes and icons in all the right places; but the only illumination was from the thousands of candles which stood in rows on every surface, and the light they gave off, soft and buttery, could be a reminder of only one place. All it needed was a few blue lights hidden in corners, and everything would have been perfect.

Everyone was seated eventually, and the service started. I was remembering times spent crouched behind trees, in the calm before fire-storms, every fibre of my soul attuned and listening for the music of life and death. A small choir sang something old and well-meant, probably the choice of Louella's mother: the archaic, carved phrases echoed round the chapel like bewildered birds trying to find their nest.

Louella's brother stood up then, and made his way to the lectern. He gave a short speech, with due emphasis on how productive a member of society his sister had been. His words were perfectly relayed around the room by the PA system, and the old woman sitting next to me started to cry, messing up the sleeve of her dress. It didn't really matter, she wouldn't be wearing it again. I couldn't believe she'd known Louella, and I wished Nearly was with me. This was what I'd been trying to tell her the night before, that our bodies are pushed into action by emotion they have no control over, and I had no patience with it any more. The real world had to learn how to deal with The Gap, or nothing would ever make sense.

Then there was more singing from the choir. At the end of it I heard stirring from the people around me. A glance at the order of service told me why: the big moment was approaching, when New Richmond's nearest stab at deity would reach down his hand and bestow the largesse of his ready-to-wear compassion. The guests sat up straighter, peered forward into the gloom, and as the final phrase of the music died into nothing around us, a figure stood at the front of the chapel and made his way to the lectern.

Like everyone else, at first I did nothing more than stare. Maxen looked stern, and distant; but that's the way we like them. We're all just looking for Daddy, and sometimes fathers are unkind. He was of medium height, wearing a dark suit, and his greying hair was swept back from his temples. The glasses he wore made his eyes oblique, as if even in the flesh you couldn't touch them, as if he'd always be behind a screen. There was something so lustrous about his power and wealth, even from that distance, that for a second I was taken aback, made to wonder whether people like me could ever really affect the world of someone like him.

The moment when I stood up reminded me of something, as if the echo of a shot I'd once fired had finally rebounded off all the mountains in the world and come back into my head for good. I guess people assumed it was part of the memorial service, at first, or that a guest had simply lost his mind. I walked with my head up and shoulders back, straight down the centre of the aisle.

The chapel was utterly silent, and my footsteps clapped like a slow knocking on some heavy door. By the time I was halfway there I began to hear murmurings, and sensed movement in the shadows over to one side of the chapel. I relied upon my prediction that the guards would not risk sending a shot off across the chapel when New Richmond's finest citizens were hunkered down on each side, and kept on walking, my eyes fixed on Maxen, his staring back at me.

When I was a few yards away I pulled out my gun, and the atmosphere behind me changed immediately. By then it was too late. Two short paces put me a couple of steps below Maxen, the muzzle of my weapon pointed squarely at his forehead. There was definite movement in the corners of the room then, as security men came out of nowhere on the peripheries of the chapel, and rifles appeared on their shoulders. They stayed out of sight of the guests, but I could feel the red points of laser sights all over my back. They had a clear shot at me, but were waiting for a signal. Like everyone else in New Richmond, Maxen had them well trained. Added to which, if they shot me there was a real danger the shells would pass through my body and make it into Maxen, travelling much slower by then, and doing a lot of damage to their lord and master. Not a risk any of them was prepared to take.

'Tell them,' I said to Maxen. 'Tell them that if anyone shoots I'll have more than enough time to spread the back of your head all over the wall behind you.'

Maxen stared down at me, his face impassive. Though only five years my senior, he looked as if he was made out of tectonic plates. His face was tired and stoic, and reminded me of something I'd seen in his wife's.

'You're going to shoot me anyway, Randall,' he said. 'So what difference does it make?'

'No,' I said. 'I'm not going to shoot you. I was going to, but instead I'm going to do something worse. I'm going to tell these people a little story, and then I'll let you live.'

'Then you'll die.'

I shrugged. 'It happens.'

Maxen flicked his eyes to the corners of the room and held his hands out. I walked the remaining steps, my gun still held on Maxen's face, and turned to face the congregation.

In front of me were five hundred pairs of eyes, all unblinking. I grabbed Maxen around the neck and held my gun up under his chin. It fit there neatly, as if it had been waiting for this moment most of its life. Perhaps we all had – me, Maxen and a gun. The crowd gasped quietly, too shocked to do anything except let their bodies unconsciously react. My head was filled with white noise, as if the circuits were burning out.

'Louella Richardson wasn't killed by accident,' I said, trying to make it as simple as possible. The microphone picked up my voice and sent it ringing out around the room. 'She was killed for fun. She was killed by a man hired by Mr Maxen.'

I don't know what I was expecting, but it didn't happen. The room was utterly silent. The eyes kept staring up at me, but I could see no change in their expression. Maxen stood stiffly by my side, the shaved underside of his chin smooth against my wrist.

I started again. 'This same man killed four other women, and some friends of mine. But the only one who lived above the hundred line was Louella, and so that's why you're here today. Not because Arlond Maxen gives a shit, but because he's guilty. It's his fault that they all died and he thinks that if he does this it will cover the smell in his head.'

Still nothing. I stared down at the faces, wondering if I'd started speaking in some foreign language by mistake. Nobody moved. There was no scandalized buzz, or indeed a buzz of any kind. This didn't seem to mean anything to anyone.

Bewildered, I let go of Maxen and leant on the lectern. I opened my mouth to speak once more, but nothing came except this, with a dawning white light in my head.

'And five years ago, he had my wife and daughter killed.'

Only then had I realized, and I found that after the realization came, I didn't have anything else to say.

'Nobody gives a shit, Jack,' said a voice, and I turned to see where it had come from. There, sitting on the end of the sixth row, was Johnny Vinaldi. 'Henna, your guys, *anyone* below the hundreds – they're all just disposables to these guys.'

This time there was a reaction from the congregation, though I don't think any of them could have been as surprised as me. Vinaldi stood up and shook his head at me. 'Sure, Maxen here cares a little bit about Suej. She was his daughter's spare. That's why he was so keen to get her back, and the real Suej died this morning, Jack, so looks like you got a tit for tat. Apart from that, no one here gives a flying fuck. They didn't come here to mourn. They came here to worship this guy.'

I suddenly understood that Maxen had never visited my Farm in the night because his own daughter's spare was there, and that would have seemed wrong to him; and in that moment I realized how many rooms there must be in *his* head, how tiny and how tightly locked.

'What are you doing here?' I asked quietly, light-headed with a sense of unreality. I knew only the sound of gunshots could make it seem real.

Vinaldi grinned humourlessly. 'What *you* should have been doing,' he said, and then he raised his hand and shot Arlond Maxen in the face.

He spun round on his axis, still upright, and before the body was on the ground Vinaldi had emptied his clip into it. Maxen's glasses skidded across the floor in the silence, and his eyes stared nakedly up into nothing.

The room exploded all around me into flares and tear gas. Out of the shadows ran six of Vinaldi's men, spraying machine pistol fire all around them, leaving behind the bodies of the guards they'd already killed, the guards who should have been parking bullets in Vinaldi and me. They were aiming now for the remaining Maxen security men, and got most of them, but they weren't the only people who fell. Maybe it wasn't deliberate, but people still died, falling to the ground like trunks in a forest which had never seen violence, surrounded by the ghostly faces of those who would be left behind. I knew that at least some of them would remember the day when the jungle rose up and came to find them where they lived, but I also knew how little difference it would make.

Vinaldi was surrounded by his men and swept away by their human shield, his mission accomplished. The room flickered with orange light, thick with smoke. I reeled into the chaos, staggering through screams and fire.

Dazed by the fact I was still alive, I wandered towards the thickest part of the crowd, unconsciously seeking cover in the parts where people were screaming loudest and panicked into blindness. I walked slowly through the forest of candles, surrounded by people having the worst day of their lives, but for me it was as if they were barely there. It felt like the whole house was burning down, as if every window was being flung open. I saw Golson in the crowd, but he didn't see me. He was too busy comforting one of the other guests, who happened to be young and attractive. Others ran past me, their clothes torn or on fire. I saw a costSlot rapidly counting down through the dollars as the garment it was attached to was consumed.

By the time I made it into the anteroom a stream of people was already ahead of me, sprinting towards the exit. I became part of the crowd again as it surged like a river in flood down the massive staircase to the entrance to the Maxens' property on the 200th floor. It didn't look like many people were sticking around for the reception.

Instead of making for the xPress with the others, I slipped out of the current and backtracked along the corridor to an emergency staircase which I knew must run from a point a couple of hundred yards away. I didn't think anyone else would know where it was – they don't get a lot of practice at emergencies above the 200th floor. I felt untouchable, and it seemed I was, because no one got in my face. A little way down the corridor I passed Louella Richardson's mother, standing by herself. Her hands were shaking but her face looked clear. She was staring straight ahead but didn't seem to recognize me.

The staircase door was unguarded, presumably because all of Maxen's men were otherwise engaged in the chaos upstairs. When

I reached it I turned and looked back the way I'd come. At the far end I could see the hurtling mass of people, hear the shouts. A smear of faces. It was all taking place in an odd land far away.

Then I opened the door and a hand immediately reached out and pulled me through.

Twenty-One

'How did you get up here?' I asked, though I'd lost most of my capacity to be surprised. Howie stood in front of me in the darkened stairwell, armed to the teeth and pumped up in a way I'd never seen in him before.

'Up the stairs,' he said. 'Sort of.' He should have looked absurd, perhaps, with spiked hair at forty and his considerable weight wrapped round with guns, but he didn't. He looked pretty formidable.

'How did you know I'd come this way?'

'I didn't. There's guys of ours on all the exits looking for you. Just dumb luck you ran into me.'

'You knew this was going down?'

'Yeah. Vinaldi talked to me last night. I'm going to be working a little more closely with him from now on.'

'Congratulations,' I said, vaguely. 'Why didn't you tell me?'

'Because you would have fucked it up, and found some way of getting yourself killed in the process. Look,' he said, putting his hand on my shoulder, 'I'm not saying I necessarily think this was a great thing to do. But I work for Vinaldi. And something else. This was the only way I could think of it going down with you standing a chance of coming out alive. You were going to try to whack Maxen by yourself. They would have cut you in half. Vinaldi did it instead, and you're still walking around.'

His face was dark, and I knew there was something else on his mind.

'But?' I said.

'But Yhandim and the others are going to come for you now, and you alone. They don't work for Maxen any more, and they hate you more than they hate Johnny. Those guys have been comrades for nearly twenty years. You killed three of them, and now the rest can't get back into The Gap. They've got a hard-on for you like you won't believe.'

I knew what was coming. Howie winced at what he had to say. 'You got to run. You got to get the fuck out of New Richmond and maybe never come back.'

We heard a shout out in the corridor then, about fifty yards away. I reached out and shook Howie's hand.

'Thanks,' I said, wishing there was some proper way of saying goodbye.

Howie said it. 'Get out of here.'

I ran.

I clattered down three flights, legs pumping like a wind-up toy, then fell out of a door onto 197. Stood there twitching for a moment, trying to work out where to go next. The nearest xPress was the obvious answer, but I had to figure that if Yhandim was already on the case, that's the first place they'd head for.

I couldn't think of anything. It had been too long. I ran for the xPress anyway.

197 looks the way the Garden of Eden would if they'd had access to nanofertilizers. I hurtled down a path through the middle of a park, past shrubbery so refined it was probably entitled to vote. Narrowly avoiding skittling a gaggle of old people, I made it into the xPress and slapped the button.

The elevator stopped at 160 and I waited inside for a second, half-expecting to hear the sound of gunfire or something equally discouraging. When none came I poked my head out the door, and saw I was on one of the chi chi shopping floors. Ahead of me stretched a long lane going east – and I knew there was another xPress half a mile away which would get me down below the 100 line.

I ran with my head up, partly to avoid the meandering shoppers and partly in the hope it would help oxygen to flood into my lungs. People stared at me openly as I passed. I guess they had people to do their running for them.

After a couple of minutes I realized I was going the wrong way, and at the next crossroads veered over into the next store-lined street. My mind was on what I was going to do after the next elevator and I didn't see Ghuaji until I was only fifty yards away and running straight at him.

He was belting up the street towards me, the very picture of a man gone rabid. Blood was running down the side of his face, and his running was crooked from the leg he was dragging behind. His skin looked like it had spent some time under ground. None of this stopped him from pulling a shotgun from over his shoulder and loosing a round straight through the crowd at me.

There were screams and a couple of people fell, but by then I was careering into an alleyway between an ice cream parlour and Emeralds R Us. There was another explosion behind me and I gathered from the face of a young woman I ran past that Hell was following after. I didn't look round. I figured I'd know soon enough if they caught me.

Then God threw me a bone, in the shape of some dweeb on a motortrike. He was pootling slowly down the lane, showing off to some giggling Mall-girls who'd never dream of shopping on Indigo Drive. I had him off the trike so fast he probably still thinks he's riding it to this day, leapt on and roared off down the middle of the street with my hand glued to the horn. The waves parted in front of me and I rocketed past hundreds of eyes all open as wide as the moon.

Don't worry about me, I thought wildly. This doesn't affect you. Just get on with your shopping.

Four minutes of moving violations got me to the xPress. The door was open, for a miracle, and I just drove the trike right in – causing a degree of consternation to the young couple who were already inside.

'You're not supposed to bring that in here,' the guy said. 'It's a violation of New Richmond road policy.'

From outside came the sound of a shotgun being fired and pellets tinkled against the outside of the carriage.

'You want your internal organs violated by buckshot?' I asked. The guy shook his head, terrified. I winked. 'So press the fucking "down" button.'

He did and the doors shut quickly enough, but they were glass and didn't hide the fact that Ghuaji was only about a hundred yards down the path. Worse, Yhandim was now running alongside, toting a large weapon of his own. My contact with him had been minimal, so far. I wanted to keep it like that.

The xPress took me down a long way. The young couple expressed a keen desire to get out quite early on, but I encouraged them to stay by showing my gun. They admired its craftsmanship and eventually agreed that it would be a shame to say goodbye before they'd had a chance to see me use it.

The elevator dropped majestically down to the 80s, and I stared out through the window at the big atrium, ten storeys of balconies draped with trailing green plants, like some biblical hanging garden. I hadn't visited the main atrium more than a couple of times in the past, though it had been one of Henna's favourite places. I should have gone more often. Too much time spent in the wrong rooms, as usual.

As the xPress started to slow I peered down below, without much hope in my heart. Sure enough, a guy with blue flashing lights in his head was standing waiting for me. I don't know how the fuck Yhandim got down faster than the xPress, but there he was. Maybe there are paths even I didn't know. His head tilted up slowly and our eyes met, and his was a hatred even I couldn't match. Ghuaji looked up seconds later, and I saw a couple of others standing around them.

I reached out and slammed the 'Open' button as we hit the floor above. The xPress groaned at the deceleration, but halted and opened its doors. I shooed the youngsters out and then shot out the controls, hoping it would take the guys a moment to work out why the lift wasn't coming down. I drove the trike out, crouched down over the handlebars and steered it unsteadily along the balcony. The sound of gunfire within seconds told me the plan hadn't worked, shells taking discouraging large chunks out of the ceiling just above my head.

I stood on the pedal and went careering along the corridor as fast as I could until I found a stairway. Turned straight into it, and went bouncing down the stairs. By then I was beginning to fancy a cigarette, but I judged it probably wasn't the time. I lit one anyway, figuring I might as well – it wasn't as if life expectancy was a concern.

I went down turns in the staircase until I started getting dizzy, and then sped out onto 65. I just drove straight through the door, which was painful and foolish, but no one was on the other side. I hurtled along the main drag towards the next down elevator, cursing the lab-rat layout of the old MegaMall. Two hundred yards from the xPress I saw a police platform hovering fast out of a sidestreet towards me. I didn't know whether they were after me because of who I was or just pure traffic offences, and it didn't make much difference. With one hand still steering the trike I shot at the platform's generator. More by luck than skill I hit it. The platform coughed and slewed into the pavement like a badly folded paper plane, spilling the cops onto the ground.

I dumped the trike outside the xPress, figuring that while it was fast, it also made me somewhat conspicuous. Then I stood thrumming and banging the walls, trying to catch my breath. I stopped the xPress two floors before I had to and made it across to another which got me as far as 24; as I tore out of the doors I heard shouts from up the street behind me but I didn't look to see who it was.

I ducked into the store where I bought my Rapt, shouting to the proprietor as I entered. He nodded with weary recognition and stepped aside to let me through into the back of his store, where a hidden stairway no one knows about dropped me another floor and into a project level where *nobody* sane lived any more. I was hoping that Yhandim would assume I was just heading straight down to the bottom, buying me some time.

23 is pitch-black darkness, filled with nothing but burnt-out warehouses that long ago used to be the Mall's staff quarters. Nobody lives there except the psychos and losers who've been cattle-prodded out of all the other floors. I ran straight across the heart of it, past fires burning on street corners. It's truly rather frightening, to be honest, and I was very happy when I saw the light of the next xPress shaft ahead. I just hoped there was going to be one along soon. I didn't want to hang around here long.

'Fucking stop right there,' shouted a voice, and I had a cardiac but kept on running. Then a shot whined past my leg and I realized running wasn't going to cut it. I stopped and whirled round.

Two guys, both around sixty. One's face was pierced and studded until it looked like a pin cushion. The other's had been in a bad fire.

'Look, what's the problem?' I gasped, barely able to speak through panting. My chest hurt like I'd cracked all my ribs at once and my legs were shaking. I kept my gun hand inside my jacket.

'No problem, sonny,' burn-face said, his voice deeper than the rumble of a distant train. 'But this is a toll road.'

'I don't have any money,' I said, wondering why I was cursed to have the same things happen to me time and time again.

'Then you fucked,' said the pierced one, who spoke with a lisp and looked denser than three bags of shit in a one-shit trumpet.

I thrust my hands into the pockets of my jacket, and found Mal's drive. I couldn't barter with that. In the other pocket, the computer chip which held Ratchet's brain. For a second I considered it, but no more. He'd helped me enough. I couldn't let go of him again.

'Don't suppose dropping Howie Amos' name is going to help?' I hazarded, beginning to panic. I was losing time, and lots of it.

Burn-face shook his head As a last resort I put my hand into my inside pocket and yanked out my wallet.

'Here,' I said. 'You can have this.'

He took it, and flicked through. There was no more than ten dollars in it, but then he found my old ownCard.

'This'll do,' he said, and they stepped aside. I didn't volunteer the information that trying to use the card would get them more police attention than crapping on Chief McAuley's head. I figured they'd find out soon enough, and it was about time they retired anyhow. I stabbed the button, leapt in, and slumped to rest my face against the carriage walls as it started to drop.

It was only when I stepped out on 8 that I realized my wallet had also held my only photograph of Henna and Angela. I couldn't go back. Memory would have to be enough.

I ran through the 8's lamp-lit streets, past so many places I knew, past the beginning of the sidestreet which led down to Howie's place. As I tore down the main drag, towards the restaurant with the entrance to the chute, I felt like I was going in reverse, as if the video of my life had reached its end an hour ago and was now being rewound, spooling past everywhere I had ever been, back towards some point where it would end again. Either end, or perhaps begin.

I skidded taking the corner into the final straight and almost lost it, but managed to stay upright and careered towards the restaurant doors. By the time I was ten yards away I could see something was wrong – there were no tables outside and no lights on behind the windows. A solid kick of the door told me it was locked. I glanced around, saw no one, and shot out the lock. Then I shoved the door open and ran into darkness, turning to slam the door shut again behind me. I hoped to Christ Yhandim and the others had gone the wrong way. At least if not then this route might get me a few extra seconds. It wasn't much, but the way things were going, a few seconds could make all the difference.

I threaded my way through the stacked tables and chairs towards the rest rooms at the back, ears tuned for any sound which might come from the streets outside. I was ready for it, and had in reserve a burst of speed which might just get me out in time.

What I wasn't ready for was a lamp being switched on above one of the tables on the back wall. It dropped a soft pool of yellow light for a couple of yards, revealing a man standing by the wall.

'Howie said you'd be passing through,' he said.

'Hello Johnny,' I replied, and swung my gun to point straight at his heart. 'You got two minutes to explain why you killed my wife and daughter for Maxen, and then I'm going to blow you apart.'

'When did you work it out?' Johnny said, slowly sitting back down. I stayed where I was, gun still held out, safety off.

'I don't know,' I said. 'Maybe just now, maybe earlier. You knew about what happened with Maxen's brother. I don't think you heard a rumour. I think you heard it from him. All the talk about atonement. Then a choice of words which in retrospect was kind of precise. You didn't put the hit on Henna and Angela, but it was you who carried it out.'

Johnny didn't say anything. Time was passing, but suddenly that didn't seem important any more. I had to understand. Dying seemed preferable to never understanding.

'Why, Johnny?'

'Maxen came to me, Jack. I was just a hood then, you know how it was. I was trying to get somewhere, but all the markets were sewn up. McAuley was tight with the old guard, and there wasn't much I could do. Then some of Maxen's guys came and found me, and took me up to see the boss. He said he wanted into the rackets, that legit money wasn't enough.'

'So you went in with him.'

'The offer didn't seem very negotiable. I sat in a very small room with several guns pointed at my head and it occurred to me that I didn't have much to lose. I say no, and he's going to ice me there and then. I say yes, and I'm going to end up running most of New fucking Richmond.'

'On the end of a leash.'

'We're all on leashes, Jack.'

'So he greased the NRPD for you.'

Vinaldi sighed. 'It wasn't like I had carte blanche, but my competitors started getting a lot more cop attention than I did. I started clearing up floors, adding them to our collection. Maxen fed capital when I needed it, worked the brass when things got out of hand. It was going good until you got involved.'

He stared at me, his face tortured.

'Why'd you have to do that, Jack? Things were the way they've always been, just a little more organized. Maxen and I could have sewed the place up, and everyone would have been happy. Less people would get killed in the crossfire every day, we'd have made money, and everything would have been cool. If you'd come to me early on I'd have put you on the payroll. You were a good cop. We could have used you. Why did you have to get nosy? Why couldn't you have just left it alone?'

I didn't have time to explain, and I don't think it would have convinced even me. The truth is I didn't know.

'Because I'm stupid, probably,' I said. 'Or because I thought I was making up for something myself.'

Vinaldi shook his head. 'So what happens is suddenly we've got problems, because you and Mal are digging too deep. Don't matter so much about me, because it's generally known what side of the line I'm on. But for Maxen, it's a problem. He can't afford anyone to suspect that New Richmond's premier white man is running all the shit.'

I could understand that. People like to feel that God and Devil are different beings. Vinaldi stopped then, and ran a hand across his face. His eyes were hooded, and when his hand came away I noticed his fingers trembling.

'So Maxen comes to me and says he wants a show of loyalty, that I got to prove I'm in with him up to the hilt. He tells me we need an object lesson. He already hates your guts because you whacked his brother in The Gap, but even he knew that had to be. If you hadn't killed him he'd have been court-martialled anyway. But now you're putting everything he owns at risk, and so it's got to happen, and he wants me to do it, Jack. It's going to be my special job.'

Vinaldi breathed out heavily, and then looked me steadily in the eyes. 'You made it easy for me, Jack. You took Phieta away from me. Maybe you thought I was just some typical wiseguy who kept a wife for show and screwed around on the side. Or maybe you were just fucking her to get closer to me. But I loved that woman. I didn't know about what was happening, but Maxen had photographs and he showed them to me. She was my wife, Jack, and she was running around with you. She didn't love me any more, even when you were gone, but I wouldn't let her go. You know what happened after she took you out of town, to the Farm? She killed herself.'

The entire city seemed silent around me then, as if nothing else happening in it mattered, as if none of it had any bearing on me. All I could do was listen, and keep my gun trained on Vinaldi's heart.

'After he showed me the pictures, Maxen pumped me with Rapt, and two of his guys took me down to your floor. They stood outside while I went in, and they took me away when I was finished. I didn't know until I was actually in your living room that Maxen had deliberately overdosed me. I didn't know what I was doing, Jack. It was just going to be a clean hit. Then the walls went away and I was back in The Gap and everything happened the way it did.'

My hand was shaking, my finger slick against the trigger. Vinaldi's chest looked like the biggest target in the world.

'You go back there, don't you,' I said. 'To the seventy-second floor.'

He looked at me. 'How do you know that?'

'Some kid I met. He's seen you standing down by the window.'

Vinaldi's head dropped. 'I can't remember what happened in there,' he said quietly. 'Leastways, most of the time. Sometimes I dream about it, and when I wake up I go down and stand outside your apartment. You're right about some things, Jack, and one of them is this: sometimes you do things which won't fit in any head. Things which are too big to forget. I gave you a hard time in front of Nearly about you thinking everything's tainted, but you were right. I tainted my own life, and I don't even remember doing it. All I know is that the shit is there, and that it ain't ever going away.'

I looked up at his face then, at the muscle twitching in his cheek. All the hate I'd nursed for him came crashing back into my head, burning the image of his face into utter clarity. I saw it so clearly that I realized it was my own, and as I started to pull the trigger it was with a feeling of utter relief.

The shot rang out in the darkness.

I let my head drop, listening to the shallow breaths of a man who'd seen me move my hand at the last minute and fire the bullet into the floor. I stood there a while, until the echoes had died away and left us alone again.

'Why'd you kill Maxen?' I asked. 'Because he'd decided he didn't need you any more and pulled Yhandim through to take you down? Because the guys from The Gap were whacking your associates and girls? Or because of something else?'

'Jack . . .' he whispered.

'Get out of here,' I said.

He stood, walked to the door.

'Good luck,' he said.

'If I ever see you again I'm going to kill you. Understood?'

He nodded once, opened the door and left.

I went into the women's rest room, removed the panel and climbed through into the pipe. Then I resealed the exit behind me, in the hope of putting off the inevitable for a little longer. I ran down the ventilation corridor as quickly as I could, ignoring a few bumps and cracks on the head. By then I didn't seem to have any processing cycles spare for worrying about a little pain. I was listening to the sound of pieces falling into place, seeing how they changed things and wondering how much difference it made.

But then I heard a faint clang behind me as they found the panel, and the shout from Ghuaji which indicated he'd heard my footsteps as I fled down the chute barely half a mile ahead of them. I hadn't expected to elude them for long, but it was still a shock.

They were good soldiers. I'd lost them but then they'd found me, and now they were going to do their job.

My father only ever said one thing which I admire. 'The race isn't over until everyone's gone home and you're left in the stadium by yourself.' He used to say it every time he lost a job. We would generally already be packing to leave for another town, and I never really understood what he meant. Not then, anyhow. As I ran breathlessly through the dank guts of New Richmond I understood all too well. I played out the game to the last, darting through cross corridors, taking a deliberately bewildering route until I got to the main shaft, then putting my hands and feet on the outside of the ladder so I could slide the floors as quickly as possible.

But I could still hear their boots thudding towards me, and as I swung off the ladder at ground level I knew the odds were against me. It seemed unfair, somehow, to have come so far, and for it to all come down to this. All I ever wanted was to escape from the noise, to find a little peace. I saw it then, that final moment, as if it had always been ordained. I saw the features of men who didn't even really know enough to hate me properly, who were simply living out their programming; saw the random expressions on their faces as they crowded round me in those last seconds; felt the channels cut through me like shafts of ice. I saw myself dying in the bowels of New Richmond, and it didn't seem too bad a way to go; and strangely, in that moment, I felt closer to my dad than anyone else in the world. However badly he fucked up he never gave in, until he chose to give it *all* up.

And then I saw something ahead of me, and the images fled as if they'd never been.

I was staring down the tunnel, half-wondering whether I could find some new route, some way which would lead me towards gaps which were too small to find. I was paralysed with indecision, my eyes flicking frantically over the smooth metal walls of the duct, when suddenly I realized I shouldn't be able to see them at all.

There was a tiny light in the distance, like a single candle fluttering in the darkness. As I stared it seemed to come closer, until it was no longer a point but an orange glow. But it wasn't coming nearer, just getting bigger; it had never been more than yards away.

The glow had a shape inside it. A figure.

I swallowed, feeling as if I had a brick in my throat, and whirled back to face the way I had come. The sound of the men coming down the ladder above told me what I already knew. There was nowhere else to go.

I turned back and stared into the light. It seemed the thing to do. Maybe somebody knew that my time had come, and had arrived to lead me through. I kind of hoped it wouldn't be Mal. I loved the guy, and hoped I'd see him sooner rather than later, but I didn't want to eat noodles for eternity.

At first the figure seemed to be made up of many flickering wings beating in time, but then it started to resolve into solidity. When I saw who it really was my mouth fell open, as if it wanted to help shed some of the tears which were forcing themselves up through my eyes. Something had happened. The birds weren't insane any more. My lips trembled so much that when I said her name it was barely audible.

'Suej?'

She smiled, and I saw that the scar on her face had gone. She looked whole, and perfect.

'We have to be quick, Jack,' she said, but the sounds behind me were forgotten as I noticed that as well as her summer dress she seemed to be wearing a ragged jacket, like those the Gap children wore.

'What are you doing here?' I whispered. 'How did you get out?'

'I found some friends,' she said. 'We're making things different. The Gap's closing. I'm the bridge.' She sounded proud, and serene, and I took a step forwards, wanting so much to hug her. She held up her hand to stop me. I stared at it, marvelling at the way it exuded light.

'You must go the other way,' she said. 'Down to the lowest level.'

'But this is the way out . . .'

She shook her head. 'Go the other way. And something else. You don't need Ratchet any more. You must throw him away.'

'No fucking way,' I said, but she interrupted me with a confidence she'd never had before.

'You *must*. Then you have to run. And they told me to tell you this: you did more than you'll ever know.'

I shook my head, not wanting to go, but her face was firm. It felt as if I was the child, as if she now held some truth to which I could only aspire.

Abruptly I realized that the sound of boots on the ladder was now much closer.

'But what *are* you now?' I asked quickly.

Suej smiled again, and lifted her hands – and then she was gone.

I lunged back into the shaft, suddenly in motion as if someone had just plugged me back in. As soon as I was into it I heard a shout from above, and I leapt down to land awkwardly on the floor below. For a second I recognized where I was, from my Rapt expedition, and then as the bullets started to spang around me I ducked into the nearest tunnel and ran.

I sprinted past places I'd never seen, over lintels and past strange doors. I saw a rusted sign which said BAGGAGE, but then I was past it and still running hard. I remembered what Suej had told me to do and thrust my hand down into my jacket pocket. I pulled out the chip in which Ratchet lived, and held it for a moment. I didn't want to let him go, but sensed that something else was calling the shots now. I placed him carefully on the ground and ran.

I spotted a familiar corner, vaulted up a couple of steps, and found myself in one of the exhaust ducts.

They were gaining on me, and I suspected I wasn't going to make it. But at least I was going to try.

I ran past an endless wall of metal, pocked with a century's wear; the sound of air rushing in my ears as I stumbled forwards, tripping and careering down the tunnel. And always behind me, and getting closer, were men running after me with only one thing on their mind. Occasionally, a bullet whined down the tunnel past me. They hadn't hit me yet, but I suspected they would.

I felt like the ghost in the machine, trying to find a way out. Trying to find the door to the outside, where there would be a sky above.

I ran, and I ran, but my lungs couldn't take it any more. My legs started going, the muscles melting into fire too insubstantial to carry me on. The footsteps were thundering louder, and my life had been too long and deep for me to find anything else left to give. I ran, but I began to fall, my feet losing rhythm, the half-seen walls around me swirling into darkness.

My feet gave beneath me and I stumbled, knowing that I had given it my best but that I had lost the race. My hands flailed out, trying to find something to hold on to, something to stop me just pitching forward onto my face.

And as I fell I felt a tiny hand grabbing hold of mine.

The hand was warm and tender, and the voice, when it came, was firm, whispering in my ear. A voice that had my own in it, and Henna's, too.

'Come on Daddy,' she said. 'It's time to leave.'

I didn't question it, but tightened my hold on the little fingers pressed into my palm. I was dragged forward, the voice still urging me on. My legs found new strength, and the pain in my chest faded away to nothing or became so loud I couldn't hear it any more. My body wrenched order from chaotic failure, and began to work in time again.

I didn't fall, but found a new rhythm. I ran down the tunnel like a child to the sea, until the walls were a blur and all I could truly sense was that tiny warmth and her voice drawing me on. As I ran I knew the footsteps were falling behind, still following but irrelevant now. All they had was hate to pull them on. There are stronger pulls.

I hurtled after Angela as if it would be my last ever run, and I felt ludicrously happy and knew that's the way it should be. I knew finally that you shouldn't lie down and wait for darkness, leaving quietly, slouching towards death. You should run, because the only real fear is that you'll *stop* running, that you'll stop *doing*, that you'll come to an end before everything else.

As I ran I felt each second stretch to breaking point as it tried to hold everything that had gone before it. Nothing was lost, nothing futile. Every thing I had done, every glance, every word, every breath shone, huge and limitless and mine. My life didn't pass in front of me – I ran in front of it. Nearly had been right. Memories are nothing more than a book you've read and lost, not a bible for the rest of your life.

I saw a light ahead, and began to notice strange sounds reverberating down the tunnel around me. I could still hear the footsteps of Yhandim and his men, but they were a long way behind me now. They would catch up sooner or later, but at least I would make it out of New Richmond. I trotted the last stretch raggedly, losing rhythm again. The joy was fading, as if it had been a fuel I was coming to the end of. It was everything that Rapt should have been, and I wished it was easier to come by.

Angela's form flickered in front of me, leading me up some staircase I'd never seen before. There was a rectangle of light at the end of the tunnel and I realized I had somehow come up another level, out of the exhaust ducts and towards the exit I knew.

The guys at the door stood there staring, mouths gaping. I was pretty impressed with my running myself, and half-expected a round of applause. As I got closer I saw that it wasn't admiration in their faces, but fear.

The noise I'd heard seemed to be getting louder, ricocheting round the walls until the whole city appeared to shake. Before I made it to the doors the men there had already turned and run.

I burst out of New Richmond, still pulled by Angela's hand. I panted through the basement and up the stairs, barely yards behind the fleeing men, and then out into the Portal to find that everyone else was running too.

I ground to a halt in the midst of chaos, hundreds of people sprinting past me out of the buildings arranged round the walls of the city. For a moment I couldn't understand, thought only that I'd started some new trend, and then a distant rumbling told me what in some sense I already knew.

I felt a tugging, and let her pull me backwards, away from the bulk of New Richmond and out of harm's way. In my mind I could still hear footsteps pursuing me, though I knew they were still down in the exhaust ducts, that Yhandim and the men who were with him were now probably being shaken off their feet by forces which were awake again.

When we were two hundred yards away we stopped, and I turned to see where she'd gone. A small shape leapt up at me as she always had, and I caught her and clasped my arms around her, and it was as if she was really there. I pushed my face into hers, smelling her mother and hearing my daughter's laugh.

Then my arms held nothing but air.

People kept speeding past me, still tumbling out of buildings which would be falling within seconds. I gazed up beatifically at the bulk of New Richmond, at its countless rooms filled with life. As the ancient pulse engines finally fired into action I knew that I had nothing to fear from anyone who still ran after me deep in the tunnels. The things that had chased me were gone.

I shouted Ratchet's name as I realized what he'd done, that the old repair droid in the basement had found the chip and Ratchet's mind had saved me once again; and I staggered backwards, laughing my head off, as the MegaMall stirred like a mountain waking up after too long a sleep.

There was a moment of hesitation, as if old machineries were striving to remember the jobs they'd once performed, and then the entire city lifted up into the air. It rose up into the sky, higher and higher, until it was finally free of the earth. Looking for old paths, new roads, and a life it could have once again.

Twenty-Two

The sky has a frost around the edges today, but is a blue which tells that though winter may not be over, spring is on the way. I don't mind either way, to be honest. Rain or sun, it's just good to see weather again.

I waited until the city had gone out of sight, standing amidst the spouting water mains and spitting cables, then hitched my way down to Northern Florida, to the beach where my mother and I used to stay. For a couple of days I just walked up and down the coast and slept in the dunes beneath the sky, and then I took a deep breath and found the condominium where my grandparents used to live. It looked older now, and battered, and nobody lives there any more; but I found a room which was more than habitable, and that's where I'm staying for now.

When I was ready I got a job in a bar in St Augustine, and one quiet night I was standing there when I saw a news report on the flatscreen hanging down the other end. An unspecified medical facility in Vermont had been attacked by a lone terrorist. Nobody knew who he or she was, and all they'd done was kidnap one of the 'patients' and disappear.

At first I just smiled, and then I laughed so loud and so long that people moved away and left me standing there alone.

I wished Suej and David luck, and hoped that some day I'd see them both again.

Nearly arrived yesterday afternoon. I was sitting by the old, empty pool round the back of the condo, remembering when there was water in it, when she marched right up behind me and cracked me round the back of the head. Very hard.

She was still extremely pissed at me, but she was also strangely determined. Suej had come to her in a dream, she claimed, and told her that she could find me here. When New Richmond put down temporarily in Seattle she'd jumped ship, and come a long way to give me a hard time. I stood there while she shouted and raved, and when she ran out of breath I took her hand and led her down the old wooden walkway to the beach.

We walked along the shore until the light began to fade. There were no lights in the old buildings we passed, looming abandoned back up behind the dunes, but birds ran along the waterline as they always had, and a group of pelicans flew first one way, and then back, above our heads.

Howie was doing well, I heard, as was Vinaldi, and the MegaMall was still on the move. Each time New Richmond landed somewhere people tried to tether it down, so they could get inside; but Ratchet was having none of it and just kept taking off again. The people inside didn't seem to mind, were happy to be flying at last.

The gaps are closing.

I would never know how much of what happened was directly Ratchet's idea, whether something had affected him a long time ago, when he'd been in The Gap, whether he'd struck some deal with the children even then; but I believed that if anyone was going to be running New Richmond, then its inhabitants could do a lot worse than the small, clear chip which now laboured somewhere deep inside it. Sometimes you have to accept presents, and Ratchet was one of those. If we are to hand ourselves over to someone unseen then I trust him more than most.

Time will tell what will happen. It always does.

Nearly still beats me up occasionally, but she's smiling now when she does it. A couple of nights ago we found ourselves sitting on the beach at midnight, full of wine and peace.

'So,' she said, leaning into me, the skin of her shoulder soft against my cheek. 'What are we going to do now?'

I kissed her softly on the corner of the mouth, and slipped my arm around her back.

'That's all very well,' she said, with a little cat smile, 'but are you sure you can afford it?'

'Well, I don't have a credit card,' I said, shaking my head sadly, playing along.

She pouted. 'You must have.'

'I gave it away.'

She looked at me for a moment, and then pursed her lips.

'I'll take cash.'

'If I had some, it would be yours.'

She sighed, and rolled her eyes. 'Alright,' she said eventually, putting her arms round my shoulders and bringing her face right up to mine. 'I'll settle for an interesting insight on the human condition.'

I shrugged. 'Hope springs eternal?'

'Good enough for me,' she said.

A week ago Nearly bought me an old book from a second-hand store in St Augustine. It's about plants, and tells you what they're called and where they're from. I'm working through it, memorizing the names. When we're out walking I look to see if I can find any of them.

When I do, I name them: for Henna, for Nearly, and for me.

Only Forward
Michael Marshall Smith

A truly stunning debut from a young author. Extremely original, satyrical and poignant, a marriage of numerous genres brilliantly executed to produce something entirely new.

Stark is a troubleshooter. He lives in The City - a massive conglomeration of self-governing Neighbourhoods, each with their own peculiarity. Stark lives in Colour, where computers co-ordinate the tone of the street lights to match the clothes that people wear. Close by is Sound where noise is strictly forbidden, and Ffnaph where people spend their whole lives leaping on trampolines and trying to touch the sky. Then there is Red, where anything goes, and all too often does.

At the heart of them all is the Centre - a back-stabbing community of 'Actioneers' intent only on achieving - divided into areas like 'The Results are what Counts sub-section' which boasts 43 grades of monorail attendant. Fell Alkland, Actioneer extraordinaire has been kidapped. It is up to Stark to find him. But in doing so he is forced to confront the terrible secrets of his past. A life he has blocked out for too long.

'Michael Marshall Smith's *Only Forward* is a dark labyrinth of a book: shocking, moving and surreal. Violent, outrageous and witty - sometimes simultaneously - it offers us a journey from which we return both shaken and exhilarated. An extraordinary debut.'
Clive Barker

ISBN 0 586 21774 6